"Shirl Henke mesmerizes readers with the most powerful, sensual and memorable historical romances yet!"
—*Romantic Times*

GOLDEN LADY
"*Golden Lady* is one of the best reads I've had in a long time."

—Sylvie Sommerfield

*Best New Western Author
—*Romantic Times*

LOVE UNWILLING
"Sensual, sensitive, a well-developed plot, plus highly believable characters . . . make this an outstanding read."
—*Rendezvous*

*Best Romance Team
—*Romantic Times*

CAPTURE THE SUN
"A beautifully written novel . . . Shirl Henke has really outdone herself on this one!"

—*Affaire de Coeur*

*Best Historical Romance
—*Affaire de Coeur*

SHIRL HENKE IS A WINNER!

CACTUS FLOWER
"Delightful and spicy, this captures the essence of the West."
—*Romantic Times*

*Best New Book in a Historical Series
—*Romantic Times*

MOON FLOWER
"A wonderful romantic epic that sizzles with Creole spice. I highly recommend both book and author."
—Karen Robards

*Best American Historical Romance
—*Affaire de Coeur*

Shirl Henke is "one of the brightest new stars in romance . . . her engaging characters and talent for storytelling will grip readers from the first page to the last."
—Katherine Sutcliffe

FORBIDDEN PASSION

Night Wind watched her glide through the water like a sleek little otter. He was surprised that she could swim. He had expected her to flounder and cry out to be rescued from drowning. Smiling grimly to himself, he shed his moccasins and breechclout and dove in after her.

"Ladies do not know how to swim, Lioness," he said as he caught up with her in several swift strokes.

She gasped in surprise, then recovered. "Conal taught Santiago and me when we were children."

His face darkened ominously. "He has taught you much—too much for a Spanish female of the noble class."

"Some Spaniard has taught you also—too much for an Apache male of the renegade class," she replied in a haughty tone as cold as his expression.

He reached out and one wet hand clamped on her arm, pulling her to him. "Come here. Take off your clothes," he whispered.

Other *Leisure* books by Shirl Henke:
WHITE APACHE'S WOMAN
RETURN TO PARADISE
LOVE A REBEL ... LOVE A ROGUE
BROKEN VOWS
PARADISE & MORE
TERMS OF LOVE
McCRORY'S LADY
A FIRE IN THE BLOOD
TERMS OF SURRENDER

NIGHT WIND'S WOMAN

SHIRL HENKE

LEISURE BOOKS   NEW YORK CITY

*For Carmine DelliQuadri,
who possesses a vast knowledge of weaponry
and just enough common sense to have married
a redheaded woman.*

A LEISURE BOOK®

April 1999

Published by

Dorchester Publishing Co., Inc.
276 Fifth Avenue
New York, NY 10001

If you purchased this book without a cover you should be aware that this book is stolen property. It was reported as "unsold and destroyed" to the publisher and neither the author nor the publisher has received any payment for this "stripped book."

Copyright © 1991 by Shirl Henke

All rights reserved. No part of this book may be reproduced or transmitted in any form or by any electronic or mechanical means, including photocopying, recording or by any information storage and retrieval system, without the written permission of the Publisher, except where permitted by law.

ISBN 0-8439-4507-9

The name "Leisure Books" and the stylized "L" with design are trademarks of Dorchester Publishing Co., Inc.

Printed in the United States of America.

NIGHT WIND'S WOMAN

ACKNOWLEDGMENTS

Setting this book in the alien and violent eighteenth-century Spanish borderlands opened a whole new world for my associate, Carol J. Reynard, and me. We were forced to create differing rhythms of language, since not a single character in our story spoke English. The idiom and flavor of Spanish and Apachean dialects have to sound different, even when the writer and the reader are using English. Carol has pointed out to me that there is a fine line indeed between authentic and stilted dialogue. We hope we have successfully walked that line.

Spaniards were the first modern pioneers in the American Southwest, arriving long after the Native Americans but hundreds of years before the first Anglo ever set foot west of the Mississippi. The research was formidable, ranging from the court politics of Charles III's Spain to the marriage customs of the Lipan Apache. How did Spanish presidios operate and what did the people of Santa Fe eat? For the vast array of resources we used, we are again indebted to the

Maag Library of Youngstown State University, and most especially to the head of reference, Mrs. Hildegard Schnuttgen, who has obtained for us not only books, but copies of obscure journal articles from decades past.

The Spanish Southwest was firmly steeped in Roman Catholicism and every facet of the Spaniards' lives was touched by their religion. But the strictures of eighteenth-century Canon Law were far different then than today. For clearing up some particularly complex problems regarding the legality of the protagonists' marriage, we are indebted to Fr. William Connell of the Diocese of Youngstown and to the Rev. Daniel Venglarik for putting us in touch with him.

Eighteenth-century firearms were primitive indeed, and the Spanish used unique longarms and shortarms. For special new challenges, exceptionally well met as always, we are most grateful to our weapons expert, Dr. Carmine V. DelliQuadri, Jr., D.O.

Chapter 1

*Outside Chihuahua City,
Nueva Vizcaya Province, 1774*

"Take care going down. I would hate to lose you, little Indian," the guard said with a guttural laugh as he shoved the boy toward a gaping hole in the earth.

Yesterday an Opata boy had fallen from the rickety chicken ladder that took the slaves down twenty feet to the first level of the mine. The rawhide lashing had rotted, causing a rung to break, even under the emaciated child's slight weight. He had broken his leg on the rock floor below. Green-Eyed Boy had watched the guard bash the child's brains out with a club.

By the young Apache's crude reckoning, he had been a mine slave for just over a year. Hate kept him alive. He choked as the cloying fumes of the torches burned his throat and eyes while he climbed down the ladder. Like a somnambulist, he stepped off the last rung and crossed the first level to the wicker basket that would lower him even deeper. Focusing on his enemy's face, he closed his eyes tightly against the rising nausea as he descended into hell. Only that way could he breathe and hold on to sanity in the gathering darkness.

The mine gasses seared Green-Eyed Boy's lungs and he coughed. Dust from the crumbly earth and rock above him fell in a fine powder. When he and the Mescalero youth behind him reached the end of the tunnel, he began chipping at the rock and passing small, silver-laden chunks to his companion. They worked in darkness, by touch alone. Many boys went blind from a combination of mine gasses and darkness. Each night, Green-Eyed Boy forced his exhausted body to stay awake long enough to stare at the bright flames of the campfire, knowing he must be able to tolerate light in order to escape. Escape was his obsession.

"Tomorrow is their holy day," he whispered to his Mescalero companion. "There will be fewer guards. Many go to worship their Christian gods. Gomez never attends the blue robe's magic rites. If he is alone in the shaft with us tomorrow . . ." He coughed and choked as he spoke the short, staccato sentences, all the while handing chunks of rock back to his friend.

Hoarse Bark was the older, but new to captivity and unused to the mine routine. "If we are caught coming up after we have killed Gomez—"

"We will die as warriors, not live as slaves," Green-Eyed Boy answered in an icy voice.

"There are high walls of stone at the outside of the mine . . . and much open ground between them and the mine pits," Hoarse Bark said unhappily.

"We will vanish with the night wind before anyone finds his body," the Lipan replied grimly.

He had prayed to the Child of the Water, asking to be freed to avenge his band. Perhaps it was his own hate rather than any vision from the supernatural that

NIGHT WIND'S WOMAN

made him so certain they would succeed. Perhaps it was the terrible nightmare of being buried alive if he spent one more day in the small tunnels. Each day he hid his sweaty, shivering terror from everyone. Only in his dreams did it roam unleashed, stalking him like some malevolent beast.

The next morning the compound guard came to unlock the adobe hut in which they slept, kicking them awake. Few other guards were about as they huddled by the fire and ate a thin gruel of cornmeal. Their hands cupped the noisome slime as they sucked it greedily into their mouths.

Usually they were fed and sent down to dig by the dimmest light of dawn, with many guards prodding the chained prisoners toward the various pits, beating them as they stumbled in the darkness. This morning it was full daylight, and the compound around the silver mine was virtually deserted. When their guard gave the signal, they licked the last of the gruel from their fingers and followed him.

As the man unlocked their manacles and called down to Gomez at the bottom of the first level, Hoarse Bark exchanged a look of expectation with Green-Eyed Boy. Gomez was new on the job and stupid. He did not heed the warning of the other guards who said, "He is the son of a white man, a half-caste, the most dangerous kind."

Gomez had only laughed. "He is a skinny, starved cur. Green eyes do not make him a white man. He is some peasant's leavings with a squaw, that is all."

The two boys climbed slowly down the shaky ladder. The guard above, red-eyed and ill from too much cheap wine the preceding night, staggered off to lie in the shade of a poplar tree. With his superior at church for the feast day, no one would reprimand him.

The conspirators had planned every move as they lay on their straw pallets at night; now they executed the maneuvers. Green-Eyed Boy dropped from the seventh rung of the ladder onto Gomez's shoulders as Hoarse Bark tripped him. They quickly brought the Spaniard to the ground. While Hoarse Bark kicked at his groin and grabbed for his club, Green-Eyed Boy gripped him with a desperate choke-hold about his neck. Gomez made only a faint gurgle as they shoved his body down to the second level, where it landed with a sickening thud on the jagged rocks. Green-Eyed Boy remembered the Opata slave as they waited for darkness.

Once during the afternoon, a compound guard came by and called to Gomez. When Hoarse Bark emitted several loud snores, the guard merely glanced down into the dim light below and laughed, sauntering away.

At dusk the two boys climbed up cautiously, armed with Gomez's knife and club. Green-Eyed Boy raised his head and scanned the area. A campfire flickered across the compound. About thirty yards away stood a string of poplars, beyond which stretched the stone wall.

The boys could hear drunken laughter from the guards sitting around the campfire. Several of them were passing a bottle of *aguardiente*. Quickly Green-Eyed Boy motioned for Hoarse Bark to follow him as he crawled over the flat, rock-strewn ground, his brown body and black hair blending into the shadows cast by the distant fire. Moving like chameleons, the two boys inched toward the poplars. Only when they reached the dark embrace of the trees did they stand up. Both were abraded and bleeding, but their skin had been toughened by rawhide whips and leather clubs.

NIGHT WIND'S WOMAN

Green-Eyed Boy quickly chose a place on the wall cast in deep shadows. "We must hurry. Soon they will miss their drinking companion Gomez and go in search of him."

Only when the young Lipan had scaled the wall did he hear the outcry from the pit. Someone had gone in search of Gomez! Hoarse Bark was taller and his larger hands and feet were not as dexterous as Green-Eyed Boy's. Reaching down to help the Mescalero, he heard a whine and then felt a sharp sting across his right side. Ignoring the pain, he yanked Hoarse Bark up and over the wall.

As they tumbled to the ground on the far side and began to run, Green-Eyed Boy faltered and Hoarse Bark reached for him. "You have been shot," the older boy grunted as he supported his companion.

Green-Eyed Boy shook free and sprinted ahead, gritting his teeth. He was free! Never, never would he go back to that pit! Just thinking of it spurred him onward with renewed fury, sweeping the pain from his mind.

After leaving the compound, the Lipan and the Mescalero had no idea of how to complete their escape, other than to steal horses and ride north. But where were there horses for the stealing?

"We must part ways, Mescalero brother," Green-Eyed Boy said, forcing himself to stand straight in spite of the wickedly throbbing wound. "Separately we can elude the Spanish more easily. At least one of us will escape."

"You mean I might, but you are too weak," Hoarse Bark supplied. "I will stay with you."

"No! I can speak Spanish well. It will be easier for me to talk with them if need be. You must find a fast pony and ride quickly. Do not argue. Already we have lost much time. I seek my father among the Spanish.

That is not your concern." With that, he turned and began to run toward the city, never looking back.

Hoarse Bark hesitated, then headed to the east through a rocky ravine that provided good cover. Perhaps if the Child of Waters smiled upon them, they would meet again one day.

With only instinct to guide him, Green-Eyed Boy zigzagged from boulder to scrub mesquite, using anything for cover. He could feel the blood running thickly down his side, but a terrible desperation drove him to fight the faintness. At daylight the soldiers could follow the trail of his blood!

Just as he rounded a stand of cottonwood trees, intent on reaching the seductive ripple of fresh, cool water, Green-Eyed Boy collided with something very solid—and moving. A burro. With a loud whump, he fell dazed to the earth near the burbling stream.

The man on the burro quickly dismounted and knelt by the boy, his coarse brown robes impeding his rapid movements. When he gently rolled the injured boy over, a knife flashed toward the man's throat.

"Utter a cry and you die, Spanish cur," Green-Eyed Boy hissed, his expression a grimace of agony as he struggled to rise, keeping the blade at the wayfarer's throat.

"I trust I may speak if I do not do so over-loudly," a soft, musical voice replied. Deftly the traveler swept the blade aside, sending it splashing into the brook. He was large and easily held the injured boy down, but again there was an odd gentleness in the doing of it that seemed to transmit a message to the child.

"You are one of the holy men," he said accusingly, giving up the uneven contest for the moment.

The big man laughed softly. "I am a Franciscan friar and a priest. As to how holy that makes me, only the Lord will be the judge of that." His alert gray eyes took in the boy's injury even in the dimness of the moonlight. "I would say you need help, my son."

Green-Eyed Boy flinched, hissing, "I am no white man's son!"

Again the gentle laughter as the friar swept the child into his arms and carried him to the burro waiting patiently at the side of the stream. As he placed the defiant boy in the saddle, he studied his profile. *Escaped slave or not, I fear you are some white man's son, may God forgive him,* the friar thought sadly.

Fray Bartolome was on his way from the City of Mexico to his new assignment at the Franciscan mission outside of Chihuahua City. His traveling companion, Fray Lorenzo, had become ill in a small village a few miles south, leaving Fray Bartolome to complete the journey alone.

When the friar and the Indian boy arrived at the mission, it proved a grave disappointment, just as the priest had feared. Along the way he had stayed at a series of missions whose primitive conditions and meager provisions were in direct proportion to their distance from the capital. "I should be grateful this is only Chihuahua, not El Paso or Sante Fe," he muttered as he looked at the dilapidated adobe with its weed-infested orchards and crumbling bell tower.

The hour was late, well past midnight, for he had lost the trail twice before stumbling on the runaway child. He pounded on the heavy oak doors. The hinges creaked, but no one responded. Shoving the doors open, he entered the courtyard and called out. Finally a sleepy youth and an elderly friar answered his summons. Neither was pleased when they saw his cargo.

"That is an escaped slave, one of the savages from the silver mines a few miles from here," young Fray Alonzo said in wide-eyed horror.

"The soldiers will come for him," old Fray Domingo added worriedly.

"He is an injured child, inhumanely treated in direct violation of God's laws and our sovereign's," Fray Bartolome replied as he carried the child into the kitchen, where a small fire burned through the night.

As the younger friar stoked up the fire and the elder one brought water and bandages, Fray Bartolome examined the child, crossing himself in horror as he looked at the scars and fresh sores on the boy's back, ankles, and wrists. The bullet had slashed a long furrow in his right side, but had not gone deep. If properly cleaned and stitched, it should heal well. "Poor little one, to have suffered so much already," he muttered as he worked.

When he had finished bathing the boy, he prepared to close the gash in his side, but just then the boy's eyes opened and he stared intently into the seamed face of the priest.

"What do you do? Sew me up like teepee skins?" the child asked as he eyed the needle and coarse thread the priest had taken from his saddle pack.

"He speaks Spanish," Fray Alonzo said in surprise.

"Look you at the eyes! Bright green as bottle glass," the old friar said in amazement.

"He is half-caste, obviously," Fray Bartolome replied, impatiently dismissing the brothers. He turned to the boy and said gravely, "Yes, I am going to sew up that wound so it will heal faster. This will hurt, so you must be very brave."

"I am Lipan. We know how to stand pain, holy man," he said with bravado. Although he did not flinch, after three stitches he again lost consciousness.

"It is really most extraordinary. This morning, when I tried to explain heaven and hell to him, I showed him the altarpiece depicting hell," Fray Domingo said in perplexity.

Fray Bartolome grunted as he unpacked his books. "Leave it to you to begin with hell."

"Well, these Indians need that for a goad onto the path of righteousness," the old friar said defensively. "But the child made the oddest reply. He said he had already seen hell. And it was worse than the altarpiece!" The old man crossed himself and rolled his eyes, then continued, "He says his gods are like our Holy Savior and Blessed Virgin. He called them the Child of Waters and the Painted Lady—"

"*White* Painted Lady," Fray Bartolome corrected. "Yes, there are some rather startling similarities." He ignored the gasp from the old friar that intimated his remarks smacked of heresy, which he supposed they did. Still, each conversation he had with the recuperating boy intrigued him more.

Green-Eyed Boy, for that was the way he translated his Lipan name for them, had been at the mission for ten days. He was strong and resilient, filling out quickly now that he was receiving adequate sleep and nourishment. But the child was an enigma. He would speak freely of Lipan religion and culture and of his life on the plains, but of his family he would only say that his mother and her people were dead.

With all of his new duties as the only priest at a crumbling mission, the last thing Fray Bartolome needed was a wary, bright, and troublesome Apache boy to shepherd. Still, he had been sent into the wilderness to minister to the farmers and soldiers in the rural areas around Chihuahua City. The boy was probably the son of one of them. That was reason enough for the priest to take an interest in Green-Eyed Boy.

Fray Bartolome was a scholar, happier in his library

at the Franciscan College in the City of Mexico than anywhere else. A large, thickset man with a robust body, curly brown hair, and clear gray eyes, he looked more like a butcher than a lover of the classics. Among the Spanish clergy in the rural north, his erudition was rare. Even more extraordinary was his fascination with the native inhabitants. Not having lived through the bloody conflicts between Spaniard and Indian, he came north with no prejudice. He wanted to learn. Did the boy?

"Will you be baptized?" he asked that afternoon in his austere study outside the chapel. He watched the boy squirm on the splintering pine chair.

"I have listened to the stories of your gods—"

"God. Three in one, but only one God, son."

The boy dismissed that with a shrug. "If I agree to the ceremonial washing," he said tentatively, "will you teach me about the white man's world?"

Fray Bartolome nodded gravely. "Being received into the Christian faith would be a prerequisite to education. Why do you want to learn about us? You have already said you wish to find the Lipans in the mountains of New Mexico." He leaned forward across the crude oak library table that served as his desk.

"I will find the Lipan someday, but there is a thing I would do first." He would say nothing more until this holy man told him what he needed to know.

It was a stalemate.

"Baptism is a serious matter, not just a ceremony, my son. You grew angry when I reminded you of your white blood, yet now you want to learn white ways. Why?"

An odd smile quirked the corners of the boy's sculpted lips. "Perhaps I long to grow religious and have your Bird Spirit fill me."

Fray Bartolome's eyes gleamed. "I should not doubt the power of the Holy Ghost, but I do not believe you. Do you want to find your father?"

"Yes, more than anything," the youth answered truthfully.

"Would you become a Spaniard to please him? You can choose between two worlds, you know. Few men have such a chance."

"No. I will never live with him. I will join the Lipan again, but if your God is as strong as you say, let His Bird Spirit follow me back to them . . . if He dares."

"I will pray on it, son."

The following week, Green-Eyed Boy was baptized Joaquín Maria Alejandro. The name of Joaquín suggested itself to Fray Bartolome the very night before the baptism. He did not know why, since it, unlike the other names, had no familiar association attached to it. But somehow it was right.

After a week of basic catechismal instructions and then his baptism, Joaquín began his lessons in earnest. Never had Fray Bartolome seen a keener intelligence. The boy was like a sponge, picking up reading and writing with skill and speed. He also went through the motions of religious observances, fooling everyone but the shrewd priest.

After nearly a year had passed, Joaquín appeared unannounced in Bartolome's study one day. The boy had missed confession for several weeks and Fray Bartolome had debated confronting him. Not that his confessions were ever of any depth, but they were at least an instrument of communication.

He smiled in welcome. "Please, sit down, Joaquín. I've missed you in the library—and the confessional.

You were not in church last Sunday either." He waited, knowing the boy would answer in his own good time.

Joaquín was startlingly well poised for an eleven-year-old, tall and mature for his age. When he looked at the priest, his eyes were dark. "I went into the city last Saturday after finishing my chores."

In his white cotton shirt, full pants, and leather sandals, the boy could easily pass for one of the numerous "civilized Indians" inhabiting the province. Few would question a green-eyed boy in peasant's garb who was fluent, in Spanish. "Why did you go alone to Chihuahua City without my permission?" the priest asked gravely.

"One of the travelers who stayed here the night before said my father was in the great City of Mexico. I wanted to see if anyone else had heard this."

"And had they?"

"No," the boy confessed flatly.

Fray Bartolome studied the boy's expression for some clue to his carefully hidden emotions. When he had tried to get Joaquín to let out the pent-up grief over his mother's death, the boy would not even speak her name. Lipan felt it dangerous and disrespectful to say aloud the name of a departed relative. He did say his mother and all his Lipan family were killed by the Spanish when he was taken to the mines. Then he had refused to say more. That breakthrough had been months ago. Now this. The priest asked carefully, "Why do you want to find your father, Joaquín? To show him what a fine, bright son he has?"

"No, Fray Bartolome," the boy replied levelly. His clear green eyes stared measuringly back. "I wish to kill him."

Chapter 2

Madrid, Spain, October 1774

Orlena was very nervous as she inspected herself in the long French rococco mirror in her bedroom. Her maid Maria fussed endlessly with the ruffles at her neck, then again smoothed the rich red velvet of her gown. Her long, dark golden curls were set back with combs and flowed in ringlets down her back.

"How beautiful! Just like your porcelain doll from France," Maria exclaimed, proud of her handiwork. Getting the active five-year-old Orlena to stand still to untangle her hair was trial enough, much less to dress her in such finery. But the normally vivacious child was strangely subdued this morning, making Maria's job far easier.

"Do you really think I'm beautiful?" Orlena asked uncertainly, her small hands running over the rich folds of her velvet skirt. The clothes were so stiff and hot! She must remain cool and not sweat like one of the horses in her brother Ignacio's stables. Today was the most important day of her life. She was meeting Don Conal Quinn, soon to be her new stepfather.

Just then her mother entered the room, beaming at her lovely daughter. "So, Maria, you have done well. You may leave us now," she said quietly to the young maid, who curtsied and left silently.

Orlena noted the glow on her Mama's face. Serafina had never acted this way with her father. Perhaps Don Conal would be kinder than her cold, unloving father, who had died nearly two years ago. She curtsied as she had been taught, then waited obediently for her mother to address her.

Serafina looked at the pale, nervous child, wanting to reassure her, but afraid encouragement would restore her daughter's penchant for disastrous pranks. They were at court, not the country estate where her husband Pedro had exiled them in his last years. Orlena must not disgrace herself in front of Conal—not to mention the king and all his courtiers!

"You do understand how important this day is, do you not, Orlena?"

"Yes, Mama. I must be presented to Don Conal. He is a very brave soldier from New Spain." Her face crinkled in childish puzzlement, but when her mother began to reiterate all the proper rules of protocol, Orlena quickly gave up the idea of asking questions—at least for the present.

While mother and daughter rehearsed, Conal waited in the specially appointed chambers, fuming. His interview with his soon-to-be stepson had gone badly. Pray God the girl would be more easily won over. With one look at Ignacio's cold, aristocratic face and pale Castillian features, Conal had known the boy could smell the stench of a mercenary clinging to him.

Damn, I come from good bloodlines, the best! The Quinns had been of a noble Irish house, but unfortunately had chosen to defy their English overlords, resulting in the loss of their lands and titles. Conal had learned at an early age that he must regain for himself what his ancestors had squandered back in Ireland. He had killed and stolen to survive, then to obtain money sufficient to buy a commission in the English army. But his fierce Irish temper had led to a disagreement with a fellow officer, a fatal one for the English peer's son. That was when Conal had first become acquainted with sailing ships. He had stowed away across the channel to France, then to Spain. Now finally, after years of living by his sword and his wits, everything was about to come to fruition—if that accursed boy and his foppish cronies did not ruin it!

He considered the Viceroy's glowing reports, which had preceded him to Madrid, praising his valor in making New Mexico safe for settlement. Let the spoiled, crafty Ignacio do his worst! The king had already set his seal on the alliance between the great house of Valdéz and Conal Quinn. He had made friends at court and had easily charmed Serafina. She was no great beauty, but she was not uncomely either, with her dark brown hair and pale olive complexion. A trifle on the thin side for his taste, but after all, she was several years his senior. She had borne her first husband five children. Fortunately for Conal, only the eldest boy and one young girl had lived. Thinking of the girl, he smiled to himself. Women he could always handle.

As if on cue, Serafina and Orlena were announced. Conal observed the small, golden-haired girl. With her fair coloring and clear amber eyes, she obviously took after the Valdéz side of the family.

"How lovely you are, little butterfly." *Mariposa.* How the Spanish word rolled off his tongue. It fit her perfectly as she made a dainty curtsy. She smiled tremulously at first, then with more spirit at the friendly, red-haired giant.

"Why am I a butterfly, Don Conal?" Her wide-eyed, childish question caused him to laugh just as Serafina was about to rebuke the girl for her forwardness.

"No, no, my dear, do not scold. It is a fair question." Conal turned from her to the child, who reached for his proffered hand with boundless confidence.

The two strolled leisurely across the room to a large window seat, richly cushioned in maroon velvet. The bright morning sunlight filtered through the heavy, leaded-glass panes like warm honey, further enriching the child's exotic coloring.

"You, little one, are like a butterfly, golden hair, eyes—even your skin."

Serafina frowned. "I have tried to keep her indoors, but the moment my back is turned, she is out at the stables, riding without any protection for her fair complexion."

"I hate silly hats," the child said, eliciting another rumble of laughter from Quinn, who watched how she turned her attention eagerly from her prim mother to him. He had heard that old Don Pedro was a cold fish, like his son. The girl was looking for a surrogate father. Good, he could use that to his advantage.

"You speak wonderful Spanish," Orlena said ingenuously. "I thought you were an Irishman. Do they not speak Irish?"

Conal's eyes darkened as he recalled his homeland. "It is called Gaelic, and yes, I grew up speaking that tongue and English, the language of our conquerors," he added bitterly. Then his eyes lit up again and he took her hand, saying gravely, "I thank you for the compliment on my Spanish. It is all I have spoken since I was but a lad."

NIGHT WIND'S WOMAN

Orlena was impressed. All she could speak was Spanish. Her brother had tutors who taught him Latin and French, but girls were not permitted such indulgences. How she longed to learn about the great wide world this man represented. She squeezed his big, callused hand.

Conal watched the way she fluttered her thick dark lashes and made a pretty little moue. Then he remembered that the Spanish word for butterfly also translated into flirt. He decided not to ask her to call him papa.

La Villa de Realización, Spain, 1775

A soft breeze swept across the orchard behind the formal gardens on her family's estate, but Orlena was not comforted by its refreshing coolness. She had been sent away from the house, even banished from the fountain in the central courtyard where she often played. Maria had been instructed to get her out of earshot of the terrible screams of her mother. It seemed hours since she had awakened to the first cry at daybreak. Now it was well onto the supper hour.

The maid had brought a picnic of meat pastries and fresh sweet peaches at noon. Maria had tried to cajole the frightened child to eat, but Orlena had refused. Looking down at the glistening, sweet fruit in her hand, her stomach now rumbled in protest, but still she could not take a bite.

"Is my mother going to die, Maria?" she asked in a very small voice, afraid of the answer.

"No, of course not, little one! She is only going to give you a new baby sister or brother. Sometimes it takes a long while. Be patient and eat your peach." Maria walked over to the child and reached for her hand. "We could walk to the stables and see your new pony," she suggested hopefully.

Orlena shook her head stubbornly. Even the beautiful new filly Conal had bought her would not distract her today.

Conal and Ignacio were both in the house, tolerating each other's presence in strained silence. Ignacio, who had lived with his paternal uncle at court the past year, had come for a brief visit. Orlena had scarcely spoken to him, for he always ignored her. Mostly he ignored Mama, too, but she and Conal had argued with him late last night. Now Mama was having the baby. Orlena was certain Ignacio's hatefulness had caused something to go wrong.

Last month, when Orlena had stolen into the kitchen for a crisp heel of bread and freshly churned butter, several of the women had been discussing Serafina's pregnancy. She eavesdropped on the conversation and then fled in fear. They said the lady was too old and frail to bear more children. She should never have been married to a lusty younger man like the Irishman.

Orlena had watched her emaciated mother grow great with the child she carried ill-concealed beneath the suffocating layers of pleated, ugly dresses designed for a lady's confinement. *I shall never have a child and let my belly grow fat like that,* she vowed to herself.

The girl had no idea why Conal's presence had anything to do with Serafina's predicament. Indeed, he had become the brightest spot in her life in the months since she had first met him at court. He laughed with her and teased her, spoiled her with outrageously expensive presents, even took her riding on her splendid new pony. Shortly after the marriage, her mother had become wan and ill, giving little time to her daughter. Ignacio had always disdained her, but since Conal had come into their lives, it seemed her brother disliked her even more. Conal was her only confidant among all the adults in her family. Perhaps this new baby would not be such a bad thing—as long as her mother was all right, she guiltily amended.

Just then, a shout went up from the house. It sounded like Conal's voice. Orlena broke away from Maria and raced pell-mell through the orchard toward the courtyard, holding her gown up in a very unladylike fashion as she leaped over rocks and logs.

Coming down from Serafina's room, Conal headed to the *sala* for a bottle of fine old Madeira he had been saving to celebrate. A son! He had a fine, lusty red-haired son, the heir to replace that puny, scheming Ignacio. Let Ignacio keep his paternal inheritance. Now Santiago Quinn would inherit all the wealth of the Guardunos, plus the sizable lands a grateful Charles III had bestowed on Conal.

Just as he lifted the glass to his lips, Orlena burst into the room, her face ashen, her breath coming in painful gulps. Taking a quick sip of the fine old wine, he set the glass down and scooped her up, tossing her into the air exuberantly. "Rejoice, little Butterfly! You have a new baby brother and we have named him Santiago for the patron saint of Spain and for my long dead father."

When he had twirled her about and set her back on the ground, she gathered her faltering courage and asked, "Is . . . is Mama all right?"

His face slashed into a wide, handsome grin. "Never better," he reassured the girl. In fact, Serafina had passed out with exhaustion as soon as the boy was born. The midwife had told him, given the size of the boy and her advanced years, that it was a miracle she had survived the birth. Now that he had his heir, he would leave her cold bed permanently. Actually, he had already done so on the very day Serafina had announced her pregnancy. Several comely wenches in the village, as well as highborn ladies at court, had kept him well entertained. But he had produced an heir!

Conal smiled beatifically and reached for Orlena's hand. "Would you like to meet your new little brother?"

Orlena returned the smile uncertainly. Mama was all right, and she had a new brother who seemed to please her idol. Just so long as the baby did not replace *her* in Conal's affections!

As she walked upstairs with him, she asked tentatively, "Does he have red hair or tan hair?" She hoped he would not be like Ignacio.

"Hair as red as mine, Butterfly!"

Orlena laughed. "Good! Then I am sure I shall like him!"

The joyous pair ascending the winding stairs did not see Ignacio. His narrowed, yellow cat's eyes brooded on their retreating figures.

Chapter 3

Aranjuez, Spain, June 1787

Orlena shivered as a draft of cool night air hit her. The hour was late and if she was found unescorted in this part of the palace, it would create a terrible scandal—almost as great as if her fiancé had been caught tearing her dress off in the woods this afternoon, she thought grimly. In retrospect, she realized that telling Ignacio had been the feckless gesture of a foolish child. Of course he would not be incensed at the besmirching of her honor. He was the one who had arranged the politically expedient marriage, was he not?

"I must convince Santiago. Conal will do anything for him," she murmured to herself, then smiled. Most of the time Conal would do anything for her, too. Hearing muffled footsteps on the carpet and low giggling, she quickly secreted herself behind a heavy drapery in a window alcove.

One of the young court gallants and his latest

paramour, the wife of a duke, passed her while busily engaged in blatantly flirtatious loveplay. The old king would never countenance this, Orlena thought sadly. Charles III had ever been a faithful husband and had led a chaste life since the queen's death a quarter of a century ago. Soon he would join her. Then the weak Prince of Asturias would be king and Ignacio would possess frightful power.

"I will not live within his cruel grasp another day," she vowed, again gliding undetected down the hallway, heedless of the opulence of velvet, marble, and gold surrounding her.

When Serafina died, Orlena had been only a child, shuffled from a maiden aunt to a series of distant female cousins at court, mostly ignored by the noblewomen and pampered by the servants. The bright spots in her childhood were those spent with Conal and Santiago. They were her real family. And now she needed them as never before!

A soft rapping on the sitting room door awakened Santiago Quinn, who in truth slept none too soundly anyway. Tomorrow his great adventure would begin. He and his papa would go to Cadiz and thence to the Viceroyalty of New Spain, where Papa would be governor of a whole province!

Santiago's deaf old servant, Rubio, snored soundly on a pallet as the boy slipped into the sitting room and opened the door to their apartments. Rubio knew what the boy did not, that Conal's appointment was really a banishment engineered by his elder half-brother, who hated Conal. But Rubio would say nothing to his young master.

"Orlena! What do you do, abroad so late—with no *dueña*, of course!" Santiago's childish voice broke in horror as he inspected her—she was clad only in a silk robe! He quickly yanked her inside the door, then

NIGHT WIND'S WOMAN

stuck his head out to see that the hall was empty and she had not been followed.

"I had to dress simply. One does not sneak down corridors at midnight with hoops and panniers," Orlena said, knowing how shocked the boy was.

His eyes glowed with amazement as he asked, "Why have you come? We already said our good-byes." His adam's apple bobbed as he swallowed hard, determined not to humiliate himself again with womanish tears, as he had yesterday.

Orlena took his small, chubby hands in hers. Still the hands of a little boy, poised on the brink of adolescence, she thought. "Santiago, I cannot let you go and leave me to Ignacio's mercy. The marriage he plans for me will be unendurable." She paused, unsure of how to explain to an eleven-year-old child what had transpired that morning between her and her fiancé, Gabriel. She began again, very carefully, "You and your papa plan a very grand adventure. I would like to share it, not languish here in this boring old court."

"So you would become a pioneer, eh?" Conal stood with one shoulder braced against the doorway.

His hair had grayed slightly at the temples and lines creased his eyes and surrounded his mouth, but he was still lean and vigorous, the handsome, laughing man his stepdaughter had worshipped since childhood. Conal looked at the lush curves revealed by her sheer silk robe. The dark amber color of the fabric matched her eyes and hair. Always the promise of beauty had hovered about Serafina's waif, but in the last two years that promise had more than been realized. He had been so occupied with the power struggle at court and enamored of a series of mistresses that he had left her and Santiago to their tutors too long.

The boy, of course, had to be educated, but when the girl had pleaded to sit in on his lessons, learning not only to read, write, and cipher, but to comprehend philosophy, history, and literature with a mind as keen as Santiago's, Conal had been amazed and indulgent. Serafina had never learned to do more than sign her name, and many women of the Spanish nobility could not even do that. He had delighted in the bright, enchanting child. Now the magnificent promise of her womanhood robbed him of breath.

Orlena ran to the doorway between the sitting room and Conal's bedchamber to embrace him with a girlish hug and a squeal of delight greatly at variance with her seductive attire. "Conal, I knew you would not be far from my brother the day before your adventure begins!"

Slowly Quinn released her and sighed. Quirking a reddish brow sardonically, he said, "Adventure, Butterfly? We are banished to a land of sand and scorpions. You would do well to remain here in the seat of power, in luxury. You cannot imagine what hardships await a gently reared woman in New Spain."

As he knew it would, Orlena's lower lip stuck out in a pout. "Oh, bother hardships!" Then she darted a glance at Santiago and her eyes conveyed a message to Conal.

"Santiago, fetch us some cool wine from the antechamber. Go slow and see you do not spill it." Conal closed the door and turned expectantly to her, waiting.

"Gabriel tried to rape me this morning." As his face hardened menacingly, she tersely described the disgusting encounter and her subsequent interview with Ignacio. She finished by saying quietly, "So you see, I must either go with you or my brother will force me into a convent here, for surely I will not wed that aged lecher." Her voice was now choked with revulsion.

Conal had always observed that Orlena had an open, affectionate nature with most people. She craved attention and love, but there was always a wariness to her, some part of her untouched, afraid, hidden away. Often he had idly speculated about how she would react in her marriage bed, concluding that there was passion in her—if only the right man unleashed it. He took her in his arms and held her, soothing her sobs.

"Ah, Butterfly, do not cry, please," he crooned. "It quite unmans me."

She looked up with infinite trust, her wide eyes unblinking, hopeful.

"It will take some craft, but mayhap we can smuggle you aboard ship!" he said with a mock sigh of surrender.

Orlena's cry of joy was drowned out by her younger brother. With a whoop, Santiago deposited his tray on the table and catapulted into their arms. In the excitement, no one noticed that he had overturned the decanter. Blood red wine dripped off the edge of the marble table and seeped into the carpet.

Chihuahua City, Fall 1787

"It has changed little in the past two years," the tall man clothed only in breechclout and moccasins said. He slid effortlessly from his horse, hidden deep in the shadows of the cottonwoods outside the Franciscan mission. Swift and silent as the night wind for which he was named, he walked to the other horse and lifted a crumpled man from its back. The rider's body was slick with blood and the horse snorted and shied nervously.

"Easy, boy, easy," Night Wind said as he soothed the horse with a melodic whisper. He turned to his injured companion and asked, "Are you able to walk?"

"I will walk," the man gritted out in pain. "But these white men, will they not betray us to the soldiers?"

Night Wind smiled as he helped his friend. "Only wait, Hoarse Bark. The priest is he who rescued me when we escaped the mines."

"The one who taught you white ways all those years ago?" Hoarse Bark echoed in amazement.

"I have visited him often over the years," Night Wind said dryly, recalling all the fierce arguments and sweet reasonableness with which Fray Bartolome had tried to woo him to pacifism. And here he was again, risking death or slavery with yet another fugitive. When they reached the side door in the mission wall, Night Wind helped Hoarse Bark lean against the cool, rough adobe. He agilely slipped over the wall and then slid the bolt on the iron gate.

"Come quickly," he commanded, helping his companion through the dense garden foliage toward a dim light burning in the rear of a low building beyond the church.

At the light tapping on his door, Fray Bartolome put aside the book he had been reading. He shoved back the massive oak chair and stood, rubbing his tired eyes, then walked to the door and opened it.

"I might have known it would be you, Joaquín. It is past midnight," he said sourly, opening the door wider to admit the half-caste and his injured companion.

"And I might have known you would be up reading even though it is well past midnight." Joaquín's expression was warm as he looked at the older man who for thirteen years had been his mentor in the white world. "I have brought a friend. I hope that was a medical treatise, not the life of Saint Francis you were reading. Hoarse Bark needs help."

"Through that door. Let us put him on my bed and I will look at him. Hoarse Bark," Fray Bartolome echoed. "He is the Mescalero boy from the mines? You have not seen him in all these years!"

Joaquín helped the priest stretch Hoarse Bark on the bed in the adjacent room. "We encountered one another by chance only this morning, Father."

As he examined the youth's shoulder, the priest grunted, "And this encounter did not perchance involve soldiers or mine owners?" One shaggy greying eyebrow arched in disapproval.

"Only their mules, several dozen destined to pull the *arrastras* at Señor Hurtades' gold mines," Joaquín said impenitently. "Hoarse Bark and his Mescaleros had the same idea I did, but the Spanish had laid a trap with extra soldiers in ambush. My men were fortunate to escape unscathed, but only a small handful of Hoarse Bark's companions were as blessed."

"Blessed!" The priest snorted as he brought a basin of clean water and bandages from the crude oak cabinet. "Your vendetta against slavery in the mines is understandable, my son, but sooner or later the soldiers will entrap you and those who follow you."

The argument was one they had often had over the years. Both men knew how useless it was, but neither would abandon his convictions. Joaquín, Fray Bartolome's brilliant young pupil, had lived for seven years at the mission, absorbing every bit of information he could about his Spanish conquerors. He had learned how to pass among them with detested disguises as a "Tame Indian." He could speak Castillian

Spanish as fluently as a scholar when the occasion suited him, yet he had spent most of his time for the past six years living with a small band of Lipans in the Guadalupe Mountains.

"Night Wind will never be caught, holy man," Hoarse Bark said, ignoring the sharp agony of his bloodied shoulder while the priest cleaned it and probed with a sharp knife for the bullet lodged in the flesh.

"Night Wind is it? Your reputation precedes you from Durango to Santa Fe, Joaquín. I have been hearing stories of an infamous raider and his band of renegades. Apaches who steal and kill. Small wonder you have had no time in the past two years to visit me and the good brothers here!"

"I will not defend how I live," Joaquín said in weary resignation. Shrugging helplessly, he added, "I am sorry I have not come to see you sooner."

The priest raised his eyes from the stoic Mescalero and stared at the tall, hard-looking young man standing beside him. Joaquín looked for all the world like an embarrassed schoolboy unable to complete his Latin conjugations.

"Hurmph. For killing and stealing you have no guilt. For neglecting your old teacher you are stricken with it." The priest broke into a sad, gentle smile. "My son, you cannot continue to move between the Apache and Spanish worlds, living as a raider. You could build a life helping the Indians. War and plunder only bring more Spanish guns."

"Yes, I plunder Spanish mines and kill Spanish soldiers. Think you if I stopped—if all those like me laid down their arms—that it would do any good? The conquerors would turn all able-bodied Indians into slaves and butcher the infirm like cattle!" Joaquín watched Fray Bartolome shake his head, and noticed for the first time the gray that tinged his dark hair.

The priest bandaged the Mescalero's shoulder after applying a poultice to the wound. Then he said quietly, "If you and those such as you would teach the others what you have learned of white civilization, a compromise might be reached. The day of the nomadic society of the hunters passed for the Europeans. So must it, too, for the Indians."

"Would you have us live like the Pueblo?" Joaquín asked with contempt in his voice.

"They live in peace and keep many of their old ways," the priest argued.

Joaquín's voice was laced with irony. "Yes, they are allowed to live in peace if they adopt the Christian religion and pay the Spanish tax collectors."

"We speak of survival, Joaquín, not the uncompromising triumph of the Indian way. As to the religion . . ." his voice trailed away as the old confusion and doubt again assailed him. "I have been too long in the wilderness and have seen too much. I do not know, my son, if God wants his sheep brought to him at the point of Spanish swords."

"You know it is wrong," Joaquín countered, then relented. "Often the Church is the only thing which stands between my people and outright destruction at the hands of the Spanish military. You saved my life—now Hoarse Bark's life—and many others over the years. If only more white men were like you and the brothers."

The priest covered the Mescalero with a coarse cotton sheet. "He needs nourishment. Come. I will warm some good hot soup to strengthen him, and you will tell me all that has passed since last you left us."

Much later, as the first pink streaks of dawn cast a soft glow of light across the earthen floor, the priest and the half-caste still sat across from one another in the front room of the cabin, which was Fray Bartolome's library and work room. Rude and bare but for the startlingly large collection of books, it served his simple needs well.

"I am sorry beyond measure for your wife's death. I will pray for her soul . . . that is, if you do not think her Apache gods would mind?" the priest said after Joaquín had told him of his marriage nearly two years ago and his wife's death from smallpox. It explained much about Joaquín's long absence. He had been grieving. The white men who brought the disease had given Night Wind another reason to hate them. Fray Bartolome sighed sadly. "Always I had hoped you would settle down and have a family."

Joaquín's drawn face softened a bit. "I have found a family, Father. When a Lipan takes a wife, even if she dies, still he is bound to her parents. I live with Slim Reed's family and provide for them."

"I am glad of their consolation, but I can see your soul is in pain," Fray Bartolome said simply.

Joaquín arched one slim black brow. "And I know you will pray to the Christian God for me as well as for Slim Reed." Gratitude for the older man's unconditional friendship was written plainly on his face.

"You have become used to white ways. Green-Eyed Boy would never have spoken the name of one departed. But I fear you have lost the Apache religion without gaining the Christian one."

Joaquín shrugged. "As you said, Father, I live between two worlds. I may be equipped by education to assume a place in the white man's world, but not by race. I am only half white. I do what I must do." He shrugged and looked away.

"You can choose another path. Leave vengeance behind, Joaquín." The priest's gray eyes glowed with intensity as he forced the young man to meet his gaze.

NIGHT WIND'S WOMAN

"When you came here an abused and mistrustful child, I convinced you to be baptized and I chose your Christian name. At first I could not think why Joaquín suggested itself to me. Now I understand. Perhaps someday you will as well." He paused, then said, "The name Joaquín is of Hebrew origin. While studying the Old Testament several years ago, I learned its literal meaning." His eyes warmed with mirth. "A very literal people, the Hebrews, with much to admire in their civilization."

"Do not let the Holy Office hear you speak so. They would have you burned as a Jew," Joaquín replied with irony. "Your tolerance for Indians has already made you suspect."

"I will take my chances. Only remember this when you next ride away from here. Joaquín means, The Lord Will Judge."

A smile curved the younger man's lips. "Perhaps your Lord has chosen the Night Wind as the instrument of his judgment."

Chapter 4

For several days as Hoarse Bark mended, Joaquín stayed at the mission. Dressed in the white cotton pants and shirt of a *paisano*, a mixed-blooded peasant farmer, he would go into the city during the day to learn about the movements of Spanish troops and shipments of gold. His nights he spent with the brothers at the mission, renewing old acquaintances with the frail, elderly Domingo and the naive, younger Alonzo. He and Fray Bartolome would argue philosophy, history, and literature far into the cool fall evenings. This was a time of respite and tranquility for his troubled spirit. He knew that when the Mescalero was able to travel, they would rejoin his raiders in the mountains and resume their guerilla war on the whites. Hoarse Bark, who had lost the last of his family in the raid when he was injured, had chosen to join Night Wind in his vendetta.

However, the last thing on Joaquín's mind as he

greeted the fruit vendors and leather carvers of the huge public market in the plaza was revenge. He wended his way across the crowded square, past mules laden with the pungent cargo of citrus fruits and chocolate from the south and stiff, odoriferous buffalo hides from the northwest. Long reddish-brown chains of chilies hung innocently in the warm morning air, their incredible potency seemingly shriveled by the sun.

He passed old Señora Quiros as she briskly stirred lime into a boiling pot filled with corn husks. Her daughter was busy at her stone *metate,* grinding the softened, husked corn into a paste, which she then efficiently shaped into thin cakes. The smell of the fresh tortillas filled the air and Joaquín stopped to buy several from her.

The pretty young *paisana* looked at the handsome stranger with liquid brown eyes that reminded him of Slim Reed. Simple trust and honesty shone forth in her round, placid face. Fleetingly he considered bedding her, but he knew the probability that her confession of lying with a half-caste stranger would come to Fray Bartolome's ears. He was one of only three priests in residence for the whole of Chihuahua City, whose population exceeded five thousand Catholic souls. He regretfully decided against indulging his sexual appetite and bought several more tortillas to appease his stomach instead.

As he munched and strolled with deceptive casualness through the huge plaza, he listened and observed. Chihuahua City was the headquarters for the military command of all the northern internal provinces. A great deal of information came through servants of the *ricos,* people who were invaluable to their high and mighty Spanish masters.

As he sat cleaning chickens in front of his small

butcher stall, one shopkeeper said, "The new governor of the province of New Mexico arrived last evening on his journey to Santa Fe. They say he is a brave soldier who received many honors from his Catholic Majesty at the Spanish court."

"Hah!" another merchant sweeping chicken feathers from his doorway snorted in disgust. "Some honor. New Mexico is full of wild Apache and Comanche. I do not envy this Spaniard his job!"

So, the most isolated of all the internal provinces was to have a new governor. *Some Spanish soldier turned courtier*, Joaquín mused to himself. Perhaps he would head to the west side of the plaza toward the military academy and barracks where an official visitor would most likely be housed. He could size up his new adversary first hand before the governor even reached his post.

When he arrived at the military headquarters, a large crowd had assembled to view the celebrity as he and his entourage departed with due pomp. Joaquín saw a large contingent of smartly dressed soldiers, obviously dispatched from the City of Mexico to serve as personal escort for the governor. No provincials ever had uniforms that matched, much less the latest in Miquelet Lock muskets. The new governor must be taking his ease for a day or two before the next leg of his arduous trek, for the soldiers were preparing for an inspection, not a journey. *A nice show of imperial authority here in the hinterlands*, Joaquín thought in amusement. Then his eyes followed those of one young lieutenant. A young woman stood in the archway of a courtyard off the commander's palace, arguing with an older woman. Their voices became increasingly strident as a boy rode up with a magnificent bay stallion in tow, rigged with a lady's sidesaddle. Stamping her foot, the imperious girl whirled

NIGHT WIND'S WOMAN

away from her frowning *dueña* and headed toward the skittish horse. Joaquín wended his way past the gawkers at the parade inspection toward the secluded garden. The beautiful señorita merited a closer look. Often he found women of the nobility to be most useful sources of information and other amusements. When he was about twenty feet from her, he could see her delicately beautiful face and the burnished magnificence of her hair. "Like old Spanish coins," he murmured to himself.

Her coloring was indeed unusual, a deep, rich gold matched by large gold eyes with thick dark lashes. Such elegant blonde perfection marked her as a Castilian aristocrat, most probably the governor's wife or a mistress brought from Madrid. Her lisping Castilian accent confirmed his guess as he heard her arguing with the boy, who had dismounted in front of her.

"Papa will be furious, Orlena. He forbade your riding this horse. Doña Inez will tell on us," the boy implored.

"Oh, bother the old harridan! Santiago, I abhor these rude colonials and their foolish pretensions. She would doubtless prefer I ride in one of the wooden-wheeled baggage carts all the way to Santa Fe! Any of His Majesty's stables would yield horses as spirited as this one and I've ridden the best of them since I was younger than you."

"But you are a girl," the adolescent protested.

"Bah! I will deal with Conal when he returns. You know he always gives us whatever we want," she replied blithely as she mounted gracefully without so much as a leg up from the youth.

Joaquín stood in the shadows, considering the girl's words. This Santiago must be the new governor's son, now brought within his grasp! "Let us see if I cannot rob him of his whelp," he whispered.

Joaquín watched the pair through slitted eyes as they rode down a narrow back street, a stupid, dangerous lark for two unarmed children. Chihuahua City was a frontier outpost in a savage wilderness where the Spanish peasantry was as capable of violence against the nobility as were the marauding Apaches.

Looking at the palace, Joaquín concluded that the governor was too well guarded to reach easily, but the road between Chihuahua and Santa Fe was a long one. He had much time to ponder his plans. For now, he decided to follow Santiago and the golden-haired woman. Somehow that one did not have the look of a bride in a May-December marriage. She was obviously too young to be the boy's mother; he concluded that she must be the governor's mistress.

Quickly crossing the plaza, he mounted Warpaint, his large piebald stallion standing untethered beyond a copse of cottonwoods. Cutting across back streets, Joaquín quickly caught up with his quarry, then followed them at a discreet distance as a plan began to form in his mind.

The haughty Europeans rode imperiously by *paisanas* toiling in small garden plots, their horses' hooves stirring up dust that blew into the women's faces. "They act as if they are two schoolchildren on a holiday," he muttered, adding a fitting Spanish oath. When they headed outside town past the large, ugly slag heaps created by the ore smelting, he was disgusted with their stupidity. The mines to the north were no place for a beautiful woman with only a boy to protect her.

Suddenly, a pair of men rode out from behind a mountain of debris, a string of pack mules trailing behind the second fellow. They were guards sent to town for supplies and their eyes lit on the golden vision materialized before them.

"Eh, Pablo, look at what we have here," the fat one said as he blocked Orlena's path. She wrinkled her nose at the stench of his unwashed body.

"Let us pass," she commanded in her most arrogant voice. When they did not move, she suddenly wished that, instead of her most elegant riding habit, she had donned the boy's disguise she had worn on her flight from Spain.

"I am the son of the governor of New Mexico, and this is my sister! Touch her and Don Conal will kill you without mercy," Santiago said as he tried to get between Orlena and the two ruffians.

The cadaverous one grinned evilly, revealing rotted black teeth. "Some high and mighty rich boy." Without warning his right arm snaked out, and the heavy whip stock he was carrying knocked Santiago from his horse. He fell to the earth in an unconscious heap.

Orlena pulled her quirt back and slashed furiously at her brother's assailant, screaming, "If you have harmed my brother I will kill you, filthy colonial rabble!"

The fat man maneuvered his horse behind her as she struggled with the thin guard. With a grunt he dragged her from her saddle. Orlena kicked and cried as she attempted to use her little whip on him, all to no avail. He pinned her arms to her sides and lifted her across his saddle like a prize of war.

"You must share with me, *mano*," the thin one said petulantly. "Let us take her behind that hill where the earth is soft with fresh mud. The boy is dead. He will not bother us."

With a grunt the fat man agreed, turning his horse to ride between the hillocks of mine refuse. His companion followed him, leading their mules. They ignored Santiago, who lay in the road.

Joaquín heard Orlena's screams and urged

Warpaint into a gallop. Pulling a wicked-looking knife from a hidden sheath beneath his trouser leg, he checked the Miquelet Lock pistol he had withdrawn from his saddlebag. By the time he found the boy struggling to rise from the middle of the road, he could see no trace of Orlena. Both horses stood near Santiago, but the woman's bay backed skittishly away when he reined in his horse.

Santiago's face was chalky with terror. "Orlena," he rasped at the hard-looking man armed with knife and pistol. "Those men, they will hurt her—"

A sharp scream, followed by a guttural curse rang out. Joaquín wheeled Warpaint toward the source of the noise. He found the girl pinned to the soft, muddy earth near a sluggish stream. Her skirts were being shoved up by a fat, greasy-looking Spaniard while another one held her arms in a cruel grip. Her hat had been knocked off and great masses of dark gold hair lay spilled on the grey earth as she thrashed.

He took careful aim and shot the fat one through the center of his back, then slid from Warpaint, racing toward the thin man, who released the girl's arms and quickly drew the knife from his belt. Joaquín jumped him and they rolled through the soft mud in a blur.

Orlena was crushed beneath the dead guard's weight, struggling to free herself from the stench of lust and death. She could feel his blood on her hand as she pushed at his body. With a final shudder, she shoved him away and sat up to view the battle raging between her other attacker and her rescuer.

Just then the slim, dark stranger rolled up over his adversary and pinned him to the muddy earth with one knee on his chest. Grabbing the long, greasy hair of the guard, the *paisano* pulled it to bare the man's neck, which he cleanly slashed from side to side. Orlena quickly averted her eyes from the gory specta-

NIGHT WIND'S WOMAN

cle, fighting down waves of nausea.

Blessed Mother, how she hated swooning women! She struggled to her feet as the stranger rose from his handiwork. After cleaning his knife on the shirt of the corpse, he carelessly sheathed it beneath a full trouser leg.

In a few lithe, silent strides he approached her, then stopped. Orlena pulled her torn blouse together and tried to hide the swell of her breasts from his piercing eyes. She could feel their cold green glare of assessment sweep her body. Pulling her muddied hair like a cloak across her shoulders to cover the irreparable damage to her clothing, she returned his bold perusal with a regal stare, then spoke. "Did you see a young boy with red hair—"

"The governor's cub is harmed no worse than you," he answered curtly in perfect Spanish. Joaquín felt a surge of desire squeeze the breath from him. The courtesan's haughty manner enhanced rather than detracted from her beauty. The sweet-faced wholesomeness of the girl in the market paled in comparison with this woman. How he would love to humble this Orlena and have her beg him for loving, as so many other fine Spanish ladies had done!

Before Orlena could decide whether he was a rescuer or another brigand, she heard the thunder of horses and Santiago's shout, "Papa!"

With an oath snarled in a strange dialect, the dark stranger slipped past her and vaulted onto the back of his magnificent horse. Wheeling the stallion around with the lightest touch of his knee, he rode in the opposite direction.

Orlena stood for a moment watching the fluid grace of man and animal meld perfectly. Then she realized that he had mounted from the right. The horse's saddle, if the strapped-on blanket and minimal stir-

49

rups could be called such, was Indian. He was Indian! Or at least, of mixed blood, a *casta*, whose finely chiseled features betrayed his heritage. Terrified, she turned and ran with her torn skirts hiked up to her knees.

Conal frantically embraced Santiago and examined him. "I should horsewhip you! Are you injured?" He examined the cut swelling into a bloody lump on the boy's temple.

Although seeing double and still disoriented, Santiago croaked out, "Orlena—the other man went to help her. Two men attacked us and dragged her there." He pointed to the path between the hills.

When Orlena rounded the hill at a run, Joaquín watched Santiago race to embrace her. The boy's father walked toward them in long, furious strides. Even from his observation point on the top of the hillock, Joaquín could sense the governor's leashed fury. They were yelling angrily. He could not discern their words from such a long distance, but he had seen enough to have his answer. The governor loved the son who was his mirror image. How would he like to see the boy raised as a Lipan?

Three hours later Joaquín's smile was calculating as he rode in a roundabout course toward the mission. He had spent the afternoon in the city learning about the new governor of New Mexico, his son, and the mysterious woman who traveled with them. His revenge would begin in Santa Fe.

Orlena sat in the hot, cramped quarters assigned her by the Commandant's wife. The room was stultifying, with its low ceiling, narrow windows, and crude plank floor. Heat seemed to radiate up from the floorboards. The rug was threadbare, and the dark pine furniture was crudely fashioned. It left splinters in her hands and tore her gowns.

As soon as she could escape Conal's scowling, furious presence, she had slipped upstairs to her room and undressed, ordering a bath. Santiago had nearly been murdered and she—Orlena forced her thoughts away from the filthy brutes who would have done such hideous things to her body. She could still smell the sour stench of sweaty wool jackets and grimy hands on her skin.

"Why do not those lazy half-caste servants bring the water," she gritted out. Orlena found herself shivering in the heat and went to lie down. She could still hear Conal's wrathful voice accusing her with deadly quiet intensity. Her adventure had nearly cost his son and her their lives. She felt miserable and guilty and defiled all at once.

Just then a knock at the door signaled the arrival of her bath water. Slipping on her robe, she opened the door to a stocky Indian servant. He walked in and began dumping the first of the two enormous pails of warm water into the hip bath near the window. She watched his straight black hair swing across his face as he bent over. The muscles bunched and rippled beneath his thin cotton shirt as he worked. When he turned, his task completed, he did not wait for her dismissal but hefted the buckets and walked past her. His expressionless face stared through her as if she were invisible.

Orlena closed the door with a shudder of distaste. She supposed she should have thanked him, but she felt unreasoningly angry at the slow, sullen Indian servants she had encountered in the long journey from the City of Mexico. Increasingly, her great adventure was turning into a greater nightmare with every mile they traveled northward.

Slipping into the warm water, to which she had

added jasmine scent, Orlena tried to relax her aching muscles, but her mind would not be still. She wondered if the Indian servant spoke Spanish. The half-caste who killed her attackers did. Perfect Spanish, not the crude dialect of the tame Indians, which she found so difficult to understand here in the north.

Every time she closed her eyes, a swarthy yet startlingly European face materialized in her mind. There was something about him, a leashed fury that baffled but also intrigued her.

In her years at the royal court, Orlena had learned that she was beautiful and that many men desired her, but she was used to playing by clearly laid-down rules, fending off amorous advances and controlling every situation. She knew the stranger also had desired her, but there was more. *He despised himself for it*! The thought made her sit up in the tub, splashing water onto the floor.

The shivering began again in spite of the noon heat. She hugged herself, feeling the tips of her breasts harden and her abdomen clench. His sneering, handsome face swam before her eyes. She could see the lean, muscular contours of his body outlined through his thin cotton *paisano's* clothes, see the smooth, catlike grace of his stride as he approached her. What would have happened if Conal had not arrived just then? Would he have touched her? Have done that terrible, disgusting thing to her that men did to make women pregnant? She forced the thought from her mind and reached for a towel. Would it be too much to hope that she could have a maid in Santa Fe—one who was not an Indian? As she dressed, she concentrated on how to placate Conal's anger and get back in his good graces.

* * *

NIGHT WIND'S WOMAN

As he rode into the deepening shadows of the cottonwoods behind the mission, Joaquín slowed his horse. Why did the richness of dark golden hair and fathomless amber eyes beckon him, as if she would suddenly materialize from behind the trees? She was the governor's woman. That alone should have been enough to cause revulsion, not lust. And she was a highborn creature of the decadent Spanish court, spoiled, haughty, and doubtless with the morals of an alley cat. He swore as he dismounted. "I would probably catch syphilis! Damn, concentrate on the governor and his son. I have much to do to capture the boy unharmed. The task will not be an easy one."

Fray Bartolome and the other brothers were just finishing their evening repast when Joaquín walked into the simple dining room of the mission, looking haggard and preoccupied. The priest saw him and smiled. "Hoarse Bark must be recovered. He has snared two rabbits and is roasting them out in the orchard over an open fire. We have beans and tortillas if you would prefer."

Joaquín nodded at the assembled men and said, "I thank you for the hospitality and apologize for being late for dinner. Perhaps some wild rabbit would taste good, though." He smiled slightly and added, "Two fat hares are too much for one skinny Mescalero to eat all by himself."

Later that evening, as they sat reading in his study, Fray Bartolome looked at Joaquín and said quietly, "You have seen him, haven't you?"

Very slowly Joaquín put the book he had been uselessly staring at down beside his chair. "I should have known you would hear. Does nothing that occurs between Durango and Texas escape your notice?"

"You have your sources. I have mine as well.

Learning that the Commandant General has as his house guest the new governor of our northern province would scarcely be a matter to be kept secret in a city the size of Chihuahua." The priest studied Joaquín. "You have fed on your hate for so long, my son. What will you do now? Waste your life in a futile attempt to kill him and be cut down by his soldiers?"

Joaquín's sculpted lips smiled, but his expression was brittle as mica. "I give you my solemn word, Father Bartolome, I do not plan to kill the governor. As to retribution . . . perhaps it comes in a way neither he nor you can imagine."

Chapter 5

Orlena swore as her riding skirt snagged and ripped on the sharp, curved spurs of a catclaw bush. Reining in the bay stallion, she struggled to free herself as Conal signaled for their caravan to stop.

"This accursed place is nothing but cactus and scorpions, I fear, a sad place indeed for a butterfly," he said as he guided his horse near hers. The low, grayish-green shrub snagged at his heavy jacket, but he pulled it free with a careless shrug. "God, but I hate this place! It rivals the lowest pit of hell!"

Orlena, who had freed her skirts, looked up at him and smiled gamely. "Ah, no. We should only be so fortunate, Conal. The lowest level of hell, Dante tells us, is naught but ice." She wiped the trickling perspiration from her brow, wishing for a cool draught of water.

He laughed heartily and signaled to the lieutenant to resume their ride. "I sometimes wish you had not cajoled me into letting you take lessons with Santiago." His eyes narrowed on her beautiful profile as she rode beside him. "You are entirely too erudite for a female."

"Why? Because I catch you out in your literary allusions?" She appeared to ponder, liking the new game that took her mind off the heat and the barren, mesquite-infested wilderness. "Or, perhaps, you mislike my bookishness for the same reasons Ignacio did. I shall be an old maid and a burden to you for the rest of your life."

His face became shuttered and somber. "Would that be so terrible, Butterfly? To spend the rest of your days at my side?"

Before Orlena could frame a reply to his oddly disconcerting question, Santiago came galloping across the rolling dusty ground, shouting to them.

"Look you, ahead! There is a line of tall poplar trees. The sergeant says it means water. Can we swim, Papa?"

"Learn one thing about this harsh land quickly, son. Water enough to keep a man alive and water enough in which to swim are not at all the same thing."

"You mean because the streams go underground during the summer and we must dig in the sand just to find water for drinking?" the boy asked.

Conal grunted in approval. "I see you *are* learning some things about survival. We will camp by those poplars tonight. By my remembrance, we should reach Santa Fe within the week."

"Thank the Blessed Virgin and all the Holy Angels," Orlena breathed.

"Do not expect too much, Butterfly. Remember, this is New Mexico."

Looking about at the jagged purple mountains surrounding them and the exotic clumps of tuna cactus and catclaw bushes at their feet, Orlena laughed. "How could I ever forget where I am, Conal?"

"Are you sorry you left Madrid?"

She shook her head, remembering the scheming plans of Ignacio and the cruel hands of Gabriel. "No, Conal, I am not sorry. Not sorry at all."

As they continued to climb to higher elevations, the oppressive heat eased. The foothills were covered with oaks, pines, and cedars, and the air was filled with their perfume. After their rude accommodations in all the smaller villages along the seemingly endless journey, Orlena began to dream of the governor's palace and sleeping in a real bed. Surely the crude architecture that typified housing along the northern course of the Rio Grande would not be repeated in the provincial capital!

When they saw the twin spires of a church in the gray haze of the distance, Orlena's heart leaped. Albuquerque had possessed no church as worthy as this! But the closer they drew, the more disheartened she became. The physical beauty of the city's backdrop was magnificent. The Sangre de Cristo Mountains reached toward the flawless azure sky to the east. The wide grassy plain rolling westward was verdant with cultivated fields and orchards. Fat cattle and sheep grazed on sparser, rockier soil.

"But the capital! It is an Indian pueblo, only larger than Albuquerque," Orlena wailed as they neared the outskirts.

"This is the Indian village, segregated to the south of the main capital. The civilized Indians who pioneered north with the first Spanish settlers live here. They are the servants and artisans of the city, Doña Orlena," Lieutenant Rodriguez said, trying to soften the blow for the beautiful Spanish noblewoman.

"There are well over two thousand souls living in the city proper. The Church of Our Lady of Light is very beautiful, and the governor's palace sits at the north side of the main street on a magnificent plaza."

Orlena observed the water of the Rio Santa Fe, which looked narrow and sluggish in the late fall drought. Her eager young escort had assured her that the river's source in the mountains was snow-fed and never went dry. Trout and other delicacies abounded in its cooler, clear waters at higher elevations.

Beyond the river lay the city proper, strung in a characteristically haphazard manner along the banks of the stream. The houses were far larger than the rude adobe huts of the *paisanos*, but still the buildings had flat, low roofs with exposed wooden rafters. The ceilings were made of woven willow boughs sealed with a paste of mud and ashes. The outlying homes had fortified towers at each corner, with gun portholes. Both Comanche and Apache made frequent raids. Their large, well-armed escort only reinforced that frightening reality for Orlena. Unbidden, the image of the green-eyed stranger flashed in her mind. But he was a civilized Indian who spoke fluent Spanish, she reminded herself. Still, something about his bearing belied his gentility, as did the swift and efficient way he had killed her assailants.

Men in decorated buckskin trousers and women with their heads and shoulders swathed in long *rebozos* came out to greet the cavalcade of the new governor. Everyone seemed friendly, but Orlena felt she was an alien in the austere frontier land. She had watched the gradual changes in the peasant population as they wended their tortuous way into New Mexico. The percentage of Indians and mixed bloods had increased, as did Indian influences in speech and dress. Handmade copper and turquoise jewelry adorned the men as well as the women. All the peasants wore moccasins instead of leather sandals.

When they reached the main plaza, she did grudgingly agree that it had a quaint charm in spite of the pueblo look of the city. The long, low governor's palace was shaded by dense rows of poplars and willows, and the Church of Our Lady with its tall towers was impressive. Even the presidio barracks looked orderly and secure.

"While I greet the mayor and his assistant and all my new functionaries, you take Santiago and decide on where you want us ensconced in the palace," Conal instructed Orlena in the midst of the noisy welcome.

Several formally dressed, officious-looking men were approaching them. All too glad of the respite from the blazing sun, Orlena nodded and motioned to her brother. Escorted by Lieutenant Rodriguez, they pulled away from the greeting committee, rode up in front of the governor's palace and dismounted. The wide porch fronting the building looked cool and welcoming. The thin, hatchet-faced woman standing in the doorway did not. She scowled and raised a beringed hand to smooth her iron-gray hair, already severely contained in a tight knot of braids.

"I am Señora Dolores Cruciaga. I am in charge of the staff of the palace. Has Don Conal arrived?" She looked past the dusty young woman and boy.

Orlena drew herself up haughtily. "I am Doña Orlena Anamaria Luisa Valdéz, Don Conal's stepdaughter. This is the governor's son, Don Santiago. I wish to inspect the palace and decide upon quarters for our family. You will show me about." Without waiting to observe the woman's reaction, Orlena turned to Santiago and said, "Why don't you go to the courtyard and wait by the fountain? I am certain Lieutenant Rodriguez will instruct a kitchen servant to bring refreshments. I will join you shortly."

By evening, Orlena had selected quarters for each of them and met all the servants, most of whom were Indians and half-castes. She decided the palace was habitable. The central courtyard was filled with flowers and palms surrounding a lovely stone fountain. All the rooms had newly whitewashed walls and polished adobe brick floors. They were surprisingly spacious and cool if one opened the mica windows to let the evening breeze inside.

She would reconcile herself to the massive, splintery oak furniture and rough, brightly dyed wool rugs. Sipping her wine, Orlena surveyed the evening meal Señora Cruciaga had the cooks prepare to welcome the new governor. After months of refried beans and tortillas, the grilled fish, roast beef, and fresh fruits were delectable. The wine was a bit sour, but nothing could be done for that. It, like most other things, was made in the province.

Don Eleazor, the alcalde, smiled across the table at her. "How do you find our city of the Holy Faith, Doña Orlena?"

Orlena took a sip of wine while she framed a politic reply. Conal watched her from the head of the table with an amused smirk on his face. "It is most unusual, but exceedingly fair. The churches are lovely and the plaza is quite grand. But I did wonder at the way the houses at the outer parts of the city are fortified like miniature presidios, with gun towers on their walls. Are the Indians such a menace?"

"Never fear, my dear young woman," Don Rubin said. As the senior officer in charge of the presidio under Commandant Quinn, the lieutenant was a self-important, boastful man. Casting a glance toward Conal he continued, "The Comanche are no longer a problem. We—er, the preceding governor and I—

NIGHT WIND'S WOMAN

dealt with them last year. To date they have held to their treaty. Our campaigns are now against the accursed Apache."

Conal swirled the thin red wine around in his goblet and said with an arched brow, "It has been my understanding that the present commandant general, and even the viceroy now, want us to set Apache against Comanche. We are to incite each to war on the other and to create dependency on us for essentials such as iron tools, knives, even crude guns and limited supplies of ammunition." His sharp gaze swept the assembly of dignitaries as he waited for a reaction.

The lieutenant smirked. "Not only do we make them dependent on us for tools and weapons, but for food and whiskey as well. That way they sink further into their own depravity."

"Soon they will either butcher one another to extinction or starve in a drunken stupor," Don Alejandro, a wealthy rancher, added venomously.

"Why, that is horrible! Giving savages guns and whiskey. What is to keep them from uniting against us in a drunken fury and killing us with our own weapons?" Orlena questioned.

Several of the older matrons around the table looked at her as if she had grown two heads. No lady interjected political opinions into the gentlemen's conversation! The most unorthodox upbringing of the governor's indulged stepdaughter created problems everywhere she went.

Conal interrupted the silence with a hearty laugh and said, "I fear she is quite outspoken for a female, but only instruct her logically and she may well surprise you."

Orlena gave him a grateful smile as the debate over Indian policy continued.

* * *

"I still think it is lunacy to arm or inebriate savages," Orlena said the next morning. "Besides, it is morally wrong to set out to kill off a whole race. The Church should convert them to peaceful ways. That is what His Majesty wishes."

"Ah, but that is *not* what the men who must survive in this wilderness wish. I rose to power from obscure origins because I fought Indians in New Spain, Butterfly."

"But you fought as a soldier, honorably. You were not a merchant selling them whiskey or weapons," she remonstrated.

Conal's eyes became opaque as he stood up, shoving his chair back from the table. Swallowing the last of his breakfast chocolate, he replaced the cup in its saucer and looked down at her. "There is much of this bloody, hellish land that you do not understand. I would prefer it remain that way."

A chill ran down Orlena's spine as Conal walked through the doorway. Never before had he been so abrupt with her and never had his face looked so coldly forbidding. His Gaelic anger she was used to—her own Spanish temper was volatile as well. They had clashed often. Many of her scandalous escapades had triggered shouting and ranting and dire threats of punishment. But Orlena sensed instinctively that this was different.

"This accursed place is to blame, so isolated and alien. Damn Ignacio and his sycophants who banished Conal to this purgatory!"

The passing days were to reinforce Orlena's feelings a hundredfold. At the idle Spanish court, Conal had indulged Santiago and her, riding with them, squiring her to balls, even taking them to the secret gaming halls of the nobility. But here his duties as governor and presidio commandant were time-consuming and

NIGHT WIND'S WOMAN

dangerous. He seldom allowed Santiago to go with him when he rode to inspect military outposts. He was becoming a stranger, preoccupied and distant.

Orlena was left entirely to her own devices, which were few indeed. The ladies of Santa Fe were crude colonials, narrow-minded and abysmally educated. She had yet to find a woman, even of the purest Spanish bloodlines, who could read and write. They sewed, gossiped, and discussed their children—when they were not at their prayers.

The men were consumed with the daily tasks of survival in this unforgiving wilderness. Even her younger brother, a boon companion of childhood, deserted her to spend hours with the soldiers, learning how to load and fire a musket, couch a lance, and wield a saber.

Señora Cruciaga marshaled the household servants like a presidio sergeant, leaving Orlena to embroider, pace the halls . . . and sweat. After her disastrous brush with death that day in Chihuahua City, she had been forbidden to ride without an armed escort, and of course the soldiers seldom had free time to perform that duty. She was at least able to cajole Conal on one of their rare evenings of dining alone to allow her to walk through the plaza and about a few specified side streets—on her solemn oath to take a well-armed soldier with her. Conal assigned a battle-toughened old sergeant of Spanish and Tlaxcaltecan blood as her escort.

The Tlaxcaltecs were civilized Indians from the far southern provinces who had intermarried with the lower ranks of Spaniards and pioneered north with them in New Mexico. Many *castas* such as Sergeant Ruiz were descended from generations of career soldiers. The thickset, swarthy man proved to be unlike most of the other mixed-bloods she had encountered.

He was actually willing to look her in the eye and answer her questions directly. She grew to like his blunt honesty and sense of humor.

They strolled across the plaza early one crisp October morning as the market stalls were opening and vendors were setting out their wares. "So many new sights—people, livestock, trade goods. It is because of the caravan to Chihuahua, is it not, Sergeant?"

He nodded. "Yes, Doña Orlena. Every day for the next week or two, the traders from Taos will come with their wares to sell in the south. Other trappers and ranchers from all across the province join them. Soon—"

"Oh!" Orlena flinched as she interrupted his explanation. A man dressed in fringed buckskins and mounted on a splendid black stallion rode slowly across the plaza. He had in tow a long procession of savages in chains, dressed only in breechclouts and moccasins. Their long hair hung shaggily below their whip-scarred shoulders, and they walked awkwardly as heavy manacles clanked about their wrists and ankles. Remembering the unconscious grace of her rescuer, she had a flash of insight about how such a one would feel encumbered with chains.

"They are most cruelly abused, Sergeant. Look you at their thinness. They have been whipped and starved!"

"They are Apaches," he replied, surprising her with the venom in his voice.

"That is no reason to torture them."

"It is enough in this land. When they capture us, it goes far worse for us. This is not a subject for a gently reared lady to consider."

She snorted in disgust at his uncharacteristic remarks. Like Conal, when the subject of Apaches was raised, his manner became shuttered and unreasoning. "No man, savage or civilized, should be treated so by civilized people. If they know no better, *we* do! Where are they being taken?"

Ruiz shrugged. "For now, to the guard house on that hill." He pointed northwest to a small promontory, where a prison with a stone tower and chapel stood. It was where condemned men were incarcerated before being executed. "When the caravan is ready to head for Chihuahua, they will be taken along and sold in the south."

"Who would dare buy them?" she questioned, almost to herself, for they were unbroken. In spite of humiliation and abuse, their fierce obsidian eyes glared with fathomless hate in otherwise expressionless faces. She shivered.

"They will not make household servants, Doña Orlena, you are right. No, some will be sold to labor in the fields, but mostly they go to the mines. They do not last long," he added impassively.

"You will not! I forbid it!" Conal thundered, nearly knocking over an inkwell from his desk.

Orlena stood her ground. "I can take the sergeant with me. Santiago has agreed to help. It is scarcely as if I wanted to take the savages into our home. I only want decent food and medicines taken to them. How can they walk across a desert hundreds of miles and live to be sold if they die of starvation or infected wounds?"

Conal's face twisted in anger. "You do not know them as I do, Orlena. They can ride a horse until it drops from abuse, then eat the carcass raw and run afoot for days. They live with wounds that would kill a white man, eat cactus, and even exist on the moisture from it when all water is absent in the desert. They will survive. All too many of the bloody bastards do."

"Father Anselmo from the Church of St. Francis has agreed to help. At this moment he is talking to the mayor. They will be here shortly."

Conal swore and began to pace across his office. Her outflanking maneuver had been well planned, for she knew how all New Mexicans felt about Apaches. Only the clergy—and a minority of them at that—agreed with Charles III's enlightened edicts regarding humane treatment of savages. She had pleaded her case to the priests at both the garrison Church of Our Lady and the parish Church of St. Francis. Only the latter would hear her out and dared to confront the city officials and the governor.

After a stormy session and much compromise, Father Anselmo was allowed to visit the prison, taking food and medicine with him. Orlena and Santiago were forbidden to accompany Father Anselmo and the soldiers. But the following evening, when the priest reported the extent of the prisoners' injuries and the abusive way the guards treated them, Orlena decided to risk Conal's wrath.

"Are you certain you wish to do this, Doña Orlena?" Father Anselmo asked again nervously as they led the patient burro up the hill toward the cold stone walls of the ominous-looking prison.

Dawn had just begun to break over the eastern mountains, casting deep purple shadows between their peaks. The air was chill and Orlena stifled a shiver. "Yes, I am certain, Father. Let that corporal of the guards try to treat the governor's daughter as they did you!" She did not add that if Conal learned she had slipped out unescorted, he would flay her.

Her haughty Spanish court manners cowed Corporal Muñez. He bobbed his head and let her pass with mumbled apologies.

Once inside the high stone enclosure, Orlena looked

NIGHT WIND'S WOMAN

at the dusty bare earth of the small courtyard. Not so much as a sprig of greasewood grew anywhere. The well in the center of the yard stank when she stood over it and peered into its murky depths. "This water is sewage!" With a swish of her skirts, she turned imperiously, motioning the priest and the presidio guards to follow her.

The windows of the cells ringing the yard were so narrow they had no need for bars. Once inside the dark interior, she could smell rotted food and excrement.

"Doña Orlena, I beg you, do not go into the cells," one young soldier pleaded. "The Apaches are dangerous."

"Are they not chained?" At his nod, she asked dismissively, "Then how can they be a danger? Unlock the first cell."

There were three men sitting on the squalid floor. Squinting to see in the gloom, she stepped into the cell and called for a torch. Even at full daylight, the windows would not give sufficient light.

Once the torch was brought, Orlena steeled herself at the horror before her. "They have been chained to the walls and allowed to lie in their own filth!" she hissed at the prison guard standing with the keys in his hand. Although he did not dare to meet her eyes, she could tell he was lazy and insolent. "I will have these prisoners taken into the compound and given clean water to scour the filth from their bodies. Then we will treat their wounds," she said, looking at the weals and abrasions covering them. "Send another two of your *soldiers*,"—she emphasized the word scornfully—"to clean up this abomination while we are outdoors. Now!"

At the flash of gold fire in her eyes, the guard nodded and slunk off quickly to do her bidding.

67

Shirl Henke

Old Shoe, a Mescalero, and Cloth Fox, a Lipan, understood Spanish. The third captive, Vision Seer, another Lipan, did not. "What does the white woman say? Why do the soldiers listen to such a shrewish one?"

Old Shoe grimaced a slight smile. "She is the governor's daughter. Her soft woman's heart has caused her to speak to the governor in our behalf. We are to be fed and bathed, our wounds treated."

The younger Cloth Fox scoffed in disbelief, his black eyes coldly fixed on the golden-haired woman. "Yesterday their own holy man could do no more than leave us some tortillas and beans, which the guards stole from us as soon as he departed." He watched skeptically as the guards unfastened the manacles from the walls and then yanked on the chain so they had to follow him, single file, from the cell.

Once in the courtyard the extent of their injuries became even more apparent. At first, none would talk with Orlena, even though two of the three understood her, but after they were offered water to wash the filth from their bodies, were given food, and had bandages and salves applied, Old Shoe spoke. "We thank you, daughter of governor. Why you do this? Only woman in black robes do this."

Orlena smiled. "As you can tell, I am not a nun, but I do believe in honorable treatment for prisoners. We are Spaniards, not savages."

Cloth Fox sneered. "We are savages. We kill enemies. Not offer softness. Spanish say one thing, do other. No honor."

Orlena turned from his bold, hostile stare, ignoring him. She looked at the quizzical expression on the gray-haired old Apache's face. "Do you think we are hypocrites—dishonorable as the guards were?" she asked Old Shoe.

NIGHT WIND'S WOMAN

His fathomless black eyes studied her. "I know not . . . yet. Your Christian God . . . His laws we not understand." He turned and looked across the compound at the soldiers. "Maybe not all Spanish understand either."

The process of removing the men from the cells and cleaning both was repeated until all ten captives had been treated. Only two others would admit to understanding Spanish, although from their gestures and expressions, Orlena was sure most of them did.

As soon as she was certain the guards would show the old priest proper respect and follow her orders in the future, Orlena departed, leaving curt instructions with the corporal of the guard. If only he knew she had far overstepped Conal's orders and was due for a reprimand herself! While she walked briskly back to the palace with one of the soldiers, Orlena considered the insolence and stoicism of the Apache. That they were insufferable, benighted savages she doubted not a bit. But as a child of the Enlightenment at the court of Charles III, she knew the white conquerors must not stoop to their level.

"I must have a bath to wash the prison stench from me. Conal will be angry enough at this morning's work," she muttered to herself after dismissing the soldier at the door to the palace.

Conal, indeed, was so beside himself with fury for her audacity and disobedience that he forbade her her dearest wish—to watch the annual trade caravan for Chihuahua City depart the following week. It would have been the high point of her dreary existence in Santa Fe. Orlena was loathe to give up her adventure, but Señora Cruciaga watched her every move. By week's end, however, she had devised a plan.

"Why did I not think of it before? Oh, Santiago, it will be just as it was when I escaped from Spain. I will

69

wear your clothes on the morrow!"

Her brother looked distinctly miserable. He had taken a terrible tongue-lashing from Conal over their misadventure in Chihuahua City. Orlena's willfulness was becoming increasingly dangerous in this untamed land. He was learning to be a soldier like his father. Was it not the duty of women to sit home and remain safe? But his sister was not like other women.

Looking at the determined set of her chin, he sighed and began to rummage through his trunks for a pair of trousers and the small clothes to go beneath one of his jackets. "You must promise me that you will stay out in the plaza for no more than an hour," he called over his shoulder.

Knowing that Señora Cruciaga would discover her absence if she were not in the dining room by ten, Orlena promised. The last thing she wanted was soldiers searching for her.

Chapter 6

Orlena wended her way slowly through the plaza's crowded stalls, eating a tortilla dripping with hot, spicy beef and chili. As she licked her sticky fingers, she tried to emulate the careless swagger of an adolescent boy, but in the press of people it was not really necessary. No one paid any attention to a lone youth who watched the chaos of departure day. Merchants, ranchers, teamsters, and militiamen had been gathering in town for weeks with their products to be sold at the great trade fair in Chihuahua City.

She watched two cursing *cargadores* first put blinders on a recalcitrant mule, then carefully strap a seemingly endless number of bundles on the animal's back. When the lead man had it loaded, he pulled on the cinch, placing one strong knee forcefully into the mule's side and yanking until he was satisfied that it was tightened enough. He then tossed the end of the strap to the man waiting on the opposite side to secure it. Two men had loaded a mule with three hundred pounds of goods in a matter of three minutes.

Orlena's ears rang with curses and shouts of jubilation. The noisome smells of deer hides and raw wool blended with the pungent spiciness of pine nuts and homemade wines. How crude and provincial, how different from the cosmopolitan markets of Spain this place was! Yet it had a certain rustic vitality that made her blood race. The cool, crisp days of autumn added to her sense of excitement. Here in this primitive land, dressed in her brother's clothes, Orlena felt truly free, at least for the few hours before she had to return to the hateful scrutiny of Señora Cruciaga.

"This is so much fun, I shall steal out often to see the city," she murmured softly, unheard over the din. She wondered about the Apache prisoners. Sergeant Ruiz had said they would be brought down to march on foot with the caravan. Her eyes scanned the bright kaleidoscope of people, goods and animals, but she did not see the Indians.

"They grow bolder and bolder. It is a great humiliation to our soldiers," Orlena overheard a shopkeeper say to a man in the blue uniform of a presidio guard.

"Pah! They will not get far. Governor Quinn dispatched twenty of our best men with Opata trackers to recapture the prisoners and their would-be rescuers. They will return by nightfall with the savages, then force-march them to catch up with the caravan. They'll be sweating in the mines by year's end."

"I do not know," the merchant replied dubiously. "The renegade called Night Wind has freed Apache slaves many times in the past years. The presidios do not deter him. He slips through army patrols like the wind blowing through the mountains."

"Every escape from Santa Fe to El Paso is credited

to this fellow. I do not even believe such a one exists," the soldier replied scornfully.

Orlena's skin prickled. Those fierce savages so brutally abused by the guards had been freed. And by the hand of the mysterious renegade raider called Night Wind! She had heard several of the mixed-blooded servants at the palace whisper about him, mooning over a deadly killer as if he were a knight in some medieval ballad!

The presidio soldier had stalked angrily away from the merchant. Orlena turned her attention back to the caravan of carts and pack mules being organized in the center of the plaza. Most of the cargo had been loaded. Soon her stepfather would arrive in his official capacity to signal the start of the great trek south. She must return to the palace well before that, lest he recognize her in her brother's clothes. She liked this new freedom far too much to jeopardize it by exposing her disguise.

Orlena retraced her steps through a narrow passageway leading between the palace and the military barracks, intent on slipping unseen into the palace. An entrance to the kitchens lay at the end of the deserted corridor. Her boots made padded sounds in the dust, but suddenly she heard another footfall, much softer and swifter. A bare, bronzed arm seized her as she tried to turn. She was swept backward and pinned against a man's chest with such force that it knocked the breath from her before she could cry out. Then a filthy hand covered her face, stuffing a foul-tasting, greasy rag into her mouth.

Kicking and flailing ineffectually, she was hoisted over her abductor's back. The walls seemed to move with blurring speed as the savage ran with her toward the rear of the passage. She caught a glimpse of his bare legs and moccasined feet before another abductor swathed her in a scratchy woolen blanket.

Orlena suffocated in the stifling cocoon. She was hefted over a wall as a pack would be tossed by a *cargador*. Her head struck something solid when she was dropped on the other side and she lost consciousness.

She awakened, bruised and sore, tied across a horse that was moving at a steady canter. The rider holding her might have been her original captor—or not. Slung upside-down, still swathed in the blanket, she could see nothing, but she knew he was not alone. The sounds of several horses filled the air with the rhythmic pounding of their hooves. Her head ached abominably and her throat and mouth were parched from confinement in the hot blanket. She was too dazed and miserable to be frightened any more. Her body limply gave in to oblivion again.

When she awakened, it was dark. She was lying on a narrow pallet in a rude *paisano's* shack. One flickering tallow candle provided illumination to the shabby single room. She had thought her earlier accommodations on the journey to Santa Fe were less than elegant, but now she was appalled at the dusty floor and peeling walls of this hovel. A rickety table and one splintery stool stood across from the bed.

Slowly she turned her head, sensing that she was alone in the room, and that it served as her prison cell. As she sat up and swung her legs over the side of the cornhusk bedding, a thrill of real fear washed through her. The wrap flattening her breasts had slipped down, and her shirt was partially undone—or rather, the fastenings were ripped free. She tried to cover her breasts with the torn shirt, but it proved useless. Her hair spilled down her back in a heavy mass. Someone had freed it from the braided knot concealed beneath Santiago's hat. They knew she was a woman! Had they

NIGHT WIND'S WOMAN

known that when they abducted her? Why would she be singled out for kidnapping?

That was how Night Wind found her, huddled on the mattress, with that bright mantle of hair falling like a cape about her shoulders. It gleamed like old Spanish gold. He was struck again by her beauty as she turned her amazed amber eyes on him. Then he reminded himself of how the Spaniards mined their gold and forgot about her beauty.

"You!" she hissed, struggling to stand, feeling frighteningly vulnerable seated on the bed.

He watched her force her numbed, bruised limbs to work. The boy's clothing no longer hid her gender. When they had unrolled her from the blanket, her hat had fallen off. Then Broken Leg had removed her jacket and torn open her shirt. Now she struggled to conceal her bared breasts from Night Wind as he insolently inspected her.

"It is all too apparent you are a woman, but the disguise was a good one. Trysting while Don Conal was busy with official duties?" he taunted her.

A combination of blind terror and unreasoning fury energized her. One small hand lashed out and slapped him for his insolence. The instant it was done, she regretted it. His eyes were as hard as glass when he reached up to rub his jaw. She took in his metamorphosis from tame Indian to savage and knew he was no one to cross. He no longer wore loose cotton peasant's clothes, but an Apache's buckskin breechclout. The wicked knife she'd seen him use in Chihuahua was sheathed at his side. His bare, muscular body gleamed bronze in the flickering light that cast his handsome face into harsh, angular planes. The anger blazing there subsided, replaced by a thoughtful expression.

Orlena instinctively took a step backward as his

Shirl Henke

eyes swept over her body. In spite of the humiliating circumstances to which she had been reduced, she forced herself to remember who and what she was. "Do not dare to touch me!" she blurted out.

His face slashed into a feral smile, revealing white, even teeth. "I will dare anything I wish," he said with studied insolence, "but you would do well to heed what I command you. Come here. Take off your clothes." His eyes locked with hers in a contest of wills, daring her to back away again. *Let her wonder if I will pounce on her like a wild panther.* Every muscle in his body cried out to do so.

Orlena fought down the urge to retreat. Savages respected only courage and possessed no civilized compassion for any weaker than themselves. She squared her shoulders and tossed her mane of hair behind her defiantly. "I undress for no man until my lawful husband commands me."

"You flatter yourself to think I would take you to wife. I bed Spanish women. I will never wed one." He glided one pantherish step nearer.

She stood her ground, rage now boiling in her veins. A filthy half-caste renegade saying *he* would not wed *her*! She could not regain breath enough to denounce his perfidy when he advanced again. This time his hand reached out and caressed the curve of her breast, a liberty no man had ever taken before. She shivered in outrage and jumped back from the feather-light caress as if scalded.

"I dislike repeating myself. Take off your clothes, unless you care not how torn they will be on your long journey with me." He stepped forward again, openly stalking her.

"I go nowhere with you," she spat, furious with herself for retreating, knowing he was only toying with her.

"Foolish little lioness," he said impatiently as one long, bronzed arm swept around her slim waist, slamming her against his body. His free hand tangled in her hair, pulling on it so that she was forced to look up into his face.

As he studied her eyes, nose, lips, each cameo-perfect feature, Orlena felt the heat and male vitality of him, pressed intimately near. Her only experience even remotely comparable to this sensation was riding a spirited stallion whose raw muscular strength she could feel beneath her body. But now she would be the one beneath this savage, cruel Apache! She began to struggle, but her arms were pinned to her sides. He held her effortlessly. Even her attempts to kick at him were ineffectual since her boots had been removed. His body was rock-hard and taut with lust as he enjoyed her writhing protest.

"Do not play the coy virgin, Lioness," he whispered roughly. Slowly, he lowered his face toward hers, imprisoning her head with his hand so she could not move. Orlena knew he was going to kiss her. His breath was warm and clean, not at all the fetid stench she expected of a savage. Then his lips were on hers, moving, brushing, teasing. She gasped in startled surprise as his tongue traced a dancing pattern across her soft mouth, then entered to collide with hers.

Orlena stiffened as his tongue dueled with hers, cunningly darting and flicking. At first she was repelled by the invasion, then pleasurable sensations began to seep through her body, seeming to move along previously uncharted pathways, down to her stomach, then curling lower. She was aware of the insistent pressure of his tall, lean body fused to hers, especially of the flesh beneath the scandalous breechclout, which rubbed shockingly just above the tingling juncture of her thighs. She responded to him in frenzied struggling, then stiffened resistance, gradually in yielding compliance.

Her body belonged to a stranger, someone who could never be a pure, highborn daughter of the Spanish nobility. When he ended the savagely gentle, shattering kiss, she was trembling, speechless, afraid she would fall to the ground at his feet if he released her. But he did not.

"Yes, you will go with me," he whispered. "For a long while, I believe." His smile was strangely bemused. The woman was an extraordinary combination of sensuality and innocence. Small wonder Conal found her diverting. As that thought took root in his mind, he let his arms drop free of her abruptly.

"I will not take another man's leavings," he said abruptly, pushing her away.

The dizzying cloud of pleasure enveloping her mind evaporated with the loss of body contact. Then his coldly insulting words struck her. She had just been violated, and worse yet, had abased herself before this Apache. Now he scorned her!

"I am no man's leavings. I will die before I become yours—you are a heathen savage! I am the daughter of the governor of this province, Don Conal Quinn, who will flay you alive for touching me!" Tears of rage and humiliation were blurring her vision and she hated herself for the sign of weakness.

"You cannot be his daughter," he rasped out with a stricken look on his face. "He has a young son—whose clothes you were masquerading in. You are his whore."

She slapped him again. This time he did not let it pass, but grabbed her shoulders in a bone-crushing grip, shaking her like a terrier worrying a rat. "The boy cannot be your brother. The time is not right," he gritted out insistently.

NIGHT WIND'S WOMAN

"Santiago is my brother," she said quickly in breathless fright. "We had the same mother. Don Conal treats me as his own beloved child, the same as his son."

He released her and turned his back to pace stiffly across the floor. Then he whirled on her with contempt—and was it relief?—in his eyes. "You are but a poor stepdaughter, brought along out of pity . . . and perhaps . . ." He appeared to consider.

As the obscenity of his line of thought sank in, Orlena restrained her urge to fly at him with claws out. Instead she spoke in the most disdainful voice she could muster. "I am Conal's daughter in all but blood—he would do anything for me, the same as for Santiago. He will kill you without mercy, you and every filthy savage who has helped you abduct me."

He ignored her threats, studying her once more. What a fiasco this day's work had been! Spotted Elk and Stands Tall had watched Santiago all week and abducted "him" when the most convenient opportunity presented itself—convenient because it was not the boy but a girl in disguise! He flushed in disgust, "What would a highborn lady be doing sneaking out in such disgraceful garb?"

Orlena felt her cheeks redden. "I wanted to see the caravan for Chihuahua City in the plaza," she responded defiantly.

He scoffed. "If Don Conal loves you so well, surely he would not deny such a simple request? Why the masquerade, Lioness?"

She bit her lip in vexation, refusing to explain any further to this arrogant savage. She countered his question with one of her own. "How did such an evil-looking renegade learn to speak such educated Spanish?"

He threw back his head and laughed. "Barbedtongued little spitfire—you prickle like a desert cactus."

"Think me a Spanish dagger and beware my spines," she replied, recalling the spiked cactus they had observed on their journey.

He walked nearer again, until he knew she could sense the heat of his body. "Better you beware *my* spike," he said softly.

Her face reddened at his crudity, but she refused to cower. "My stepfather is the governor. He will pay any ransom to have me returned unharmed," she said, attempting to infuse self-assurance rather than supplication into her voice. Then the thought hit her. "You intended to kidnap my brother and hold him for ransom!"

He neither admitted nor denied her accusation. "But you stole his clothes and sneaked from the palace. I repeat—a lover's tryst?"

"I have no lover!" she replied with such outrage that he believed her.

"Then why the disguise? If you are Don Conal's daughter in all but blood—why would he not escort you to the plaza when he sent off the caravan?"

"Conal will pay you well for my return," she replied evasively.

"He sounds like a tyrant then, forbidding his innocent stepdaughter the right to attend a great festival," he persisted.

"He is not a tyrant! He is wonderful and kind and good, and he loves me!" Orlena cried in frustration.

He loves me! Her words ate into his soul like acid. "I shall write a letter to your beloved stepfather, Lioness."

"If you harm me, Conal will see you repent in hell! I promise you."

"Do not make promises that neither you nor Conal

can keep," he whispered softly, then vanished through the door.

"You cannot keep her," Spotted Elk said in amazement. "Kill her and let us leave before the army's Opata scouts track us here."

Night Wind sat before the fire, deep in thought. "No, I will not kill her. She will serve my vengeance well."

"She is only his whore," Stands Tall said in disgust, "not the son. I am sorry for the mistake. The governor will not care that we take her with us. She cannot become a warrior to fight the Spanish."

Night Wind's face slashed with a slow smile as he spoke. "No, she cannot become a warrior as can the boy. We will one day capture him, but for now I have a use for her."

He sat before the fire with his writing instruments, carefully composing a letter to Conal Quinn.

Conal:

I hold your beloved stepdaughter Orlena. She is very beautiful. I commend your restraint in not taking her virginity yet, but I will relieve you of that burden on your conscience. When I return her to you, she will have been my creature. Think long on that every time you gaze at her perfect golden body and know you that I learned its every secret.

Night Wind

Orlena sat alone, cold and hungry, huddled on the lumpy pallet. Ignoring her growling stomach and aching head, her mind raced over the day's horrifying events. How was she to escape? She had no idea of how far they had traveled while she was unconscious. She had overheard the presidio soldiers say the rene-

Shirl Henke

gades hid in the Sangre de Cristo Mountains northeast of the capital, but she could not be certain that was where they had taken her. Conal and his soldiers had scant chance of finding her before she was dishonored by that hateful renegade. She had to flee his frightening touch before she was ruined, not only physically but spiritually.

What had transpired between them earlier terrified her worse than being raped by a band of cutthroats. Then, at least, she would have fought and died quickly. But the handsome half-caste with the perfect Castilian accent would exact an even higher penalty. Every time she closed her eyes she could see that chiseled face with its arresting eyes piercing her soul, reading her innermost thoughts and fears. The clean vitality of his scent hung in the air of the room. "I must not let him touch me again," she whispered into the silence of the night.

Locked in a windowless, adobe-walled room, there seemed little chance of escape, but just then the wooden door opened and a burly Apache entered. He carried a crude pottery bowl filled with brownish gruel that he set on the table, along with a gourd full of brackish water.

Orlena stood looking past him through the open door. The dim light of a campfire flickered down the hill. Three figures huddled around the fire. Were there any others? She looked at the impassive savage and decided to attempt communicating with him. "I need to go outside. I cannot breathe in this closed-in place a moment longer."

His fathomless obsidian gaze gave no indication that he had understood a word she said. Then he pointed at the food and turned to where a cracked chamber pot stood in the corner and motioned to it with a crude, unmistakable gesture.

NIGHT WIND'S WOMAN

She reddened in mortified fury and reached for the bowl of refried beans, hurling them toward his expressionless face. He dodged the missile effortlessly and walked out the door. The shards of broken pottery lay about the floor with bits of the sticky beans adhering to it. Her stomach let out a fierce rumble and she collapsed on the bed in defeat.

Shortly, the door opened with a sharp crack, and Night Wind stood silhouetted in it, an impatient scowl on his face. "A foolish waste of valuable food, little lioness. Your spoiled Spanish temper will bring you only hunger here. Perhaps you will be more willing to eat tomorrow?" He shrugged indifferently and walked toward the pallet.

When he sat down beside her, Orlena jumped up, her fatigue and hunger forgotten. "I will not lie with you, you—filthy renegade," she hissed, placing the small table between them and arming herself with the pitiful water gourd.

He made no move to rise but merely regarded her with the disgust a parent might show for a dim-witted child. "Now you will spend the night thirsty as well as hungry. I care not, but understand this—for as long as you are my prisoner you will obey me. And I will keep you until I tire of you."

"You said you were going to ransom me." She tried to put assurance into her tone of voice.

"No, you said it. I did not."

"I will not let you take me." She spat the words out in a breathless, terrified voice as her knuckles whitened on the gourd handle.

"I am not going to rape you, Lioness," he replied softly. "I do not force women, but there are many of my men who do not share my feelings. Having lost their own wives and sisters to the whites, they rape Spanish captives whenever the chance arises. If you would have me protect you from their lust, you must obey my commands. If my men believe you are my woman, they will not touch you." He waited for her to digest this.

"What do you mean, 'believe I am your woman'?" she asked suspiciously. "Ransom me and let me return to Conal."

His face lost its patient expression. "You are my prisoner. I will do what I will do. Come and sleep on the mattress with me or sit all night in that rough chair. This will be the softest bed you will have for many nights."

"I would rather lie on jagged rocks than beside you," she ground out.

"You will get part of that request sooner than you realize," was all he replied. Then he lay down on the pallet and rolled over.

Orlena waited at the table until the candle was almost gutted out. His even breathing seemed to indicate that he slept. Silently she rose with every muscle in her body screaming in protest. Each step across the dirt floor was made with stealth. *I must get that knife from its sheath and plunge it into his heart.*

Without making the slightest sound, Orlena knelt beside the pallet. His body was sleek and sinuous even in sleep, like a splendid wild animal's. She took a deep breath to steady her trembling hand and reached for the knife belted securely at his narrow hip. Suddenly, his iron-hard fingers clamped on her slim wrist with bone-crushing force and he pulled her across his body. Before she realized what had happened, she was lying atop his chest with her arms pinned behind her.

Night Wind lay on his back, holding her effortlessly. She felt soft, and her golden hair was scented with jasmine, even though the smell of the filthy blanket clung to her clothes. Her breasts strained against his bare chest and he could feel her heart pound. His own responded by accelerating. They lay for a breathless moment suspended in time as both assimilated the new and powerful sensations rioting through their bodies. He had vowed to go slowly, to seduce her and make her beg for his touch, but her effect on him was unlike that of any noble lady he had conquered in the past. "I could take you right now," he whispered hoarsely in her ear.

When she began to flail and kick, he twisted onto his side and threw one long bronzed leg across her lower body. His hand tangled in her hair. "There, you see how easy it would be?"

Orlena was panting now, fighting the terror welling inside her. She could feel the burn of his gaze as he looked down between their bodies. Sweet Mother, her half-torn shirt had come open in their wrestling and two puckered pink nipples lay bare before his lustful eyes. "I will not beg for mercy," she forced herself to reply.

Slowly he pulled her closer, until her breasts pressed against his hair-roughened chest. "Mercy is a hypocritical notion of white men. Lipan do not pretend such an alien feeling. We hate—and we love—honestly."

"I hate you, you filthy, brutal, savage—"

"You begin to repeat yourself, Lioness," he interrupted. "I said I chose not to force you. But if you persist in trying to kill me, I might decide to let Broken Leg have you. He asked for you tonight."

Instinctively she knew he referred to the squat, ugly man who brought her dinner. She shivered in spite of herself. Something inside of her snapped as she asked bluntly, "If you do not desire me and do not choose to ransom me, then why do you not just give me to him and have done?"

Shirl Henke

"Time will give us both the answer to that, Lioness. Do not further try my patience in the meanwhile." He released her hands and rolled onto his other side, his knife secured beneath him, his back to her.

Orlena lay scrunched between the adobe wall and his hard body. Her wrists were numb and every inch of her body ached with exhaustion. As she wriggled onto her back and attempted to cover her breasts, she knew he lied about not desiring her. Lust had been plainly visible in his face only moments ago. But for now she had a reprieve. Sleep claimed her almost instantly.

Chapter 7

The little Frenchman watched the wind tangle the woman's golden hair as she struggled to keep her precarious seat. Her little burro climbed a steep, rocky incline in the fastness of the Sangre de Cristo Mountains.

"What will you do with her, *mon ami*? Sell her to the slavers to ransom back?" Pascal asked Night Wind in serviceable Spanish with an oddly lilting French accent.

"No, I will not do that," the half-caste replied with narrowed eyes fastened on the troublesome woman.

"You will kill her then," Pascal said flatly, "when you have tired of her."

"I will not tire of her for a good while yet, but when I do . . ." He stopped, not completing the sentence.

Blaise Pascal looked at Joaquín, the man now called Night Wind, whom he had first met as the Green-Eyed Boy in a Lipan camp fifteen years ago. "The woman is beautiful, but headstrong and dangerous. She almost escaped you yesterday."

Night Wind's mouth hardened into a parody of a smile. "Why do you think I have her riding one of your burros? Mounted thus, she cannot escape a horseman."

"Already she has lamed one of your finest stallions and nearly gutted Spotted Elk before you subdued her. She is too much trouble and probably a hellcat to bed as well."

Night Wind looked at the deceptively benign face of the fat little Frenchman. "Just what are you leading up to, *mon ami*?"

Pascal shrugged his shoulders expressively, curious about the raider's uncharacteristic behavior. "I might be able to contact the new governor and arrange a ransom."

"For a goodly share of the proceeds," Night Wind interjected. "No. I will not ransom her."

"Then she must be as changeable as a desert wind, turning from haughty bitch to hot-blooded woman in your blankets. Morena will not like this one, Joaquín."

Night Wind's eyes hardened as he replied icily, "Do not call me Joaquín when we are with my people. As to Morena"—he paused—"she understands our relationship well enough. Orlena has naught to do with her."

If the French trader was puzzled about Night Wind's plans for Orlena, she was even more confused. Smiling like a cat teasing a sparrow, he had told her the first night as he pulled her against him, "Body heat makes blankets work better." It was true that the farther they climbed into the mountains, the colder the nights grew. Hating herself for it, she awakened the next morning huddled closely against him, with his arm draped possessively across her breasts. He seemed to take perverse delight in touching her intimately, although he did not again demand that she disrobe.

As Orlena relived last night, she feared that he planned something more insidious than rape. He had held her next to his hard, naked body, his flesh scalding her with its heat as he caressed her breasts and hips with his slim, deft fingers. He tangled his hands in her hair, drawing her to him for one of those searing, humiliating kisses. Prepared for what his lips and tongue could do, she had forced herself to remain rigid and unresponsive, her mouth tightly sealed.

After a few moments he had stopped his amorous attention with apparent indifference. Long after he slept soundly she lay wide awake, exhausted and trembling. *What does he want with me if not to ransom or to rape*? The question had hammered at her since they rode off from the isolated adobe hut with the renegade trader two days before.

At first she had hoped that Pascal, a white man, would intervene in her behalf. But he was a Frenchman, trading with the Apache and Comanche in Spanish territory. If the Spanish soldiers ever caught him in New Mexico, they would shoot him, he informed her in casual good humor. A brief conversation with him in her best court French had given her an idea, however.

She found out that they were riding northeast toward Elk Mountain to throw the presidio troops off their trail before shifting to a southerly route. If she could just break away and head due south, she might encounter Spanish soldiers scouring the mountains for her. But one of Night Wind's men had stopped her. They struggled over his knife and she accidentally stabbed him. Then the stupid horse she was riding had stumbled and thrown her. When the tall half-caste had yanked her roughly to her feet, she had almost prayed for a quick death. But he had perfunctorily examined her for injuries and then seated her on one of Pascal's burros!

Orlena cursed the plodding, foul-tempered little beast that smelled even worse than she did. After three days without a bath, she was filthy. The hot, parching days in the sun had wind-blistered her delicate golden skin until it peeled painfully; the cold night air drove her to seek the most unwelcome body heat of her captor.

As if conjured up, Night Wind reined in his big piebald stallion alongside her. He inspected her bedraggled condition, finding her distressingly desirable in spite of burned skin, tangled hair, and torn boy's clothing. In fact, the shirt and pants outlined her flawlessly feminine curves all too well now that she had discarded the binding about her breasts.

Orlena watched his cool green eyes examine her and felt an irrational urge to comb her fingers through her hair in a vain attempt to straighten it. Instead she said waspishly, "Why do you stare at me? To take pleasure in my misery?"

He chuckled, a surprisingly rich sound, vaguely familiar. Indeed the eyes, too, seemed familiar, but that was only because in his swarthy face such an obvious white man's feature stood out.

"Look you ahead. Relief for your misery is at hand. Your bath awaits." He gestured to a dense cluster of scrub pine and some rustling alders. They ringed a small lake of crystal-clear water fed from some underground spring.

Orlena's first impulse was to leap into its cool, inviting depths, but her reason quickly asserted itself. She fixed him with a frosty glare and replied, "A lady requires privacy for her ablutions. Also some clean clothes to wear afterward."

"Unfortunately for you, my men and I travel light. We have no silk dresses in our saddlebags."

"Then you should not have abducted me," she snapped as her burro skittered, smelling the water.

"You should not have worn your brother's clothes and my men would not have taken you by mistake," he replied evenly as he dismounted by the water's edge.

Her eyes narrowed. They were back at the original impasse. "Why did you want Santiago?"

His face became shuttered once more as he considered his plan gone awry. "I did not plan to kill him," was all he would say.

Or ransom him either. Orlena was certain of that much. His motives regarding both of them centered on Conal in some way. Before she could argue further he strode over to the burro and swept her from it, tossing her into the deep clear water. At first she shrieked in shock as her blistered, sweaty body met the icy-cold water. But when she began to swim, the cold became refreshing. However, her clothes and boots were a decided impediment. With a couple of quick yanks she freed the boots and tossed them onto the bank.

Night Wind watched her glide through the water like a sleek little otter. He was surprised that she could swim. He had expected her to flounder and cry out to be rescued from drowning. Smiling grimly to himself, he shed his moccasins and breechclout and dove in after her.

"Ladies do not know how to swim, Lioness," he said as he caught up with her in several swift strokes.

She gasped in surprise, then recovered. "Conal taught Santiago and me when we were children."

His face darkened ominously. "He has taught you much—too much for a Spanish female of the noble class."

"Some Spaniard has taught you also—too much for an Apache male of the renegade class," she replied in a haughty tone as cold as his expression.

He reached out and one wet hand clamped on her arm, pulling her to him. "Come here. Take off your clothes," he whispered.

Her eyes scanned the banks. As if by prearrangement, the Lipan and Pascal had vanished downstream. She could dimly hear them unpacking the animals and making camp, but a thick stand of juniper bushes and alder trees provided complete privacy. She jerked free and kicked away from him, but he was a stronger swimmer. In a few strokes he caught up to her, this time grabbing her around her waist.

"You will drown us both if you are not sensible," he said as he struggled with the shirt plastered to her body.

"I told you the last time you asked me to disrobe that I would never do it for you," she gasped, flailing at him. Blessed Virgin, she could see through the water! He was completely naked! "No!" The cry was torn from her as he finally succeeded in freeing her from the shredded remnants of her shirt.

"You are burned and filthy. If you do not cleanse your skin properly you will become ill," he gritted out as he began to unfasten the buttons on her trousers. She continued struggling. "I am not going to rape you, little Lioness," he whispered roughly.

"I do not believe you," she panted. "You only waited, tricked me—"

He silenced her with a kiss. It was most difficult to remain coldly rigid with her lips closed when she was gasping for breath and flailing in the water. The hot interior of his mouth was electrifying as he opened it over hers. His tongue plunged in to twine with hers in a silent duel. Orlena pushed at his chest ineffectually as he propelled them effortlessly toward the bank where shade from an overhanging alder beckoned.

The sandy soil was gritty and full of rocks away from the water's edge, but an uneven carpet of tall grass grew out of the water and up the gently sloping bank. He carried her dripping from the water and tossed her on it. Before she could regain her breath or roll up, he seized her sagging, loose trouser legs and yanked, straightening her legs and raising her buttocks off the ground. Unbuttoned at the top, the trousers slid off with a whoosh, taking with them the ragged remains of her undergarments.

He looked down at her naked flesh, sun and wind burned, covered with scratches and bruises. Orlena shivered as the dry air quickly evaporated the cold water from her skin. She tried ineffectually to cover herself with her hands as she rolled to one side, unable to meet his piercing gaze. He reached down and scooped her into his arms again.

"Now, I am going to let you swim for a few moments while I get some medicine from my saddlebags. I do not think it wise to try to escape with no clothing. You are already burned enough!" With that he tossed her back into the icy embrace of the water and strolled off, heedless of his own nakedness.

Orlena fumed as she treaded water, watching him carry off the last remnants of her clothes. He was right. Where could she go in the mountain wilderness, naked and afoot? In only a moment he returned, leading the big black-and-white stallion. He took something from the buckskin pouch on what passed on Apache mounts for a saddle and waded back into the shallows. "Spanish ladies seem to set great store by this," he said mockingly, holding up a piece of what looked to be soap—real soap! "It is not the jasmine scent you favor, but it is all I could find for our unplanned bathing." He held out the soap for her inspection. The unspoken command was in his eyes as he waited, waist-deep in the water, for her to come to him.

Orlena warred within herself. She could not outrun him and had nowhere to go, yet she hated to let him humble her by begging for the soap—not to mention having to expose her nakedness once again to his lascivious green eyes in order to reach the bribe. She treaded water, careful not to let her breasts bob above the surface.

"Toss it to me. I can catch quite well."

He smiled blackly. "Allow me to guess. Conal taught you. No, Doña Orlena, you must come to me—or stay in the lake until that lovely little body turns blue and freezes at nightfall." With that he sauntered toward the shallows, tossing the soap casually from hand to hand.

"Wait!" Orlena was growing cold already and the sun was beginning to arc toward its final descent beyond the mountain peaks to the west.

He turned with one arched black eyebrow raised and said, "I will meet you half way, but you must do as I command. I have already given my word not to take you against your will. Unlike your Spanish soldiers, the word of a Lipan is never broken."

That a savage could talk to her thus made bile rise in her throat, but she was trapped in the freezing water, hungry, naked, completely at his mercy. "I suppose I must trust your Apache honor," she replied through chattering teeth. Was it only the cold that made her shiver?

NIGHT WIND'S WOMAN

Very slowly she swam toward him. Very slowly he walked across the smooth lake bottom toward her. Orlena watched the sunlight filtering through the trees trace a shifting design on his bronzed skin. His arm and chest muscles rippled with every step he took. He had taken off the leather headband along with his other apparel and his wet black hair hung free, almost touching his shoulders. Without the band, he seemed less Apache, more white, but not less dangerous.

"Come," he whispered, watching her, knowing what this was costing her Spanish pride. Waiting for her, touching her without taking her, was exacting a price from him as well. He observed the swell of her breasts swaying as she moved through the clear water. Darkened almost bronze by soaking, her hair floated like a mantle, covering her as she touched bottom and rose from the water.

He reached out and drew her to him, unresisting at first, until he pushed back the wet heavy hair from one pale shoulder. "No," she gasped, but it was too late. He had one slim wrist imprisoned. Slowly he worked a rich, sensuous lather against her collarbone, moving lower, toward her breast. When his soap-slicked fingers made contact, she forgot to breathe. The tip of her breast puckered to a hard, rosy point and the tingling that began there quickly spread downward. When he released her wrist, Orlena did not notice. His free hand lifted the wet hair from her shoulder and he spread the lather across to capture her other breast, gently massaging both of them in rhythm. She swayed unsteadily in the water. Although it was still cold, Orlena Valdéz had become hot. Night Wind cupped her shoulders and then worked the sensuous, slick suds down her arms.

She stood glassy-eyed and trembling in the waist-deep water, studying the rippling muscles beneath the light dusting of black hair on his chest. It narrowed in a pattern that vanished beneath the water. Just as her eyes began to trespass to that forbidden place, she felt a jolt as he reached that selfsame location on her! Quickly and delicately, he skirted the soft mound of curls and lathered over her hips, then around, cupping her buttocks.

"Raise your hair and turn," he commanded hoarsely, maneuvering her like a porcelain doll into shallow water. He could feel the quivering thrill that raced through her as he performed the intimate toilette. His own body responded, hard and aching, but he ignored his need and massaged the delicate vertebrae of her back, down past her tiny waist to the flair of hips and rounding of buttocks. "Now, kneel so I can wash your hair."

Like a sleepwalker she responded to his slight pressure on her shoulders and knelt with her back to him. He lathered the masses of hair, massaging her scalp with incredibly gentle fingers. Orlena imagined her maid back in Spain performing this familiar ritual, but this was not Maria and she was far from Madrid, alone in a foreign land, the prisoner of a savage!

His voice, low and warm, with its disquietingly educated accent, cut into her chaotic thoughts. "Lower your head and rinse away the soap."

Orlena did so, working all traces of the lather from her hair. Then she rose from the water, eyes tightly closed against the sting of the soap, and began to squeeze the excess water from her hair. Night Wind watched the way her breasts curved as she raised her arms above her head. Her waist was slim, her skin pale; she was so fragile and lovely that it made his heart stop.

He had used many white women over the years, but

NIGHT WIND'S WOMAN

none had any more claim on him than to assuage his lust, more often to please his masculine pride. A despised Apache could seduce a fine white lady, have her begging him to make love to her. Make love! Those other times had been more acts of war than love to Night Wind. Never had he played a waiting game, balancing gentleness with iron authority. Never before had he taken a white woman's virginity. And it was still far too soon, he knew, for that to occur unless he forced her. The feelings she evoked were dangerous and he did not like them. The anger betrayed itself in his voice.

"Now, I have bathed you. You will bathe me."

Orlena's eyes flew open and she blinked in amazement. "Surely you jest, but it does not amuse me!"

"So, I can play lady's maid to you," he said in a quiet deadly voice, "but you will not be body servant to a dirty savage."

She reddened guiltily, recalling her thoughts of Maria a moment earlier. He held out the soap in one open palm, waiting once more.

"No! I will not—I *cannot*." She hated the way her voice cracked.

"Yes, you will and you can—else the young deer Broken Leg is now roasting will not fill that lovely little belly tonight."

Ever since her first temper tantrum with the bowl of beans and the water gourd, she had learned the power of hunger and thirst over human pride. She had not been fed all the following day, only given water, until they camped last night. By then the mush of bean paste had actually been palatable. Now the fragrance of roasting meat wafted on the evening breeze. She salivated and her stomach rumbled. They had broken their morning fast at dawn with cold corn cakes and water, but she had eaten nothing since.

97

"I have clothes for you, in Warpaint's saddlebag," he motioned to the horse grazing untethered nearby. "Or, you can stay here all night, freezing and starving."

With a remarkable oath she had overheard a Spanish sailor use, Orlena stalked over to him and grabbed the soap.

Forcing her hands to remain steady was nearly impossible as she flattened her lathered palms against his sleek dark skin and began to rub in small circles across his chest, then down the hard biceps on his arms. His chest was lightly furred with curly black hair. Trusting the steadiness of her voice only slightly more than that of her hands, she said curiously, "All the other men are smooth skinned. Why do you—"

"You may think me a savage, but I am half white," was the stormy reply. Then he added in a lighter tone, "You have never seen any man's bared chest before, have you, Lioness?"

She stiffened at the intimacy of his voice, hating herself for her stupid words. "Of course not!"

"Then how did Conal teach you to swim—fully clothed?"

A small smile warmed her face as she recalled being a little girl with a toddler brother, cavorting in the pond at the villa in Aranjuez. "In fact, we all wore light undergarments. I was a child and never thought on it. But I do not remember him furred as are you."

He frowned. "Conal's hair is red. It would not show as easily as dark hair. Body hair is considered ugly among my people."

She looked up suddenly. "Then the Apache must think you uncomely indeed," she said with asperity.

"No. The Lipan accept me as one of their own," he replied with an arrogant grin, adding, "Women, red or white, have never found me unattractive."

"Well now you have met the first one who does," she hissed.

"Liar," he whispered softly, watching as she lowered her eyes and busily applied herself to the disconcerting task he had set her.

Orlena felt the steady thud of his heart, angry at its evenness when her own pulse was racing.

Night Wind was having a far more difficult time looking calm than the furious, golden-haired woman before him could imagine. Lord, her small, rounded breasts arched up enticingly as she raised her arms to lather him. Intent on winning this contest of wills with her, he clenched his fists beneath the water to keep from caressing the impudently pointed nipples. Smiling, he watched how she bit her lip in concentration as she was forced to touch his body. She kept her eyes fastened on her busy hands, not looking up into his face.

Orlena could feel him shrug and flex his muscles as he turned, allowing her such casual access to his body. She thought she knew it well from lying wrapped in his arms the past nights. She was wrong—how much different this was, with both of them naked, slicked by the cool water and warm sun.

"Turn so I may wash your back." She tried to emulate his command and was rewarded with a rich, low chuckle. When he did not move at once, she added, "You do not, for a surety, fear to turn your back on a mere female?"

"Not as long as my knife and any other weapons lay well beyond your reach," he replied with arched eyebrows. Then kneeling in front of her he added, "It will be far easier for you to wash my hair than me yours."

His thick hair was coarse and straight, shiny black as a raven's wing. She worked a rich lather into it, finding the massaging motion of her fingertips on his scalp soothing. Angry with herself, she shoved his head under the water abruptly, saying, "Rinse clean."

He came up coughing and splattering her with droplets. "You try a man's patience overmuch, Lioness." Then a slow smile transformed his face as he said with arrogant assurance, "Wash below the water, also, as I did to you."

She dropped the soap with a splash, but he quickly recovered it in the clear water. When he handed it to her silently, she moved around him and began with his back. Touching his tight, lean buttock made her quiver with a strange seeping warmth in spite of the cold water. She finished quickly, forgetting to breathe as he turned around to face her again.

His eyes burned into her as he took her wrist and began to work her small, soapy palm in circles around his navel, then lower, beneath the water. When she touched that mysterious, frighteningly male part of him, she could feel its heat and hardness.

In spite of his best resolution, Night Wind let out a sharp gasp and his hips jerked reflexively when he closed her soap-filled little hand around his phallus. Orlena jumped back, jerking her hand free. At first she was uncertain what had happened, but then she realized what it was, and a small smirk curved her lips.

So, he is not as indifferent to me as he would pretend. On a few occasions when she escaped her *dueña*, she had seen animals mate in their stables. Always the male's staff had seemed an ugly, threatening thing to her. But those were merely horses and dogs. This was different . . . frightening, yes, but not ugly. . . .

She dragged her thoughts from their horrifying direction. Blessed Virgin, what was happening to her? She surely had not found the naked body of a man

NIGHT WIND'S WOMAN

pleasing! And a savage at that! Like mares and bitches, women had to subject themselves to male lust in the marriage bed. But she knew well from her own mother's plight what the consequences were—a swollen belly and an agonizing childbirth. She backed away from him, clenching the soap unconsciously in her hands.

Night Wind struggled with his desire for her, but at last let her go, deciding the game had been played out long enough for now. Then he realized that she continued slowly backing away from him, all the spitting fury and innocent sexual awakening of moments ago evaporated. Her face was chalky, and she wrapped her arms protectively about her body as if warding off a blow.

"I did not intend to frighten you, Lioness," he said softly. "I gave my word not to force you, and I will keep it."

"I see evidence to the contrary," she spat, but refused to look at his lower body, clearly outlined beneath the water.

One long arm shot out and grabbed her wrist, prying the soap from her fingers. "We are both clean enough," he said gruffly, pulling the shivering woman behind him as he splashed to the bank.

Feeling her resistance, he released her in the shallows and said, "I have cloth to dry you and an ointment for your burns."

"And what of the small matter of clothing? You have destroyed the pitiful remnants of Santiago's shirt and trousers."

"I have more suitable garments—women's clothes with which to replace them," he replied reasonably, ignoring her as he pulled a long cloth from the piebald's saddlebag and tossed it at her.

Orlena dried herself carefully with the rough cotton

towel, wincing at its abrasion on her tender skin. In a moment he returned from another foray into his pack with a small tin. "Pascal says this is a miracle cure for sun and wind burn. It will serve until the women of my band can tend you."

She eyed him suspiciously. His hair and chest were still wet but he had slipped on a pair of sleek buckskin pants and his moccasins. He held out the ointment like a peace offering. "Come here." A smile played about his lips. "After all, I need not repeat the rest of the sentence. You are already rid of your clothes."

"You promised me women's clothing," she replied with rising anger, but still she clutched the towel protectively in front of herself.

He waited until she approached, warily, then commanded, "Raise your hair first so I may treat your shoulders."

Still holding the towel draped around herself with one hand, she lifted her hair up with the other. Santiago's thin shirt had been ripped on the brushy shrubs and trees as they rode and her skin was both scratched and sunburned. His fingers were calloused, yet warm and soothing as he spread the salve with surprising gentleness. The sting evaporated magically, but she did not voice her appreciation, only turned to let him minister to her throat and arms, then her hands.

When he tipped up her chin to touch her windburned cheeks and nose, she was forced to meet his eyes. Again a sense of recognition niggled, then vanished as she observed his reaction to her.

"Ah, Lioness, you are too delicate for New Mexico. You should have stayed in Spain," he said with what almost sounded like regret in his voice.

She looked at him oddly, puzzled and afraid. Of him . . . or of herself? She honestly did not know.

Chapter 8

That night Orlena helped Pascal serve the savages their evening meal of freshly roasted meat. *They know Night Wind took me bathing with him like a common body servant!* she thought miserably. Of course, since they already thought she was his whore, what did it matter if he had rewarded her with the scandalous outfit she wore?

She angrily shoved the low-cut peasant blouse back onto her shoulder. Every time she reached forward it gaped open, revealing her breasts, which showed all too clearly anyway through the thin white cotton. The bright red skirt hung almost a foot above the ground, revealing her slim ankles and the perfectly horrid leather sandals that flopped on her narrow feet. Naturally, Night Wind had given her no undergarments!

Gritting her teeth, she tossed her thick plait of hair over her shoulder and bit into a hunk of venison. The juice dribbled down her chin and she wiped it away with her fingers. After a lifetime of taking table linens for granted, Orlena Valdéz had been reduced to a sorry pass indeed! She ignored the impassive savages as her hunger, combined with the first decent food she had eaten in days, erased the last vestiges of her ladylike decorum. She squatted by the fire and greedily stuffed bits of meat into her mouth with her fingers. *Just like a peasant, a savage!*

Blaise Pascal watched Night Wind's beautiful captive. She had been singularly subdued since returning with him from the lake, dressed in the *paisana*'s clothes. The clean blouse and skirt were far more flattering than the filthy boy's trousers, to his way of thinking, but she was a Spanish noblewoman, Conal's ward. The Frenchman could well imagine how she hated the crude garments.

Orlena could not cook, could not build a fire or perform the easiest camp chores. Even when starved into working, she was clumsy and ill suited to the tasks. Yet Pascal was forced to admire her spirit. Most men backed away from the Night Wind in mortal terror. This slim woman defied him like the lioness he had named her.

The shrewd Frenchman had been observing the interplay between them ever since Joaquín had dragged her kicking and struggling from the adobe hut three days earlier. Her open defiance and temper tantrums had been quelled. Thirst, hunger, and exhaustion were natural pacifiers. Now, noting the charged tension in the air since they returned from their bath, he wondered what other natural pacifier her handsome captor might have used on her.

No, not so, he decided with a grim chuckle, glancing from the half-caste to Orlena. Each was too tensely aware of the other, each coiled like a tightly wound watch spring, ready to snap. Sacred Blood, how he

NIGHT WIND'S WOMAN

would love to have watched them bathe—if he had dared!

Rubbing his leg where the stump was attached to the wooden peg, he spoke to her. "Did the ointment help your burns?" His black eyes glowed as he stared at the lushness of her curves revealed through the thin garments.

Orlena looked at him with narrowed eyes. "Yes." Quickly she turned her back on his lascivious gaze and began to gather up the few crude cooking utensils Pascal used to prepare their meals. She could hear the Frenchman's low chuckle and hated herself for having to endure his knowing smirk. "Look to your manners lest Night Wind cut off your other leg and you must hop on two stumps," she said tartly.

"I did not cut off his right leg, Lioness—a bear's mauling caused the leg to rot. Blaise sawed it off himself," Night Wind said as he walked silently into the light of the campfire.

Orlena's eyes widened and she nearly dropped the heavy kettle she had been scouring with sand. She did not want Night Wind to hear her use his name as if he were her protector! Ignoring his smirk, which indicated that he was thinking along precisely the same lines, she said to Pascal, "You could surely not have cut off your own leg?"

The fat little Frenchman laughed, revealing a blackened row of teeth with several missing. "I sawed it off with this." He unsheathed a wicked-looking long knife that gleamed in the firelight. "When I finished the unpleasant task, I sewed off the blood vessels with deer sinew. It was a while before I walked again."

Orlena felt her gorge rise as she imagined the grisly operation. Once she would have scoffed in disbelief, but after months in this wilderness, she believed anything was possible! Even the renegade trader's absurd name. "I believe your story as much as I believe your name. Blaise Pascal, indeed!"

He and Night Wind both laughed. Then Pascal looked at the half-caste. "She knows for whom I am named. Beware, Night Wind, for you have a dangerously educated woman here."

"So it would appear," Night Wind replied darkly.

"It is scarce a sign of great erudition to know of the famous French philosopher and mathematician," she replied stiffly, "but I still do not think it is your true name."

"The family name Pascal is quite common in the north of France. My father, an impoverished tutor to a noble family, had dreams of grandeur for me. He chose the name Blaise. And, after all, is not every man's life a gamble?" He shrugged. "What were my chances of surviving this?" He thumped his leg, severed just below the knee. "Or, who would have believed Conal Quinn's ward would become the Night Wind's woman?" He looked warily from Orlena's outraged face to the half-caste, gauging his reaction.

"You know not to speak of Quinn, Pascal," he said quietly. The threat hung palpably in the air as he rose in one fluid movement and walked toward the horses.

"You know my stepfather?" Orlena asked with hope soaring in her breast.

"I have known Don Conal for many years, but as your lover warned me, it is best left unspoken." His voice had lost all its earlier taunting joviality and was hard now.

She looked at Night Wind's departing figure. "I am not—" She bit back the denial, aware that Night Wind's protection brought her a certain degree of respect. She looked at Pascal with contempt now, saying, "You are afraid of that renegade, like everyone

NIGHT WIND'S WOMAN

else. Better to fear the wrath of Governor Quinn when he catches all of you!"

Pascal spat in the dust, then stared at her with keenly assessing eyes. "Oh, I know the treachery of Colorado Quinn, never fear, Doña Orlena, but you would do well to realize that one"—he pointed at Night Wind—"is far more deadly."

"He is the treacherous one, the kidnapper of women and boys! How dare you call Conal bloody, you traitor!"

Pascal regained some of his good humor at her righteous anger. He was beginning to understand why Joaquín had kept her. "I am no loyal son of the Spanish Crown. As I am a Frenchman, I can scarce be called a traitor."

"You sell guns to the savages. That is a betrayal of all civilized men," she said, shoving the kettle and spoons she'd just scoured at him.

He shrugged. "I sell guns, medicines, iron pots, whiskey—whatever men can purchase, whoever they are. Their gold is the same to me. A man must live in this harsh land. The philosopher was right. Life, death, morality—it is all a gamble."

"There are those like Conal who possess honor," Orlena said with disgust.

"You will find honor has a much different meaning in New Spain than in Madrid. It did for Don Conal. So will it once more," he added cryptically as he packed up the cooking supplies.

She Who Dreams sat staring at the rising ball of orange fire, her black eyes glowing like the sunrise. White Crane slowly emerged from the wickiup and knew at once that She Who Dreams had had a vision during the night. The sweet fragrance of sotol bread baking on the hot coals of the campfire drew his attention. He walked past his wife and scooped up one of the roasted cakes. Eating in silence, he looked about the awakening Lipan encampment. She Who Dreams would speak in her own good time after she had mulled over her message from the spirits. Always it was this way. She was a powerful medicine woman, his wife, and White Crane took great pride in her gifts.

Suddenly the old woman turned from her trance and looked at him. Her round face was creased with a frown of puzzlement. "Night Wind returns to us this day."

"That should mean great rejoicing, my wife, yet your heart is troubled. Is he injured by the Spanish?" White Crane asked as dread filled his heart.

She shook her head quickly. "No, he is unharmed, other than by the hatred that always consumes him," she said softly. "But he brings a captive with him, a white woman. There is much about her I do not understand, but I do know this—she is important to Night Wind's future."

White Crane frowned now. "For good or for ill?"

"This I do not know. When I see her and speak with her, then I will know," she said with quiet assurance as she rose and began to scoop the hot sotol cakes from the ashes of the fire. "Come, eat more. This will be a day of many trials. I am certain of it."

Knowing they had reached Night Wind's Lipan camp in the isolation of the Guadalupe Mountains made Orlena certain she would face many trials. Three days earlier, the Frenchman had left them, heading west onto the Staked Plains to trade with the hated enemy of the Apache, the Comanche. Night Wind and his raiders took Orlena south. As they neared the village, her dread increased.

NIGHT WIND'S WOMAN

On the surface, nothing changed between the half-caste and his captive. Yet since that night in the lake when they had bathed each other, a subtle difference had permeated their relationship. Although he drew her into his blankets to sleep each night, he no longer taunted her by exploring her body. They slept together to share body heat, but he turned his back to her and fell instantly to sleep. Or so it seemed to Orlena, who in spite of exhaustion lay awake and trembling with the unpardonable feelings he had evoked in her.

And now they were at journey's end. She had no idea what he planned to do with her once he reached his home. Bleakly, she realized that after the days of hard riding in the impenetrable trailless mountains far south and east of Santa Fe, Conal could never find her. What would these savages do with her? Would the half-caste simply turn her over to them to abuse and kill? Orlena doubted that. If he had planned rape, he or his raiders could have had their way long before this.

But she had overheard stories about the Apache women, whose cruelty to captives was said to exceed that of the warriors. As they rode slowly down into the narrow ravine where brush arbors were strewn along the banks of a twisting crystal stream, Orlena darted nervous glances at Night Wind.

His impassive face told her nothing. She concentrated on guiding the hateful little burro behind his big piebald stallion as they descended the steep, rocky trail under the watchful eyes of fierce-looking sentries armed with bows and lances. The camp was small, not more than a few dozen brush arbors. These varied in size, some of them accommodating only two people, others elongated and large, obviously meant to shelter numerous children.

There were lots of children, playing naked in the

warm autumn sunshine. Women clad in simple buckskin tunics worked about the camp, pounding fruits and cactus hearts in stone bowls, drying strips of meat on racks and scraping deer and antelope hides. That much she had observed in the pueblos near Santa Fe, but no tame Indians camped here. Breech-clouted warriors sharpened lances and fletched arrows. They looked barbarous and menacing, with their bronzed skin glistening in the sun. Their silver and copper earrings, arm bracelets and necklaces reflected brilliant flashes of light. The men wore their long hair loose, held off their faces with leather headbands. Their chores were quickly abandoned, as were those of the women, when they saw Night Wind's band of raiders riding slowly toward the camp.

Orlena concentrated on keeping her head held high and her spine stiff. She must betray no fear to these fierce people! Feeling dozens of pairs of eyes on her—awe-filled children, squinting old women, even speculative glances from young men—Orlena stared straight ahead, her eyes fixed on the jagged peak of a distant mountain.

The language spoken was unintelligible to her, but she knew it to be the Lipan dialect Night Wind spoke with his men. The voices were excited and everyone was obviously rejoicing at the return of the raiders. She did not dare consider how they felt about Night Wind's captive.

When they reached one of the smaller arbors in the center of the camp near a curve in the stream's headlong rush down the canyon, Night Wind stopped and slid effortlessly from his big horse. An older man and woman stood outside the shelter. He embraced the man with great warmth and then nodded with grave formality and respect to the gray-haired woman.

NIGHT WIND'S WOMAN

"It is good that you are here," White Crane said simply.

Night Wind looked at him with a smile, saying, "And of course, She Who Dreams knew I was returning this day." It was not a question. His mother-in-law always knew such things.

White Crane nodded. "She also said you brought a captive white woman." He looked up at the golden-haired girl on the burro. "She has the glow of the sun in her hair. Her unusual beauty may cause trouble."

Night Wind smiled grimly, looking about the gathered crowd for one particular face. "Quick Slayer is absent. Trouble will wait until he returns."

White Crane grunted, then turned to his wife. "See to the captive. I would know what you can learn from her. I will speak with our son-in-law."

She Who Dreams nodded and waited until Night Wind turned to the girl, ordering her to dismount from the burro.

Orlena considered defying him, but only fleetingly. Surrounded by savages who spoke no Spanish, the half-caste was her only slim connection with civilization. She dismounted with as much grace as her aching posterior and the short, thin skirt allowed.

The old woman walked up to her and inspected her with shrewd but kind eyes. She was several inches shorter than Orlena and had a round face and plump body. Her salt-and-pepper hair was plaited into a thick braid that hung down her back to her waist. When she reached with one chubby brown hand to touch Orlena's chin, turning her face one way, then the other, the white woman fought the urge to cringe in fear. *Is she measuring me for some insidious torture device*? She stood ramrod straight, with her fingernails biting into her palms, scarcely daring to breathe.

"You have courage to hide your fear," She Who Dreams said softly in thickly accented Spanish. "Come with me. Not harm Night Wind's captive— unless he say."

Smothering a gasp of outrage, Orlena stood stock still, her eyes turning back to where Night Wind and the old man sat beside a campfire. Would he have this woman harm her? Who was she? His mother? Somehow Orlena doubted that, for there was no resemblance between them.

"Come," She Who Dreams repeated, losing patience as she watched the haughty set of the girl's patrician features. This was no *paisano*'s daughter but one born to privilege and power among the hated Spanish.

Just then a thunder of horses heralded the arrival of more men. A small band of warriors rode in with a long string of captured ponies trailing behind them.

"I see my respite from Quick Slayer is all too brief," Night Wind said as he stood up wearily. Looking over to where She Who Dreams and Orlena stood at the door of the wickiup, he swore in Spanish. Without even turning toward his old rival, Night Wind knew his eyes had found the golden-haired woman. *His* woman.

Quick Slayer's face hardened in anger when he saw White Crane and Night Wind conferring. Then he saw the woman and knew the raiders had brought a great prize to the camp. Well, so had he—many fine ponies stolen from a big ranch outside El Paso. He studied the woman, insolently ignoring Night Wind and his father-in-law. Slowly now, he kneed his mount and rode up to where She Who Dreams stood with the golden one.

He had wanted to take Slim Reed to wife, but this fat old hag who claimed the powers of a medicine man

NIGHT WIND'S WOMAN

had denied him—her and her foolish husband. They had let the maiden wed the half-blooded white man with green snake's eyes. But now Night Wind had another woman, a slave. Slaves could not choose as could free Lipan women. He slid off his big gray in front of the golden one.

When he stretched out his hand toward her hair, Night Wind's voice halted him. "Do not touch her, Quick Slayer."

Just then, Orlena attempted to strike him, but he turned to face the advancing pair of men, laughing at her puny effort.

"I have never seen a golden woman before, Night Wind. I would buy your slave for many ponies. Look you at my prizes and choose three of the finest." His harsh face was impassive.

"She is not for sale, Quick Slayer, no matter how many ponies you offer." Night Wind's green eyes locked with his enemy's black ones in pure, icy hate.

Observing the exchange, Orlena could not suppress a shiver of revulsion. Even though she did not understand the language, she could guess what they said and felt their mutual hate like a palpable thing.

"If you will not sell her, you will have her live as a slave in this camp. I say such a one must undergo the test of the knife. What says Night Wind's honored father-in-law?" He turned to White Crane. "Will you let your medicine woman put her to it? If not, you must plan to kill her."

White Crane looked at She Who Dreams and the woman nodded with assurance. "She must take the test. I will learn much that way," she replied.

Vision Seer and Cloth Fox watched Orlena from across the crowd, amazement written on their faces. When Night Wind's raiders freed them, they had been escorted by one called Hoarse Bark to the stronghold.

They had neither seen nor heard of their rescuer's whereabouts since.

"Why has he captured the governor's daughter and brought her here?" Cloth Fox asked in amazement. "It will mean danger for all of us from the Spanish soldiers."

Vision Seer scoffed. "Already Quick Slayer makes trouble—he is the danger, not the foolish Spanish, who can never find us."

"But why does Night Wind bring her among us? To create dissension? Or does his white blood call to him for such a mate now that his first wife is dead?" Cloth Fox's face hardened.

"That is not for us to know, but the woman helped us when we were at her father's mercy. Without the food and medicine she brought, we would never have withstood the escape," Vision Seer replied as he walked toward the confrontation. Reluctantly, Cloth Fox followed.

"I would not have her marked, Mother of my Wife," Night Wind said quietly to She Who Dreams. Although direct speech between a son-in-law and mother-in-law was permitted, the rules governing it were quite strict.

She nodded and motioned for two of the other women to lay hands on Orlena. Just then, Vision Seer approached White Crane and said, "I would speak. This woman is the daughter of the new Spanish governor, Colorado Quinn. She saved our lives while we were imprisoned in their village."

White Crane's eyes widened in horror and he turned to Night Wind, with an abrupt signal for the proceedings to halt. "Come with me," he said to Night Wind and turned to enter the wickiup.

"She is not his daughter by blood," Night Wind said without preamble. "Her father is dead. Conal Quinn did but marry her mother. Her capture was a mistake, but now I mean to keep her." His green eyes glowed in the darkness of the wickiup.

White Crane considered for a moment. "She Who Dreams said the captive's life was intertwined with yours. There is much more to be learned, but for now, she must face the test if you would keep her safe in this camp." He turned and stepped outside into the bright light. "Let the test begin. Vision Seer, I will consider your words about her after this is completed."

Orlena listened to the exchange, recognizing the two Lipan prisoners. Had they interceded on her behalf? Then the women again reached for her and her knees turned to water. Should she fight? She knew instinctively that crying or pleading would be worse than useless. There were far too many of them to resist. Stoically, she let the two younger women lead her. The old woman walked to the center of a large clearing and picked up a long, wickedly curved skinning knife from where it lay beside a large antelope hide. With it in her hand, she waited impassively while Orlena's two guards brought her to a large boulder that lay by the edge of the stream bed. They pushed on her shoulders until she reclined against the rock. Then the old woman walked up to her. Orlena willed herself not to look at the knife.

"Be still. Not move, no matter what," she said quietly in Spanish.

The two young women held Orlena's arms and one pulled on her hair, stretching her over the boulder until her throat was bared and arched, vulnerable to the knife. At least it would be quick and clean, no slow torture, she thought as she lay frozen, staring at the incredibly azure sky overhead.

Everyone in the village, from the oldest woman to the smallest child, gathered in a large circle around the boulder. Except for the yips of dogs and an occasional nicker from a horse, the assembly was deadly silent.

She Who Dreams stood to the right of Orlena and lay the razor-sharp edge of the knife against her throat. Its blade caught the sun and gleamed with silver fire as she withdrew it from Orlena's throat and raised it in an arc, then again lowered it to slide it across the taut white skin.

If I swallow, she will slice my throat open! Orlena fought to breathe as the knife slid across her throat for a third, and yet a fourth time.

Night Wind watched Orlena's ordeal with seeming detachment, glad now that on the long journey from Santa Fe she had learned to curb her fierce, spoiled temper.

After four passes had been made, She Who Dreams withdrew the knife and the women raised Orlena up. Dazed and sun-blinded, she blinked and tried to orient herself, glad she had the boulder to lean against for support, lest her knees give way. She had passed some kind of test apparently, for the whole crowd buzzed in what seemed like approval, even the cynical Cloth Fox. Only one face looked angrily at her—the tall, menacing man who had apparently initiated the confrontation.

Quick Slayer glowered at the girl, then shifted his anger to Night Wind. "You have won, for now. When you tire of her puny white body, I will buy it—for one pony!" With that he turned and left.

"She has great courage, and if what Vision Seer says is true, a good heart as well," White Crane said.

Night Wind scoffed. "She has a stiff Spanish spine."

A voice interrupted them, saying, "That may be, but she still possessed the compassion to save these men and Old Shoe."

NIGHT WIND'S WOMAN

"Hoarse Bark—Mescalero brother! It is good that you have found your way safely here with the freed prisoners." Night Wind embraced his old friend, now his chief lieutenant when he raided Spanish mines and garrisons.

Night Wind looked from the Mescalero to the golden-haired woman, who was being led toward them. She walked as regally as a queen, although he suspected the terror she kept at bay inside her. Knowing such buried fear intimately, he grudgingly felt his respect for her grow.

"Her future is linked with yours. I would speak with her, Husband of My Daughter," She Who Dreams said, standing well back from Night Wind.

"Do this and tell White Crane what you learn," he replied with a formal bow. Night Wind watched as his mother-in-law escorted Orlena into a wickiup across the clearing.

"I, too, would learn more of this golden woman," White Crane said. "From you."

Seeing the tension between White Crane and Night Wind, Hoarse Bark quickly excused himself. He was burning with curiosity but knew he would have to wait to learn what had gone awry in Santa Fe.

They sat in silence for several moments as White Crane prepared a pipe and inhaled from it, then handed it to his son-in-law.

"So, she is beloved of Colorado Quinn. You stole her in vengeance?" His black eyes were shrewd and measuring as he waited for Night Wind to reply.

"No—that is, not at first." He swore silently and gathered his scattered thoughts. "I sent my men to steal the Quinn's son—a youth. He would make a fine Lipan warrior one day."

A look of puzzlement crossed the old man's face. "But they stole a woman in his stead."

"She was dressed in her brother's clothes, out for a lark in the crowds, watching the caravan leave. My men dropped a blanket over her in a dark alley...."

The old man understood. "And when you found their error, you decided to exact another form of vengeance against the Quinn?"

"I will not harm her. She will come to me," Night Wind said defensively, hearing the reproach in White Crane's voice.

"She aided Vision Seer and the other prisoners. That is a debt which the Lipan must honor," he said gravely.

"Orlena Valdéz is my captive. She has passed the test of the knife. I may keep her as my slave." His intense eyes now met White Crane's squarely.

"She has courage," he nodded, "and beside Spanish pride, also a good heart. Only beware, my son, that you do not fall victim to your own revenge."

Chapter 9

"Stir and put in bowls," She Who Dreams instructed Orlena, handing her a crude wooden spoon that she had withdrawn from the iron kettle over the fire. A savory stew of buffalo, freshly killed from the fall hunts, simmered with wild onions, celery, and dried sage.

Even as the angry protest formed on her lips, Orlena felt her stomach growl. How many times had she gone without food because she refused to serve her savage captors first? Biting back her retort, she took the spoon and stirred the stew. After days of dry spitted rabbits and cold tortillas, this was heaven! She served it into the dishes, which she and the older woman then carried to Night Wind and White Crane. Of course the women would eat their men's leavings!

This was her first opportunity to observe savage Apaches in their own environment. She had never seen their women before and was somewhat taken aback by the way they looked and behaved. She had expected beaten, cowed creatures who slaved while the men sat idly about drinking mescal and lording it over them. If this woman, who spoke passable Spanish and smiled freely with her husband and Night Wind, was typical, their lot was not horrid—for savages. The women she had seen around the scattered campfires were clean, as well dressed and adorned as the men and seemed cheerful and well fed. Certainly She Who Dreams was not wasting away, even if she did have to serve the men first! Still, Orlena, who had been raised with servants to wait on her every whim, was furious that she must become one in this detested place.

Night Wind watched Orlena dish up the food and then bring it to him. Smiling slightly, he reached to take the bowl from her hands. When she looked about to drop it on his head, he flashed her a quelling look and she handed it to him.

"She is not used to our ways," White Crane said as he blew on the steaming chunks of meat and vegetables before spearing them with his knife.

"Do not let her get behind your back with a grinding stone or a knife," Night Wind replied sourly.

White Crane only chuckled as he watched the Golden One cross the clearing.

"Come. We eat now," She Who Dreams said to Orlena, as she squatted comfortably beside the fire. The women were just out of earshot of the men, who were seated on the grass beside the stream.

Taking a bowl and filling it, Orlena looked about for a spoon but found nothing. Pascal had crude utensils with him when he cooked for them on the trail. After he left them, they had existed on dry foods such as spited game and corn cakes. She watched the old woman pick carefully through the chunks of stew and extract a fat onion, popping it into her mouth. She followed suit with a piece of meat, then some other unidentifiable vegetable, probably a wild potato. The men used their knives and Orlena knew the old woman had one, too, but did not deign to use it. Perhaps it was a form of courtesy, since no one in the camp would ever turn *her* loose with a knife! Her stomach knotted with hunger. She reached into the bowl with her fingers and ate.

"How are you called?" She Who Dreams asked between bites.

"Orlena Valdéz."

"I am She Who Dreams, Lipan Medicine Woman. I know Night Wind brings white woman. Have dream." She allowed the girl to digest that fact along with her food, then asked, "What means Orlena Valdéz?"

"Golden One is a literal translation from the Latin for Orlena."

She Who Dreams nodded approvingly and waited.

"Valdéz is my family name. We are of a noble house in Spain." At the Apache's puzzled look, she considered how to explain, but it seemed hopelessly complex. She settled for a sop to her own badly battered pride. "I am related to the great king of all the Spanish, who lives far away and yet rules here."

She Who Dreams smiled. "Not rule *here*." She swept her hand across the vast magnificence of the mountains that surrounded them.

Unable to argue the point, Orlena changed the subject. "Where did you learn to speak Spanish?"

"Night Wind teach wife. She teach me."

Orlena's chest inexplicably tightened for an instant. Then the surprise and hurt were replaced by an onrush of anger. So, he was married. "How many women does he have? Do they all speak Spanish?"

121

She Who Dream's eyes shrewdly watched the flashes of jealousy and anger in the Golden One. "Lipan men have only one wife. She who was my daughter dead now. Night Wind has no woman—except you." She looked speculatively at Orlena, who reddened beneath the scrutiny.

"I am his captive, not his . . . his woman." After she said the hated words, Orlena remembered Night Wind's warning about others in his band who might take her by force. If only she understood his motive, who he was, why he kept her without violating her.

When She Who Dreams returned with the men's bowls, Orlena walked with her to the stream to clean them. All around her, up and down the twisting creek, women washed crude cooking utensils, even bathed small children. Everyone spoke the Lipan dialect. She wondered how many of them understood her language. "Does anyone here but you speak Spanish?"

"A few—young warriors who ride with Night Wind. He teach them."

"How did he learn himself? Did his Spanish father teach him?" Orlena pretended casual indifference as she scoured the bowls with sand from the creek.

She Who Dream's face became shuttered. "Night Wind tell you of white father—if he choose. Blue Robes teach him speak . . . and speak silent messages." She made a few signs to indicate writing.

"He can read and write as well as speak perfect Castilian! Where are these Franciscans—Blue Robes? Did they raise him?"

She Who Dreams shrugged. "Part of his life with Blue Robes in south. Part with Lipan. Night Wind's band all dead, killed on plains. Blue Robes teach him white way. Then he find this band."

Orlena felt as if she were looking at a half-woven tapestry. Parts of Night Wind's life were revealed;

NIGHT WIND'S WOMAN

many were obscured in the unfinished weave. *Why should I want to know about him*? an angry voice asked. "Know your enemy," she muttered beneath her breath as he approached.

"Until She Who Dreams can teach you how to build a temporary shelter, we will sleep in my blankets. I have found a place with privacy. Come."

"Everyone bids me come and go as if I were a burro," she said angrily as she stood to face him.

He laughed. "Your temperament does present marked similarities." Before she could make an angry retort, he reached out and grabbed her hand, pulling her with him. When she tried to resist, he turned and hauled her up, slinging her across his shoulder with effortless ease.

Seeing the looks of amusement on the faces of many observers, Orlena subsided. *Blessed Virgin, I will not put on a spectacle to entertain them!*

He carried her across the stream, splashing through the shallow, icy water until he located a copse of low growing Texas madrones. Within their shelter lay a stand of tall grasses and a small pool of water.

"It is not part of the rushing stream. The sun has warmed it a bit. If we hurry, we can bathe before the cool of evening." His eyes glowed like a cat's in the gathering darkness as he placed her on her feet before him.

"I do not wish to act as your body servant again," she said with as much hauteur as she could manage while moving away from him.

He backed her against the trunk of a tree and stood with scarcely an inch between their bodies. "You smell of burro and wood smoke."

She wrinkled her nose. "And you simply stink." she spat, trying to slip past him.

"We both need to bathe, I will not deny it." Deftly

unfastening the drawstring at her neckline he slipped one shoulder of her blouse down to reveal a proudly uptilted breast. Quickly he pulled the other side of the blouse down, baring her other breast and imprisoning her arms at her sides. She could feel his hot gaze on her breasts as he leaned nearer, lightly brushing her nipples with his crisp chest hair until they hardened into tight points. Something warm and drugging, like mulled wine, stole over her, erasing the chill of the twilight air. She stood very still, afraid to breathe as he held her in thrall.

Then, without touching her further, he turned and kicked off his moccasins and removed his breechclout. "Either undress, Lioness, or be thrown in the pool with your clothes on. I will not share my bed—or my body's warmth—with an unwashed woman."

She gasped in outrage and before she could think, kicked with all her strength at his backside. He was bent over, tossing his scant clothes on top of his moccasins. Her blow sent him headlong into the pool with a resounding splash. With lightning speed he surfaced, shaking droplets of water from his shoulder-length hair, which clung like spilled ink to his head. "If you run, one of my men will catch you," he said softly. "I do not think they would care if you were as filthy as a pig." With that warning, he emerged casually from the water and walked over to his saddlebag to extract a bar of soap, totally ignoring her and his own nakedness.

Orlena watched the last of the setting sun's rays play on his rippling, lean muscles. He was hard and rangy, yet elegantly proportioned and taller than the other Apache men. Again she wondered about the finely crisscrossed scars that marred the perfection of his back and shoulders. Were they some sort of test of manhood that half-castes had to endure? None of the

NIGHT WIND'S WOMAN

full-blooded Lipan men were so scarred, only Night Wind and the Mescalero, Hoarse Bark.

Slowly, hating herself, but knowing he would let her freeze or worse if she did not follow his orders, Orlena finished undressing and slipped into the cool water. After he had sudsed himself, he tossed her the soap with supreme indifference.

"Just like the food. Apache women must always take their men's leavings," she muttered.

He laughed. "There is plenty to go around, Lioness. Only wait and observe the Lipan way. You will have ample opportunity in the days that follow."

Again that night he held her in the thick soft furs he had heaped together as their sleeping pallet. Again he caressed her lightly, experimentally, then fell sound asleep with his arm draped possessively around her. Orlena choked back acid tears of humiliation as he slept peacefully. Earlier by the pool, when he had bared her breasts and teased them, she had responded wantonly, feeling them tingle and harden, sending a surge of heat and desire coiling lower in her body. Beneath the furs, he again touched them, cupping them with his hands and running his fingers lightly down her belly, as if he knew what she felt. She was losing control of her own body, her own feelings, her morals—to a lowly half-caste, a savage!

Dawn came all too soon. Orlena awakened when something soft and heavy was flung on top of the thick beaver pelts that served as a blanket. She sat up in a daze, then realized she was naked beneath the warm pelts and grabbed them up to cover her breasts.

Night Wind smiled at her disarrayed beauty. "I have brought you presents. They should fit." He held a pair of women's laced boots in one hand and gestured to the skirt and shirt of buttersoft deerhide that lay atop the furs. "The days grow too chill for your *paisana*'s garb, and such a costume is impractical anyway."

She touched the soft garments gingerly. "Who did they belong to?" she asked, dreading the possibility that they were his dead wife's.

"She Who Dreams has a niece named Sweet Rain who is about your size." Then he added quietly, "When a Lipan dies, all her possessions are buried or burned with her." He turned and walked through the trees toward the camp without another word.

"Why is it always as if he can read my very thoughts?" she whispered furiously to herself, not wanting to dwell on how much he may have cared for his Lipan wife.

The clothes fit her perfectly, and Orlena had to admit that they were warm and comfortable. The laced boots were snug and provided her sore feet far more protection than the peasant's sandals had. She used the small bone comb the Frenchman had given her to detangle her hair and braided it in one fat plait. If not for her fair coloring, she could be an Apache squaw, she thought unhappily, wondering what the day would hold for her.

As she walked across the clearing toward their campfire, Orlena observed the Lipan women at work preparing and serving food. "Why do the younger women take food from the cookpots of the older ones and carry it to other shelters?" she asked She Who Dreams as the old woman deftly shoved sotol bread from the ashes onto a wooden plank.

"They are daughters of family. Each shares mother's cookfire. Takes food from it to own husband and children."

"Do the daughters always marry men living so nearby?" In spite of herself, Orlena found the Apache customs fascinating.

NIGHT WIND'S WOMAN

She Who Dreams smiled. "Not like Spanish. Lipan not send daughters away. Man come to live with wife's family. Night Wind come to us when he married she who was my daughter," she said with both pride and sadness in her voice.

Orlena did not want to hear more about Night Wind's lost love, so she asked no more questions and fell to helping She Who Dreams with the morning cooking. Over the next few days she learned much about Lipan life and acquired new skills so menial they would once have appalled her. Yet all the Lipan, except the very young and the very old, contributed to camp life. As Night Wind's slave, she had to do the bidding of his mother-in-law. In truth, Orlena was coming to a grudging liking of the insightful older woman, whom all of the band seemed to revere as a seer and a healer.

A few days after their arrival, Orlena was busily pounding dried mulberries and strips of jerked venison together as She Who Dreams had shown her. Sweat ran down her temples and pooled between her breasts in spite of the cool fall day. She stopped to wipe her brow, only to see Night Wind and several other young men ride into the camp laden down with young deer and large strings of rabbits. As they rode through the camp, the men stopped here and there, distributing fat rabbits and large chunks of the deer carcasses to various people, mostly lone women and old men. Of all the hunters, Night Wind had the most game and gave the most away. Generosity and a sense of community permeated the village in spite of the harshness of their lives.

Several *paisano* men and women, "tame Indians" of mixed blood, were also slaves, owned by various families. Although they worked hard, none seemed abused. She wondered if they, too, had passed the test of the knife. She refused to consider what happened to captives who failed it. At least a half dozen of the younger children definitely were pure Spanish, or half-caste, yet had been adopted into the tribe and were raised as Lipan. It had crossed her mind fleetingly that perhaps Night Wind had intended to raise Santiago that way, since it had been her brother and not she he had wanted to abduct. He had said he did not plan to kill or ransom Conal's son. But why? She feared to ask Night Wind about Conal. In fact, all the Lipan—even Blaise Pascal—had called him Colorado Quinn, the bloody one. They hated him for his service to the Spanish crown. Even She Who Dreams' face took on a remote, expressionless mien when she heard Conal's name.

When Night Wind rode up to her and slid from Warpaint, she continued grinding the meat and berries until he spoke to her. "White Crane tells me you please She Who Dreams."

"Why do you speak so seldom with her? It seems you avoid her just as the others avoid mentioning their dead relatives," she said, pausing to rub her aching back.

He smiled, glad to have her drawn into Lipan life, but finding the custom of mother-in-law avoidance difficult to explain to a European. "Among the Lipan, it is considered a form of respect for a son-in-law not to have direct dealings with his wife's mother. Brothers and sisters and cousins of opposite sex also do not speak to each other. We have very strong laws against blood incest—and there is no dispensation from a church that ever changes the rules."

As he spoke, she saw a strange, haunted look flash across his face. It was such an arrestingly handsome face, stormy in anger one moment, then slashed by a blinding white smile the next.

"I was educated by two men—White Crane has been my Lipan father and sponsor with this, my people, now that my own band is dead. As to the other, he is a remarkable Franciscan priest, a scholar, but a man with more questions than answers—more compassion than condemnation. I have learned much of both worlds." He paused and the sad, haunted look again flashed, then vanished.

"Yet you would be Apache, not Spaniard, even though you have studied both," she said quietly, knowing that her own people would never accept a half-caste as more than a menial, while the savages granted even those of wholly foreign blood equal rights. It rankled her sense of superiority and she disliked considering it in this new light.

"You, of course, think the Spanish way the only way," he said with a scowl. "Look around you." Across the river two women were scraping a large buffalo hide from the recent fall hunt on the plains. A young warrior, probably the husband of one of the women, was helping them lift and pull on the heavy hide. "Here men and women work together. Everyone, rich and poor, contributes. Daughters are as valued as sons in our society. A man does not leave his estates to a male heir, for no one owns the land. The family is everything—and each daughter stays with her family, enriching it by the husband who comes to live with them and the children they together give the family."

"She Who Dreams told me about your marriage customs," Orlena said stiffly. She was no wife, only a lowly slave, so lowly he would not even take her as a man takes a woman. The instant the thought surfaced, she gasped in mortification at her own admission and dropped her stone pestle into the bowl. She stood and then bolted for the trees, running swiftly as a deer in her boots and the soft doeskin clothing.

At first, Night Wind watched her in perplexity, seeing the blur of tears in her amber eyes. He had no idea what had triggered the emotional explosion. Perhaps it was the sudden realization that Conal had never been a true father to her. Perhaps neither had her natural father. Feeling a stab of guilt, he rose and ran after her. She could not get far on foot in the rugged mountains.

Then he heard horses whickering and the pounding of hoofbeats, followed by an outcry. Hoarse Bark came running across the river toward him calling out, "She has taken one of White Crane's ponies and ridden off like a demon! I stopped the sentries from shooting her, saying she was your woman."

With a snarled oath, Night Wind raced toward the compound, calling to Warpaint. The large black-and-white stallion raised his head and trotted obediently toward him. Not waiting even to place a hackamore on the piebald, he swung up and kneed him into a swift gallop in the direction Orlena had gone.

Hoarse Bark called out, "I will follow with weapons and remounts."

Dread filled Night Wind's senses as he realized the direction Orlena had taken—due south toward the rocky, uneven ground where her horse could stumble and throw her, breaking her neck. It was also the place where the caves honeycombed the earth—hiding places for the spirits of mischief and evil, the Apache said, always avoiding them. Night Wind did not fear the Owl Spirit or the Coyote, but the other . . . His mind froze at the thought. He urged Warpaint on, focusing only on finding Orlena quickly.

Orlena had been a superb rider ever since she was a small girl, sneaking off with Ignacio's horses, riding bareback. Later, Conal had lavishly indulged her with the finest Spanish barbs. When they were at home in Aranjuez, she had ridden astride with him and Santiago. Of course, this half-wild Apache pony was a far cry from the beautifully trained horses in the Valdéz and Quinn stables. Luckily she had remembered to mount from the right as she had watched the Lipan warriors do—and luckily, the first horse she grabbed for had a hackamore on and was a filly of reasonable temperament. Now, the unfamiliar countryside blurred by her as she leaned over the horse's neck, clinging like a burr and urging her faster.

Tears choked her and the thorny cactus and brushy mesquite tore at her arms and legs, catching on the soft doeskin clothing. If she had worn thin cotton, she would have been bloodied by now in her headlong, reckless dash, but such thoughts were farthest from her mind as she sped south, with no destination, simply wishing to escape from Night Wind.

The terrain grew more uneven, with sharp outcroppings of rock poking up through the brushy, high desert floor. Just then, the filly stumbled as the ground suddenly seemed to give way beneath them. Waist-high in dense mesquite, she could see nothing but the prickly thorns and greenish browns of the vegetation as she was thrown clear of the floundering horse. The little red-and-white pinto cried and thrashed, backing up and regaining her footing, only to race away, leaving Orlena laying dazed and bruised in a large patch of mountain juniper.

She was hopelessly lost in this trackless wilderness, which was doubtless filled with poisonous snakes and other deadly wildlife. Shaking her head to clear it, she struggled to her feet, pulling prickly pear spines and bits of brush from her doeskins. The filly was nowhere in sight and she was completely disoriented. Without thinking, she simply put one foot in front of the other, heading toward the trampled brush where the horse had stumbled.

Suddenly the earth seemed to swallow her up. She was falling, scrambling for something to grab hold of, finally clawing some grape vines that broke her rolling, bouncing descent into the bowels of the earth. Orlena screamed, not realizing that she called out for the very man she had been fleeing.

Night Wind heard her scream his name and the air rushed from his chest in a painful constriction. The little filly had just raced by him, headed back toward camp. Orlena had been thrown!

"If only she had not—" His words were cut short by another cry, echoing as if from far below. With horrifying certainty he knew she had fallen into one of the caves honeycombing the area.

He reined in Warpaint and dismounted, his throat dry, choked with terror as he called out her name. No answer now. Taking a deep breath he called again—and again, walking cautiously toward where he knew the earth's crust was treacherous. Unspeakable terrors lurked below.

Orlena awakened slowly to the sound of his voice, somewhere high above her. She was in a dark place, covered with rocks and debris from her fall. A few thin shafts of light penetrated the gloom to reveal to her straining eyes the interior of an underground cavern. But one unlike anything she had ever read about or imagined. Slender, spiky stalactites glowed with an eerie, dim light that seemed to radiate from within them. The small tunnel she had fallen into was part of a labyrinth, with numerous openings into yet more tunnels running in every direction.

She struggled to stand up, coughing and choking in the thick dust as she shook free of the rocks and silt from her fall. She could still hear Night Wind's voice calling to her from a great distance and she looked upward toward the light. Blessed Virgin, how far had she tumbled! The dim shafts of sunlight winked like distant stars. When she took a step forward, her leg buckled beneath her, sending her to the hard rocky earth again with a hoarse cry of pain. Her leg—God and all His Saints, had she broken it?

Again Night Wind's voice rang out, ragged and breathless, but nearer. Without a thought for why she had fled him she called out, feeling the welling scream rip from her throat.

"Orlena!" He was at the opening in the earth, tearing frantically at the leathery vegetation. The entrance was small. "Orlena?" He waited, his heart hammering in his chest.

"Night Wind. I am here. I have hurt my leg. I cannot—" A gasp of pain echoed up to him.

Frantically he looked about. No one had found his trail yet. He could not leave her there alone. But could he go down after her? Blood pounded in his head, almost blinding him with its driving fury. Sweat drenched his buckskins in spite of the cool mountain air. And he trembled like an aspen leaf in a spring storm. Taking a deep breath he called to her, "I am coming, Lioness. Only wait a moment."

He looked over to where Warpaint stood, waiting patiently. He must only hope Hoarse Bark would be along soon and find them by sighting the well-trained piebald. Slowly he grasped a handhold of the dry, twisted vines and wrapped them about his arm, testing their strength. "How far below are you? I can see naught but blackness from here," he called out, realizing how raspy his voice must sound.

"The vines and some rock outcroppings broke my fall. It seems to be quite far. I—I cannot see you, only a few thin shafts of light from above. That and the light from the cave. Oh, Blessed Virgin, Night Wind, it glows in the dark down here!"

He had heard tales about the glowing rocks—great jagged lances that grew from the ceilings and floors of these caverns. They were considered sacred, forbidden places where the Owl and Coyote spirits dwelled, perhaps the passageway to the Underground from which the First People journeyed to the earth. Night Wind no longer believed in Apache lore or religious taboos. His fear was far more immediate and palpable, born in that year of darkness and hell in the silver mines of Nueva Vizcaya.

"Watch for falling rocks as I descend. Can you stay clear?" he called down.

"Yes. I can move, just not very fast, I fear."

She feared! Every breath rattled in and out of his lungs as he climbed into the inky depths. His hands were so wet with sweat, the vines slid through them. Then his footing slipped on the rocky walls of the cave and he dropped several lengths before breaking his fall. He grappled for a foothold, then clawed at the rocks with both hands as he heard the vines snap above him. Their ladder out of this hell had just given way! Clinging like a tick to the flank of a horse, he struggled to find breath as Orlena called frantically.

"Night Wind, are you all right?"

He was frozen with terror, unable to answer her for several moments until he slowly won the war with his rebellious arms and legs. When the trembling subsided sufficiently for him to resume his descent, he called out, "I am unharmed."

Inch by agonizing inch, he lowered himself further from the light by sheer will, focusing not on his enemy's hated face as he had done in the mines, but on the tawny beauty of the golden woman below. "Orlena, Lioness, I come for you," he whispered.

NIGHT WIND'S WOMAN

When his feet finally reached the floor of the cave, she was there, clinging to him, sobbing as she wrapped her arms about his neck, molding her soft curves against his sweat-drenched body. Orlena could feel him trembling, feel the violent, shuddering breaths that racked his lungs. It seemed that as she calmed, he became more rigid with terror, as if her fear had somehow been absorbed by his body.

"Night Wind? What is wrong?" Surely he did not care for her enough to be frightened that she might have died! In the weeks she had known him, ever since that first fierce bloody fight in Chihuahua, he had been a man afraid of nothing. But now the arrogant, ice-cold renegade, who she knew had faced death calmly a thousand times, trembled like a schoolboy in her arms.

Finally, taking several deep breaths, Night Wind put his arm around her and took a step into the shaft of light from above. Seeming to draw strength from the sweet fragrance that was uniquely hers, he looked at the honeycombs spread before them. Dimly glowing spikes grew from the floor and ceiling. It was as the medicine people had said. For a fleeting moment, he wondered if they were right about the evil ones supposedly dwelling there.

The spirits had frightened him as a nine-year-old boy, when he was first lowered into the blackness to dig from sunrise to darkness. The Green-Eyed Boy had been terrified of being lost in the Underworld filled with malevolent gods. But gradually, when no Owl or Coyote appeared to devour him, he came to realize that the enemy was within himself, eating at his guts, twisting them until every breath, every moment brought a far greater agony than the blows from the guards' whips when they forced him to climb down into the mines. The dark underground became his demon. Still it remained inside him.

Orlena understood that he was struggling with some hidden torment that she did not comprehend. "Night Wind," she spoke his name softly, feeling his hold about her waist tighten. Her leg throbbed wickedly, but she was otherwise unharmed. Her hands stroked the now-familiar contours of his lean, hard body, finding him, too, unscathed but for minor cuts and scratches.

"We must get out of here," he rasped out at last, looking about for any vines or handholds on the walls ascending toward the light. "Can you climb if I help you?"

She gasped when she moved her injured leg. "I will try."

Without releasing his hold on her, he grasped the wall beneath the opening with his free hand. Nothing. There were only a few jagged rocks, too loose and far apart to use as footholds for climbing. The vines had all broken far above them.

With a repressed shudder, he whispered, "We must wait for Hoarse Bark and the others. They will track us and find Warpaint." With a sickening wrench of dread he knew that could take hours. He might have to spend a night underground. But he was not alone. There was the woman.

Odd. He should have been furious with her for running away so foolishly and blundering into this deadly mess, but her presence was his one slim link to sanity. He pulled her with him to sit on the ground in the small shaft of light from above.

Night Wind said nothing; Orlena was afraid to speak. They huddled together in silence for what seemed an eternity. Each time the light shifted as the course of the sun arced to the west, he would follow it across the rocky cave floor.

NIGHT WIND'S WOMAN

Emotionally and physically exhausted, Orlena lay her head against his shoulder and dozed. Suddenly, her head snapped up as she heard voices calling in the Lipan tongue, then in Spanish. "Night Wind, your friends are here!" She pounded on his chest, but he seemed to be in a trance.

Then, suddenly, a hoarse cry broke from his lips, guttural and low, like a wounded animal in unbearable pain. "Hoarse Bark! We are here! Bring no ponies past where Warpaint stands. Watch for holes in the earth!"

Each word, each sentence seemed torn from him as he stood up, trembling at first. Gradually, he grew steadier as he heard the voices from above. He held Orlena in his arms as Hoarse Bark explained that they were braiding vines together into a stouter rope which would support their weight.

It took hours to locate sufficient materials. All the while the others worked, Hoarse Bark continued to talk to Night Wind, seeming to understand that the one-sided conversation was essential to his friend.

Finally, the rope was lowered and Night Wind grasped it, tying it about Orlena's waist. She looked at him but quickly let the protest die on her lips. The dim light striking his face reflected his implacable expression. Now his hands were firm and steady, his movements sure as he whispered, "Hold yourself away from the sharp rocks with your arms as they raise you." Then he called out to Hoarse Bark, and she found herself being slowly pulled from the abyss.

When she reached the entrance, the Mescalero's face was black with hate as he glared at her. Saying nothing to her but continuing his words to the man below, he rapidly untied the rope and shoved her toward his two companions. One of them was the squat, ugly Broken Leg, who held her far closer against his body than necessary to prevent her possible escape.

By the time they had Night Wind out of the cave, it was twilight, yet even in the gathering darkness she could see the glazed look of terror etched across his face. Silently, he nodded his thanks to the Mescalero. Some unspoken message seemed to be exchanged between the two men.

Speaking in broken but intelligible Spanish, the Mescalero said, "Walk with care. Do not fight Broken Leg. Earth is weak over caves." With that, the ugly Lipan yanked her behind him and started back to where their horses were tethered.

Biting her lip against the pain in her sprained leg, she cast a glance back at Night Wind. Hoarse Bark walked beside him, continuing their earlier conversation in a low voice, neither touching him nor expecting any reply. The bold raider, leader of these dangerous renegades, walked in stony silence like a somnambulist, his eyes fixed unseeing on some distant point. Lazarus returned from the dead could not have had eyes filled with more torment.

Chapter 10

Santa Fe

Bone weary and covered with grime, Conal Quinn rode into Santa Fe. He had just spent three stinking weeks combing every filthy scorpion-infested mountain range north to south, every trail or pass the renegades were known to use. The expedition had been in vain. Now he understood how that bastard had received his name. He had vanished like the night wind at a hot, still desert sunrise.

Conal reached one hand to the leather tunic he wore, sensing rather than feeling the letter from the renegade. He had carried it with him when he set out in search of Orlena. His beautiful, innocent butterfly was suffering the abuse and revenge of that filthy savage. Part of him longed to rescue her and take her back to civilization where she could forget the shame she must surely have endured. Yet another part of him feared he might find a woman so broken in body and spirit that death would be a welcome respite. He had steeled himself to kill her quickly if necessary. He forced from his mind the possibility that the savage's boast might come true. His Orlena, proud and independent, would never willingly submit to a half-caste's touch. Yet the letter seemed to burn through his very skin with its hateful message.

"I will kill you, Night Wind, mongrel cur. And you will die so slowly, you will beg me for the mercy of death as no prisoner of the Holy Office ever did!" he swore beneath his breath as he dismounted in front of the governor's palace.

Santiago had watched the weary, filthy line of soldiers ride in without his sister, and his spirits had plummeted. He had been so sure that his father would find her! He must, for the boy could not bear to live with his guilt.

Conal watched the freckled face of his son crumple with hopelessness as he walked toward the door. "We could find no trace in any direction," he said tonelessly.

"If only I had not given her my clothes. It was me they wanted, not my sister!" His voice caught on a sob, but he forced himself to squelch such childishness. He was a man now, even if his father had refused to let him accompany the soldiers on the mission.

Conal sighed. He had been hard on the boy the morning he learned of the escapade, when Orlena had not returned from the market. But then Night Wind's message had been delivered and he realized the intent of his enemy. Thank all the Saints he had not captured Santiago!

"You are not to blame. If not your clothes, she would have stolen some servant's rags just to gain her own way. Orlena was always willful," Conal said to the boy.

NIGHT WIND'S WOMAN

"Do not speak of her in past tense—as if she were dead. They can ransom her, can they not?"

"Has any message come while I was away?" Conal asked his son as they walked into the cool, dark interior of the palace. He had not told Santiago of the letter he had received the day after Orlena's abduction.

"No, none," the youth replied sorrowfully. "Does that mean . . . that she is truly dead?" he forced himself to ask.

Conal's face darkened and his eyes narrowed. He ushered the boy into his library off the main *sala*, away from the curious ears of the servants. Taking Santiago firmly by the shoulders, he said, "You have spent months in New Spain now. You have heard what captives of the savages must endure. Would you wish her alive in such circumstances?"

The brutal question stunned the boy, leaving him speechless with horror. He turned from his father's stony gaze and walked over to the courtyard window. "I will never give her up. I will search until I find her, or until I am dead, too. You will not stop me this time, Papa. I will go—with you or without you!"

Conal faced his son, the pride of his life, and saw an implacable stranger. "Perhaps it was wrong of me to keep you here," he replied wearily. "Send Sergeant Ruiz in to me. I will have a reward posted in every presidio and villa from California to the Mississippi River, enough to tempt St. Peter himself to betray the Night Wind. Then we will ride out once more—together."

Santiago nodded tightly and turned to do his father's bidding.

Quick Slayer watched Night Wind's woman from his hiding place behind some large rocks near the spring. She was filling water skins with several of the other women. Ever since Night Wind had brought her to their camp he had desired her. He watched the sun gild her dark golden hair with burnished splendor. Even her skin, at first reddened and burned, now glowed a soft golden color. Pulling at his groin to ease its ache, he considered how he could wrest her from his hated enemy.

Night Wind guarded her each night, taking her to his blankets in the privacy of the sturdy wickiup She Who Dreams had helped the captive construct. During the day, she was always in the meddlesome old woman's company or with other of the younger women, doing camp chores. For a slave, she was treated far too well, he thought—until he considered how such exotic beauty could inflame a man, especially one with white blood in his own veins. Small wonder Night Wind protected her!

Orlena had spent the days since their ordeal in the caves steeped in misery. No one would explain Night Wind's bizarre behavior to her. He would not speak of it, and Hoarse Bark seemed to exude hate toward her ever since the incident. The bold Apache renegade Night Wind was human after all—afraid of the dark! Small wonder his teasing tongue and insolent manner had turned to stony silence. Yet she felt perversely bereft, actually missing their arguments and the coiled sexual tension that had radiated between them like summer lightning.

What is wrong with me? The strain of this hellish captivity is unhinging my mind! When Sweet Rain and Little Doe left the stream, Orlena dawdled, heedless of being alone. Since they, like everyone else, seemed angered with her, she was glad to be quit of their company. Not that she entertained any more foolish ideas about running away. Deep in the fastness of the

NIGHT WIND'S WOMAN

Guadalupe Mountains, surrounded by deserts and fearful underground caverns, she knew escape to be futile. Orlena held fast to the dream that Conal would yet rescue her. For now, it was her only hope.

Orlena stood up, and swung the two heavy water skins as expertly as any Apache woman, one to each side of her shoulders on their wooden yoke. After a single halting step, she heard a crunch of gravel from the rise over the hill. Earlier Orlena had felt an eerie sensation, as if someone watched her. Quickly her golden eyes darted across the jagged horizon. The stream was strewn with boulders and a trail twisted downward toward their camp. Now the other women had walked out of hearing. She was alone. Or, was she?

Swallowing the sudden bile of fear, she squared her shoulders beneath their heavy burden and began to walk toward the trail.

When Night Wind saw Sweet Rain talking with She Who Dreams, he looked about for Orlena. She had not returned with the other water gatherers. Swearing, he stalked over to the girl. After bowing politely to She Who Dreams, he asked, "Where did Orlena go? She is not in camp."

Sweet Rain's pretty round face puckered with a frown. "That one still sits lazing upstream." Secretly, she had been glad when her companions agreed to leave the white woman alone. They had all hurried back to camp.

An oath escaped Night Wind as he turned toward the path along the twisty stream. He began to run, some instinct urging him to do so. "Surely she would never be so foolish as to try an escape again?" he muttered to himself. But that was not his true fear.

When he crested the hill and turned the bend where the stream burbled, he saw what he had dreaded.

"Quick Slayer! You die for this!" His cry rang out as he leaped toward the sandy bank where the big Lipan wrestled with Orlena. She was bloody and bruised, and had obviously fought valiantly. Her doeskin skirt had been pulled up, baring her long, silky legs to the cool evening air as she thrashed and kicked in vain, unable to scream because her assailant's meaty hand covered her mouth.

Hearing his enemy, Quick Slayer shoved the girl roughly aside, nearly pushing her into the water in his haste to free his knife. Just as he did so, Night Wind was on him and they rolled across the soft, sandy ground, each straining for an advantage, locked in a struggle to the death.

Orlena sat up by the water's edge, dazed and breathless. Her body burned with scratches and abrasions, but she forgot her own pain, watching transfixed as Night Wind and Quick Slayer fought. In a matter of moments a small group of Apache, mostly men, had gathered. Obviously they had followed Night Wind after he ran to find his captive.

Gathering her torn clothing protectively about her, Orlena stood up and looked across the clearing to White Crane. Surely he would help his son-in-law? But no one moved to intervene as the two antagonists broke apart and rolled to their feet, knives gleaming evilly in the twilight.

"I challenge the Night Wind for his yellow-haired slave," Quick Slayer said loudly.

Night Wind could hear Orlena's hissed intake of breath. Quick Slayer's intent was clear, even though she understood but a few words of the Lipan dialect. "I told you never to wander about alone," he ground out in Spanish without taking his eyes off Quick Slayer's knife. Then he replied to his adversary in Lipan, "Night Wind accepts your challenge. Prepare

NIGHT WIND'S WOMAN

to die for touching my woman." With that he crouched low and waited.

Quick Slayer was brawny and large, but surprisingly agile in spite of his size. His knife arced up and slashed at Night Wind's throat, coming heart-stoppingly close before his foe deflected the blow. They circled each other, like a bear and a cougar, Night Wind still in the defensive, crouched position, seeming to wait for the heavier man to spend his energy uselessly. He parried all of Quick Slayer's slashing attempts at a swift kill, but as the fight continued, he received several superficial cuts that began to bleed freely. Ignoring them, Night Wind began to grow more aggressive, watching for openings, drawing blood from his enemy. As he weaved and parried with the grace of a cat, Night Wind taunted the big man.

"You have always hated me. This is your chance. Why do you not end it as you have often boasted you would?"

"I will kill you, white man, son of Blue Robes and their foolish gods! Then I will possess your slave." Even as he spoke, Quick Slayer again feinted low and then arched high with his knife.

But Night Wind deflected the thrust with his own blade while his left hand snaked out with blurring speed to seize his foe's wrist. With the knives locked high above their heads, they strained, each unable to break free until Night Wind's yank on Quick Slayer's arm sent them both tumbling to the earth, where they again rolled in the sand. Now it caked to their sweat-and-blood-slicked bodies.

Quick Slayer's blade came dangerously close to Night Wind's throat, but by sheer strength he forced the other man's hand back. They remained in a stalemate of rolling twists, each unable to finish the other until Quick Slayer suddenly broke free and reached out with his left hand to splash a clump of wet sand from the stream into Night Wind's face.

Night Wind felt the sting of gritty sand in his eyes and was momentarily blinded. Just as quickly, the sharp agony of Quick Slayer's blade sliced into his chest. Opening eyes blurred with tears, he focused on Quick Slayer's knife as he withdrew it and again raised it, this time to plunge into Night Wind's throat.

Orlena watched Quick Slayer blind Night Wind and deal what looked to be a killing blow, but before she could do more than cry out and reach for a small rock, White Crane and Hoarse Bark restrained her.

"He will not be dishonored by a white woman," the Mescalero gritted out.

Night Wind heard Orlena's scream as the blade neared his throat, but he concentrated on moving his own knife, an incredibly painful task with the puncture wound in his chest. Even through his sand-blurred eyes, he could see that Quick Slayer's total attention was on the final kill. His whole lower abdomen was exposed as he raised his body over Night Wind.

Night Wind's knife gutted the Lipan, slashing from left to right, then ripping upward toward the heart. As he dodged the blade aimed at his throat, Night Wind could hear Quick Slayer's grunt of surprise. Still not relinquishing his impaling hold on Quick Slayer, Night Wind rolled up over the dying man. The pain in his chest was suffocating him and a red haze was forming behind his eyes, but he succeeded in pinning Quick Slayer to the earth. The larger man choked on his own blood in a long, slow death rattle. Night Wind prayed to the Child of the Water that he could hold on long enough to see Quick Slayer die. His prayer was answered.

NIGHT WIND'S WOMAN

Then he felt Orlena's soft, small hands on him and heard her sobbing voice call his name in Spanish. Hoarse Bark caught him as he fell. Everything went black.

"Do not let her tend him, old woman. She will kill him, even if Quick Slayer's thrust fails," Hoarse Bark said to She Who Dreams.

Orlena stood at the door of the wickiup watching the two argue. Although she could not understand their words, she knew Night Wind's Mescalero friend hated and mistrusted her ever since the incident in the cave. "Now I am doubly blamed because that brute attacked me and Night Wind had to fight him." She sighed and waited to see what She Who Dreams would do. Sweet Rain and several unmarried maidens who hoped to win Night Wind's attention had volunteered to nurse him.

"I am Night Wind's woman. It is for me he fought. I have the right to care for him," she said boldly to She Who Dreams, interrupting Hoarse Bark's diatribe.

"You are his slave. He captured you. Much Spanish pride. Why now you want to tend Night Wind?" She Who Dreams' shrewd black eyes measured Orlena.

She felt herself flush beneath the scrutiny of Hoarse Bark and She Who Dreams, one hostile, the other directly curious, not judging but waiting for a reply.

"I—I feel a debt. He saved me from that terrible sav—from Quick Slayer." She could not stop her shudder of revulsion at the memory of the big, brutish Apache.

She Who Dreams smiled sadly, recalling how Slim Reed had shared Orlena's feelings about both men. "You do what I show. We make Night Wind strong again." With that, Hoarse Bark was dismissed.

He felt a surge of fury, but realized how useless it

was to show his anger among these Lipan who gave their medicine woman a great amount of power. He stalked off after hissing at Orlena, "If he dies, you die."

"Hoarse Bark hates me because I tried to escape. Before that he did not—"

She Who Dreams interrupted Orlena. "Brothers— Hoarse Bark and Night Wind. They know same pain, come from same place."

"They are both scarred, yet none of the other men here are," Orlena said consideringly as she followed She Who Dreams to her medicine pouch in the wickiup. "Where did they come from? You must know."

"If Night Wind wish, he tell you," was all the old woman would say as she began to mix an herbal poultice to prevent an infection from developing in Night Wind's wound.

"Get cool water from creek. Wash Night Wind. Too much heat in body bad. Kills," she said as her busy hands worked with a mortar and pestle.

Orlena examined Night Wind's still, pale figure lying on the pallet. He did not feel feverish yet. "How do you—?" She broke off the question, knowing it to be useless. The medicine woman seemed to know everything. Did she indeed have visions that foretold the future? Orlena grabbed a large waterskin and ran to the stream to fill it.

As darkness fell, Orlena became frightened, watching Night Wind's unconscious body in the flickering light from the fire. He had indeed developed a fever. What if he died? For all the times she had cursed him and wished him dead, the very real prospect now filled her with dread. She would be alone, surrounded by enemies, without the protection of the one man in this wilderness who had actual contact with civilization.

NIGHT WIND'S WOMAN

Yet, as she softly sponged his body with cool water, Orlena knew her feelings were not as simple as choosing the lesser evil between two unthinkable alternatives. The coiled tension of Night Wind's body was relaxed by unconsciousness now. Those piercing, mocking green eyes were closed. She touched his face and felt the rasp of beard on his cheek, and was reminded of his white blood. Night Wind. Had the Franciscans given him another name? What of his Spanish father?

Her confused thoughts were interrupted when She Who Dreams entered the wickiup with a steaming bowl of dark, pungent liquid. "This cure fever," she said without preamble as she indicated to Orlena that she should feed the liquid to the unconscious man with a crude spoon made from bone.

"What is it?" she asked. The oddly familiar fragrance was not nearly so unpleasant-smelling as the poultice on his chest.

"Bark of cherry tree. Boil in water," She Who Dreams explained as she piled thick pelts like pillows behind Night Wind's back, propping him up.

Obediently, Orlena spooned the cherry bark infusion into Night Wind's mouth. She Who Dreams showed her how to stroke his throat to assist swallowing, but still he choked and only about half the liquid went down. The Lipan woman seemed satisfied. After checking the poultice and probing the evil-looking wound, she grunted and left Orlena to her vigil.

The evening was cool, but Night Wind burned with fever. Orlena and She Who Dreams had been sewing a tepee of large, well-tanned buffalo skins for the winter months ahead, but it was not yet finished and they resided still in a summer brush hut the Apache called a wickiup. Before, she had dreaded the lack of privacy and close confinement of sharing a tepee with Night

Wind, but now . . . She sponged his face as he grew restless and began to murmur.

At first the words were low, indistinct, spoken in Lipan; but then he began to use Spanish. Orlena bent low, both to restrain his thrashing and to hear what he said in the grip of this terrible nightmare.

"Mother, no! The Spanish rock gougers will—" An anguished cry tore from him, that of a small boy. "Why? Why do you do this? You traitor! I will avenge the death of she who was my mother! My uncles, all those you have butchered. I swear it! You will beg for death before I am done with you." He coughed and choked as Orlena tried desperately to spoon more of the fever medicine between his parched lips.

"I will live on my hate . . . live on my hate," he rasped out, seemingly stronger in the grip of delirium. A series of convulsive shudders shook him as he cried, again in Lipan, then in Spanish, "No! Do not take away the light. Do not put me in the hole again! Coyote and Owl wait down there. I am strong for my ten years—I can work anywhere—anywhere but this hole!"

All through the night his feverish ranting revealed his past. Wiping scalding tears from her face, Orlena listened to a broken and disjointed tale of unspeakable terrors, of a boy betrayed by the Spanish, his whole family massacred and he, the lone survivor, sold into slavery in the mines outside Chihuahua. She had heard stories about how Indian captives were forced to labor for the gold and silver that enriched Spanish coffers, about the conditions under which even small children lived and died. Orlena shuddered as he relived the horror of seeing a Spanish guard bashing in the skull of a Mescalero boy who fell from a ladder and broke his leg.

Now she understood the scars that crisscrossed

NIGHT WIND'S WOMAN

Night Wind's back—his and Hoarse Bark's. They had been mine slaves together as children.

Small wonder they both feared and hated those caves to the south! She pictured a terrified little boy, beaten with a rawhide lash and tied into a basket that lowered him to the deepest bowels of the earth to dig from dawn to darkness in tiny rabbit-warren tunnels. Orlena shivered just thinking of it.

Night Wind had good reason to hate the Spanish father who must have abandoned him and his mother to such a horrible fate. Only hate had sustained him through the ordeal of the mines.

"Thank the Blessed Virgin for that priest who saved him!" There were some of her people who acted as befitted civilized men. But the bitter lesson she was learning since coming to New Spain was that men like the good friar were rare; men like those drunken mine guards in Chihuahua City were far more numerous.

"No, not the dark. No. It . . . it is me. I see things, feel things the others do not. Please, Mother! Mother! Help me. It is wrong to call your spirit back to this evil place. . . ." his voice faded and he shuddered, transported into childhood once again.

"I am here, my son. Do not fear. Soon you will be free of this place. Do not fear." Orlena's voice was choked with tears as she whispered low, wishing desperately that she could speak the words in Lipan, but in his fevered state, Night Wind did not know the difference. Her soft voice and touch seemed to soothe him, for he lapsed into a deep, dreamless sleep.

"Now you know why Night Wind fears caves," She Who Dreams said matter-of-factly as she entered the wickiup the following morning.

Orlena sat up, rubbing her eyes. She had been curled up close to Night Wind, whose fever had finally broken toward dawn. "What? How did you know—?"

Her voice trailed off as she realized that the old woman had deliberately left her alone with Night Wind through the night. She knew he would rave in his delirium and that was her way of letting him tell Orlena about his past. Of course, there were still a great many unanswered questions, especially pertaining to Conal Quinn. Why had Night Wind tried to abduct Santiago, and why had he kept her when she was taken by mistake? Orlena was not certain she wanted to know the answers.

She Who Dreams cleansed Night Wind's wound. She issued terse instructions to Orlena about how to soak the poultice off with clean water, then reapply the sticky paste after bathing the tender skin. "Good. Not red. Not puff up." She watched Orlena's trembling hands as the girl gingerly followed orders.

"Will he live?" Orlena held her breath.

She Who Dreams smiled serenely. "Yes." The word spoke volumes, as if she had always known Night Wind was in no danger! Perhaps she had.

Once the poultice was in place, Orlena looked up hesitantly. "Why does Night Wind hate Conal Quinn? Did Conal . . ." her voice faded with the horror of it, but she forced herself to ask, "Did Conal sell him into slavery in the mines?" Impossible as it was to imagine her Conal doing such a monstrous thing to a small boy, she *had* to know. If true, it would explain so much, but at the same time leave so many more painful questions unanswered. She waited.

"I think Night Wind tell you . . . some day," came the cryptic reply. She Who Dreams stood up with surprising grace for one so rotund and advanced in years. Scooping up her medicine bag, she departed, saying, "Later I bring food when Night Wind awake. You sleep now."

Orlena was emotionally and physically exhausted.

NIGHT WIND'S WOMAN

After once more bathing Night Wind's now cooled body, she lay down beside him and fell instantly to sleep.

It must have been a nightmare that awakened her, for she was falling down, down into a bottomless black pit one moment, the next bolting upright on the soft fur pallet. When she collected herself, Orlena looked at the man lying beside her. Bright green eyes, no longer clouded with fever, stared intently at her.

A dizzying surge of joy infused her body. "You *are* going to live! She Who Dreams was right," she cried, unable to explain her elation, unwilling to analyze it.

"How long have I been unconscious?" he asked as his good arm came up and his left hand touched the hole in his chest.

"Lie still," she scolded. "You had a fever all night. She Who Dreams saved your life. I want to learn her healing skills."

A ghost of a smile tugged at one corner of his lips. "Surely not so you could apply them to me?"

She gave him a disdainful look and scooted away. The old hateful arrogance had returned. "You must be recovering," she replied waspishly, ignoring his question.

He rubbed his head. "I remember having dreams . . . nightmares. You were having one just now, were you not?" His expression was troubled and confused.

"Yes, I . . . I was falling down a well—a pit really." The instant the words escaped her lips she could sense the tension radiating from him.

"You were imagining the mine shaft—the silver mine in Nueva Vizcaya," he accused her. He had told her everything, babbling in feverish confusion! He swore and tried to sit up.

Orlena's cool hands gently restrained him. "No! You'll start your wound bleeding again."

"What did I tell you?" he asked flatly.

She tried to avoid his piercing eyes, but he reached out with surprising strength and caught her wrist in his left hand. Dark fingers squeezed painfully on the delicate bones.

"Stop. You are going to break my wrist!"

"Poor reward. She save your life," She Who Dreams said as she stood in the doorway. "Eat." Although the command was meant for Night Wind, She Who Dreams gave the bowl and a small spearing knife to Orlena, obviously intending her to feed the wretched ingrate!

When the old Lipan woman had departed, Orlena set the bowl down and rubbed her aching wrist. Surprising her, Night Wind took it in his hands and gently massaged the red marks. "I am sorry. I did not intend to hurt you, Lioness. Your nightmare was startlingly similar to mine. I must have told you a great deal," he prompted.

Her eyes were liquid gold with tears when she looked down at him. "I know that you hate white men for killing your family and selling you into slavery. You described the mines. . . ." She paused and shuddered again at the image of a beaten, starved child shoved down into a black hole to dig until he died. "You spoke of a Fray Bartolome who rescued you. That explains your formidable education."

"Is that all?" His eyes searched her face for some clue to the rest. He had a niggling remembrance of crying out for his mother—and being answered. He did not like that thought at all! But her words quickly caused the memory to desert him.

Boldly she looked down at him and said, "I already knew you hated Conal—but did he kill your family?" Her voice cracked on the question. It must have been a battle; Conal was a soldier fighting grown men,

NIGHT WIND'S WOMAN

deadly savages, not children!

"He led the Spanish soldiers." he replied tightly.

She gasped in horror. "But the mines—he did not take you there? Surely, children were always to be baptized and taken into private homes—"

"You will defend him when Satan himself comes to claim Conal's black soul," he said with a cold smile. Without another word, he reached for the bowl and knife.

Not wanting to pursue the hurtful conversation further, she took the food from him and began to feed him after plumping up the furs to elevate his body.

When he had eaten about half the rich meat, each chunk soaked in bone marrow, a special delicacy of the Apache, he gently pushed her hand away. "Enough. I am weary. Eat yourself, Lioness."

A grudging smile tugged at her lips. "Are you certain you can trust me with the knife while you sleep?"

He merely grunted and stretched back, instantly asleep. Orlena watched his handsome face in repose. With the hardness and coldness gone, he was a startlingly beautiful man. That old familiar feeling of heat and ache pervaded her senses again as she remembered how his hard body had felt stretched against hers, how his kisses tasted, how much she wanted—a gasp ripped from deep in her throat, closing it off. Orlena squeezed her eyes shut but silent, burning tears flowed down her cheeks nevertheless. *I love him! I want him to touch me, to love me as a husband!*

I bed Spanish women. I will never wed one. His words came back to taunt her. What was she thinking of—a lady of the Spanish court, the nobility, enamored of a half-caste savage, son of some *paisano* who had deserted an Apache squaw! Pride stiffened her spine. She gathered the food bowl and knife up with trembling fingers, and left the wickiup.

Over the next several days, Night Wind regained his strength with amazing speed. In Spain, Orlena had seen many men sicken and die of dueling wounds far less serious. She nursed him under She Who Dreams' skillful guidance, each day cleansing the poultice away and replacing it. By the end of a week he no longer needed the evil-smelling medicine. She Who Dreams instructed Orlena to assist him outdoors to enjoy some bright fall sunlight, which she assured the girl was the best healer of all wounds.

Leaning heavily on her—perhaps more than necessary, she thought—Night Wind walked outdoors and smiled up at the bright autumn sun. The radiance of his handsome face transfixed her for a moment.

Night Wind had noted the change in Orlena since his injury. At first he had feared she understood that he was using her in his quest for vengeance, but it seemed he was wrong. Her soft woman's heart was only touched by the suffering of a small boy. She refused to consider Conal guilty of his crimes, and for now that suited Night Wind's purposes perfectly. Still, why did it disturb him so that she had such faith in the Irishman? He pushed that thought aside and said to her, "Let me rest here for a while. Then when everyone is busy with their chores, you may help me walk to the stream so I may bathe the stink of sickness from my body."

He smiled at her widened eyes, which revealed much. So, she remembered their last encounter with mutual bathing, did she? The desire to take her had grown like an ache inside him, ever since he first laid eyes on her, dressed in Santiago's clothes, with that

NIGHT WIND'S WOMAN

mane of curly hair spilling like molten gold down her back. Her silky skin and jasmine fragrance had incited him from the first time he came near her and every moment since, even when he was angry enough to kill her. He wanted her. Soon he would know success. He had vowed not to force her, and now he knew she would not resist.

Orlena watched him sit gracefully on the soft furs. His eyes followed her as she nervously began to shell pecans, placing the sweet nut meats into a large bowl for roasting, then gathering the sharp shells into a neat pile to be discarded where no one, particularly a child, could cut himself on them.

Several boys nearby laughed as they wrestled with an older man who was playfully showing them how to pin an opponent in a fight. Ever since her arrival in the Lipan camp, Orlena had been amazed at the time and attention children received, especially from the grandparents and all older members of the band. Grandmothers and great aunts taught sewing and cooking to girls, and wizened old warriors patiently sat stringing bows for small, chubby-handed boys. Having been raised by governesses and tutors much of her life, Orlena had treasured her outings with Conal. Such indulgences were a rarity among Europeans of the upper class, and she knew it. But here, everyone adored children and even the oldest, most respected chiefs such as White Crane spent hours caring for small children and instructing youths.

Night Wind observed Orlena as she looked longingly at the children. For the first time he wondered about her childhood. Had she been lonely? European children often were. It would explain much about her devotion to Conal. But the poisonous reverse side of that thought ate at him. What motive was there for

Conal's possible devotion to her?

"Come, I think we should seek the cooling water." Without waiting for her help, he rose and scooped up several soft buffalo robes. Reaching for her arm, he walked toward the sheltered area downstream where the water was deep enough for bathing.

Trembling, Orlena walked with him.

Chapter 11

"Come here. Take off your clothes." His words were softly spoken, taunting yet gentle. Night Wind had stripped and waded into the lapping water, which was warm from the noonday sun. The pool was a long walk from camp and very private. They had stopped to let him rest several times. Now he felt strengthened as the stream refreshed him.

Orlena's throat collapsed on itself, leaving her speechless as she stared at his swarthy beauty. Bronzed muscles rippled as droplets of water slid over them. He splashed and then laughed, a warm, rich sound, so at variance with the first time he had said those words to her.

I bed Spanish women. I will never wed one. As those bitter words flashed through her mind, Orlena felt an overpowering urge to flee from his burning magnetism. She could easily outrun him in his weakened condition, but to what end? *This is your fate. Why do you fight against it?* Slowly, she began to pull off her doeskin clothing.

Night Wind stood waist-deep in the stream. His breath caught as he watched the golden vision before him. He could sense her fear and hesitance, yet feel the innocent power of her newly awakened desire as well. She would come to him, willingly, as he planned so many weeks ago. Yet, at that moment, vengeance was the furthest thing from his mind. He watched the soft sunlight filtering through the aspen leaves, bathing her body in a golden glow. She was slim and fine-boned, perfectly formed, a delicate aristocrat, a European lady. Before, he had always felt contempt for the Spanish women he bedded, women who disdained him even as they desired him, women who betrayed their husbands and family honor to satiate their own lust.

For all her youthful pride and temper, Orlena was nothing like that. She was truly innocent. He ached to touch her silky skin, now tinted by the sun yet pale compared to his bronzed body.

When she unfastened her skirt and let it fall in a heap beside her moccasins, she turned away from him, overcome with shyness and a terrifying wave of embarrassment. Next to the Lipan women, she was thin and pale. What if he felt disgust or pity? Then her pride reasserted itself. After all the times he had watched her with his lust held so tightly in check, she knew he must desire her. She pulled the rawhide thong from her braid and shook her hair free, letting it float about her shoulders in gleaming masses. With her chin held haughtily high, she forced her eyes to meet his and began to wade into the creek.

Night Wind walked toward her with his arms outstretched, palms up. She was so lovely, with her high pointed breasts, accented by pale pink nipples.

NIGHT WIND'S WOMAN

His gaze sketched a brief look at her flat little belly and the soft golden curls between her slim thighs. Then he reached for her cool, trembling hands and clasped them in his large warm ones, gently massaging her sensitive inner wrists and raising one hand, then the other for soft, wet kisses.

When he pulled her against his body, a languid heat began to overwhelm her senses. She grew dizzy and clung wordlessly to him, her hands gliding up his hard biceps to cup over his shoulders. She raised her head to his face and waited for the mind-robbing kiss she knew was coming.

Night Wind's heart hammered as he felt the soft brush of her small, perfect breasts. Her nipples hardened as they rubbed in sensual innocence against the mat of hair on his chest. He bent down and kissed her, at first with the fierce, hot hunger of his long repressed need, then with increasingly gentle, exploratory caresses, letting his lips and tongue taste and tease hers.

Orlena felt a primitive thrill when Night Wind savaged her mouth. Oddly unafraid, she arched against him and returned the kiss in breathless pleasure. When his lips softened and his tongue darted and flicked, hers answered. She could sense his reaction, and it fueled her boldness as she ran one small hand up and buried it in his straight, shoulder-length hair. It felt coarse and thick. When he left her mouth to trail kisses down her throat, she let her head fall back instinctively. He buried his face in the golden cloud of her hair, grasping great handfuls of it and raising it to his lips.

"You smell of jasmine still," he whispered hoarsely.

"It is only your memory. My perfume is long bathed away," she replied with even more difficulty.

"Let me test further," he murmured, lowering his head to one arched little breast. His hand cupped it, raising the hard tip like a treasured chalice to his lips. The contact of his hot mouth sent a shudder of ecstasy through her and she whimpered incoherently. He moved to the other nipple and duplicated the magic. "The jasmine is your skin, which holds its own perfume," he whispered.

Heat was coiling low in her belly now, like the warm, sweet honey she and the Lipan women had scooped from the bee trees in the valley. Darts of pleasure lanced from her breasts to her belly, then lower yet. She could feel the persistent pressure of his erection rubbing against her. His hips gently rocked hers in an ancient rhythm as he held her buttocks in his hands and again centered his mouth on hers for a long, slow kiss.

As they kissed, he carried her deeper into the creek, until she floated weightlessly against him, her feet barely touching bottom. "Let us bathe—quickly," he said, breaking off contact and leaving her so breathlessly bemused she could scarcely tread water. She watched as he moved with the grace of an otter to the bank for a bar of the Frenchman's soap. Remembering the way they had sudsed each other on the journey to the stronghold, she flushed with anticipation. When his hands glided over her shoulders with the silky lather, she shivered and closed her eyes. When he cupped and teased her breasts in circular caresses, she felt her breath stop. He worked lower, raising one slim leg, then the other, and laving them. When one warm, strong hand reached between her legs, she gasped and threw her arms about his neck, holding on to him in a whirling vortex of pleasure.

"You are quite, quite clean—but for your hair, Lioness," he whispered as he lowered her into the water to soak the heavy masses of curls. As he worked suds through her hair, he massaged her scalp, then

NIGHT WIND'S WOMAN

rinsed the glittering dark gold. He watched as she shook her head and opened her eyes to stare at him, dazed with passion. "Now," he whispered, his voice washing over her as smoothly as the soap lather, "it is your turn to wash me." He placed the bar in her hand and closed her nerveless fingers around it.

Nodding slowly, she remembered to breathe and then began to rub a lather between her palms. Her hands trembled as she massaged the soap across his hard chest with its black, curling hair. She remembered the first time—how touching his flesh so intimately had affected her. This time the feelings grew even stronger. Night Wind was like an exotic aphrodisiac she had read about in that forbidden book she had sneaked from Conal's library. What magic hold did this barbarian have upon her? She no longer cared.

Night Wind forced his breathing to slow as her hands burned a languorous trail from his head down to his waist. She was careful with the soap around the healing knife wound. He flexed his shoulder and chest muscles, showing her that the wound was no longer painful. He could sense her hesitation when she reached his lower body. Gently, he guided her soapy hand to his hardened phallus. After a few tentative strokes, he emitted a sharp gasp of pleasure, clenching his fists at his sides. Orlena felt the thrill of power wash over her.

"We are clean enough," he said, scooping her into his arms and splashing through the water to the bank. He knelt and placed her on the thick, soft buffalo robe spread across the ground. When he lay beside her and took her in his arms, Orlena rested her head against his chest. He tipped her face up to his by twining his finger against her scalp and pulling gently on her thick wet hair as he kissed her slowly, drawing her tongue forth to duel delicately with his as the caress deepened.

Night Wind rolled over her, shifting his weight to his elbows and raining soft, wet nips, licks, and bites down her throat and over her breasts. He felt her arch up against him, eager for more. With a feverish moan, he obliged her, then moved lower and lower, across her belly to the downy fur between her legs.

Orlena's fingers twisted in his long hair, urging his burning mouth onward until he reached that most private part of her. She stiffened. He silenced her protests by retracing the path back up her body. But his hand dipped lazily between her legs, feeling the creamy evidence of her desire. Again, she moved involuntarily. He smiled against the valley between her breasts and murmured low, "It is time, I think, Lioness."

Orlena felt him grasp her wrist and guide her hand to stroke him again. She knew somehow what would come next, and her body tensed. He crooned soft Spanish love words in her ear, kissing her and sliding her trembling legs apart with his knee. Slowly, oh, so very slowly, he guided the tip of his shaft against the core of her body, using the heavy moisture of her excitement as a natural lubricant, slicking his way ever deeper inside the tight opening. When he touched the barrier of her maidenhead, he stopped with a trembling, shuddering breath and again kissed her.

Orlena felt a primitive instinct urging her to arch upward against him, wanting to feel more of the hot, melting ecstasy his body was giving hers, but he stilled her with one hand holding her hips, knowing how she felt. "We have time . . . much time," he whispered into her open mouth.

Then, after regaining some measure of control, he made one fast, sure thrust, breaking the barrier even

NIGHT WIND'S WOMAN

as he muffled her cry of surprised pain with his kiss. Once deeply embedded, he held his lower body very still and continued kissing her.

None of the other white women he had lain with had been virgins. The only one he had ever taken was his Lipan wife. Remembering her pain, he tried to still his madly racing desire for Orlena, his frail, delicate lady. He must not cause her any more hurt than necessary. Concentrating on that, he moved a tiny bit, experimentally.

Orlena was aghast at the sudden change from intense pleasure to sharp burning, but once his shaft impaled her, the pain dissipated quickly. He seemed to stretch her body, filling her with heat and a gnawing, aching need. She felt an instinctive desire to rub against him. When he began to move, she moved, too, finding to her amazement that the spiraling, dizzying ecstasy was returning with each longer, more intense stroke. She held tightly to Night Wind and returned his kiss with desperation, soaring, needing, but not comprehending what, or why it was so.

Night Wind's heart nearly burst with pleasure at her response. Her initiation into womanhood would not be the slow, painful ordeal it was for many women. She was a lioness, passionate and strong, in spite of her delicate lineage. He thrust harder and she matched him, stroke for stroke, panting and whimpering, all the want and frustration and fear of the past weeks exploding now, centered on seeking the relief which only that essential male part of him could give.

He concentrated on his evaporating control, struggling to regain a measure of it lest she take him over the brink and rob herself of completion, something he wanted never to happen for as long as she was his woman.

My woman! Did he whisper the words aloud? Night

Wind did not know, but he could sense the beginnings of her climax. Her amber eyes flew open as she stared through an unfocused haze at his face. He rose high above her, his hips pounding in primal, urgent rhythm now, his face exultant like a dark, beautiful god, savage and splendid as he spilled his seed deeply within her quivering flesh.

Orlena watched her love through the blinding explosion of her release, feeling at last the freedom from her hunger, the answer to her need. Then, when she sensed he was joining her in surfeit, a renewed thrill swept through her. Radiating from where their bodies joined so beautifully, it spread outward in ever-widening ripples that left even her fingertips tingling.

He collapsed on her, panting and sweat soaked. Only then did she remember his injury. Barely two weeks ago, he had lain near death! Had this taxed him so dearly that the fever might again return? Her hands began to caress his back softly and she murmured against his cheek, into his damp, clean hair. "You must lie back and let me warm you lest the fever return."

He chuckled low and raggedly. "Lioness, you already have kindled a fever in me, one I fear only you can assuage." He rolled off her and drew her against the length of his long, hard body. "Do not fear. I am well. She Who Dreams' medicine has worked. So has yours."

Orlena puzzled over that for a moment, then reached up to place one small hand on his chest to inspect the wound. It seemed well enough, although she knew he was still weak. "Only rest for a while before we are missed and must return to the village."

He smiled. The afternoon was warm and there was time, much time—if he chose to allow it, a troubling voice niggled. Ignoring the future, Night Wind slept, relaxed and at peace for the first time since the abduction of his spitting lioness.

"You have need of skin lodge before cold come," She Who Dreams pronounced the next day. "We finish now." With that she trundled down the hill to where a large buffalo hide was staked tautly across a level stretch of earth.

Already Orlena had learned how a hide was cured to buttery softness by using a paste of buffalo brains to soak it. Then all the hair and residue was scraped cleanly away with a sharp adz. It was killing labor that took days. The men about camp assisted the women with all the strenuous work of daily life, but the boring drudgery of scraping the heavy hides after they were turned and staked was left to female hands—and backs.

After several hours at the grueling chore, she paused to rub the deep ache in the small of her back. *Blessed Virgin, I am using muscles that I never knew I possessed.* Doggedly, she returned to work.

As she toiled, Night Wind watched her slight figure from across the creek, where he and several other men were making the hard leather shields that the Apache found so useful against Spanish bullets. White Crane also watched as Orlena struggled with the difficult task.

"She is too weak for Lipan life," Night Wind said flatly, almost as if attempting to convince himself.

Pausing as he stretched a layer of hardened cowhide over the shield, White Crane replied, "She has learned much in the past weeks. Only give her time. She Who Dreams is a fine teacher."

"But Orlena is Spanish, from their land across the great waters, a land where she had servants to wait upon her. She could never withstand this life."

The old man grunted. "Is it her you fear for—or yourself?" At the younger man's startled look, White Crane smiled. "Your vengeance has been blunted. You no longer think of returning her to Colorado Quinn, do you? Or is it that you do not wish to remember your plan now that you have lain with her?"

Feeling the heat steal into his face, Night Wind retorted angrily. "Lying with her was part of my plan. As to the rest"—he made a dismissive gesture—"I must return her whether I would wish it or not!"

White Crane let his young companion stalk away, understanding Night Wind's confused feelings. She Who Dreams had already seen a vision. Orlena and Night Wind's lives were fated to be intertwined. As he had predicted from the first, vengeance was a double-edged blade that had already turned on the half-caste. White Crane only prayed to the Child of the Water that both troubled young people would find peace, a peace he knew neither had seen before they came together.

Orlena saw Night Wind's black, scowling look as he stalked away from White Crane. After their interlude in the water yesterday afternoon, she had returned to camp dazed and shaken as the enormity of what she had done—what had been done to her—sank into her rational mind. Yet that night, as they lay in their blankets, alone in the stillness of the night, he touched her and she turned to him once more.

What she had instinctively feared ever since that encounter in the adobe hut had come to pass. She loved a man who was not only her social inferior, but a hunted outlaw! And she was as powerless to control her physical passions as she was to control her wayward heart. What kind of life was this for the proud Orlena Valdéz—to become an Apache squaw! Yet she could never return to Conal and Santiago now, to

NIGHT WIND'S WOMAN

Santa Fe and the censure of Spanish society. Women who survived captivity among savages were so much human garbage, relegated to cloisters where the good sisters hid them from prying eyes.

Even if she could, did she want to leave Night Wind? He was still an enigma to her, a man who had abducted her by mistake and for some obscure reason chose to keep her. *He only lusts after me, much as Gabriel did.* But quite unlike that repulsive nobleman's, Night Wind's touch did not repel her! *I love him, but he does not love me.* That was the most painful fact of all for her to face. Swallowing her tears, she reapplied herself to her work. She was Night Wind's captive and had no choice about what he did with her. But come what might, Orlena Valdéz would survive, one day at a time. Brooding on the future gained her nothing.

Still the tantalizing thoughts trickled into her mind as she worked. What if he *did* come to love her? He was educated, half-Spanish. Many such half-castes lived lives of relative prosperity among the *paisanos* of New Mexico and other rural provinces. Would Night Wind give up his hatred of whites? If so, he could lead a civilized life, even become one of the *ricos*, mixed-blood ranchers who populated the countryside. How quickly life changed people! Only a few months ago, when she began her journey from Vera Cruz through New Spain, she would have been appalled beyond reason at what now seemed an unattainable dream!

As Orlena brought their evening meal into the wickiup from She Who Dreams' cookfire, Night Wind watched her natural grace. She set out the sotol bread and roasted venison. Her soft doeskin skirts and flexible moccasins allowed her great freedom of movement as she knelt on the hard-packed earthen floor.

"Soon it will be too cold to sleep in this summer

shelter. How does our lodge progress?" Night Wind took the green willow that skewered a large, juicy chunk of meat and pulled off a generous bite with sharp white teeth.

"It is almost finished. All the hides are prepared and ready to be sewn together. Tomorrow, She Who Dreams will show me how to select lodge poles from strong young saplings," Orlena replied, eyeing him uneasily. Why was he so grim tonight?

"That is difficult work for women. Green saplings are difficult to cut. I will go with you. Such soft hands will soon be ruined doing camp chores," he said, reaching out to clasp her wrist and examine her reddened skin and broken nails.

"I am scarcely going to be invited to the Viceroy's ball this fall, so the condition of my hands does not signify," she replied, snatching her hand away from him.

"Ah yes, balls and teas, lace fans and silk stockings, velvet-lined carriages and soft linen bed sheets. You have given up much, Lioness."

Her eyes widened at his knowledge of such things. "Surely the Franciscans had no velvet upholstery or linen sheets. There is not a carriage in all of New Mexico," she scoffed. "Where have you learned of such things?"

His face became shuttered. "No, the good brothers in Chihuahua City live a simple life, much as New Mexican *paisanos*, but farther south there are great Spanish cities, are there not?"

"And you have seen them?" she asked incredulously.

The racial and social superiority her surprise implied raised his hackles. "I have 'visited' the City of Mexico more than once, Doña Orlena. Dressed in civilized clothes, I have gained entry to all manner of

NIGHT WIND'S WOMAN

places." *And women*, he added in silent arrogance, as a sop to his ego.

Somehow she could picture him in courtier's garb, with his hair clubbed back. His arrestingly chiseled features and striking green eyes might allow him to move among the powerful, especially considering the education he possessed. Among the ill-educated colonials, he would stand out as a paragon of erudition! "What do you do, spy on them and then rob them?" she asked acidly.

"Something of that," he replied with a grim smile.

"This war on the Spanish will only end with your death. Why do you not end it now? With a pardon from the governor, you could begin again—"

"A pardon you would beg from your beloved Conal?" he asked with fury etched tautly on his face. "Do not bargain overmuch on your ability to sway him where I am concerned. He will not heed you."

"Why? Because you have dishonored me?" she shot back, stung at his refusal to consider her pretty, implausible dreams.

He barked a harsh, mirthless laugh and set down the skewer of venison. "Yes, I have dishonored a Spanish noblewoman, the illustrious governor's step-daughter! I recall well the wrath of Colorado Quinn, which you have reminded me of since the day I abducted you. But look you, how well he controls this land your Spanish king claims. The governor will never find us in our stronghold."

Orlena quivered with fury. "You blame Conal for everything that ever befell you! He was only a soldier, fighting his enemies, just as you and Hoarse Bark fight the whites! You do not know him as I—"

"No! For a surety I do not know him as you do," he growled low. "But mark me well, I know him for what he *is*! Only pray you never do!" With that he stood up and stalked out of the wickiup.

She bit her lip to stem the flow of tears—weak, foolish tears, for an insufferable barbarian who did not deserve them! Dispiritedly she cleaned up the remains of their meal and then rolled up in their bedding furs. In spite of her resolve, she cried herself to sleep.

Night Wind left that night with Hoarse Bark and a handful of young Lipan warriors. Although no one would tell her, she knew he had gone to raid the Spanish settlements.

Each day Orlena found her eyes scanning the horizon for his big piebald stallion. Each night she lay alone, astonishingly bereft to be without the comforting warmth of his body next to hers. Sleep came only after long hours of fitful tossing. Although she would not admit it, she ached for his return.

"Lodge is warm, strong. Snow, wind will not enter. Good," She Who Dreams pronounced their work. Although he had left in anger before cutting the lodge poles for her, Night Wind had asked White Crane to assist with the task. Now the buffalo-hide tepee was finished.

She Who Dreams was right, Orlena thought with pride. The skins were tightly sewn and stretched securely over the tall poles, creating a warm, dry haven from the bitter nip of frost in the autumn air. Nothing she had ever done in her life before had given her this sense of accomplishment. *If only Night Wind returns to sleep in it with me.*

She Who Dreams helped her young charge move her simple camp utensils and bedding into the lodge. Little Doe and several other young women brought fragrant, newly cut cedar boughs to soften the sleeping pallet. Upon these she piled thick pelts, which served as the warmest blankets. The women were polite and shy, communicating with her by means of a broken mixture of her Lipan and their Spanish, mostly by simply improvised sign language. They were friendly and curious about Night Wind's strange, yellow-haired slave, but Sweet Rain remained openly hostile. She was cousin to Quick Slayer and followed Lipan mourning customs by cutting her hair and wearing old clothes. His immediate family mourned him, but Quick Slayer was a troublemaker in the band, disliked by most. Two elderly men had taken his body away for burial at a distant site, so his angry spirit would not return to wreak havoc in the encampment they had recently chosen for a winter shelter.

Orlena felt certain Sweet Rain's dislike of her had little to do with her cousin's death and far more to do with her desire for the man who had killed him. The comely Lipan woman wanted Night Wind for husband and Orlena, even as a lowly captive, stood in her way. Knowing how he despised her Spanish blood, she was certain he would choose another Apache wife. Perhaps it would be Sweet Rain.

That dismal thought caused her to reach carelessly into the coals for one of the sotol bread ash cakes and burn her fingers. With a hiss of pain, she drew her fingers out and sucked them. Blessed Virgin, the first time she had ever tried to cook alone at her own campfire she could not even perform the simplest tasks without injuring herself!

Suddenly she felt a cold draft and the skin flap of the tepee door opened. Tall and forbidding, dressed in buckskin leggings and weighed down with weapons, Night Wind stepped inside.

He looked down at her, sitting by the fire, holding her fingers in her mouth, looking more beautiful than any woman he had ever seen. As she scrambled to her feet his eyes swept the tepee, noting how neatly it had been arranged. When his gaze rested on the large single pallet piled high with skins, she colored, but remained silent.

"I am hungry. She Who Dreams will give you some of the rabbit stew she was cooking when I rode in," he said as he sat down and began to strip off his knives, pistols, and a quiver of arrows.

Just as simple as that! Not a word of greeting or explanation after a week's absence!

"I have prepared *my own* meal," she said smugly.

His mouth twitched a bit as he looked down at the burning sotol bread in the coals. "I do not think it is any longer edible."

"Oh, Blessed Virgin!" Orlena swore as she reached a small knife and her fingers into the coals to retrieve the blackened cakes, which were now sending billows of smoke up the opening at the lodge's apex. She burned her fingers once more and abandoned the ash cakes, which were now truly ashes.

Mutinous golden eyes flashed at amused green ones. Then Night Wind's expression sobered. "I have missed you, Lioness." He reached out and took her burned fingers in his hand, kissing the reddened tips softly, then pulled her into his arms before she could protest. He held her in a tight embrace, seeming to study her face for a moment suspended in time.

Orlena inhaled the scent of her lover, reveling in its heady effect on her senses. He smelled of horse and leather, faintly of tobacco, but most of all, the male musk excited her, making her heart race in her breast. Wordlessly she raised her face to his and opened her mouth for his kiss.

Her spontaneity pleased him and the honest longing in her eyes revealed the depths of her feelings. *I have done what I promised Conal I would do*, he thought as

NIGHT WIND'S WOMAN

he kissed her with fierce passion. Then why did the taste of her raise such a bittersweet ache in his heart?

When he finally broke off the long, ardent kiss, Orlena breathlessly asked, "Are you yet hungry? I will go to She Who Dreams for that rabbit."

He laughed and looked down at the sleeping pallet. "Yes, I am hungry. Very hungry. Very hungry," he said. Kneeling on the furs, he whispered, "Take off your clothes."

Santa Fe, November 1787

Blaise Pascal sat in the small cantina and took a deep drink of the potent mescal. It was foul stuff, but anything would be acceptable if it cleansed the grit from between his teeth. Sacred Blood, he was sick of cold and wind and sand! He had planned to spend the winter back east in the balmy gulf climate of New Orleans, but when he arrived in San Antonio he had read the poster of the New Mexico governor: five thousand pesos for the capture of the Lipan raider Night Wind! That was more than a year's pay for a provincial governor. That golden-haired woman Night Wind had kidnapped must mean much to Conal Quinn if he would offer such a fortune for her rescue, for surely that was what prompted the reward.

Pascal debated little on the ethics of betraying his companion, but long over the danger of doing so. If Night Wind ever found out who gave Quinn the information, it would be most unhealthy for him in all of New Spain. He spat on the earthen floor in disgust. He did not give a fig for all of New Spain. With that much money he could return to civilization, where French was spoken—to New Orleans. Damn this wind-cursed, scorpion-ridden desert. Let the stupid

Spaniards have it! He signaled the barkeep for one more drink.

The governor's palace was impressive by New Mexican standards, the Frenchman thought as he paced the polished adobe brick floor of the antechamber where he had cooled his heels awaiting Don Conal's pleasure for several hours. The walls were whitewashed over smooth plaster and hung with several passable paintings. He was wondering idly if the governor's stepdaughter had done any of the decorating, when a cold-faced soldier called his name.

He limped on his peg leg into Quinn's receiving hall, remaining passively unimpressed with the Spanish trappings of authority. He and Quinn had known each other nearly thirty years ago when the Irishman was naught but a young mercenary whose star had not yet risen.

Giving the tall, red-haired man a thorough inspection, Pascal said, "You have changed little. A bit of gray, some wrinkles. But one thing has changed—your purse is grown fatter."

Conal's eyes narrowed as he stared at the fat, oily little man. He sniffed in repugnance. "I see you, too, have changed little, still preferring to sell soap rather than use it."

Pascal ignored the jibe and came straight to the heart of the matter. "Yes, I still trade with Indians . . . and renegades." When Conal's hands tightened on the back of his heavy oak chair, the Frenchman laughed. "I see you are still quick of mind. That is a quality I always admired in you. It is doubtless why you are now governor."

"And commandant general as well. I can have you thrown in that cesspool on the hill until you tell me where Orlena is."

"Ah, but you will not do that. You will take the

NIGHT WIND'S WOMAN

information I can give you and pay me. No white, not even one with my formidable contacts with the Apache, knows how to find Night Wind's mountain strongholds. I think your chasing after shadows these past months has proven that."

"Is Orlena alive?" Conal's eyes glittered with a cold, unholy light. He would stick the fat pig until he squealed in agony if he did not tell the truth.

"When last I saw her she was quite unharmed. Of course, that was two months ago." He paused, knowing how dangerous the Irishman was, gauging his anger and his desire for the woman.

"If you were involved in her abduction, you know what I will do with you, Pascal."

"I would never have been so foolish as to come here if I was involved. I met Night Wind and his raiders in the mountains and rode with them a short while. He had a blonde woman with him. When I read your reward notice in San Antonio, I knew she was your woman. I, too, am very quick, Don Conal. But, alas, I am not grown rich . . . at least not yet."

"What can you tell me of Orlena if you do not know where Night Wind's stronghold is?" Conal asked with tightly reined anger.

"There are many things about the mysterious renegade half-caste that I have learned over the years of traveling from Nueva Vizcaya to Texas—things which would enable you to bring him to heel. He, like you, has a vulnerable spot."

Conal's face hardened. "All his Lipan family are dead," he said flatly.

"Ah, yes, but there is another family," Pascal said, watching the startled shift of Quinn's eyes. "I do not mean blood kin, but rather the man who raised him, educated him. For Fray Bartolome Moraga, the renegade Night Wind would give his life." The fat man's eyes glistened with anticipation. He could feel the soft gulf breezes and smell the sweet scent of gardenias. "For five thousand pesos, I will tell you where to find this priest."

Long shadows played over the big audience hall as Conal paced. He must plan this with utmost care. If only so much time would not be lost! And if only he could be as certain as Pascal that the priest meant enough to Night Wind to trade Orlena for him. Quinn shuddered, thinking of how she might return, soiled by that filth, all the fire and laughter of his Butterfly snuffed out.

Then again he considered. Her marriageability was now destroyed, along with her reputation. Might she not consider—

"Papa, Sergeant Ruiz said you have word of Orlena!" Santiago burst into the room, his face ablaze with joy. After all the weeks of feckless searching through the bitter onset of winter in the mountains, at last the boy saw some hope.

Conal motioned for his son to sit on one of the tall, straight-backed oak chairs. "What I have learned may or may not bode well for your sister," he began very carefully. "She is held deep in the Apache strongholds to the south. We cannot find her, but must draw that bastard who took her away from his lair. Tomorrow we ride to a Franciscan mission in Chihuahua City."

Chapter 12

Guadalupe Mountains, January 1788

Orlena sank down onto the thick pelts piled carelessly near the big cookfire in She Who Dreams' tepee. Although it was early afternoon, she felt bone weary and exhausted. Carefully scrutinizing the wood she had gathered for the fire, she began to sort the drier pieces from those dampened by exposure to the snow outside.

"You cold. Here drink." She Who Dreams offered Orlena a crude gourd cup filled with a hot spicy brew made of water boiled with an assortment of herbs and juniper berries.

Orlena sipped as She Who Dreams fed the fire with the dry kindling. The younger woman grimaced at the bitter taste of the drink, but it was warming on such a cold, windy day. *Blessed Virgin, what would I give for a cup of hot chocolate!* She looked up when she felt the kindly older woman's eyes on her.

"Go to your tepee and rest. I will bring stew for the

evening meal," She Who Dreams said in Lipan. Over the past months, Orlena had proven an apt pupil, as she spent hours working at She Who Dreams' side. They conversed in both languages now, although Orlena could speak the Apache dialect with far less fluency than She Who Dreams spoke Spanish.

"I do not need to rest. There is much work to be done," Orlena said peevishly. She did not add that several of the younger women, incited by Sweet Rain, had already derided her for her weakness and lack of skill in performing camp chores.

"Food cooks. You have gathered firewood enough for the night. I think there is a more important thing you must do." She Who Dreams looked at Orlena with shrewd, assessing eyes, waiting.

"I have sewing to do, yes, and a great deal of dried corn to grind," Orlena said as she began to rise.

She Who Dreams' leathery hand stayed her. "Sit back. We must talk." Then she switched to Spanish. What she had to discuss was better spoken in Orlena's native tongue. "For two moons you use no bloody rushes."

Orlena's face crimsoned. When her first monthly time came upon her in the wilderness, she had no menstrual cloths and had to ask She Who Dreams what the Apache women did. Matter of factly, the old woman had explained the practice of using soft, absorbent cattail fiber, which was then disposed of very carefully, for such blood was considered taboo among the Apache.

"No. I have had no courses for . . ." Orlena paused to remember. Only two times since she had been a captive had she bled. "It has been nearly three months, I think." She Who Dreams was not making idle conversation just to embarrass the girl, for that

NIGHT WIND'S WOMAN

was not her way. "Why do you ask me this?" Orlena questioned forthrightly.

"You hungry all time . . . and tired much." She was stating the obvious, but the foolish Spanish must not tell their girl children the simplest facts of life. Already she had learned from Orlena that they had no puberty rite for daughters at the onset of their menses. Rather than a natural cycle heralding the beginning of fertility, it seemed to be viewed by the whites as a stigma to be ashamed of and hidden. Shaking her head at the foolishness of Orlena's people, she sat down beside the girl. "Night Wind take you to blankets for two, three moons?"

A sudden surge of heat tinted Orlena's cheeks, but she stared defiantly back at She Who Dreams. "I am his captive. He does with me as he wills."

"He force you?" She Who Dreams already knew the answer, but she needed to gain Orlena's honest admission before she could put forth her plan.

Hanging her head, the younger woman whispered, "No. He did not force me. He . . . enticed me. I came to him, after weeks of refusing." She raised her head. "I will never be free of him now. He has taken my innocence and holds me prisoner while he goes off to raid and kill among my people." She blinked back tears, having grown unduly emotional of late.

"You love Night Wind?" Again, She Who Dreams asked a question to which she already knew the answer.

"It does not signify what I feel. I am only his slave," Orlena replied bitterly. Night Wind had been gone for nearly two weeks. Always when he left her, she feared for his life, even knowing that he was revenging himself against the Spanish. She loved him and he despised her for her white blood.

"Better you marry. Before baby comes. I think you love Night Wind. Baby will help two foolish young people."

Orlena dropped the gourd, spilling the now cool drink on the earthen floor. Her amber eyes dilated until the pupils were black with fear. "Baby! I am with child?" She felt her numb fingers clasping her swollen breasts. Although she had never had the symptoms of pregnancy explained to her, she had come to understand the ultimate consequences of lying with a man. How stupid, how blind not to realize this would happen! She had vowed never to fall into the trap of marriage and childbirth after what had happened to her mother. A hysterical bubble of laughter escaped her lips. She was pregnant by a half-caste who did not care a fig for her! She would bear an Apache child without even the blessing of the church!

She Who Dreams watched Orlena's face. "Nothing to fear. Night Wind will marry you. Good provider for children."

"I am a slave, not a wife. One of the hated Spanish. He will not marry me. It is against your laws anyway. Because I am not Lipan, he cannot wed with me." Orlena stood up, unable to staunch the flow of tears any longer.

Before she could flee, the old woman restrained her, holding her gently. "You will be Lipan. I have no daughter. Night Wind have no wife. White Crane speak with other leaders. You be"—she searched for the Spanish word—"adopted, made our daughter. Then Night Wind will marry you." She nodded at Orlena, having settled that issue.

"But—" Orlena's words died on her lips. Over the months she had come to love the old woman and her husband, White Crane. To be adopted by them would be an honor. "I would be proud to be the daughter of

NIGHT WIND'S WOMAN

She Who Dreams and White Crane, but that will not make Night Wind wish to marry me," she added very carefully.

She Who Dreams snorted. "Hate make him blind. Baby change that. You see." She watched Orlena, knowing the girl did not believe Night Wind could care for her yet. But there was something else troubling Orlena. "Why you fear baby?" she asked bluntly. Whites had such strange customs that even someone of her sagacity could not fathom them.

Orlena's hands touched her belly gingerly as she turned from the searching black eyes waiting for her answer. "I never wanted a baby—that is, I never wanted to become pregnant and endure the birthing."

She Who Dreams shrugged philosophically. "Some pain, but great joy at new life." Watching Orlena's face she knew that there was much the girl had not told her. "Tell me why you have this fear of baby." She urged Orlena to sit once more and then recline on a pile of skins, while she poured another steaming gourd of amber liquid.

Gradually, as the soothing herbal drink relaxed her, Orlena told the story of her mother's frightening ill health during her pregnancy and the horrifying daylong labor that nearly cost her life. By the time she finished the narration, Orlena was trembling with the vividness of her memories, locked away inside her since she was a six-year-old child.

She Who Dreams understood now. She ran her hand gently over Orlena's golden head, again marveling at the gleaming color of the fat plait of hair. "You not like mother. You strong. Work hard, breathe free." She indicated the soft doeskin clothing the girl wore. Once, long ago, several Spanish ladies were captured and brought to their summer camp on the plains. Dressed in hot, tight clothing, they could scarcely walk and could not take a deep breath of air or perform the simplest chores. "You young. Mother old when brother born—not strong like Lioness."

At the mention of Night Wind's pet name for her, Orlena flushed. She had been lonely for him, eager for his return to her bed! How foolish such a wish was. Of course now it was too late to undo what their coming together had already wrought. *I can never return to my family*, she thought bleakly, but said nothing to She Who Dreams.

Several nights later, as she tossed fitfully beneath the warm covers, Orlena considered the flurry of activity the chief's wife had set in motion. The tribal leaders had conferred and agreed that Orlena would be considered from that day the daughter of White Crane and She Who Dreams. As soon as Night Wind returned from his raid, he would marry her, as this was the wish of his father and mother-in-law. That he might refuse was never considered—by anyone but Orlena.

Hearing the pounding of hoofbeats, Orlena huddled deeper beneath her fur covers. Her heart raced as she heard voices. The raiders had returned by the light of the full moon. A sudden gust of icy air filled the warm lodge as the flap was pulled back and Night Wind stepped inside. Had anyone told him of her change in status? Of their impending marriage? She rolled up and blinked, focusing her eyes in the dim light from the smoldering coals in the fire pit.

Night Wind stirred them up and tossed on more wood, then warmed his frozen hands over the rising heat. When he turned to Orlena, he felt the old familiar wrench in his heart. It was the same each time he returned after an absence from her. What witchery was her hold on him? Angry with himself and his body's surging needs, he began to strip off his heavy winter clothing in the warm tepee.

"I am cold. You must warm me, Lioness," he said softly as he pulled back the furs she held up to her chin.

Orlena watched the firelight dance against his naked flesh, reflecting rosily off his hard, sinuous muscles as he climbed into the pallet with her and took her into his arms. "Aah! You are cold," she gasped. But quickly that changed as she warmed him to feverish desire.

"You cannot ask this, White Crane! You know of my plan for the Spanish woman. She is Quinn's beloved!"

White Crane studied his distraught and angry son-in-law. "I ask it. She who was Orlena Valdéz among the Spanish is now Sun in Splendor, my daughter. She will be your wife, as is the custom of our people. You will obey my wishes in this?" The old man's creased face looked like tanned leather, but his black eyes glowed with keen insight. He knew Night Wind would not refuse him, even though he and She Who Dreams had agreed not to tell the young man of his impending fatherhood. One surprise at a time.

Outside the oblong council lodge where the two men conferred, Orlena sat wordlessly, her heart frozen in dread. They were not telling him of the child; at least that small consolation comforted her. But he was still being cornered, forced into the marriage. She had been a lowly captive. Now she was White Crane's daughter. As his son-in-law, Night Wind had no honorable recourse but to do as the chief asked and marry her.

Would I ever have dreamed I would want to marry a savage in a heathen ceremony? For better or for ill, she was a part of this savage scene now, and the Lipan were the only family she would ever again know. A lump of misery welled up in her throat as she thought of Santiago and Conal, now lost to her forever.

At that moment, Night Wind stepped outside the lodge, his face darkened with fury. He strode over to her in a few long-legged steps and took her forcefully by the arm. Automatically her chin went up and she walked stiffly beside him, refusing to humiliate herself by making a scene. She could feel curious eyes on her as numerous of the villagers stood and stared, eager to know what White Crane and Night Wind had discussed in the council lodge.

When they had walked out of earshot, he said, "So my Lioness will whelp in the summer." His voice was low and controlled.

A thrill of anger coursed through her. "White Crane promised not to tell you!" she blurted out, then her breath caught. "You will not marry me." She hoped the tight misery in her chest did not carry in her voice. "I told them you would refuse."

"I will marry you, Lioness," he replied softly, feeling her stiffen in surprise. "I cannot refuse White Crane."

She forced out a tight little laugh. "You did refuse—that is why he told you about the child." Her face flamed in humiliation as understanding washed over her.

"It was not my plan to keep you here. . . ." His voice trailed off in confusion. How could he explain to her what he did not comprehend himself?

"Then send me home—back to Conal and my brother," she said quickly, determined not to beg or debase herself further.

His face hardened and he hissed, "Still you prattle of that cur Quinn! You cannot go back to him. Think you the fine nobility of Santa Fe would accept the red bastard growing in your belly? That your noble Conal would?" Scorn laced his voice now. "We are bound together by blood, Lioness. It is too late for either of us to look back. We wed tomorrow night, as soon as She Who Dreams and the other women make their preparations."

His voice sounded hollow. He was doing this out of a sense of duty to his family, not out of any love for her. That wounded her more than she had ever dreamed it would, even though she had assured her foster mother that Night Wind did not wish this match. "You are right. I cannot return home. You have seen to that. Now it seems your hatred of Conal has turned on you, trapping you in your own web of deceit and violence!" With that she broke free of his grasp and turned back to her lodge, where she knew She Who Dreams and several of the village women made wedding gifts.

"I did not know the depths of the hatred eating his soul," White Crane said sadly to his wife. "I had to tell him of the child and actually shame him into the marriage."

She Who Dreams watched her husband puff disconsolately on a pipe as they shared a simple meal in their tepee. "I have seen many confusing visions, my husband, but know this. As the years stretch ahead, Night Wind and Sun in Splendor will be separated. Theirs will not be an easy path to travel, but they are fated to love. Beyond this I cannot say, but my heart tells me it is enough."

Nodding, the old man was content. She Who Dreams' medicine was very strong, her visions always true. Smiling, he said, "Night Wind did bring me three of his fleetest ponies this morning, along with six fine antelope hides and a splendid skinning knife he received from the French trader."

"He will take good care of his wife and their children. Have no fear. Both are proud and afraid to confess their feelings. White blood must cause much foolish blindness!"

At her words, her husband chuckled. "I warned him when he brought her here that his vengeance would turn on him. He, too, is half white and half foolish."

Orlena nervously ran her hands over the delicate quillwork on the satiny white buckskin dress. When She Who Dreams and Gray Fawn had brought it to her earlier, she had shed tears of gratitude. The dress was incredibly elaborate, with yards of long fringe and intricately patterned quills. The buckskin took weeks of preparation to achieve the snowy white color. The dress was to have been Gray Fawn's, but her wedding was not to be held until spring, when her groom came from another band of Lipan. She shyly explained that she could sew another gown before then, but Sun in Splendor needed one now. Such generosity touched Orlena deeply.

"What do I do at the ceremony?" she asked Gray Fawn. She Who Dreams had vanished into the large council lodge earlier to complete the preparations.

"Only follow your husband's instructions," Gray Fawn said in Lipan. "It will be very simple."

When her foster parents escorted her into the midst of the assembly that night, Orlena was not at all certain how simple it would be. She could feel dozens of pairs of eyes on her and knew that even more of the villagers waited outside in the chill evening air, for the lodge was too small to accommodate them all. Most marriages took place outdoors during warmer weather, but in this strictly chaste society, few had her reason for a hurried ceremony!

NIGHT WIND'S WOMAN

When Night Wind saw her, he was rendered speechless by her beauty. If the simple, tanned skirts and tunics of his people suited her well, the exotic white dress was perfection itself! Her skin, darkened by the autumn sun, glowed against the snowy dress with its brightly colored green and bronze designs. Her hair was plaited in two large coils on either side of her head, each intricately fastened with feathers and quills. Burnished gold, it did indeed shine like the sun in splendor!

Orlena gazed at her husband to be, splendidly attired in fitted buckskin leggins and a fringed jacket weighed down with quill work and heavy copper ornaments attached to the long ends of the fringe. The suit was a rich tan color that contrasted with her white clothing. The barbarous magnificence of his tall, dark body robbed her of breath.

Night Wind walked up to her and clasped her hand, taking her from where she stood between White Crane and She Who Dreams. Leading her over to where the marriage basin stood, he slid off his moccasins, indicating that she should do likewise.

Orlena looked uncertainly at the large bowl on the ground. It was about six feet in diameter, made of hardened cowhide and filled with several inches of water. Night Wind guided her by the hand to one side of the basin, then he walked to the position directly across from her. He stepped into the water and she followed his lead. As he walked in a clockwise pattern around the basin, he motioned for her to circle in the opposite direction until they had each returned to the spot where they began. Then he stepped into the center of the warm water and pulled her to his side, guiding her to step out of the basin midway between their points of entry.

She Who Dreams waited by the edge of the basin

with a soft fur pelt to dry their feet. They donned their moccasins once more and turned to face the assembly.

White Crane said, "I have given my daughter, Sun in Splendor, to the Night Wind as wife. No longer do they walk separate paths. Now their lives are joined together. They begin their journey through life purified by this water. We are bound as family for as long as they both agree to live as husband and wife."

With that, the ceremony was ended and everyone began to smile and talk. Several of the tribal leaders and shamans nodded. She Who Dreams beamed at Orlena. The younger women began to serve food—a spicy steaming stew full of venison chunks and wild onions, mounds of pounded buffalo jerky mixed with dried fruits and suet, a candy of wild honey and dried raspberries, as well as the staples of corn mush and sotol bread. Looking up at Night Wind's unsmiling face, Orlena decided that she was not hungry in spite of her recent voracious appetite.

"Must we stay for the feasting?" she asked in a timid whisper, hating the break in her voice as his stormy eyes turned to regard her.

"It is expected. There will be dancing. The celebrants will wish us great fertility, which does not seem necessary under the circumstances," he added caustically.

Orlena bristled. "You abducted me, you seduced me, and you got me with child! I do not think this an appropriate time for recriminations," she hissed in Spanish.

She Who Dreams hid a smile behind her hand. So, the Lioness had not lost her claws. It was good, for Night Wind was an arrogant man who would soon tire of a submissive wife.

Night Wind's face was ominously shuttered as he sat down abruptly, motioning Orlena to do the same.

NIGHT WIND'S WOMAN

When the foods were presented, she was supposed to offer him each dish and let him eat first. After a terse exchange in Spanish, and her uncertain look over at her foster parents, Orlena did as she was bidden.

The feted couple ate and drank, watched the ceremonial dances, and then, as soon as he could do so without dishonoring his in-laws, Night Wind stood up and walked over to White Crane. "I wish to take my bride to our lodge now, Father."

Smiling, White Crane inclined his head. The feasting and dancing would go on long into the night. If only these foolish young ones could share the joy. But he trusted in his wife's visions. With the fulness of time and the birth of this child, all would be well between them.

"Enjoy your pleasures now, for soon you will be denied them." he whispered with a chuckle to Night Wind.

Overhearing, Orlena reddened as she followed Night Wind from the long brush arbor. Not as warm or windproof as the hide-covered tepee, it nonetheless served when a large crowd gathered. They left the noise and warmth behind and walked out into the starlit night, now husband and wife by the law of the Lipan. Moonbeams reflected on the thin crust of newly fallen snow.

The ceremonial wedding garb was beautiful, but not warm. Orlena shivered and Night Wind wrapped his arm about her; then, almost as a reflex action, he scooped her into his embrace and stalked quickly across the silent village to their lodge.

"Soon we will not be able to lie together. Let us enjoy what is ours while we can, Lioness," he whispered, nuzzling her ear.

When he set her down and reached to untie the flap of their tepee, she asked, "We are married by your laws. Why can we not . . . ?" White Crane had said the same thing earlier.

"Once a woman is visibly pregnant, she can no longer make love with her husband. It is a religious taboo and supposedly protects the unborn child," he replied as they entered the warm lodge.

That bit of Apache folklore dismayed her. As he had said, the only thing they truly shared was making love. At times, she almost dared to hope he was coming to care for her, so intense and sweet was his passion. Now that, too, would end. *And I will grow fat and ugly, mayhap die in this cold wilderness, alone, in the agony of the childbed.*

Never would she confess her cowardice to Night Wind, or even worse, her need for him. "How soon must you seek your pleasures elsewhere?" she asked tartly.

He chuckled mirthlessly as he began to undress. "You reason like a Spaniard. Now you are Lipan, at least by adoption. Lipan men are not faithless husbands who keep mistresses like the Spanish. Nor are we allowed second wives, as are the Mescalero and other Apache."

"No, but when you are gone from this stronghold, spying and raiding among the Spanish, will you be so faithful?" The minute she blurted the question, Orlena knew she did not want to hear his answer.

Night Wind looked at her stricken face and reached for her, taking her in his arms and crushing the heavy, ornamented dress as he held her tightly and kissed her lips roughly. Then, abruptly, as if the civilized Spanish side of him had gained control over the savage Apache side, he released her. His breathing was erratic and his green eyes glowed in the flickering light. Orlena watched him, fascinated and fearful at the same time.

NIGHT WIND'S WOMAN

"The dress is very beautiful. If you do not want it damaged, you had best remove it," he said as he unlaced his buckskin shirt. After peeling it over his shoulders, he tossed it across a buckskin robe and began unfastening his leggins.

Orlena complied, slowly lifting the heavy dress over her head with loving care, then spreading it carefully across one of the willow backrests sitting by the door of the lodge. In spite of the warm air, she felt a sudden chill, standing naked before him. Her breasts were already growing heavier and her waist had thickened a bit, although as yet no telltale bulge marred her belly. After all their nights and days of loving in the past months, she was suddenly self-conscious, afraid of the changes in her body.

Sensing her uncertainty, Night Wind raked her with a scorching look of desire. His hands cupped and hefted her breasts, teasing the distended nipples until they contracted into tight rosy buds.

"Take down your hair. I would feel its silk and see it flow freely down your back," he commanded.

As she reached up to fumble with the quills and feathers holding the braids in the intricate hairdo, he helped her, pulling the ornaments free, then unplaiting her waist-length hair until all of its mass floated like a golden cloud about her upper body. He took a fistful and inhaled its fragrance, let it drop back over her breast, then reached up and swept all of it back from her temples until it cascaded down her spine, the curly ends brushing her buttocks enticingly.

He groaned and ran his hands down her sides, over the satiny curve of her hips, grasping her buttocks and massaging her firm tight cheeks, pressing her against his body. His lips brushed and teased her neck and throat; then he lowered his head and suckled her breasts, alternating from one to the other. At her sharp moan of pleasure, he picked her up and lay her on their pallet, now piled even higher with lavish new pelts and sprinkled with sweet-smelling herbs and dried flowers.

As he leaned over her, his hair fell like a black curtain, obscuring his face from the light. Orlena reached up and combed her fingers through the inky mass at his temples, pulling it back, studying the harsh beauty of his sculpted face. The wide, sensuous mouth was parted and his forehead furrowed in concentration. Hesitantly, she released his hair, letting it fall as her fingertips explored one high cheekbone, then slid down to caress the strong line of his jaw. Beyond the dark, compelling handsomeness of his face lay something familiar, but the thought was quickly banished as he lowered his mouth over hers, brushing and teasing her lips, allowing his tongue to dip and dart in and around her mouth, tasting her, exciting her to mindless passion.

"You are so perfectly formed, all golden, my Sun in Splendor," he whispered. His tongue curled cunningly into one tiny ear while his hand roamed over the swell of her breast, past her waist, around her hip, then moved across her thigh to tangle in the dark golden curls between her legs. "Everywhere, sunlight," he said huskily as he touched her wet aching flesh and felt her legs spread, eager for his penetration.

Her hands slid feverishly up and down the hard, scarred length of his back, her palms pressing into the taut, rock-like curves of his buttocks, urging his body to meld with hers. "Now, now, please, husband," she whispered boldly.

Night Wind sank into the sweet, hot void of her flesh, so yielding, yet so tightly sheathing his pulsing shaft. The pleasure was as blinding as the sun; he closed his eyes tightly to concentrate on prolonging

NIGHT WIND'S WOMAN

the ecstasy. His mind cried out for control, yet his body continued its deep rhythmic thrusts, driven to wild, sweet abandon by his wife's response. *My wife.* In that surge of passion, the idea no longer appalled him, but rather infused his very soul with a burst of joy.

Orlena felt his heat and hardness, the desperate possessive drive that caused him to ride her so fiercely, yet it did not frighten her. She reveled in it, in her husband's need, reflecting her own. The simple Lipan marriage rite had touched her deeply with its beauty. She asked nothing, wanted nothing more from life than to have this bond between them continue. *Let it never be broken*, she prayed. Did she ask her Christian God—or that of the Apache? As the shuddering bliss of her release washed over her in shattering waves, Orlena Valdéz, the Sun in Splendor, did not care as long as her prayer was answered.

Feeling her convulsive pleasure and the soft cries of ecstasy she muffled against his shoulder, Night Wind made several swift, long strokes and exploded, deeply embedded inside her. His eyes were yet closed tightly, but the image of her delicate face floated through his mind as he collapsed, breathless and spent, over her silken flesh. Gathering a fistful of her hair, he gently pulled her head into the curve of his shoulder as he rolled onto his back. She curled against his side like a sylph and put her arm across his broad chest.

Slowly, as the haze of pleasure dissipated, her fears and insecurities rose anew. Sensing a calmness and acceptance in her husband that had not been present earlier, she quashed her private misgivings and asked a harmless question. "I could not understand all the Apache words White Crane spoke. What did the ceremony signify?"

His hand cupped her shoulder, tangling in her hair,

rubbing it unconsciously as he spoke. "We entered the water in a very prescribed way, I from the north, you from the south. Each of us circled the perimeter of the water, then we met in the center and stepped out of it facing the east."

"Where the sun rises each day," she said with partial comprehension.

"The east is more than that to us—it is the beginning of all warmth and light, of life, renewed with each dawn." *Like you, Sun in Splendor.* "We entered the purifying waters alone and traversed it in opposite directions, then joined together in the center."

"It was very beautiful," Orlena said with a catch in her voice.

"It was not a binding marriage in your one true church," he replied cryptically.

Her heart skipped a beat. "Do you consider us married, Night Wind?"

"Yes, but I am more Lipan than white, in spite of Fray Bartolome's influence. What do you believe, Doña Orlena?" Some self-punishing part of him, the half-caste rejected by Spanish civilization, had to ask. He was amazed to find he held his breath, awaiting her answer.

"Yes, I believe we are married, husband," she answered him, this time speaking haltingly in the Lipan tongue.

He tightened his embrace, holding her against his heart in the still silence of the night.

Chapter 13

An idyl of honeymoon closeness between Night Wind and Sun in Splendor began the night of the marriage and continued in the following days. If they could not confess their hopes or fears to each other, they could communicate in the oldest language, the language of love.

Once his resentment over being coerced into the marriage passed, Night Wind felt an odd sense of relief in being bound to her. Now the dilemma of returning her to Conal for revenge was ended. She was his wife, the mother of his child, and he would keep her. Hatred of the Spaniards no longer held him in thrall. Although he had not relinquished vengeance, he found it amazingly easy to focus on the present and his golden wife, not on the dark and bloody past. Yet he feared for the future. She was European, an aristocrat, not meant for the hard and dangerous life of the Apache. Night Wind was sure of her passion, but did she love him? Did he love her? The answer to both questions eluded him.

Orlena, too, experienced confused feelings. She had long admitted to herself that she loved Night Wind, but feared to speak the words aloud to this proud, aloof man who still remained such an enigma to her. He desired her and felt bound to her even as he was bound to her foster family. But duty and desire were not love. Adding to her insecurity were the sweaty, terror-filled nightmares in which she heard her mother's screams of agony echoing across the courtyard of their estate in Aranjuez. She Who Dreams assured her that she would not have such a difficult birth, but a lifetime of fear was not easily set aside.

The jeering contempt of Sweet Rain and a group of her friends did not soothe Orlena either. Sweet Rain continually reminded her of how unfit she was to be a Lipan woman. Nevertheless, others, older women like She Who Dreams and many of the younger married women, offered friendship after her adoption and marriage.

Little Otter, a young wife who was exceedingly pregnant, shyly introduced herself to Orlena as she filled a water skin at the stream one chilly morning.

Squatting awkwardly, for her ungainly belly allowed her no grace, Little Otter stuck the neck of her water vessel into the current. As it inflated, she smiled at Orlena, who was kneeling with two larger skins for She Who Dreams' cookfire.

In halting Spanish, the Lipan girl said, "Good morning," then lapsed into slow, simple sentences in her native tongue. Her shiny black hair was braided in a sleek plait, and her loose, comfortable tunic and skirt were plain but clean and soft, sewn with great care. "She Who Dreams has sung your praises. She was very sad when her daughter died. You fill an empty place in her heart. I would like to be your friend."

Returning the guileless smile, Orlena practiced her broken Lipan, "I want to be your friend. How are you called?"

"I am Little Otter, daughter of Stands Tall and Oak Woman. And you are Sun in Splendor, daughter of White Crane and She Who Dreams." Her brown eyes sparkled with curiosity as she gazed raptly at Orlena's hair.

Orlena laughed. "How strange! Where I was born, a woman's identity lies with her husband, not her parents. Are husbands not important to the Lipan?" she asked, only half jokingly.

"Oh, very important," Little Otter replied solemnly. Then a slow smile spread across her face as she patted her protuberant belly. "Without them we would have no babies!"

Seeing the joy and contentment on Little Otter's face sent a stab of jealousy through Orlena. "You do not fear the birth?" She asked the question tightly, her fingers unconsciously splaying across her own stomach.

"Why? My mother and She Who Dreams will be there. They have birthed many babies," she replied with puzzlement as she struggled to lean far enough out to finish filling her waterskin.

"Here, let me help you. You should not work hard," Orlena scolded as she took the heavy skin and tugged it from the stream.

"Hard work is good for me. It makes me strong," Little Otter said as she took the container from Orlena and stood up, unconscious of her ungainly appearance.

"She Who Dreams told me I had nothing to fear, that I was strong . . . but with Spanish women . . ."

Orlena struggled for words to convey the concept of confinement and the pampering that generally accompanied pregnancies for those of her class.

Little Otter looked around as they began to stroll from the stream to camp, careful that no one could overhear them. "You already carry Night Wind's child?" At Orlena's uncomfortable nod, Little Otter continued without censure, "You must be very careful. Do not let anyone know until your belly grows. Once you tell, you cannot lie with your husband."

Orlena's face suffused with color. "Night Wind has explained that to me."

"Of course, a few women are eager to sleep alone." Little Otter looked at Orlena and then let slip a girlish giggle. "But they are married to ugly, fat men who are bad lovers!"

Thoroughly engaged by her newfound friend's candor, Orlena, too, laughed in spite of her embarrassment and her fears.

Over the next days, Sun in Splendor and Little Otter became fast friends, helping each other with chores and sharing confidences. Little Otter was appalled at Orlena's explanations of how Spanish noblewomen stayed hidden indoors and took no exercise while pregnant. She Who Dreams and Little Otter both exhorted her to forget the foolish ways of white women. Small wonder they sickened and died, in their hot stiff clothes with their muscles grown flaccid from laziness!

Taking their lessons to heart, Orlena found she felt a renewed burst of energy in the days that followed. Outside of an exceptionally voracious appetite and a slow but steady weight gain, she had no actual ill effects from being with child. Remembering her mother, listless and thin, taking to her bed and saying all food made her ill, Orlena felt sad for Serafina's fate and prayed her own would be different.

There was a great deal Europeans could learn from the Apache. Already she had watched She Who Dreams skillfully set a boy's broken leg with green willow branches and a stiffened cowhide binder to hold the bones together as they knit. A man bitten by a rattlesnake, who would have been resigned to die in any Spanish settlement, was cured with an herbal poultice and a strong, evil-smelling drink to counteract the deadly venom. She still recalled vividly the miraculous fever-breaking properties of the cherry bark infusion She Who Dreams had given Night Wind. Her thinking had undergone a complete reversal in less than six months, but that never occurred to Orlena. She was caught up in the hard work of village life and the sensuous web of her husband's caress.

Little more than three weeks after her marriage and her befriending by Little Otter, the two women worked together late one afternoon on tanning a large buffalo hide. It was a splendidly perfect skin that Little Otter planned to make into a sleeping robe to celebrate her husband's return to her bed. For over an hour after their midday meal, the two women toiled, scraping with their adzes. Orlena noticed that her friend worked more slowly and paused often, but assumed it was merely because of her advanced pregnancy and her consequent awkwardness. Then the dark-haired girl emitted a sudden gasp and dropped her scraper onto the large hide. Straightening up from her task, she rubbed her back and looked up at Orlena. "Sun in Splendor, I think you must call She Who Dreams."

Orlena went pale. "You are going to have the baby?"

Little Otter continued rubbing her back. "I have been having the baby all morning, but now I believe it is wise to consult She Who Dreams."

Panicked, Orlena shot up and ran across the village. It was a sun-kissed day with no wind, a most propitious day for a birth—but then so was the day Santiago was born in Aranjuez! She ran faster.

When the breathless girl yanked open the tent flap, She Who Dreams was already gathering her medicines and charms. Looking calmly at Orlena she said, "It is time. We will go to Little Otter now and you will assist me."

"Me?" Orlena's voice squeaked! Women who had not borne children were never allowed to witness a birth in Spain.

With considerable trepidation, she followed She Who Dreams back to where Little Otter continued working on the staked hide. She had been joined by her mother, Oak Woman. Every few moments Little Otter would pause and rub her back, then resume her task. The girl's words finally sank in—Little Otter had been laboring with the baby all the while they labored at the tanning!

"Should she not go into her tepee and lie down?" Orlena asked She Who Dreams.

Smiling serenely, She Who Dreams shook her head. "Foolish. Lying down only makes the coming of the child take longer. She should walk now, I think."

Little Otter obediently rose with assistance from Oak Woman and Sun in Splendor. The three women ambled along the edge of the stream. After about thirty yards, Little Otter again stopped and rubbed her back, this time pausing longer. A slight beading of perspiration dotted her forehead and upper lip in spite of the chilly February air.

"Now you will drink this," She Who Dreams said, approaching Little Otter and her two helpers as they stood by the creek. She offered the girl a gourd filled with a steaming herbal brew. Little Otter drank it in a few swift gulps and handed the container back to the old woman.

This process of walking and drinking the medicine woman's offerings continued for several more hours. Her friend was obviously in pain, but still she kept doggedly walking. Afraid of upsetting Little Otter, Orlena held her peace and offered her arm when her friend faltered. *The herbs in the drink must possess some sort of pain-numbing property*, she thought as she noted the way the brew seemed to relax Little Otter. For a prospective grandmother, Oak Woman remained calm, saying little but simply patting her daughter's arm from time to time.

About mid-afternoon, She Who Dreams reached a decision and said matter of factly, "Now we will go to the lodge."

Entering the tepee Little Otter shared with her husband, Strong Bow, Orlena helped Little Otter kneel on the bed of skins. Oak Woman and She Who Dreams began preparations, assisting the girl in taking off her skirt and tunic. Orlena watched in fascination as Little Otter's distended abdomen hardened and moved with a powerful contraction. No wonder her back ached! Every muscle in her torso seemed to be pulling her apart.

Oak Woman held one of Little Otter's arms, and She Who Dreams motioned for Orlena to take the other to help the girl support her weight. Then the old medicine woman spread Little Otter's knees and set a wide low basin between them.

"Now, you push down. Let go and the little one will arrive quickly," she instructed.

Little Otter began to grunt, panting for breath as she followed instructions. Sweat soaked her body now, but a fire warmed the lodge, keeping her from taking a chill. Both of the older women spoke in steady tones, soothing the girl and urging her on with her labor, for that was what it appeared to be—bone-jarring hard work, but not the mysterious, terrifying agony Orlena had imagined from her mother's screams.

Suddenly, after one long, hard push, a gush of water came pouring into the basin, filling it nearly to overflowing. Clucking in apparent satisfaction, She Who Dreams deftly replaced the full basin with another one until all the birth waters had been expelled. She Who Dreams removed the basins and placed a soft, clean deer pelt between the girl's legs. Then she examined Little Otter's belly again. Now the outline of the child could be clearly seen, lying with head pressed low in the birth canal, curled up with legs tucked in its belly.

"Good. The baby is in the right position. Now, push more. It will not be much longer," She Who Dreams instructed. Little Otter's grunts became more feral now, harder and louder with rasping breaths between them as she worked to expel the child.

Orlena was too engrossed in watching the mystery of life unfold to be frightened for her friend or herself. She held firmly to Little Otter's arm and felt every muscle in the girl's strong young body work in singleminded unity.

A sound of pleasure came from She Who Dreams as she held the crown of the baby's head in one leathery old hand. With the other she kneaded and stroked Little Otter's belly, helping the natural rhythm of the contractions as first the head emerged, then in several more hard, driving pushes, the shoulders.

Orlena found herself craning her neck, intent on seeing the infant emerge. What sex was it? Was it well formed and healthy?

Little Otter took an enormous breath and gave one final push. The baby girl slid into She Who Dreams'

NIGHT WIND'S WOMAN

arms and gave a lusty squall. As Little Otter squatted lower to accommodate the short length of the umbilical cord, She Who Dreams laid the infant on the soft pile of pelts between the mother's thighs. Then she tied off the cord and cut it.

The baby continued crying fiercely all the while, causing the two old women to exchange a smile. The medicine woman then awaited the swift expulsion of the afterbirth, which she carefully examined. Once assured it was intact, she laid it on another, larger piece of cowhide.

"How perfect and beautiful she is," Orlena breathed in awe, oblivious of the fact the child was a bloody, sticky mess!

After instructing the two women holding Little Otter to assist the exhausted new mother in stretching out on her pallet, She Who Dreams washed the infant gently in warm water she had set aside in a bison-horn container. The baby gradually quieted, almost magically. Now all four women beamed.

"See how she kicks. She is strong and fine," Little Otter said with glowing eyes as she watched.

Remembering how disappointed her mother had said her father had been at her birth, and how much Conal had wanted a son, Orlena had a fleeting fear that Strong Bow might not be as pleased with the girl child as the mother was, but she said nothing.

She Who Dreams turned to Orlena and said, "Make haste and bring water from the stream so that Little Otter may cleanse herself and then present the little one to Strong Bow."

Looking from the exhausted new mother to She Who Dreams in amazement, Orlena only nodded and did as she was bidden. Outside the lodge, Strong Bow stood nervously awaiting word of his wife and child. He was a pleasant-looking youth with a wide, earnest face and shy manner. Uncertain of whose role it was to make the announcement, she smiled to reassure him, and then scooped up two big waterskins and their leather carrying strap and raced for the stream.

When she returned with the water, she fully expected that she and Oak Woman would have to assist Little Otter with her ceremonial washing, but the smiling mother sat up and reached for the coarse piece of buffalo cloth, eager to perform her own bathing.

"Oak Woman has gone to bury the afterbirth," She Who Dreams said to Orlena. "It is very bad magic to let any mischief makers find it." Turning to the large buckskin pouch sitting against the far wall, she unlaced it and pulled out a buttery soft yellow tunic and skirt. "When she is cleansed, you may help her dress for Strong Bow," she said to Orlena.

The new father's face was alight with love and joy as he took the infant from Little Otter. "She is as lovely as her mother," he said solemnly. "I will present her to the sun and the four winds now." Gingerly he carried the wriggling bundle from the lodge to perform the ritual of initiation. As Lipan custom dictated, Little Otter must stay in the tepee for four days.

"Now is her time to rest—after her work is done, not before," She Who Dreams explained to Orlena. It seemed to make sense. As the two of them observed Strong Bow's proud presentation of his daughter to the sun, and in turn to the north, south, east, and west, She Who Dreams whispered to Orlena, "Do you still fear the baby in your belly?"

It was as if a great weight had been lifted from her and she could breathe freely once again. "No, no, I do not." Her hand pressed against her abdomen and she smiled as Night Wind walked up to join the happy assembly watching Strong Bow and his infant daughter.

NIGHT WIND'S WOMAN

The look on Orlena's face was radiant. When his father-in-law had informed him of She Who Dreams' plan to have his wife assist in the birth, Night Wind feared for her delicate Spanish sensibilities, knowing what he did of how the European nobility shielded ladies from such matters. Now he could see that his mother-in-law had made the right decision.

"Strong Bow is a very happy man," Night Wind said softly to Orlena, almost musing to himself. Would he feel such joy on seeing his child, with more European blood than Lipan?

"I . . . I am happy for them," she said hesitantly, uncertain of how to express what she felt. "Among the Spanish, a son is more prized than a daughter. I had feared when the baby was a girl . . ." Her voice faded away as she realized how little she understood these complex people whom she had once branded ignorant savages.

Night Wind smiled arrogantly. "A daughter stays with her parents and brings another provider for their old age. We do not pass on land through our sons, but tradition through our daughters."

Orlena felt a twist of pain. Night Wind obviously favored Lipan society and despised the Spanish. By indirection, such contempt struck her and her baby as well. Wanting to hurt back, she said impulsively, "When I was but a girl of five years, long before my brother was born, Conal Quinn loved me, just for myself."

His demeanor turned from arrogance to ice. "Colorado Quinn never loved any but could give him return in gold or silver. Think you your mother's lands and wealth did not go to him by the generous hand of your king?"

That was an indisputable fact, but monstrously unfair and misleading to Orlena's mind. "Conal loved me—he loves me yet as much as Strong Bow loves *his* daughter!" With tears shining in her eyes, she turned from him and walked away, her carriage stiffly erect and her step deliberate.

He swore beneath his breath in Spanish. As if her white blood were not enough, Conal would ever be between them!

Just then hoofbeats sounded from downstream in the sheltered valley where the band wintered. Night Wind saw Hoarse Bark, a sentry that day, swing down from his horse. Knowing his friend searched for him, he walked clear of the assembly and waved.

"This message came for you through the Opata who scout for the presidio in Santa Fe," the Mescalero said, handing a rolled oilskin container to Night Wind.

"It is from Quinn," Night Wind said flatly as his eyes saw the signature at the bottom.

Hoarse Bark knew the message could be only ill news, but he was not prepared for the surge of fury that blackened Night Wind's face as he crumpled the paper and ground it under his foot.

"He has Fray Bartolome! He is holding him in Santa Fe in exchange for Orlena. If I do not return her unharmed, he will kill a priest!"

"One of the Blue Robes? Surely not even Colorado Quinn would do this insane thing—they are holy men among the Spanish, are they not?" Hoarse Bark asked.

"Quinn has no religion but his own," Night Wind said softly, his eyes narrowed in calculation, running down a mental list of everyone who knew of his bond with the priest. "There is but one way to counter this," he added finally.

"Surely you will not give up your wife and child?" Hoarse Bark said in surprise. He had not favored the fragile-looking Spanish beauty, but over the months she had spent among the Apache she had proven herself. When Night Wind had told him his reason for agreeing to the marriage, he had been certain that the proud half-caste had accepted the woman.

"I keep what is mine. But there is yet another way to bargain with Quinn. Come. We ride for Santa Fe this night!"

"Blood and bones of St. Peter, it is cold in this hellish wilderness! Does the wind never cease?" Ignacio Valdéz, Conde de Plasencia and Marqués de San Clemente, paced the hard adobe bricks of the governor's receiving room. Damn the accursed Irish trash, keeping him waiting when he had presented papers signed by the hand of Manuel Antonio Flores, the Viceroy of New Spain himself! *I am no longer a boy for you to bully, you cheap foreign charlatan.*

Indeed, Ignacio's power at court had grown greatly with the death of the old king and the ascension of his son as Charles IV in 1788. The former Prince of Asturias had remembered his young companion and rewarded him. When Ignacio wished to pursue his errant sister to New Spain and retrieve her from Conal Quinn's grasp, he was given royal letters of recommendation to assure him a smooth course as he went about his task.

He had found several wealthy and powerful men at court who remembered Orlena's legendary golden beauty. If he could but reclaim her intact, fit virginal property for marriage, his star would rise even higher. And then, too, there was the matter of revenge. Conal had taken his mother, his mother's ancestral estates, and now had even stolen his own sister! He would see the arrogant Irish braggart crawl.

Inside his audience chamber, the governor dismissed several alcaldes who had come with their usual bribe in lieu of the taxes owed by their districts. Being governor of such a venal backwater of the Spanish crown did have its monetary rewards. But all the money he extorted from the provincial officials and merchants could not compensate for his return to this hellish place, nor for the threats to his son or the abduction of Orlena.

Orlena! He looked at the elaborate royal seal on Ignacio's letter of introduction and commendation. As if he needed introduction to that impudent cur! Charles IV could commend him to the devil for all Conal Quinn cared. Yet the man had not only the distant ear of Madrid but viceregal backing from Flores in the City of Mexico as well. And now he was here to reclaim his sister.

Conal ran calloused fingers through his reddish gray hair and sank into the heavy leather chair behind the long oak table. His message regarding the priest had gone unanswered by Night Wind. It had been simple enough riding to Chihuahua City, locating the obscure mission and abducting the cleric. No one in Nueva Viscaya even knew who had done the deed, but the bold lover of savages was proving a troublesome nuisance.

The soldiers at the governor's palace who were holding him under house arrest had become increasingly in awe of the scholar, and the servants were aghast that even the governor would dare imprison a holy man of God. If only word about an exchange of the priest for Orlena would arrive, then he could at least make assurances to Ignacio that his sister remained unharmed and was merely a political prisoner. The real reason for Night Wind's vengeance and the nature of it he must keep secret from the deadly courtier. God's Bones, he was in enough royal disfavor already!

NIGHT WIND'S WOMAN

"Well, little is to be gained by stalling the royal emissary any longer," he muttered with a sigh as he stood up and motioned to the soldier standing at the door. "Show Don Ignacio in."

"You have done what!" Ignacio exploded, again jumping up to confront Conal across the heavy table. "Kidnapped a priest—a scholar from the Franciscan College in the City of Mexico! You are even more of an idiot than I imagined. All your brains can be held on the edge of your sword!"

"Best beware the edge of my sword, my lord Ignacio," Conal replied in a deadly quiet tone of voice. He did not rise but held his temper under iron control, realizing how the ascension of the Prince of Asturias to the throne had increased Ignacio's arrogance and self-importance. At thirty, he was no longer rail-thin, but thickened at the waist from a rich courtier's life. His pale face had been mottled red with fury ever since Conal had told him of Orlena's fate. At first he had not planned to inform Ignacio of his scheme with the priest, but when the interview had gone badly, he relented and explained about his "house guest." The indulged and scheming youth was even more livid now.

Then his mercurial temperament suddenly shifted and Ignacio sat down once more. Pale, beringed fingers drummed on the polished wood of the table. His yellow eyes reminded Conal of those of a cornered jaguar—calculating and deadly.

"So, the governor of New Mexico has taken a cleric under the legal jurisdiction of the Church, and holds him for ransom in return for some savage. Think you, how will such a deed look in my report to his excellency, the Viceroy? If I report your blunder, that is."

Shirl Henke

"You want your sister returned for your dynastic alliance. This is the only way to handle matters. You know nothing of this wilderness," Conal said with contempt. Blood of the Martyrs, this bastard could have him relieved of office and jailed at whim!

Ignacio scoffed and waved his hand in a swift angry gesture of dismissal. "I give not a fig for Orlena now. What Spanish nobleman will touch the leavings of a band of filthy savages! Her usefulness to me for a marriage is at an end." *But her usefulness in destroying you has only begun, Irishman!*

"I have told you, this half-caste renegade is in revolt against the crown. He is holding Orlena in return for the freedom of Apache mine slaves. She was not simply taken as a female captive to rape and kill. Night Wind will not touch her." *If only I believed that!*

"It matters not. Everyone will believe she has been dishonored. Merely by living months among the savages she has been tainted. You abducted my sister, ruined her chance for a splendid marriage, and now you have let her fall prey to renegades. As if that were not indictment enough, you have abducted a priest. I think, *Don Conal*"—Ignacio stressed the name contemptuously—"you had best prepare yourself for a return to what you doubtless do best—riding about the deserts and mountains, killing savages."

Finishing his evening prayers, Fray Bartolome rose on stiffened knees and looked out into the courtyard below. The governor's palace was a handsome prison, he had to admit. He had never been this far north. New Mexico was awe-inspiringly magnificent country. He would actually have enjoyed the journey in spite of being brought against his will if it were not for the reason precipitating it. Joaquín had kidnapped Conal's stepdaughter in revenge! And now he, as well as the innocent girl, was a pawn in their ugly warfare.

He alternately prayed for Joaquín's soul and Orlena Valdéz's safety and railed at the cruelty of both men who had done such perfidious deeds. Of Conal he expected no better, but of Joaquín he had hoped for so much more.

"I am an old fool who believes in the face of all odds that an embittered, abused boy can be redeemed even after he has grown into an outlaw," the priest muttered to himself.

A light tap on the door interrupted his reflection and he turned from the window as a tall, sallow-faced young man, elegantly garbed in satin breeches, sauntered into the room. "Good evening, Father. I am the Count of Plasencia, Ignacio Valdéz," he said arrogantly, perfunctorily bowing from the waist to the priest.

Fray Bartolome's face became grave as he nodded. "You are related to that poor child the Apaches are holding," he said carefully, instinctively not trusting this fop with the cold yellow eyes.

"My sister, alas," Ignacio replied, daubing a lace kerchief at his brow in feigned distress. "I wish you to understand that I had nothing to do with your abduction. Indeed, I have only last evening arrived here and learned of Orlena's fate this morning. The governor has greatly exceeded his authority in holding you—as you well know," Ignacio added while he measured the priest's shrewd gray eyes. This one would not be awed by his rank or deceived with cajolery. He would be blunt. "However, Father, I wish to know what reason you have for sheltering runaway Indian prisoners. I understand this Night Wind who abducted my sister was such a one."

Although tall, Ignacio could not match the broad shouldered mass of the priest. Fray Bartolome locked eyes with the courtier and paused a moment as his troubled expression gave way to one of rebuke. "My reasons are as old as our holy faith, my son. When Caesar—be he Roman emperor or Spanish king—enslaves nine-year-old boys to dig in the mines, the church must protest. Our government is committing atrocities in the silver and gold mines of Nueva Viscaya and Sonora. I've seen small children with whip scars on their backs, our Blessed Savior only knows what scars in their souls. Joaquín, the one now called Night Wind, came to me shot and beaten, starved and filled with hate. Should I have turned a ten-year-old back to that hell on earth?"

"Your duty is to save their benighted souls, not to incite them to rebellion against royal authority," Ignacio answered coldly.

"My understanding of the policy of the Council of the Indies, in conjunction with his majesty Charles III's decrees, is that the Indians are to be civilized, made Christians, and brought into our society as peaceful free subjects, neither butchered wholesale nor enslaved."

The priest met Ignacio's insolent stare with steady assurance as the courtier said, "No matter how well intentioned the laws, the reality of dealing with savages must allow for some harsh measures."

Fray Bartolome smiled tolerantly. "I believe those were almost your stepfather's very words to me on the subject."

Ignacio's face hardened. "Conal Quinn is an opportunist, an unscrupulous mercenary who has overstepped his office. I will reclaim my sister, see your renegade Indian hung, and . . ." he paused to stress his last words, "I will bring the Governor of New Mexico before the Viceroy and see him stripped of his rank!"

NIGHT WIND'S WOMAN

When he had stalked out, Fray Bartolome considered everything he had learned. He and Joaquín and that innocent girl were caught in a power struggle between two utterly ruthless and cunning men. "I only pray, Holy Mother, do not let Don Ignacio learn Joaquín's secret!"

Chapter 14

The Jicarilla scout was a small, squat youth, whose round face belied his trail-seasoned skills. A member of the presidial Indian militia, he was required by law to serve the Spanish government in return for the protection the army supposedly offered his village. In fact he, like numerous other conscripted Indians, was a spy for Night Wind's raiders, giving them information regarding troop movements and mine shipments from Santa Fe to Durango.

Juanito had been ransomed by the Spanish from the Comanche, who had captured him from his own people. Thinking the Jicarilla grateful for his salvation from the archenemies of all Apache, his Spanish superior trusted him. But the Jicarilla, like the Mescalero, were closely allied with their Apache kin on the plains, the Lipan.

Now Juanito stood in the deepening twilight beneath a cottonwood grove south of Santa Fe. A man

NIGHT WIND'S WOMAN

dressed in the simple white cotton clothes of a *paisano* with a large sombrero shadowing his face walked casually by and stopped. "Juanito, it has been a long time since last I saw you."

"Nearly six months. Your yellow-haired captive, she must keep you well occupied," the Jicarilla replied in a whisper.

Night Wind shrugged. "She has caused me much trouble."

"I have heard about the holy father Quinn holds under house arrest.

"Have you seen him? Is he harmed in any way?" Night Wind asked with dread in his voice.

"He is allowed brief morning walks in the courtyard of the palace. I have talked with the servants and he is treated well enough. Will you trade the woman for him?"

"No. But Quinn will trade Fray Bartolome for his cub," Night Wind replied grimly.

"So that is why you wanted to speak with me," the Jicarilla replied in a hushed voice. "Ever since the girl was taken, Quinn allows his son to go nowhere without a large armed escort."

"I do not plan a battle, my friend, but I will need some information from you. Where does the boy go? How many soldiers accompany him? Everything about his habits, his daily routine—any vulnerable time or place where I could reach him without raising an alarm," Night Wind said as he gazed around the deserted adobes that lay scattered along the winding banks of the river. Somewhere in the distance a coyote howled in the still evening air.

Juanito sighed. "What you plan is very dangerous."

A smile slashed across Night Wind's face as he replied, "And have I not lived with danger all these years?"

The Jicarilla considered. "The first of each month they ride to Taos for the trade bazaar. I think the governor collects his bribes from the Indians selling their wares that way. While Quinn and his leeches *tax* the merchants, he lets the fire-haired boy wander among the crowded market stalls, with guards to protect him. I do not think he wishes his son to know how he steals from the people—or from his own king," Juanito said with contempt.

"Next week is the first of the month. I think we will be waiting in the Taos bazaar with a special bargain for young Santiago."

He forced down the tears, weak, foolish woman's tears. Soon they would be at Night Wind's stronghold. The arrogant butcher had told him this only last night. Again he cursed himself for his stupidity in falling for the trap. Papa would be insane with grief now. First Orlena, now him—both prisoners of this evil half-caste who spoke Spanish as elegantly as Ignacio.

Tied to his horse for the past days' journey, Santiago had little to do as they rode but think. He focused on the enigma of his captor. Night Wind was well educated, yet of mixed blood. He hated the Spanish, yet revered the priest his father was holding. The raider's reputation was fearsome, yet he had treated Santiago without rancor in spite of several feckless attempts to escape, including braining one of his guards and breaking the leg of a good horse. Santiago regretted the horse's death, but was unrepentant in his desire to escape. His captor seemed not only to accept this, but to take pride in his willful temerity, saying Santiago reminded him of Orlena.

When Night Wind mentioned Orlena's name, Santiago had tried to leap at his throat. The boy recalled with humiliation how effortlessly the bronzed savage had subdued him. *At least I will see Orlena this day.* He prayed fiercely and desperately that her spirit was not broken. There was something mysterious about this half-caste, something that made him more than another renegade Apache. As they rode, the boy pondered. Who was the Night Wind?

"But why did they leave so suddenly, in the middle of the night?" *Without a word to me?* Orlena paced the small confines of Little Otter's lodge. Watching her young friend contentedly nurse her infant, Orlena was happy that Strong Bow did not ride with Night Wind and his group of raiders.

"I heard my husband say Night Wind received a message—white man's writing. But often his spies send such. It must have been very important for him to leave so suddenly." Little Otter hesitated as she rocked Shining Pebble, her bright-eyed daughter. "Sun in Splendor, did you and Night Wind quarrel before he left?"

Orlena sighed. "Always we quarrel."

Little Otter smiled reassuringly. "All husbands and wives quarrel. It is natural."

"Perhaps, but we have so much that stands between us . . . my stepfather, who was kinder to me than anyone, is Conal Quinn, the governor." Beside Night Wind, only her parents knew of her background. She looked at Little Otter with a mixture of pride and fearfulness on her face.

"And you revere this man, Night Wind's sworn enemy." Little Otter digested that disquieting fact as she tucked her daughter into her beautiful new cradleboard. "I understand why you would quarrel—yet he has kept you with him, fought to save you from Quick Slayer, and married you. In spite of this barrier, he cares for you. I know you love him." At Orlena's flush, Little Otter only nodded sagely and continued, "When he returns, put the past behind you. Do not speak of Quinn. Your future is here." She reached over and touched Orlena's slightly swollen belly.

"Perhaps you are right. I do not know. Night Wind is a man of many secrets, filled with bitterness. It is not easy for him to love . . . I am not at all certain that he *can* love." Her voice had faded to a pained whisper.

Before Little Otter could respond, the sound of voices raised in great excitement interrupted the two women. Orlena was the first one out of the tepee. She saw Night Wind leading his men into camp, surrounded by curious and agitated villagers.

He had a new captive. Was it another woman? Then she recognized the slight figure tied to his horse. "Santiago!" The cry was torn from her as she raced toward the crowd, rudely pushing and elbowing aside women, children, even large men in her path.

When Night Wind saw her approach, he swung down from Warpaint and restrained her before she could reach the boy. "He is unharmed, Lioness," he said quietly.

She yanked free of him as if he were a leper, scorching him with blazing golden eyes. "Is it not enough that you have me? Does your hatred of Conal know no limits?"

Night Wind had no chance to answer before the boy, recognizing his sister's golden hair, cried out, "Orlena! Holy Mother and all the Saints, *you are alive*!" He struggled to dismount with his hands tied.

Orlena helped him down under Night Wind's baleful stare. "I am alive and well. And you? What have they done to you?" She examined his face where several bruises discolored his eye and cheek, then turned to his wrists, chaffed by the rawhide bindings.

NIGHT WIND'S WOMAN

Night Wind interrupted, "This is touching, but as you can see, his injuries are superficial. It seems he shares your unrealistic penchant for escape, Lioness. He received the bruises and cuts from falls. The wrist bands were essential to keep him from harming any more of my men! The cub is a fighter," he said with grudging admiration.

"Why have you done this, Night Wind? He is only thirteen years old!"

"Bartolome is nearing fifty, a priest and a friar who did naught but succor those who came to him for refuge. Your beloved Conal holds him prisoner—in exchange for you."

A look of incredulity washed over her face. Could this be true? With a sinking certainty, she looked at Santiago's crestfallen face and knew it was. "And so, you have taken my brother in exchange for the priest. Where will it end, Night Wind?"

"Ask Quinn," he replied tersely as he took Santiago by his bound wrists and led him toward Hoarse Bark's small lodge. Orlena stalked furiously behind him.

"Bring him to our lodge, not the Mescalero's," she demanded.

He paused and looked at her with a caustic smile playing about his lips. "Surely you would not want his innocent eyes to see . . . what he would see."

Santiago looked from his red-faced, furious sister to the tall, hard-looking renegade with dawning comprehension. When Orlena let out an oath and slapped Night Wind, he let go of Santiago and grabbed her roughly, pulling her against his body and securing her hands behind her back. She struggled and kicked as Santiago also launched himself at his sister's lover, clubbing awkwardly with his bound fists.

Holding the slim woman with one arm, he cuffed the youth, knocking him to the ground. "Enough!" He turned to Orlena. "If you would not see him harmed, do not incite him to foolish bravery."

Realizing that Santiago could be seriously injured, she ceased her struggles. "Let me release his bonds and tend his injuries. Or is that beyond your fine Lipan sense of honor?"

He shrugged in acquiescence and released her silently, noting that a number of curious spectators had followed them across the camp. Looking around, he said, "Go about your work. My wife will see to my new captive."

As they disappeared, Orlena knelt down and pulled a small dagger from her belt. She cut the bonds on Santiago's wrists, then quickly replaced the blade beneath her tunic before her impetuous brother could repeat her early mistakes. "Come with me," she said, not meeting the crestfallen expression on his face.

Santiago followed his sister to one of the larger skin-covered lodges. He noticed the assured way she walked and the Apache clothing she wore. But for her golden plait of hair and pale skin, she could have been one of the savages! As they neared the tepee, she even exchanged words with several women in their strange, harsh language.

When they entered the lodge, the boy looked around, curious about how the fearsome Apache lived in spite of his righteous anger. On one side of the circular skin wall, two woven willow backrests sat with soft skins thrown over them. A large buckskin pouch sat between them. In one corner lay a pallet covered with rich pelts. More were piled near the door. A fire burned low in the center of the lodge, with its smoke curling eagerly toward the small opening at the apex of the poles.

"Sit down while I get my medicines," Orlena com-

NIGHT WIND'S WOMAN

manded as she began to rummage through a large buckskin bag.

"It is warm in here ... and clean," he added, almost to himself. The surprise in his voice was evident. Many of the *paisanos'* adobe huts were not nearly so well kept as this portable dwelling. He watched his sister's hands as she nervously selected several herbs and added them to a small bowl of water.

When she approached him with the healing paste and began to smear it on his cuts and bruises, he looked at her and worked up his courage.

"You have a knife—give it to me and let us escape. I can steal horses—"

"Do not be foolish," Orlena retorted sharply as she continued her work. "We are hundreds of leagues in the mountains of southern New Mexico. Even if we could get away from this village, where would we go? What would we eat or drink? The nearest Spanish settlement is many days of hard riding from here."

"You dress as one of them and speak their language ... and ..."

"And I am Night Wind's woman," she finished the sentence softly. "I cannot return to Santa Fe, Santiago. You will be ransomed, but Night Wind will keep me. Even if I were free, women who have been captives are treated differently. You know that."

"We could go all the way to the City of Mexico—or back to Madrid! No one there would know what had happened here, Orlena."

"Yes, they would." She hesitated. How could she tell a thirteen-year-old boy this? "I—I am married to Night Wind," she began.

"Married! How? By some medicine man of the savages? You were not blessed in the church—you are not his wife," Santiago protested stubbornly.

Taking a deep breath, Orlena said quietly, "Night Wind married me by tribal law . . . and I carry his child, Santiago."

"He raped you! I will kill him!" His freckled face looked so hurt and vulnerable that it tore at her, but she grabbed him before he could dash outside and again attack Night Wind. Hugging him closely, she said, "No, he did not . . . force me. I . . . he . . . oh, Santiago, it is too complicated to explain, but I cannot go back with you. You must tell Conal that I am well treated and wish to stay here. You and your father have a different road to travel than I now," she added softly.

Burying his head on her shoulder, Santiago hugged her tightly and finally the tears he had held back in front of the men poured out. "Orlena, my sister, why has this happened to you? If only I had not let you wear my clothes. I should have told Papa—"

"No, hush, little brother. None of this is your fault. The hatred between your father and Night Wind is old and bitter. We have been caught up in it, but perhaps some good may yet come of the accident which brought me here."

His head shot up and he studied her face. The half-caste was educated and, he supposed, from a girl's point of view, handsome. "Do you want to be his wife, Orlena?" he asked, not sure how he should feel about her relationship with the renegade.

"I . . . do not know," she replied evasively. "Sometimes I want to kill him . . . yet other times, he can be kind. He has endured much at the hands of the Spanish, Santiago, yet he has not harmed me or you."

"He kidnapped us both!"

She sighed. "Yes, but Conal kidnapped his friend, the Franciscan who saved his life and educated him. It

A Special Offer For Leisure Historical Romance Readers Only!

Get Four FREE* Romance Novels

A $21.96 Value!

Travel to exotic worlds filled with passion and adventure—without leaving your home!

Plus, you'll save at least $5.00 every time you buy!

Thrill to the most sensual, adventure-filled Historical Romances on the market today...
FROM ▙ LEISURE BOOKS

As a home subscriber to the Leisure Historical Romance Book Club, you'll enjoy the best in today's BRAND-NEW Historical Romance fiction. For over twenty-five years, Leisure Books has brought you the award-winning, high-quality authors you know and love to read. Each Leisure Historical Romance will sweep you away to a world of high adventure...and intimate romance. Discover for yourself all the passion and excitement millions of readers thrill to each and every month.

SAVE AT LEAST $5.00 EACH TIME YOU BUY!

Each month, the Leisure Historical Romance Book Club brings you four brand-new titles from Leisure Books, America's foremost publisher of Historical Romances. EACH PACKAGE WILL SAVE YOU AT LEAST $5.00 FROM THE BOOKSTORE PRICE! And you'll never miss a new title with our convenient home delivery service.

Here's how we do it. Each package will carry a 10-DAY EXAMINATION privilege. At the end of that time, if you decide to keep your books, simply pay the low invoice price of $16.96 ($19.98 CANADA), no shipping or handling charges added.* HOME DELIVERY IS ALWAYS FREE.* With today's top Historical Romance novels selling for $5.99 and higher, our price SAVES YOU AT LEAST $5.00 with each shipment.

AND YOUR FIRST FOUR-BOOK SHIPMENT IS TOTALLY FREE!*

IT'S A BARGAIN YOU CAN'T BEAT! A Super $21.96 Value!

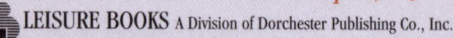

▙ LEISURE BOOKS A Division of Dorchester Publishing Co., Inc.

GET YOUR 4 FREE* BOOKS NOW— A $21.96 VALUE!

Mail the Free* Books
Certificate
Today!

4 FREE* BOOKS A $21.96 VALUE

Free Books Certificate*

YES! I want to subscribe to the Leisure Historical Romance Book Club. Please send me my 4 FREE* BOOKS. Then, each month I'll receive the four newest Leisure Historical Romance selections to preview for 10 days. If I decide to keep them, I will pay the Special Member's Only discounted price of just $4.24 each, a total of $16.96 ($19.98 in Canada). This is a SAVINGS OF AT LEAST $5.00 off the bookstore price. There are no shipping, handling, or other charges.* There is no minimum number of books I must buy and I may cancel the program at any time. In any case, the 4 FREE* BOOKS are mine to keep—A **BIG** $21.96 Value!

*In Canada, add $7.95 US shipping and handling per order for first shipment. For all subsequent shipments to Canada the cost of membership in the Book Club is $19.98 US plus $7.95 US shipping and handling per order. All payments must be made in US dollars.

Name _____

Address _____

City _____

State _____ Zip _____

Telephone _____

Signature _____

If under 18, Parent or Guardian must sign. Terms, prices and conditions subject to change. Subscription subject to acceptance. Leisure Books reserves the right to reject any order or cancel any subscription.

Get Four Books Totally F R E E* — A $21.96 Value!

(Tear Here and Mail Your FREE* Book Card Today!)

PLEASE RUSH MY FOUR FREE* BOOKS TO ME RIGHT AWAY!

Leisure Historical Romance Book Club
P.O. Box 6613
Edison, NJ 08818-6613

AFFIX STAMP HERE

NIGHT WIND'S WOMAN

is a long, bitter tale ... I do not know all of it. T'would serve naught to speak of it even if I did."

She resumed her attention to his bruised face. "Night Wind said you tried to escape several times."

He puffed out his thin chest and replied, "Once I knocked my guard off his horse and rode for miles before they caught me. I would have made away if my horse had not stumbled and broken his leg. I was sorry about the horse, not the guard," he added impenitently.

Orlena chuckled, her mood lightening as they talked like conspirators of old. "I also tried to escape several times. Finally, when they learned how well I could ride, they put me on a burro!"

"A burro!" In spite of their circumstances in this hostile world, the image of his proud, elegant sister mounted on a burro brought a twitch to his lips, then a burble of laughter.

Hearing the laughter erupt, Night Wind restrained his impulse to enter the lodge. He had faced the worst when Orlena came charging toward her brother like a lioness defending her cub. The boy had intelligence and courage, and he loved his sister—that was evident. The half-caste swore at Conal Quinn, who had begun this bitter tangle so many years ago. How would it all end?

"We go hunting for elk this fine morning. Do you wish to go with us? I will teach you to hunt with bow and arrow," Night Wind said to the boy who sat hunkered, shivering before the open campfire. It was barely dawn, but Santiago had been unable to sleep for the past several nights. He brooded over his sister, who lived in the lodge a scant fifty feet from where he slept in Hoarse Bark's tepee. Orlena was considered by these people to be Night Wind's wife. She carried his child. Worst and most confusing of all, as he observed the relationship between the renegade and his sister, Santiago realized that she considered herself Night Wind's woman. She had come under his spell.

Now, looking up at the tall, commanding presence of the half-caste, he could understand why it was so. "I have never hunted with bow and arrow," he said uncertainly, his youthful curiosity piqued by the offer.

Night Wind's handsome face split in a smile. "If you can fire a musket, you can learn to fire an arrow—they strike with far more accuracy, once you master the technique." Night Wind watched the boy agonize, looking over to the lodge where Orlena slept. She had been tired the past weeks as the child began to grow in her. He let her sleep and slipped quietly from their pallet many mornings. The boy was over-protective of her and jealous. He wanted to change that and win the loyalty of Conal's cub. "What say you?" he asked again, showing the boy a splendid bow made of Osage orangewood.

Hypnotically, Santiago stood up and reached for the bow, running his fingers along its gleaming length. "It is beautiful," he whispered in awe. Then with a truculent look, he asked Night Wind, "What makes you so certain I will not shoot you with one of those arrows?" He gestured toward the quiver slung carelessly over the half-caste's shoulder.

Night Wind laughed. "You and your sister are much alike. As I treated her, I shall treat you—and never turn my back to provide you an easy target. Is that fair? Or do you wish to stay a prisoner in camp doing women's chores?"

That brought an end to the boy's ambivalence. "I will learn to shoot. But mark me, Night Wind," Santiago said with a tone of voice old beyond his

NIGHT WIND'S WOMAN

years, "do not turn your back and present too tempting a target."

They rode all morning, into brushy, rough terrain, far from the sheltered valley where the band wintered, patiently stalking the fleet elk. Hoarse Bark, Strong Bow, and Cloth Fox accompanied them. As they traveled, Night Wind patiently explained to the boy how the tracking was done, what signs to watch for, and how a small group of men could cooperate to flush a fat deer or elk for one man's easy shot. It was understood that all meat taken was to be shared.

While Cloth Fox, a surly fellow who refused to speak Spanish, rode ahead with Hoarse Bark, the friendly young Strong Bow helped Night Wind give Santiago a bit of target practice. Each man smoothly nocked an arrow against a tautly drawn bowstring and let fly at a small maple sapling, hitting it dead center. Carefully coached by Night Wind, Santiago followed suit. Several arrows went far wide of the mark.

Gritting his teeth in frustration, he said, "If only I had my Miquelet Lock, I could hit the smallest twig on that tree!"

"But how quickly could you fire a second shot?" Strong Bow asked innocently. He quickly nocked and let fly six arrows in blurringly rapid succession. Each found its mark.

"I understand what you mean," Santiago said grimly. "Let me try again."

Having been well trained with long and short arms, Santiago possessed a natural marksman's eye. Allowing for wind and distance were concepts he had already mastered. Hitting a stationary target did not prove too difficult. When the others returned with one large elk and said they had sighted another a short distance away, Santiago was eager to try his new hunting skills. He had been given a pair of soft moccasins, enabling him to walk more quietly than in hard-soled boots, but he quickly learned how many skills he had yet to master. Kicking a rock and snapping a dead twig, he sent the first elk into flight. The second encounter proved even more disastrous, for he was able to get near enough for a clean shot. A slight movement by the animal combined with his own nervousness led him to wound the elk and send it into frenzied flight. Cloth Fox brought it down with one clean shot.

"Quinn's cub has much to learn before he can be Apache," Cloth Fox said contemptuously in perfectly clear Spanish.

"He will learn well enough," Night Wind said, giving the Lipan a quelling look.

"This morning he draws a bow for the first time—and hits his target with little practice," Strong Bow added.

Over the next weeks, Santiago practiced with the bow and with a war lance. He joined the other boys of the camp in their games, learning to run and wrestle, to swim in cold winter weather, impervious to the icy water.

"The boy grows more Lipan each day. It will be a hard thing to return him to his father," White Crane said to Night Wind as they sat watching the children cavort about the central campfire one evening.

"Once I wanted to make him Lipan, to teach him to hate the Spanish, to kill whites. Now, I must send him to Conal for Bartolome," Night Wind replied.

The old man lit his pipe and took a long draw on it. "You would not make him a renegade risking death, even if you did not have to ransom him for the Blue Robe," White Crane said levelly. "He is brother to your wife. His heart is like hers—good. We do not return evil for good."

NIGHT WIND'S WOMAN

"If we return him to Conal, is that not evil?" Night Wind asked. The question had caused him anguish during the weeks since they had abducted the boy.

"You ask this not only about Santiago, but about your woman also." It was not a question.

Looking up from the fire to meet the clear brown eyes of his mentor, Night Wind said with a sad smile, "She Who Dreams is not the only one who sees into men's hearts and minds." He sighed and took a pull from the soothing tobacco himself. Exhaling the fragrant smoke, he pondered. "I fear for Sun in Splendor. She is still Orlena Valdéz, and her life in Spain would have been better than sharing our danger. But Conal lured her here and now... I have added to her hardship. She is too delicate to grow old traveling from the mountains to the plains, moving lodges and building wickiups."

"Yet you would not be parted from her or your child," White Crane supplied. "There is another answer. You are right—the Quinn is evil. But you are half white. You could leave this life and live among the Spanish. This would be good for Sun in Splendor and for Santiago."

"I will never live as a white man! You know why!" Angrily, Night Wind stood up and strode off into the gathering darkness, feeling the old man's sorrowful eyes follow him.

"You have received no word from Conal about the exchange?" Orlena asked Night Wind early one morning. They had just made love in the warmth of their bed of thick pelts. Her amber eyes were still heavy lidded with satiated passion as she stroked the hard muscles on his chest, listening to his heartbeat.

"These things take time. Especially in winter, when travel is slower. My men must send my message through several intermediaries to reach Quinn. Then he must reply."

"Santiago is becoming very fond of you, Night Wind," Orlena said hesitantly, uncertain of how to explain her confused feelings.

"Like sister, like brother," he teased and nuzzled a fat golden curl away from her cheek. "Are you afraid I will make an Apache out of him?"

"Have you not done so with me?" She pulled away from him and sat up, holding a fluffy fox fur against her bare breasts.

He looked up at her beautiful profile, unable to read her thoughts. "Would you choose to return with him, Lioness?" he asked softly.

"No. I cannot. But I am a woman, and he will be a man. It is different for Santiago."

"That is not what I asked you, Sun in Splendor—wife. If you could choose without penalty, what would you do? Remain with me . . . or return to be Conal's darling?" Hurt and anger warred within him. He had enslaved her body, but did he hold any part of her heart? Gently, he reached one long-fingered hand up and turned her chin so her eyes met his.

They gleamed with unshed tears. Her hand softly caressed his in an unconscious gesture of conciliation. "Things now are not what they were. It is useless to pose hypothetical questions. I do not know what I would do if I could choose the circumstances under which we met." *Unless you loved me. Then nothing else would matter.*

Chapter 15

The weather had warmed a bit, hinting of spring. Santiago and two other youths, Swallow Hawk and Yellow Deer, decided on a great adventure.

"I thought the caves were forbidden. My sister told me a fearful tale about them," Santiago said, remembering Orlena's story about falling through the ground.

"We do not go south, but north. I know a place where grass is plentiful. Great sheep with the round horns abound. They are easy to kill. Their meat is sweet and juicy," Yellow Deer said. Being sixteen to the other two youths' mere thirteen, he carried the day.

In the afternoon, Night Wind noticed that Santiago was missing, as were the fleet bay pony he had given the boy, and his bow and arrows. Half fearful the youth had tried to escape once more, he sought out

White Crane, who often oversaw the boy's activities.

"Those young rascals took off on a hunt of their own, I would bet. Swallow Hawk and Yellow Deer are gone, too. Best you follow them lest harm befall. She Who Dreams had a vision of a bear last night. I do not like it."

A few questions of the women washing clothing by the stream gave him their direction. Quickly he picked up a trail. After a few hours, Night Wind's annoyance turned to genuine concern. The foolish boys had headed toward a cave-infested stretch of mountains, not the below-ground caverns to the south where the earth gave way, but dangerous enough if they were tempted into one of the openings in the hillsides.

Just then his worst fears were realized. Warpaint began to shy and prance nervously. Only two things affected the seasoned horse so—a puma or a bear. Pumas were creatures of the night and seldom attacked men unless they were starving. Spring meant the end of a winter of sleep for the bears in their lairs. Such hungry giants were deadly.

Santiago and his companions had just found out how true that was. A large black bear was peacefully fishing in a stream when the boys crashed through the woods, stumbling on him completely unawares. Although Swallow Hawk managed to hold his seat on his pony, Yellow Deer's bolted out of control and Santiago was dumped to earth a scant few yards from the frightened and foul-tempered beast.

Landing on his back with the wind knocked from him, he struggled to sit up and reach for an arrow, only to find his bow was still attached to the galloping bay's blanket strap. His arrows were spilled across the ground. Quickly he pulled a small knife from his belt,

NIGHT WIND'S WOMAN

woefully underarmed for the confrontation. Swallow Hawk let fly two arrows, wounding and further enraging the animal without even slowing his shambling approach to the crouching boy.

Santiago knew with a sweep of his eye that there was no refuge in the stream or the brushy woods on its bank. Bears were surprisingly fleet for such clumsy-looking beasts, and they even climbed trees! He stood and readied himself for the deadly claws as the animal reared up on its hind legs and swatted. His blade connected with one paw, slashing a wicked cut in the bear's pad, but the impact of contact sent the knife spinning from his numb fingers. Preparing for the embrace of death as several more arrows from Swallow Hawk proved ineffectual, Santiago stood tall and took a deep breath.

Just then a shot rang out, deafening the boy. Before his eyes the shaggy black monster fell backward, with a splattered red hole squarely between its eyes.

Night Wind stood with his musket still smoking. "Sometimes a bullet works better than a bow," he said quietly as the boy ran toward him.

Dropping the gun, he hugged Santiago to his chest fiercely. "You were very foolish, but very brave, little brother."

Night Wind entered the lodge where Hoarse Bark and Santiago sat, eating in companionable silence. Taking a large bite from a skewered slab of beef, the boy wiped the trickling juices from his chin with one brown hand. Were it not for his curly red hair, he looked as dark as a warrior. His skin was bronzed by the sun until all his freckles seemed to merge into a solid tan. He wore an old buckskin shirt and leggins with high moccasins laced over his muscular calves.

In the scant three months he had stayed with them, the boy had adapted well.

"I would speak with the brother of my wife," Night Wind said to Hoarse Bark, who immediately arose, taking with him a fistful of sotol cakes and a skewer of the roasted beef, freshly butchered from their small herd.

Santiago looked at the water-stained roll of paper in Night Wind's hand. "You have word from my father." It was not a question. Neither was it full of the defiance or joy both would have expected when the youth had been captured.

"Yes. He will make the exchange of Fray Bartolome for you. Next month is the feast of Our Lady of Lights. Santa Fe will be full of revelers from all across the province. The roads will be filled with people. In the confusion, we will arrange your return and the priest's safe release."

"You suspect my father of treachery, do you not?" Over the months, Santiago had heard too many stories of how Conal Quinn had risen to glory. He could no longer ignore his father's bloody past.

Night Wind shrugged. "I took your sister. He took Bartolome. Now I took you. It is an ancient fight between the Spanish and the Apache." He paused, studying the youth. "Your father loves you, whatever his faults. He will be overjoyed to have you back."

"And I suppose I must go. Back to hot leather armor, stupid heavy saddles, satin dress breeches with shoes that pinch my feet—and books. I hate Latin! I would rather stay here and be a warrior. I killed two fat elk last week," the boy volunteered eagerly. Then, seeing the set expression on Night Wind's face, he subsided with a long sigh. "No, I suppose I must become a Spanish gentleman and learn Latin. Even French," he added with a shudder. "I will miss

NIGHT WIND'S WOMAN

Orlena . . . and you and everyone here who has taught me."

Night Wind felt his chest constrict. The injustice of it all! Why must his world be so cruelly divided? "About Orlena . . . your father doted upon her back in Madrid, even took her to New Spain. Would he treat her well if I sent her back with you?" The words were wrenched from him, but he had to consider what was ultimately best for her and their child. One day soon the Spanish would own this land in truth. His child could be on the victorious side, even if he could not.

Santiago was stunned. It had seemed to him that Night Wind was devoted to Orlena. He knew, even though she had never said so exactly, that she loved the half-caste. His eyes narrowed as he replied, "You took her and made her pregnant. My father could not hide what has happened to her—even if he wished to. She is your wife. You should marry her in the Church. When the priest is ransomed, he can do this, else she will be forever disgraced in the eyes of white men." He paused, unable to read the shuttered face of the man who had become his hero over the past months. "Do you not want Orlena, Night Wind? What of your child?"

"What I want and what is best for them are not the same," was the cryptic reply.

"You will marry her," Santiago insisted with dogged determination.

"If the lady agrees, yes, Little Bear, I will wed her in your Church."

Since Santiago's encounter with the black bear, his bravery in facing death had earned him the name Little Bear among the Lipan. Now he would leave all his wild freedoms behind—and his sister as well—to return to his responsibilities as the governor's son. At that moment, both Night Wind and Little Bear thought life cruelly unfair.

Every son and daughter of the Church loved a fiesta, whether they were *ricos* or *paisanos*, pure-blooded or *castas*. The numerous holidays scattered throughout the year involved far more than piety, although each began with a religious procession. Statues of saints were carried across the plaza, and a solemn mass was said. For days before, farmers and ranchers, miners and soldiers gathered in Santa Fe awaiting the feasting, music, and dancing that always accompanied the celebration.

Fray Bartolome alone worried about the future as he looked out on the plaza crowded with crude wooden carts and spirited horses. Peasants in simple white cotton clothing and gentlemen in silver-trimmed wool suits ambled about in a spirit of camaraderie.

If Chihuahua City had seemed a wilderness to Fray Bartolome, filled with barbarous men, New Mexico was far worse. So far from the royal arm of law and order, the isolated north was an island of political corruption.

Living in the governor's palace under house arrest, he was allowed to perform mass daily in a small private chapel. After that, he stopped by the kitchens to eat a simple meal and talk with the servants. Then he availed himself of Quinn's library. Although meager by his standards, it contained some surprisingly fine, if not pious works—a smattering of Greek mythology, Roman history, even the highly suspect if enjoyable adventures of Cervantes' Don Quijote. Although the Irishman was well read and glib, it was for the education of his son Santiago that he had brought the extensive reading materials. The priest wished devoutly to meet both the boy and his sister.

In listening to servants and soldiers gossip, Fray Bartolome learned that the new governor had taken the license for bribery inherent in his office to new heights. His extortion of bribes in lieu of the unrealistically high royal taxes was exceeded only by his brutality in dealing with the Indians, both Comanche and most especially all the various tribes of Apache. Long before he had sailed in triumph for Spain, Quinn was known among the Indians as Colorado, the Bloody One. Bartolome had seen first-hand the extent of his perfidy with Joaquín, but now that Orlena and Santiago had been taken, Quinn was as dangerous and unpredictable as a cornered cougar.

The priest had been summoned that morning to the governor's office. His heart filled with dread, Bartolome waited while he overheard Quinn receiving a payment from one of his lieutenants. Why had he been asked to wait in these private chambers? Had the exchange of the boy for him been completed? What of the young woman Joaquín held?

Fray Bartolome feared what would ultimately befall the star-crossed life of his brilliant pupil. Quinn's treachery knew no limits and brought forth an answering savagery in Joaquín that made the priest heartsick.

The governor's large oak desk was filled with papers. Perhaps if he could find some damning evidence of Conal's blatant corruption among them, he could have him recalled from office by the viceroy. Checking the door, he walked over to the papers and began to scan them quickly with a scholar's practiced eye.

Amid requisitions for presidio payrolls, letters of recommendation for officers' promotions, and various tax collection documents, one single sheet of paper caught Fray Bartolome's eye. He had taught the beautiful penmanship to this writer—he would recognize Joaquín's hand anywhere, even if the missive had not been signed.

Before he could read it, the heavy door to the office moved. Quickly slipping the small paper into the folds of his robe, he moved away from the desk and stared calmly out the window.

Conal dismissed the pesky Sergeant Ruiz, who had just collected taxes from the outlying ranches, a fat bit of coin he could put to excellent use outfitting the men he would use to hunt down and kill Night Wind once Santiago was safe. He looked at the stiff back of the priest and muttered an oath, damning the ill fortune that brought Ignacio Valdéz to New Spain at precisely this time.

"The viceroy's emissary feels I have done you a grave injustice," he said impenitently to Bartolome.

The Franciscan turned and affixed Quinn with shrewd gray eyes. "I can see how concerned you are with his excellency, Don Ignacio. I doubt you have summoned me to impart that bit of news," he added drily.

"No. I have other, more pressing problems. I will deal with Valdéz later. Your savage has finally responded. He will return my son for your freedom. We make the exchange during the feast celebration. He has chosen the place."

Bartolome considered, not liking Quinn's apparent calmness. "Night Wind's word is good. If he says he brings the boy unharmed in honest exchange, he will do so. But what of you, your excellency? Will you lay a trap once you have the lad?"

Conal shrugged, then laughed. The harshness of the sound disturbed the priest, sending a chill of premonition down his spine.

NIGHT WIND'S WOMAN

"You did well with his education, Priest," Conal said coldly. "He sets up the conditions most carefully. I must give you to his intermediaries and take back Santiago somewhere on the crowded road between here and Taos. He will choose when and where. I like it not, but he yet holds Orlena. I would not see her further harmed else I would certainly entrap him."

"Night Wind is a man of honor. He keeps his word," the friar rebuked him.

Conal's fist smashed the thick oaken table, sending loud reverberations around the room. "I reserve honor for civilized men who deserve it. Stinking savages are lower than curs. They possess no honor!"

"And no souls?" Bartolome probed.

"What would you do, turn me over to the Holy Office for uttering heresy? I know the Church has bestowed souls on these black, conscienceless animals. As a soldier, 'tis none of my affair what you do with them in the next world—I must deal with them in this one. Be ready to travel within the week. And rejoice, Father. Soon you will be reunited with your student. Would that he had not proven such an apt pupil."

It was nearly midnight and the tallow candle on Conal's desk had almost burned out. He did not want to have it replaced now because this meeting was secret, between him and Lieutenant Terris.

"You are certain this Jicarilla is the one?"

"Yes, excellency. In the past months, I have had two men from the village following all the Indian militia as you instructed. This Juanito is the one who rides out alone often. One of the village women saw him talk with a man who she thinks was the half-caste, only days before your son was taken."

"Good. Have the Jicarilla followed closely at all times from here on. Do not allow him to escape. I will have need of him shortly. That will be all for now, Lieutenant."

"Will it be soon now?" Santiago asked as Night Wind scanned the trail below. They were on a particularly desolate, rough stretch of terrain on the Taos end of the Royal Road.

"Yes. I see your father's men. Fray Bartolome is with them and no others lie in wait to give chase anywhere along the trail." Night Wind set down the glass he had used to identify the riders from the mountain where the renegades hid. "This road is rough for an old man used to riding only mules, but he will have to do his best." Night Wind looked at the boy and felt profound regret wash over him again. "We have opened many doors these past months, Little Bear," he said quietly.

Mute with misery for a moment, Santiago struggled to clear his throat and then said, "I will never forget what you and White Crane and all the others have taught me. I . . . I will miss my sister, too. When the baby is born, I would know . . ." His voice choked off. Parting from Orlena had been very painful, and now he was finding, inexplicably, that parting from Night Wind was proving even more so.

"We will meet again. You will play with your nieces and nephews, Little Bear. I swear this to you, and a Lipan never breaks his oath. But for now you must be Santiago again. Tell your father as little as possible. It will be easier that way."

"Think you so? I do not! I will try to allay his fears about Orlena. I do not believe he will heed me, though," Santiago added gloomily.

NIGHT WIND'S WOMAN

"It is time to go. Look you, they approach the place I have marked." Night Wind embraced the boy one final time and then stood on the craggy hillside watching him descend, a small, solitary figure against the bleak landscape.

Sergeant Ruiz looked ahead and saw two of Night Wind's Apache raiders riding around a sharp bend in the trail. Putting up one hand, he waited as the party of twenty heavily armed soldiers stopped behind him with the priest. The Lipans would signal for the boy to walk free when Fray Bartolome was clear.

Conal watched the emissaries approach through slitted eyes, darting glances at the sharply rising bluffs around them. *He could be hiding anywhere.* A slow smile spread across his face as he thought about the Jicarilla, Juanito. Night Wind would yet curse the day he had stolen Santiago Quinn.

Fray Bartolome observed Quinn with an acute sense of unease. Why was he so calm? Earlier, when the exchange had first been arranged, he had been as tense as an overwound watch. Something was amiss. He smelled a trap. Both men were desperate and dangerous, alike in their blood lust. He said another prayer for the innocent youth beginning to climb down the hill after he had urged his mule toward the Lipan riders. *Precious Savior, preserve the boy and his sister, I implore in your name.* In spite of his misgivings, no additional soldiers materialized from behind the rocks and scrub brush to thunder down on their small group.

As soon as the priest reached the two Lipan men, Santiago approached the soldiers, walking slowly. But Fray Bartolome had no time to ponder how odd it was that the youth did not run to his father. The exchange went smoothly. On Night Wind's signal, the Apaches took off at a canter that the priest's mule was hard pressed to match. As soon as they clamored up the twisting, rocky path to the summit of the hill, Night Wind appeared with a fresh horse for Fray Bartolome.

They rode until well past midnight, stopping for nothing. Finally, beneath the light of a brilliant spring moon, an enchanted scene appeared. Seeming to materialize out of nowhere, the small hidden valley was graced by a twisting silver ribbon of water with lush stands of rustling oaks along the banks.

"We will camp here and rest your weary bones, which I know are far better suited to kneeling in prayer or hunching over a book," Night Wind said as he reined in beside the exhausted priest.

Arching his bushy brows, Bartolome said, "And your bones do not in the least need a respite from the jarring of that demon?" He motioned to the heaving piebald as he dismounted.

This was their first opportunity to speak since the headlong flight had begun that noon.

"You are unharmed—other than by the ride?" Joaquín asked in seriousness as one of his men built a fire and the others began to rub down the sweat-soaked horses.

"I am unharmed, yes, in body. Conal Quinn can do naught to me, Joaquín—at least not to my spirit. But you . . . you have done so," the older man said quietly.

Joaquín's eyes clouded with resignation. "You charge me with my sins in taking the boy. He enjoyed his time with the Lipan. We did him no injury. Come, let us speak of this thing in the house." He walked toward a dense stand of oaks, whose dark branches embraced a small adobe building. At the priest's surprised look, he added, "It belonged to a family of sheep ranchers. They all died of smallpox some years ago. I have been using it as a rendezvous point."

Lighting a small tallow candle on the crude wooden table, Joaquín motioned for the priest to sit down on a sturdy oak chair.

"It is you who should sit, I think," Bartolome responded.

"As I did when I was your pupil in school?" He walked over and placed one moccasined foot on the seat of the chair, then turned to Bartolome. "I told you only that I would not kill Quinn. I also swore I would be revenged."

"Enough!" The priest pulled from his robe a rolled-up paper and slapped it down on the table. "You take your war to women and boys now! Even if I were to excuse the abduction of Santiago because you wished only to save my life, I can never excuse this. This is evil. The man who wrote this thinks and acts as Conal Quinn would!"

Joaquín paled as he recognized his letter to Conal, written so long ago, a lifetime ago. "That was a mistake," he said quietly.

"What have you done with the girl? Do you deny seducing her? Using her, an innocent child, as a pawn in your revenge?"

Joaquín met the priest's accusing gray eyes levelly. "She is at our wintering place in the Guadalupes. I have married her, Bartolome. She carries my child. I will never give her back to Conal."

The Franciscan stopped and stared, speechless for a moment, then threw back his shaggy head of graying brown hair and roared with laughter. "You have had the scales of fortune reverse themselves well enough! You stole this girl and she stole your heart. I imagine that was not in your plan, eh?" He looked at Joaquín with a delighted grin slashing his face. "A child, you say. If your tribal elders permitted a marriage, they must have accepted her."

"Orlena is Sun in Splendor, daughter to White Crane and She Who Dreams," Joaquín replied with evident irritation in his voice. He did not enjoy feeling the fool this explanation seemed to make him.

Sensing the ambivalent feelings boiling beneath the surface of Joaquín's carefully controlled facade, the friar sat down and waited until the younger man did the same. "I think there is much to this tale that I would know, but we will have some time to sort it out later. Only know this. I am happy for you. You have been alone for too much of your life. Now you have begun to learn love instead of hate. I think you will find it far more sustaining."

"I have not said I loved her," Joaquín replied defensively. "She carries my child and I would not dishonor her."

"You also said you would never return her to Conal. That was not revenge speaking. You can hide your feelings from yourself, Joaquín, but you have never long hidden them from me. You care for this Orlena Valdéz—and for her brother, I think."

"Santiago is a fine boy. As unlike Conal as—"

Joaquín's words were interrupted by the pounding of hooves and an outcry from the sentries. Fearing they had been set upon by Conal's soldiers, he leaped up and raced for the door. "Hide yourself in the trees behind the cabin and pray as you have never before prayed," he called out as he vanished through the door.

A small group of riders were dismounting by the flickering light of the fire. As they drew nearer, Night Wind could see they were Lipan. His men exchanged hearty greetings with them. Suddenly, one small figure darted from the group and ran toward him as he walked into the circle of light.

"Night Wind! I had to come." Orlena's arms reached out to him and enveloped him in a fierce embrace.

Chapter 16

Joaquín embraced her tightly for a moment, then roughly gripped her shoulders and held her at arm's length. "What are you doing here? It is days from the stronghold through dangerous territory. If you care not for yourself, think of the child."

"I do care for our child, with all my heart," she defended. "I knew you would be angry, but I had to come. White Crane and She Who Dreams understood. They gave me escort. I did not ride alone, Night Wind."

Scowling, he looked at several younger warriors, including Strong Bow. "So, you have enlisted your malleable parents in this madness. Why, Orlena?" He placed one arm protectively over her shoulders and began to walk away from the group, out of earshot.

Orlena's thoughts were jumbled and all her carefully rehearsed speeches deserted her. One look from those angry green eyes and her mind spun dizzily.

"I . . . I needed to know the exchange was made safely, that my brother is all right," she began hesitantly.

He scoffed, "Santiago is back in Conal's loving arms. Does that reassure you?"

His sarcasm cut her and she blurted out, "I did not ask of Conal, but only feared for my brother and my husband." The minute the words escaped her lips, she wished to call them back. Her pride demanded it. Her pride also demanded she look him squarely in the eye and face whatever scorn or pity Night Wind might reveal.

Predictably, his expression was shuttered and hard. "I have told you we are both well," he said flatly.

"What of the Franciscan? Is he here?" Orlena waited for his reaction, knowing he would be wary of her motives, as he was of all she did.

"Bartolome is in the cabin. When it is safe, I will arrange escort for him to return to Chihuahua City—after the bishop in Durango has been informed of Conal's actions."

"I rather imagine the bishop will be informed quite soon by this lady's elder brother," Fray Bartolome interrupted. He had followed Joaquín from the cabin, worried about what ill news the riders might have brought. Then he saw the blonde woman run into Joaquín's arms and knew she was his new bride.

Orlena looked up at the towering giant of a man with a bushy dark beard streaked with gray. He looked fierce and formidable and his words about Ignacio jarred her.

"You do not appear as I had imagined you," she said with a gulp, all her inbred Spanish pride suddenly deserting her.

"And how, Doña Orlena, did you imagine me?" His gray eyes glowed warmly.

She responded hesitantly, "Oh, slight and stooped over from much studying." Turning her small pointed chin up, she smiled at him and was rewarded with a rich chuckle. "You said Ignacio has come from Spain?" She bit her lip in vexation. Wherever her older brother went, trouble followed.

"Yes, he arrived in Santa Fe while I was a *guest* of your stepfather. It appeared the two do not share any family loyalties," he said drily.

"Ignacio hates Conal," Orlena replied baldly. "He has come to ruin him and to drag me back to Spain for a monstrous marriage that would benefit him."

"You still have not explained why you came here," Joaquín interrupted.

Orlena looked from her husband to the priest, then back to Night Wind. "I would like to speak privately with Fray Bartolome."

"To confess your sins, Lioness? You have committed none. They are all mine, as the good father has already reminded me," he said with a wrenching mixture of defeat and sadness in his voice.

Orlena put one small hand on his chest and felt his heartbeat accelerate. "You mistake me, Night Wind. I do not wish to confess, only to learn . . ." Her voice faded.

Fray Bartolome watched the exchange and realized what Orlena sought. She was Conal Quinn's stepdaughter—and his renegade enemy's wife. Dare he tell her the truth? He looked at Joaquín's hard, cold face, suddenly filled with vulnerability and pain. *He has not told her.*

"There is much to be said for a willing pupil," the priest interjected, smiling in reassurance at her, then looking at Joaquín. "Once, many years ago, I had a very bright pupil, eager to learn, a delight to teach. He grew up to be a fine man. Flawed, human . . . but a

NIGHT WIND'S WOMAN

fine man. And now he has chosen a fine woman for his wife." He paused and looked at Joaquín reassuringly. "I will tell her of my favorite student. There are some things she must hear only from you, my son . . . when you are ready to tell her."

Joaquín nodded silently and walked away, vanishing into the darkness like his Apache namesake. Fray Bartolome escorted Orlena into the cabin and offered her a chair. One of the men had brought fresh water to drink while they were outside. A pouch of jerked beef and dried fruit lay beside the cooling refreshment.

"Here, sit. You and your babe must be weary."

Orlena felt the heat rise to her cheeks. "The Church has not blessed our union. But I do not want you to blame Night Wind. I . . . I came to him willingly." She met his eyes and saw no condemnation, only the faintest hint of a mysterious smile.

"So, you love him. And he, I believe, has come to love you as well. Joaquín should not have stolen you from your family—"

"That is part of what I wish to learn about." Orlena interrupted him, leaning forward, the food and water forgotten. "You call him Joaquín. You educated him to be white, but he chose to be Apache. His hatred has something to do with my stepfather. Father, I have always loved Conal Quinn, since childhood. Yet I have learned things about him since coming to New Spain —things that frighten me."

The priest looked at her wide golden eyes, filled with confusion, as vulnerable as Joaquín's had been the first time they met. He began very carefully, "Sometimes a man can be two men. When you grow up in one world and then are forced to leave it and enter another, this can change you. I left the cloistered world of books in Santander and sailed to New Spain where I ended up ministering to Indians and peasants who live impoverished lives in a frightful wilderness. This has changed me. Conal Quinn came to this strange new world as a youth, out to make his fortune as a soldier, without the constraints and blessings of the Church which have sustained me. The man you met in Spain and the man he has become again in New Mexico are not the same. To Conal Quinn, Indians are not people. They are animals, to be used as such."

Remembering the scars on her husband's back, his feverish nightmares about the mines, she shuddered. "I must know. Was Conal in charge of the soldiers who . . . who killed Night Wind's mother and burned his village, who sold him into slavery?"

Her anguish was a palpable thing. Bartolome could feel her pain reach out to him in much the same way a young boy's pain had those long years ago. "Yes, Orlena, Conal Quinn sold children into slavery in the mines of Nueva Viscaya. But they were Apache children—not human to him, people without reason, people without souls."

"He was so kind to me. I was five when he married my mother. My father never loved me or Ignacio. Poor Ignacio. No one ever loved him, I suppose. And he learned to love no one," she added with a shudder as his cruel yellow eyes flashed before her.

"But Conal became your champion?" Bartolome asked gently. "A man can be two people, as I said. Only remember the good part of him. Forgive the evil and put it behind you. Teach Joaquín to do the same. You are the only one who can reach him—you do know that, do you not?"

Orlena looked startled. "I am not certain of that at all. He has shown me kindness and treated me fairly after I came to his people, but"—she paused in stricken pain, then whispered—"he was forced to wed me by the law of his people. He never has said he loves me. Joaquín"—the name sounded alien on her tongue—"my husband never has spoken of love, only duty," she finished sadly.

The priest reached across the table and took her delicate hand in his. He could see the callouses on her palms and the abrasions from rough work. Joaquín should take her to a safe place, make a secure life for her. Living as Apaches would bring them both to early graves. "Your husband loves you, Orlena. He is a hard and solitary man. You know of his childhood, the pain and humiliation he endured in the mines. But there is more. Only remember now what I have said, for I know him well. In time he will tell you the rest and you must accept it, no matter how bitter the truth. Nothing worth having is easily gained, else we would not value it."

As they sat in reflective silence for a moment, Joaquín walked through the door. Seeing the friar holding Orlena's hands in earnest conversation, he felt a sudden flash of resentment. *What has he told her that her devilish mind can use against me?* "Several of the warriors from my band who have never seen a Blue Robe want to meet the prodigy of wisdom and tolerance I have so often described," he said with a wry twist to his mouth.

"So, you have filled their heads with fairy tales and now I, a man of clay, must appear to disillusion them," Fray Bartolome said, laughing. "Let us leave your wife to rest and refresh herself. Then we must see to sleeping arrangements, for this shelter will hold only the two of you."

Now Joaquín did smile openly. "Ever blunt and practical, Priest," he said affectionately as they left Orlena sitting alone at the table.

She chewed the dry, spicy jerked meat, softened

with sips of water, all the while thinking about the friar's words. What did Night Wind—or Joaquín—have to confess to her? *You must accept it, no matter how bitter the truth.* The words haunted her. What had the priest meant? He knew another side of her husband, the white side, that she had never really seen.

Her back ached from the long ride and she was tired, but before she rested, she must eat some more. Ever since the child had begun to grow in her, her appetite had grown with it! Reaching for the pouch full of meat and fruit, she saw a rolled piece of paper lying on the edge of the long table, partially covered by the water bucket. Curiously, she pulled it from beneath the rusty container belonging to the luckless *paisanos* who had long ago toiled in this valley.

The paper was new, obviously not left by the adobe's former owner. Some intuition told her not to read it, but her curiosity won out. It had been so long since she had seen anything to read. The script was beautiful, easily legible, as if composed with great precision. Then she saw the salutation, to Conal. Her eyes raced to the signature of Night Wind, then rose with dread to read the message in its crushing entirety.

"I may yet take one or two of your young men, especially Strong Bow, I think, down to that stream and baptize them," Fray Bartolome said as they walked back to the adobe. "Failing that, I will certainly put the blessing of the Church on your marriage to Orlena."

Joaquín grunted. "If not one sacrament, another. You toil overlong in the vineyards, Blue Robe." His voice was oddly light and teasing. If Bartolome approved of the match, might it not be a good idea to wed in the Church?

When he stepped inside the door, he suddenly

froze, nearly causing the larger man behind him to knock him over.

"What is wrong, Joaquín?" His eyes went from his stricken friend to Orlena, who was holding Joaquín's letter to Conal crumpled in her hands. "She can read?" he whispered in amazement and horror. Virtually no Spanish ladies learned more than to sign their names. He had never in his fifty-odd years encountered a literate female. What had he done, carelessly leaving the purloined letter lying on the table after their argument?

"Yes, Bartolome—Orlena can read," Joaquín replied sadly. "Lioness, what I wrote at that time, what I intended then—"

"You intended to seduce me—to *use* me and then send me back to Conal. When did you think to complete your vengeance—before or after your child was born? Would you deign to keep it, having such contempt for my Spanish blood?" Her voice crackled with fury, but her eyes overflowed with burning tears that she made no attempt to staunch.

Joaquín walked toward her slowly, agonizing over what to say, intent only on holding her in his arms. He could never let her go! Too late, perhaps, he realized that fact.

"Do not touch me, Night Wind—Joaquín, whoever you really are. I will not fall under your spell again." She backed away, hurling the balled-up paper at him.

Ignoring her outburst, he moved after her, desperately needing to absorb the pain he had inflicted on her. He reached out and pulled her rigid, unresisting body against his own. Running his arms up and down her back, he buried his face against her neck, whispering low, "I love you, Lioness. Yes, I did plan to use you for my vengeance, but I did not know this would happen between us."

So long Orlena had prayed to hear his declaration of love. Now she had it, but could she believe it? She felt numb and exhausted, buffeted like a galleon in a hurricane, unable to think rationally with this man, her lover, *her beloved*, holding her so possessively, murmuring love words in her ear, kissing her neck. The urge to cling to him nearly overwhelmed her, but pride held her back and she kept her hands clenched into fists at her sides.

Just then, shots erupted in the still night air. Shouts and hoofbeats echoed from down the valley as a large number of riders came thundering into their camp.

Night Wind quickly pushed Orlena beneath the table, ordering, "Remain here under cover. Do not come out unless I call you!" He turned to the priest, who had returned from outside to warn him. "Stay with her!"

All he carried was the knife at his waist. His guns, his hunting bow, every weapon, lay across the clearing at the campfire where chaos now erupted. Sweeping the scene with a quick glance, he could see more than a dozen Spanish leathercoats mixed with a good number of Indian militia—the hated Comanche. No wonder the sentries gave no warning!

Slipping from the adobe hut into the shelter of the trees, he made a quick decision. Everyone would be killed if resistance continued, but the heavily armed soldiers could never catch a lightly mounted Apache. "Flee to the mountains and scatter," he cried out. "Return to the stronghold!"

Even over the battle's din they recognized their leader's voice. The Apache evaporated into the night, one or two at a time. Several lay dead, sprawled grotesquely on the bloody earth. Their bodies were quickly obscured as one fleeing Lipan kicked dust over the coals, extinguishing the eerily dancing flames of the campfire.

Suddenly Night Wind felt the prick of a knife blade at his throat. Another blade flashed across his chest and was positioned low on his abdomen. Both Comanche were set to draw blood, yet apparently were under orders not to kill him. Using the advantage, he kicked at one man and knocked the other's blade clear of his throat, spinning to the side to escape the deadly trap. Several more of his foes jumped him. He could not count how many before darkness descended on him.

A bucket of water splashed across Night Wind's face, then a second caused him to cough and choke as he slowly opened his eyes. The fire had been relit and illuminated the grisly carnage about the camp. Conal Quinn stood towering over him with a look of feral satisfaction radiating from his harsh face.

Joaquín struggled to focus his eyes on his hated enemy. Giving his aching head a vicious shake to clear it, he began to rise, but strong Comanche arms held him fast as Conal placed one booted foot on his chest.

"So, Night Wind, after all these years, we meet again. I do regret the circumstances," he said grimly, looking over to where two of his guards were escorting Orlena and Fray Bartolome from the house. "But you will pay dearly for taking her and my son."

"How did you find this valley?" Night Wind asked calmly, his heart seized with terror for his band hidden in the winter stronghold.

"Juanito would not tell Sergeant Ruiz where you had taken the priest, even under extreme duress. But when we brought his wife and children to the guardhouse . . . he did not want them disfigured." He gave Joaquín a vicious kick and spun to face Orlena, who stood frozen in horror at his words.

"You would torture a woman and her children?" she said, incredulously. So much evidence had already damned Conal; this was but another example of the two men inside him that Fray Bartolome had described to her.

"What has he done to you, Butterfly?" Conal asked, ignoring her revulsion at his earlier words. "I did not expect the good fortune of rescuing you so soon."

Night Wind broke free of the two Comanche and lunged at Quinn's back, but was quickly recaptured. It took three men to subdue him, and that only after Conal had threatened, "Hold, or I will kill the priest!"

At once Night Wind ceased his struggling. He stood quivering with rage. A thin trickle of blood ran down his temple and several bruises discolored his face. Hate radiated from his eyes as he watched Quinn turn and reach for Orlena's hand, pulling her from Fray Bartolome's protection.

"Come here, Butterfly. This filth cannot harm you again, nor can his renegade allies," he added with a cold look of contempt at the Franciscan.

"Night Wind did not harm me, Conal," she replied quietly, resisting his attempt to enfold her in his arms.

"How can you say that when he kidnapped you and sent me word of his plans to abuse you in revenge against me? I will take you home, never fear. You will forget this as if it were only a brief nightmare." He held her close, hearing the struggle of the infuriated captive behind him.

As he turned to gloat at the half-caste, Orlena again pushed away his arm. "I will not ever forget my time with the Lipan, and it was not a nightmare, Conal. Finding out that you sold children into slavery was the true nightmare," she said.

NIGHT WIND'S WOMAN

Conal's expression turned from triumph to fury. "What I did to some Apache animals years ago has nothing to do with you, Orlena. I have already told you that life in this hellish place is lived by different rules. You will forget the past."

"I cannot! Even if the good people of Santa Fe would allow me to reenter their society, they would not accept my child, and I will not reject it." Her hands protectively cupped the slight swell of her belly as she pressed the loose buckskin tunic about it, revealing her pregnancy to Conal.

A flash of fire shot from his eyes as he snarled at her, "You do not seem at all shamed. Would you keep the child as a remembrance of your rape?"

"Night Wind did not rape me, Conal. I came willingly to him," she said in a whisper.

His hand lashed out and he struck her with all his strength, knocking her backward into Fray Bartolome's arms.

Night Wind broke free of the Comanche holding him and grabbed Quinn by his neck, which he would have snapped but for the rapid recovery of the two guards and a soldier. As they restrained him, Conal turned, rubbing his throat.

"So, she was your squaw. Well, I have reclaimed her now, Green-Eyed Boy." Quinn spat the words at the half-caste. "You had your way with a foolish virgin. I hope she was good, for now you will pay for your pleasures."

"You always were a coward, Irishman, murdering men in their sleep, then selling their women and children for Spanish gold," Night Wind flung back, straining to lunge again at his hated enemy.

"The woman and child in question were mine to do with as I pleased," Quinn said with contemptuous dismissal.

Night Wind hissed a guttural oath in Apache as the older man's fist smashed into his midsection. He coughed, but did not double over in spite of the wicked blow.

"Once I swore to kill you. I am yet alive to keep my oath."

Orlena's eyes flashed from one tall, slim man to the other. Their coloring was startlingly different, Conal with his fair skin and curly red hair, Night Wind bronzed, with inky straight locks. But both arrogant, chiseled faces matched in profile as two pairs of icy green eyes glared at each other.

She felt the breath sucked from her body and nearly fainted as Fray Bartolome supported her. "Blessed Virgin, Conal is his father!" she cried.

"His baptismal name was Joaquín Maria Alejandro Quinn," the priest replied sadly.

Chapter 17

"I give no Apache bastard my name," Conal snarled at Bartolome.

"God gave him life through you—your name went along with the act," the friar replied calmly as he faced the livid mercenary.

"You sold your own son into that living hell?" Orlena whispered, almost in disbelief. The horror of it all made her violently ill and she choked back bitter bile as she looked at Conal, truly seeing him for the first time in her life. The blinders of childhood were removed now, and Bartolome's words made sense. So this was Joaquín's darkest secret—sharing the blood of a monster like Conal Quinn!

Conal saw her recoil from him and swore again, looking with disgust at her thickening figure. Damn the savage, he had kept the promise made in his letter! He turned back to his half-caste son. "I will kill you for this—so slowly that you will beg for death before I am done!"

"You cannot kill your own son—any more than he can kill you. This insanity will send both of you to your eternal damnation!" Fray Bartolome thundered. Setting Orlena gently aside, the big Franciscan strode boldly to where the two men confronted each other. Several of the soldiers crossed themselves in fear. Even the Comanche, sensing the aura of power about the white holy man, backed away.

Conal laughed harshly. "You would damn me, Priest? I am already bound for hell."

"To send him there, I would join him," Night Wind added.

"Stop it! Both of you may be damned until the end of eternity for all I care, but I will not let you destroy your son." Orlena turned from Joaquín to Conal. "Or your grandson!"

"Let me marry you and give the church's blessing to your child," Fray Bartolome asked Orlena. When she looked back to Joaquín, the priest's level gray eyes fixed on him as well.

"I forbid it!" Conal shouted.

"Would you have me return to Ignacio in Santa Fe carrying a bastard?" Orlena interrupted, suddenly needing to have the words spoken before a priest. *I love you*, Night Wind had said. Did he? Did Joaquín Quinn love her?

Conal considered her words. So the meddlesome Franciscan had told her of her brother's arrival. *I must deal with Ignacio's wrath when he finds Orlena pregnant by a savage. God and all the Saints preserve me, if Ignacio learns the savage is my bastard!* "Bind him securely to one of those saplings until I decide what to do," he ordered the guards. "Watch the good father. Upon threat of death for his renegade compatriot, I do not think he would do anything rash. Wait for me, Priest," he barked to Bartolome.

Then he strode over to Orlena and said, "Come with me to the adobe. You must rest, lest you harm your babe," he added sarcastically.

Orlena watched the Comanche guards roughly lash Joaquín to a tree, using rawhide bonds that bit cruelly into his arms and chest. He never looked at her. Turning, she walked to the adobe hut. Conal was seated inside, sipping from a small silver flask.

"This is good *aguardiente*, but in your condition, I doubt you should indulge," he said, wiping his mouth with his cuff.

"You must let Father Bartolome marry us, Conal. That way, no matter what else you do, you can tell my brother I am not dishonored. The priest can give him assurances as well." She waited in dread, knowing there was little hope of saving Night Wind's life. But if Conal was afraid enough of Ignacio, this might be a way to delay the inevitable. Perhaps Fray Bartolome could come up with a plan.

Conal observed her Lipan clothes and sun-gilded skin. She had become the Apache's creature, even as he had boasted! "We both have problems, it would seem, Orlena. You are unwed and swelling with a bastard's bastard."

She glared at him with contempt. "If Night Wind is a bastard, 'tis you who made him so. It would go ill to repeat the mistake in a second generation." His eyes flashed fire, then became cold green shards, reminding her eerily of Night Wind. Why had she never noted it before?

"Let us put aside the morality of Apache by-blows for the moment and consider more significant problems. We both face your devious brother and his political machinations. What should we do, I wonder?" He wanted her to beg, to plead—if not for her lover's life, then at least for her own reputation.

"You toy with me, Conal. But it will not work. I know how well-favored Ignacio is now that the prince is king. He wants me alive for his own designs, and he blames you for my escape. He is a very clever and vengeful man, my elder brother."

"So am I, by all the saints!" Conal swore, leaping up from his chair. "I loved you, indulged you, risked my very neck spiriting you from Madrid to the colonies. And you betray me with a half-caste renegade!"

Orlena felt the hysterical laughter begin to bubble up in her. "The irony of it, Conal. Long ago Ignacio accused us of being lovers, and I struck him for the obscenity of the idea. But he was right, wasn't he? You wanted me that way—not as a daughter, but as a mistress!"

"I would have had you as wife if the Church allowed it! More fool I. You obviously prefer the sweet caress of filthy red hands." He swept her from head to foot with disgust in his eyes. "Now you must crawl before I will take you as mistress."

"But you know I will not crawl and that galls you, does it not, Governor Quinn? Best beware my brother or you may not remain governor for long."

He took two quick strides around the table and raised his hand to strike her, then stayed it at the last moment. She stood her ground, unflinching.

"What serves this?" he sighed wearily. "The renegade will be executed. I will be hailed as a savior and you will be disgraced. Make no mistake, Orlena, when I bring the infamous Night Wind back to Santa Fe in chains, Ignacio will not have power enough to suppress the adulation I shall receive." Again he waited, letting his words sink in, gambling that he could strike a bargain with her.

NIGHT WIND'S WOMAN

Orlena sagged in defeat. He was right. Here in the wilds of New Mexico, he was a military hero and Ignacio merely a foppish foreigner. He had outmaneuvered them all. "You would see your own flesh and blood die that horrible death?" Her voice broke as she realized how a raider such as Night Wind would be punished—beaten, starved, caged up like an animal, then hung and decapitated, his head stuck up on a pike above the presidio guardhouse. "What kind of a monster are you?"

"One willing to make you a bargain," he said coldly, once more in control. "I will let the priest wed you—which will not only save your honor, but also keep you from Ignacio's clutches. He has yet another bridegroom awaiting you back in Madrid."

"If I am so soon to be a widow, how will this marriage help me?" she countered with narrowed eyes. This new Conal was unreadable—truly two men, as Fray Bartolome had said.

"I will release your husband. He will make another of his miraculous escapes. But you shall not be a squaw for him any longer, Orlena. You will do *exactly* as I say if you would save his life." He waited.

"Pray, continue," she prompted in a tight voice, already dreading what he would say.

"You shall wed my bastard here and now, then tell him you have done so to save yourself from disgrace. You must convince him that you despise him and all Apaches. Your brother Ignacio has made you a splendid offer—the brilliant life of a Spanish noblewoman in the City of Mexico. You will await your delivery with the priest in Chihuahua City, then travel south to join Ignacio. The child will be placed in an orphanage. But mark me, Orlena, you must make him believe this, or I will kill him *and* his bastard!"

Orlena stood with her fists clenching the back of a

rough oak chair. The room spun crazily and she felt ill. *I love you*—his words came back to her again. Perhaps he did, but if she did this to save his life, he would hate her forever. "Why should I trust you, Conal? I could do as you bid and you could yet kill my husband."

"Ah, but you do not see the future, Orlena, my beautiful golden Butterfly." He walked over to her and touched her sun-kissed cheek, feeling her flinch in disgust. "The Apache has marred you, but when you are delivered of the babe and your skin is again pale and soft, you will be a beautiful woman. I will let your lover live and I will let you keep your child. In return, knowing I have granted you all of this, you will await my pleasure . . ."

Her face was chalky and her hands clammy. Her stomach churned as she fought to keep down the bits of dried meat she had eaten earlier. "You want me as your whore."

"You were that savage's whore! You will endure my touch or I will not only kill him, I will first lock him in a small, dark box for days, rather like a mine tunnel. It would mayhap bring back memories of—"

"No!" she choked out with a shudder. "I will make the bargain, Conal. Only see that you keep your word. Night Wind must ride free. In return, I will await you in Chihuahua City."

He stared at her beautiful face, blanched white beneath her sun-darkened complexion. He had truly frightened her, mentioning the sweat box and the mines. *I shall have to remember that.*

The sergeant walked toward the tree where Night Wind was bound. With a dark scowl he said to the Comanche guards, "Release him and bring him to the adobe."

Roughly they cut the rawhide lashing, which left his wrists and chest abraded with red weals. He rubbed his numbed hands, struggling to regain circulation. Whatever Conal planned, he must be prepared to face his hated enemy.

It was a cruel irony that after all those years of focusing his hate on the father who had betrayed him, now he was far more concerned with what would happen to Orlena. He cursed himself for writing that arrogant, hateful letter to Conal. How blinded by his blood-lust he had been! That hate had grievously hurt the woman who loved him, the woman he loved most dearly in the world! Admitting he loved her had come too late. Now Conal would exact his revenge on them and their innocent child. He tried to clear his head as he walked slowly toward the adobe hut.

Fray Bartolome stood at the door, his face grave. "I have been given permission by the governor," he said in perplexity, "to marry you and Orlena. Beyond that, his excellency will say nothing further."

What game does Conal play now? Both men exchanged the unspoken question as their eyes met. They entered the building under the guns of several Spanish soldiers and the Comanche militia. Conal and Orlena were in the center of the room. The second in command, Lieutenant Terris, stood beside them. Joaquín quickly took in the three armed guards crowding the perimeter of the small area. With all the others surrounding the building, there was no chance of escape for them.

He then centered his attention on Orlena, trying to read her expression. She appeared pale, but calm. If only he could make her understand how bitterly he regretted hurting her! "Father Bartolome is to give us the Church's blessing, Orlena," he said, reaching one hand out palm up, praying she would take it.

Shirl Henke

She stepped forward and placed her ice-cold hand in his, saying nothing. *Oh, please, Night Wind, forgive what I must do!*

Conal filled the silence. "I am allowing this marriage to save Orlena's reputation. She is a Spanish noblewoman and must be protected—unlike an Apache squaw who needs no benefit of clergy to whelp!"

Night Wind fought the urge to fly at the cruel, mocking face and smash it, but he knew how useless the attempt would be. "Let us be wed then. I assume this is the last request of the condemned man, but what of my wife and our child after Spanish justice has dealt with me?"

"We will discuss that after the priest has done his office," Conal replied smoothly, nodding to Bartolome.

"Whatever is to be, this child and your woman shall be blessed by the Church," the Franciscan said sadly. He motioned the young couple to kneel on the rude, bare earth.

Joaquín felt the stiff coldness of Orlena's hands as he assisted her. She looked up at the priest, not at him. Sharing the pain he knew she must feel, he covered her hand with both of his.

The exchange of vows was brief and simple. With their future so precarious and the past so confused, neither of them could appreciate the ceremony as they had their Lipan marriage. Each spoke the words in a strained voice. When he had finished the prayers and bade them stand, the priest looked warily at Conal.

"I think we can give the bridal couple a few minutes in which to talk in private, eh, Father?" He motioned to the lieutenant, who dismissed the guards. Everyone filed out but Conal, who paused in the doorway. Smiling, he said. "Do not take overlong. You have

NIGHT WIND'S WOMAN

little left to say each to the other."

When they were alone, Joaquín looked at Orlena with a question in his eyes. Reaching for her hand, he said, "Come here, wife. We must at least have a bridal kiss. I would have you understand my heart."

Orlena felt she would shatter if he kissed her. Every fiber of her being cried out to fling herself into his arms and confess Conal's blackmail, yet to do so would consign the man she loved to a ghastly fate. Whether he loved her or had used her did not matter now—only saving his life and their child's life! Pushing free of his hypnotic touch, she turned and walked around the table, taking the moment to steel herself. *I must do this quickly, lest my courage fail me.*

Joaquín looked at her stiffened back, afraid his callousness had lost her, even for these last few bittersweet moments. Then she faced him again, and he was riveted by the cold scorn on her face.

"I would have you understand *my* heart, Joaquín," she said with contempt. "I was your plaything, the instrument of your vengeance, the vessel for your lust. But no longer. Conal has come for me even as I said he would. I wed you to save disgrace, but I can be free of you now, even if I cannot be free of your seed growing in my belly. The child will be given to the sisters to raise. I wish never again to see you or the child. Ignacio awaits me in the City of Mexico, where I shall be a respectable matron with a mysteriously absent husband. Mexico is a very entertaining city for a woman without a *dueña*." She paused for breath, watching the look of amazement on his face change to shuttered expressionlessness. *Blessed Virgin, he has believed me!*

Joaquín felt a band of iron tightening about his chest. "So, my Lioness has been a consummate actress all these months. But know you this, Spanish whore, you came to me, not to gain advantage then—but to satisfy your own lust! And you enjoyed my crude passions—you shared them!" With that he was around the table, slamming her hard against his body. Before she could make a sound, he kissed her, savaging her mouth until she whimpered in pain. Then he shoved her back against the table in disgust. "'Tis a pity Conal gives us only a few moments, or we could satisfy our carnal cravings one last time. Think on that in your silken bedchamber in Mexico!" He turned and stalked out the door, slamming the loose, rotted wood on its rusty iron hinges.

Orlena crumpled on the table as silent sobs tore her throat raw. *He will live. He will live.* She repeated the thought over and over like a litany to hold off insanity.

Quinn stood outside the hut, lounging casually against a tree as Joaquín emerged. Dawn was seizing the sky with faint purple and orange fingers. He could see the bleak pain the younger man held carefully disguised beneath his scornful anger. "I assume the lady has told you her pleasure," he said, not expecting a reply. He motioned for two of the guards, who led Night Wind toward the dense stand of pines by the stream. As they disappeared behind the trees, he watched with a slow, bitter smile twisting his face.

Then he turned to Bartolome. "Offer Orlena comfort, Priest, and prepare to ride out after a brief respite. I will provide you safe escort back to Nueva Vizcaya."

"What of the Apaches?" one Comanche militiaman asked when the holy man had vanished inside.

Shrugging in disgust, Conal replied, "Take what you will from their bodies. The renegade Night Wind goes with me."

With great enthusiasm, the Comanche began their grisly mutilations, crying "*Aaa-hey*" each time their busy knives claimed another trophy.

"Sergeant Ruiz," Conal called out, ignoring the barbaric chaos around them. "As soon as these allies of our sovereign are finished, bring the girl and the priest out. You will accompany them to Chihuahua City. Take half the regulars with you. Report back to me in Santa Fe as soon as you have completed your mission."

Inside the hut, Orlena's fingers dug into the coarse cloth of the Franciscan's robe as the Comanches' blood-curdling cries echoed through the dawn. Bartolome held her. "Do not listen. There is nothing you can do. I will pray for their souls."

"Night Wind—he was freed?"

Bartolome did not know how to respond to the girl. "I do not know for certain. Conal did not turn him over to his tribe's ancient enemies. Two soldiers took him across the stream. His horse is tethered there." He much doubted that Conal would let his half-caste son live after all that had passed between them, but the priest could not extinguish what slim hope Orlena held now. She had sustained enough tragedy this night.

When they entered the shadows of the trees, Night Wind's guards knocked him to the ground. One knelt beside him while the other kept his pistol trained on him. The kneeling one produced a length of the same rawhide cord that had bound him earlier. The Spaniard tied his hands tightly in front of him and then looped the remaining line around his neck. With the choke rope firmly in place, he yanked his captive up. "We await the commandant's pleasure," the sergeant said with a feral grin slashing his face, revealing rotted teeth.

From his hidden vantage point, Joaquín watched

Fray Bartolome and Orlena ride south from the valley, escorted by Sergeant Ruiz and a dozen men. *South to the rich life you were born to live, Lioness.* He wondered how many of his men had escaped. Four bodies were visible around the campfire. Neither Hoarse Bark nor Strong Bow were among the dead as far as he had been able to see. They would know to ride for the stronghold, but he doubted that the Lipans could return with enough men to free him before Conal had him back in Santa Fe. His fate awaited him there and he would accept death, perhaps even welcome it. *If only I could take Colorado Quinn with me.*

Joaquín's thoughts were interrupted by that hated voice, now oily with sadistic pleasure. "So, you have said your farewells and seen her ride away. She returns to the life you would have robbed her of."

Joaquín let his face relax into a taunting smile as he stood unbowed before Quinn. "I have robbed her of the one thing that no courtier in Mexico can restore," he said arrogantly.

Before he could mask his own fury, Conal lashed out with a wicked punch to Joaquín's jaw. The half-caste's head snapped back as the soldiers held their choke rope tightly.

Two pairs of icy green eyes glared at one another. "We have each had some measure of vengeance, Irish cur," Joaquín said.

Regaining his composure, Conal replied, "Yes, but when you think of your mongrel child in an orphanage, your wife with a succession of foppish lovers, and your head hung from the presidio guard house, whose revenge will be the sweeter?" He turned on his heel and ordered the sergeant, "Mount him on the piebald and see that you do not let loose of his leash on the ride back to the capital."

NIGHT WIND'S WOMAN

When Joaquín carelessly mounted Warpaint and stared impassively ahead, Conal pulled his bay beside the black-and-white stallion. "I will give you something else to contemplate on the journey north. I am given to understand that you mislike dark, closed-in places . . . such as mines. We have a sweat box at the prison in Santa Fe. You are tall for an Apache, but I think we can squeeze you into it."

Joaquín did not flinch, but holding his face and body still took every ounce of will he could muster.

As they rode, Conal brooded over his revenge on his renegade son, cursing the day he had spilled his seed in the half-caste's Apache mother. Orlena had been so stupid as to believe he would free the bastard—that he would keep *her* as mistress! He had wanted her for long years, but never, never would he touch this arrogant savage's leavings. They both would pay and so would their child.

Chapter 18

Blaise Pascal hated Spaniards, especially officious fops like the viceregal emissary who had summoned him to the palace. He had been terrified when Quinn rescinded his travel pass and placed him under arrest pending the outcome of his negotiations over the priest. Now, after months of waiting, he was dragged before yet another Spanish functionary. And he was no nearer to the five thousand pesos than he was to freedom.

He watched the lace-frothed cuffs of Don Ignacio's shirt rustle across the pages of documents spread before him. The arrogant youth sat behind Conal's table in the audience chamber, reading papers and making notes while he let the Frenchman stand and wait. Finally, without even deigning to look up, he spoke.

"You are said to know about this renegade who took my sister." Catching Pascal's start of surprise from beneath his lowered eyelids, Ignacio added, "Yes, the governor's stepdaughter is my sister. I have journeyed far to reclaim her. His carelessness in allowing her capture by Apaches is most distressing."

Pascal thought the icy man before him would have been more distressed if his cuffs fell afoul of the inkwell on the desk, but he replied cautiously, "I did not realize, excellency, who you were. I am most regretful about your sister's kidnapping, but I had nothing to do with the tragedy."

"But you do know of the man who took her? That is why my stepfather has authorized payment of a sizeable reward to you—pending the safe return of Orlena. Pray, tell me, Monsieur Pascal, how you came to know Night Wind—and Conal Quinn. Omit nothing in your tale, or you will live to regret it, I assure you."

Conal Quinn's harsh military bearing made men fear him. Ignacio Valdéz's manner was effete by comparison, his voice lisping, and his appearance languid. Yet the hair on Pascal's neck prickled in warning. Here was an adversary every bit as devious and dangerous as the Irishman. "I will begin with the circumstances of the half-caste's birth, excellency..."

Conal threw down the letter, every fiber in his body taut with rage that he struggled to subdue as he paced the polished brick floor of his private office.

As soon as they had arrived in Santa Fe, he had placed Night Wind in the foul prison at the top of the hill north of the city. For that much, at least, he had felt some grim satisfaction. Then he had gone to the governor's palace, pondering how to deal with Ignacio's wrath. Immediately Señora Cruciaga had come running out the front door, practically falling at his feet in entreaty, gasping, "Oh, Don Conal, it was not my fault! Those lazy guards, they do not stand watch as they should, or it never would have occurred."

For a fleeting moment, hope had flared in his chest that something fatal had befallen the viceroy's emissary, but when the woman handed him a letter with trembling hands, he realized that Santiago had not rushed out to greet him. Hours later, as he sat in his quarters, he reread the letter with consuming bitterness.

Papa:

I have left Santa Fe of my own free will to join the Lipan again. My sister dwells there and I long to be with her. I grew to love that life and the people even as Orlena has. I would be a bridge between Spanish and Apache worlds so that each can live in peace and freedom.

Forgive the hurt I have caused you in doing this, and please do not harm Night Wind's friend, the holy father, if you hold any love for me.

With regret,
Santiago

"If I hold any love for you," he echoed hoarsely. "Everything I have ever loved has been stripped from me as if I had been born cursed—my family's wealth and title, my homeland, my position at the Spanish court—then Orlena and now you, the son of my blood, my heir, my mirror image—you choose to live with savages!"

He grabbed the inkwell on his writing desk and hurled it across the room. It crashed against the far wall, splattering the freshly whitewashed surface with

NIGHT WIND'S WOMAN

a jagged black explosion that perfectly matched the torment in his soul.

Ever since they had arrived in this hellish place, he had watched his son grow apart from him, questioning his dealings with the pueblos, the *paisanos*, and the merchants who paid him in lieu of dearer taxes to the crown. Like Orlena, the boy had a soft, idealistic streak in him that insisted the enlightened Europeans must deal honorably with animals like the savages. At first he had dismissed the disillusionment and puzzled hurt in Santiago's eyes as the natural process of growing into manhood, but the youth had become someone he did not know. Like Orlena, Santiago rejected him and clung to that half-caste renegade!

Well, his bastard lay in chains up on the hill, at his disposal as Governor of New Mexico. "This I swear to you, Santiago, be you alive or dead by now in your quest to rejoin those whoresons—I will kill every Apache from here to Texas and see your damnable idol Night Wind reduced to a glassy-eyed, cringing piece of offal who must be dragged to the executioner's block!"

The whip bit into his back, reopening old scars which had been reduced to thin white lines since his childhood in the mines. Now once again they oozed crimson as he hung with his wrists manacled from the ceiling, his chest flattened against the rough adobe wall. With every blow of the short leather whip, his face slammed against the gritty surface until his cheek and lips were as bloodied as his back.

Conal watched from the end of the long row of dank filthy cells, standing near the door so as to breathe more freely. God and all his Saints, how he hated the stench of savages! But he relished the punishment being meted out to the renegade, who hung silently on the wall. Conal knew what he was thinking. *He prays for the beating never to end rather than to endure what will follow it.*

Joaquín did attempt to focus his mind on the pain of here and now. Anything was better than contemplating the small black box he had been shown upon his arrival at the prison. Barely the size of a coffin, it was made of cast iron with tiny, narrow breathing slits on the sides. No other light could penetrate its cloying confines, only the heat of the blazing spring sun, baking its hapless victim to a slow, agonizing death. Of course, long before he died from lack of water or shock, his mind would retreat into the oblivion of madness. No amount of physical pain could equal the terror of the beast within him, the beast from the bowels of the mines.

"Cut him down and put him in the box while he is yet conscious," Conal ordered.

Weakened as he was by the brutal beating, the half-caste still fought with amazing strength as they dragged his manacled and chained body toward the central courtyard of the prison. So great was his frenzy, it took four men to hold him in the box until the heavy ring of the iron lid was finally flung down and latched. At once the noise of his protest ceased. The silence was eerie and the prison guards and Conal's soldiers all backed away from the half-caste in the sweatbox.

Only Quinn remained, unafraid. Walking up to the box, he kicked the side with the toe of his hard-soled leather boot and said, "Remember, your beginning will be your end—alone in the blackness of hell."

Sergeant Ruiz, who had been patient and courteous to Orlena back in Santa Fe, now escorted her in hostile silence. He was polite to Fray Bartolome, but studiously ignored her. "I am a fallen woman to him, Father. Why do the Spanish soldiers, even those of mixed blood like the sergeant, hate Apaches so much?" she asked the priest as they rode toward Chihuahua.

They had been traveling hard for four days now, and the friar paused to rub his aching back as he considered how to explain bigotry to a woman who had grown up so enmeshed in its web that she could not see where the sticky threads began and ended. "Ruiz is a half-caste, yes, but one whose roots are far to the south among the reduced Indian tribes. He is probably Tlaxcaltecan or perhaps Opata. To an Indian, does an Irishman such as Conal seem different from a Spaniard such as Ignacio?"

Fighting fatigue and depression, Orlena struggled to focus on his line of reasoning. "I suppose to an Apache, all white men are enemies. They do not differentiate one European from another."

Fray Bartolome answered, "Yet you and I know Europeans have warred against each other for thousands of years. Just as our cultures are different, so are those of the Indian tribes. A man whose Tlaxcaltecan great-grandmother wed a Spanish soldier thinks of himself as part of Spanish culture even if he retains a vestige of tribal identity. To a Tlaxcaltecan, an Apache is the enemy—wild, free of all restraints, defying the very Spanish government that pays his wage. Apache and other untamed tribes raid his village. They rape and kill the mixed bloods as well as the Spanish. It is war."

"But the Lipan fight for their own land, for their freedom, asking nothing from Spain but to be left to hunt and gather their crops in peace. My husband's vengeance came only after he was most hideously abused by his own white father and the corruption of the Spanish government."

Bartolome shrugged in helpless consternation. "Yes, that is true, but neither side is right to kill, Orlena. There is no justification for what they both do. I know not how to stop it."

They rode on under the bleak scrutiny of Sergeant Ruiz, ever southward, farther from the mountains of New Mexico, away from her Apache lover.

Orlena swayed in her saddle, limp with exhaustion. The sun hung suspended on the horizon, but still the sergeant pressed onward, wanting to put as much distance between his small party and the Apaches as possible.

Suddenly, the woman slid silently from her horse to the hard, dry earth. Instantly Fray Bartolome dismounted and dropped to his knees beside her, cradling her head in his lap as he examined her for injuries. When the sergeant reined in his horse and turned it about to ride back to the stragglers, the priest looked up at his set face and said, "You must stop for the night! Can you not see she is ill? A woman with child cannot ride like a soldier. I adjure you to heed me for the safety of your immortal soul."

As the sergeant looked down at them, Orlena moaned and doubled over, holding her abdomen. A dark stain of blood spread slowly through her buckskin clothing. Bartolome crossed himself and said a swift silent prayer for the soul of the child he knew she was losing; then he picked her up and carried her to a small cluster of piñon pine by the side of the trail. Stretching her out behind the privacy of the small, spreading trees, he ran back to his horse and took the water flask and a blanket from the saddle.

Ruiz debated. His orders were clear. He was to deposit the priest and the woman at the mission in

Chihuahua City and return to Santa Fe as quickly as possible. But he was responsible for her life, he supposed, even if she had fallen from the governor's favor and become a savage's squaw. Shrugging, he gave the order to dismount and make a dry camp for the night.

Orlena could feel the tightening cramp begin at the base of her spine, then radiate outward in every direction, squeezing the breath from her with wave after wave of agony. Fray Bartolome's hands were gentle as he bathed her sweat-soaked brow with water, murmuring low, comforting words to her. "Oh, Father, why? Why is God taking my baby?" she whispered hoarsely, then bore down on another, sharper contraction. Tears streamed down her face as she felt the new life, so fragile and unformed yet, leaving her body. Night Wind's child, her last link to him, erased in this trackless desert. How could a merciful God be so cruel?

"I do not know what the Almighty wills, daughter, but I do know what human cruelty has wrought," he replied to her agonized question.

Desperately, he searched his scholar's orderly memory for the books he had read on medicine, especially midwifery. Mostly written by Jews, they were prohibited by the Church, but their inclusion on the Index had never been sufficient reason for the Franciscan to forego reading them. "Remember Maimonides," he muttered to himself as he felt Orlena gasp for breath. Before the infant, nearly five months along, was expelled, he quickly baptized its soul. He was certain the body would enter this world devoid of life.

The babe was so tiny, yet so perfect, it wrung his heart. A girl, with Joaquín's coal-black hair and Orlena's cameo-perfect features, now placid in death. Death before life. *Why, oh Lord?* Forcing aside his doubt and grief, he said prayers for the infant, all the while working carefully to see the mother safely delivered of the afterbirth. Joaquín's daughter had died, but he would not lose his wife, too. If only he remained alive to mend their painful parting some day.

Before Orlena regained consciousness, the priest wrapped the babe in a clean cloth and walked over to where the soldiers had pitched camp. "I will need a small grave dug. Deeply and quickly," he said to Ruiz.

"The woman?" the sergeant asked impassively.

"She will live, in spite of what you and your commander have done to her."

The adobe shacks straggling along the river south of Santa Fe were rude and small, as impoverished as the inhabitants. Santiago hid in the thickening shadows, waiting to be certain he was not followed as he now knew Juanito had been followed. The Jicarilla scout and his wife and children had been imprisoned by Conal. It was hard to reconcile this stranger's actions with his father, for Conal had the woman raped and then threatened to torture the boys. Juanito finally told the governor about the hidden valley in the mountains where Night Wind would take Fray Bartolome after the exchange. The Jicarilla had died from his wounds in prison last night. Torturing him had yielded nothing until his family was arrested.

"If only I can convince the others to help me," Santiago whispered to himself. The darkness of night descended quickly in the New Mexican mountains. With the stealth he had practiced in the Lipan camp, the youth crossed from tree to tree until he reached a small building on the far outskirts of the Indian settlement. He knocked lightly on the door and waited, holding his breath.

NIGHT WIND'S WOMAN

A thin shaft of pale amber light spilled out as a woman cracked the door open. Her round, flat face was expressionless until he said, "I am come from the prison—Juanito died last night."

Her face crumpled as she asked, "What of his wife and children?"

"She who was called Yellow Bird is dead by the Spaniards' hands, but the children are unharmed—for now. The prison holds another, one who can free your nephews and avenge your sister's death. Night Wind."

The door swung open and an old man with long gray hair and rheumy, opaque eyes motioned him inside. "You are Quinn's cub. Why do you come here to tell us this?"

Sighing, the boy replied, "It is a long and bitter tale . . ."

"While I lived at Night Wind's camp, I learned of his system of spies among the presidio scouts. My sister is wife to the Night Wind," Santiago proudly explained as he stuffed heaping spoonfuls of beans into his mouth. In the two days since he had escaped from the governor's palace, he had eaten little, for he had been unable to sneak much food from under the watchful eye of Señora Cruciaga. He had hidden in the stables the first day, then traveled that night to the prison on the hill where he had been told Conal was holding Juanito and his family. What he learned there only strengthened his resolution to rejoin the Lipan. The following afternoon, Conal had returned with Night Wind. He watched their entry into the city from afar, knowing his bright red hair would betray him as the governor's runaway son if he tried to get closer. When the soldiers took Night Wind to the prison, Santiago knew what he must do.

"Even now they torture him. Soon they will kill him and place his head on the presidio wall if we do not act."

The old man, who was named Silver Hair, considered the boy's long and incredible story. His daughter and son-in-law were dead and his grandchildren in mortal danger. Could he trust Colorado Quinn's son? The boy obviously had learned much during his time with Night Wind's band. Perhaps he truly knew his father for the man's worth now. But dared they attempt to rescue Night Wind?

Guessing the old man's thoughts, Santiago said, "If my father hears that a red-haired boy was seen on the Taos road tomorrow, he will postpone killing Night Wind, to ride himself in pursuit. While he is off on this fool's errand, we can do as the Night Wind himself did last spring, when he took a dozen Apaches from that place."

"I will send word to our village in the north. We can have enough warriors to get into the prison, but how will you lure Quinn to the Taos road?" Silver Hair asked.

Reaching for a knife sitting on the rude table, Santiago began to slice the long red locks from his head. "Back in Spain we have a curious custom. It is called wearing a wig."

"I do not want him to die . . . yet. Remove him from the box for the night and chain him in the cell. Let him ponder his return to it on the morrow." With that he walked away.

From somewhere in what seemed a far distant place, Joaquín could hear Conal's voice and echoing footsteps. The tremors that wracked his body and the tight dizzying paralysis of his breathing forced him to concentrate on the pain of his lacerated back and then

NIGHT WIND'S WOMAN

on Conal's face—his father's face, the hated enemy who had given him life and then so brutally taken it from him again. And now a second time. In the mines, concentrating on his hate and eventual revenge kept him sane. He learned to work in the dark, confining tunnels and to avoid the worst abuses of the drunken guards. He had survived a living death. He had escaped the beast.

But now, caged in the tight black confines of the sweatbox, the beast was again seizing hold of him. The old tricks he had used—pain and hate—no longer worked. Instead, a vision of his golden Spanish wife floated before him. But the look of love in her bright amber eyes quickly turned to burning contempt. Then Orlena evaporated, and the old clawing terror began pulling him down the twisting, writhing tunnel, dragging him to the bowels of hell . . . to insanity.

He knew he had screamed several times when the fear won out. Yet he persisted in recalling Orlena, her rich warm laughter and soft silken skin, the deep gold her eyes turned as they smoldered with passion. Each time she would bring him back from the abyss. Why she should be the instrument of his salvation, the thin thread connecting him to sanity, he did not know. She had ultimately betrayed him. And her betrayal was even more cruel, more devastating than that of his father.

As the guards unfastened the clasps and swung the heavy iron lid of the coffin open, he looked up at the twilight sky and squinted his eyes. After a full day in the blackness and heat, the soft light and cool air were a shock to his system. They dragged his dazed body up from the box. Staggering behind them toward the prison's interior, he was struck by a blinding realization. *I see Orlena because she has taken Conal's place!* Now he understood that his need to punish her exceeded even his need to kill Colorado Quinn.

They chained him to the wall in a small, filthy cell and doused his body with fetid water to revive him. He shivered in the chill evening air as his bloody skin dried. Several hours must have passed, for he lapsed into unconsciousness until a noise awakened him. A guard carrying a bowl of thin corn gruel opened the cell door and set the bowl before the prisoner. With the manacle chains barely long enough for him to reach it, Joaquín struggled to pick up the noisome food. He debated whether to throw it at the smirking soldier or bolster his strength by consuming the liquid. Living to face more days in this private hell held little appeal, but then he thought of Orlena and it stayed his hand. He raised the bowl to his lips, held his breath against its stench, and drank the slop.

Just as the guard reached down to retrieve the bowl, a thudding noise caused him to turn. Joaquín shoved his manacled leg out with every ounce of his waning strength, tripping the startled soldier, who went crashing to the hard stone floor.

A scuffle was going on in the narrow passageway beyond his cell door. Suddenly two men burst into the dark chamber. Before the stunned guard on the floor could rise or sound a warning cry, he was dispatched with a knife by a Jicarilla scout whom Joaquín recognized in the flickering torchlight. He was Juanito's brother, Manuel. Several other Jicarillas were with him, moving swiftly and silently as they dragged soldiers' bodies into the room and threw them against the wall. One, who had searched all the corpses, had the key to the manacles and had begun to unlock them when a thin, youthful figure slipped into the cell.

At first, Joaquín could not discern his identity in the poor light, but he sensed the boy was not Apache. His

NIGHT WIND'S WOMAN

hair was shorn nearly to his scalp and looked dark at first. Then he stepped closer and Joaquín recognized him. "Santiago! What are you doing here?"

"What does it appear I do? I have brought friends to free you and Juanito's children. It seems my father just received word that a red-haired boy was seen riding along the Taos road this afternoon," he said with a boyish chuckle. "He and half the soldiers in the presidio are scouring the countryside searching for me!"

"He is free. Let us go quickly," Manuel said as he helped Joaquín stand. Without the heavy chains, he moved with more ease, but the agony of his stiffened muscles impeded his normal speed.

"He was whipped before they placed him in the box. Look you at the blood!" Santiago whispered in horror, all traces of his earlier adventuresome enthusiasm gone from his voice as he took Joaquín's arm and placed it across his thin shoulders.

"We must hurry before the sentry on the wall returns from his rounds," one of Manuel's cousins said, ushering Juanito's wide-eyed children with him.

Silently, the group evaporated into the shadows beyond the light cast by the torch on the wall. The corridor was narrow and short. Soon they were outside in the chill night. A coyote yipped in the distance, but no other sound broke the silence as they moved swiftly across the prison courtyard, keeping to the wall, out of the light. They flattened themselves against the rough adobe bricks as the guard paced slowly by on the wooden walkway overhead. When he had turned the corner, they climbed one by one up the rickety ladder and dropped silently to the earth on the opposite side.

Joaquín's whole body screamed in protest as he followed the others. Gradually, as they moved along the brushy ground, circulation began to return to his cramped arms and legs. He ignored the rippling pain of his lacerated back. They finally reached a thick stand of trees over a mile from the prison where a number of horses were tied. Among them was Joaquín's big piebald.

"How did you get him? Surely one without Lipan blood cannot steal a horse such as Warpaint," Joaquín said as he stroked the animal's muzzle, mustering his strength to swing onto his back.

Santiago grinned again, his elation once more returning. "I did steal him, truly—yesterday, late in the night. It was simple. The stables were almost deserted when the governor and his soldiers rode out. Conal has already lost his son. When he returns, he will find he has lost his prisoner and his prize horse as well!"

That Santiago no longer called Conal father was not lost on Joaquín. Swinging up onto the big piebald's back, he said, "You do not wish to return to your father?"

"Never. I am Lipan now. I would return with you to the stronghold where my sister awaits us."

Joaquín's face darkened, but he held his peace. "There will be time enough for you to rejoin Orlena. For now, come. Let us ride from this place of death!"

Chapter 19

"What do you mean, he's escaped! I left him half dead, manacled to a wall in that prison!" Conal was livid. He had ridden all night to Taos and back, scouring the countryside for Santiago. It seemed the redheaded boy reportedly seen on the road had simply vanished. Now, dusty and disheartened, he returned to the governor's palace, hoping for a good day's rest for his weary bones. Instead, the smirking Ignacio awaited him with this unbelievable news.

The courtier seemed as pleased as a Persian cat. He now had Quinn precisely where he wanted him. "Mayhap you were negligent—first you let Orlena be abducted, then your stripling vanished, also abducted you say." He paused with patent disbelief on his face. "Now a dangerous renegade has escaped from the prison in the dead of night while you and your soldiers were off on some highly improbable chase to retrieve your younger son...."

Conal's hand stopped in mid-course as he reached for the decanter of brandy on the cabinet in his office. "What do you mean, *younger* son?"

Ignacio waited a beat, letting the implication sink into his enemy's gut. Then he twisted the verbal knife, answering softly, "Why, only that you had two cubs here in Santa Fe—for a while. An interesting coincidence, is it not? Joaquín Quinn being the fearful Apache raider Night Wind? Your bastard has conveniently escaped while you were away."

Conal took the decanter and poured a generous portion of the harsh local *aguardiente*, swallowing it in one burning gulp. Then, replacing the glass on the cabinet, he turned to the satin-clad fop before him. "At least my sons, born on either side of the blanket, are men!" His eyes raked Ignacio's soft body and pale face, now flushed with anger at the insult.

Conal's green eyes were as hard and cold as glass. "Night Wind is one of many whelps I have got on Indian women over the years I have served in New Spain. But mark me, I hate him and one day I will kill him. If you get in the way of my vengeance, you will pay with your life, viceregal favor or no. I am still governor of the province. Leave me now. I have much to do if I am to capture the renegade and his savages."

He walked past Ignacio, but the younger man's voice stayed him. "You will not be governor in a fortnight."

Conal turned with narrowed eyes. "You overestimate the political power of a royal lap dog in New Mexico, Ignacio. I have rescued Orlena and sent her south to Nueva Vizcaya. You would do well to return to the City of Mexico and await her. The north is not safe for you."

Ignacio's face twisted with hate. "Yes, you have rescued my sister—with her belly filled with your half-caste bastard's child! If word of her dishonor reaches the capital, I shall never arrange a marriage for her—and do not think such scandal will help your prospects either. They are dim enough now, I warrant. You are being recalled—for corruption. It seems you have been most remiss in the matter of tax collection. I have found witnesses, documents—" He raised his hand to halt Conal's menacing steps toward him. "It is too late! Harm me now and your head—not your bastard's—will hang from the presidio gates! I have sent full documentation of your misdeeds to the viceroy, along with a letter in which I pleaded for protection, lest you take reprisals against me for exposing these irregularities. You may try to clear your name—but harm me and the wrath of his majesty, the viceroy, and the Council of the Indies shall descend on you!"

"I will not kill you—yet, Ignacio, but mark me well. When I have dealt with my bastard son, I will turn my attention to you. The Blessed Virgin and all God's angels will not be able to protect you from me. They do not live in New Mexico—but Satan does."

As Ignacio quit the room, he felt a shiver of fear slice through his gut. He must leave Santa Fe at once!

The escaping renegades rode through the night and all the next day, stopping only to relieve themselves and water their lathered horses. Food, what little there was of it, was consumed while riding. When they reached the foothills of the Guadalupes the following evening, Night Wind signaled the exhausted group of riders to stop by a stream and make camp. "We are in our own lands now. The Spanish soldiers do not know this place," he said simply as he slid from Warpaint's back.

Santiago had been watching the half-caste ride in

the lead all through the day, seemingly impervious to his bloody back and battered body. The boy himself was aching and exhausted, dejectedly feeling that he could never be a Lipan warrior. *How can he endure such pain and continue riding?* he had wondered again and again.

Now as they dismounted, Santiago rushed over to catch Night Wind as he began to silently slide to the ground. "Bring water, quickly!" he cried to Manuel as he laid their leader on the ground.

"His back must be cleansed and packed with a poultice lest he get the poison fever that kills," Manuel said. "We must ride for the stronghold as soon as our horses can stand to travel."

"She Who Dreams will know what to do," Santiago assured himself, remembering her miraculous healing skills. "But how can he ride through the high passes? He is unconscious now."

"You will tie me to Warpaint," Night Wind whispered through cracked lips. "Now, give me water that I might revive myself, then tend the horses. I would speak with Santiago."

When Manuel walked away, Santiago turned to Night Wind. "I go with you to the stronghold. I will learn to be a Lipan warrior," he said with dogged determination.

"Once that would have given me the greatest pleasure, little brother," Night Wind said sadly as he sat up and drank from the fresh cool water of the mountain stream, then poured the icy libation over his head and shoulders to clear his mind. He must explain very carefully to his brother, once the hated supplanter, now the rescuer to whom he owed his life.

Santiago's face held a puzzled expression. "Why say you, *once* it would have pleased you?"

"Once I saw you as an enemy."

"Because I am white? Conal's son? Orlena told me he did a terrible thing to you long ago. I would be with my sister and you now, Night Wind. You, not Conal, are my family." His earnest green eyes locked with Night Wind's. "Is it not a sign that you and I share such strangely colored eyes?" the boy asked, not wanting to hear what he feared the half-caste was going to say about his living among the Lipan.

"It is not strange, Santiago, little brother . . . for we *are* brothers. Conal Quinn is father to me as well as to you." He watched the boy's face blanch in incredulity.

"But he sold you into the mines when you were a boy! Hoarse Bark was there with you!"

"Yes, and I would have had my vengeance on him through you. When I took Orlena, it was you I sought—to make into a warrior who would kill white men. That was to be my revenge on our father."

Santiago digested this in confusion. Part of him was horrified at Conal's perfidy, part of him overjoyed that his idol was also truly blood kin. "Then perhaps . . . perhaps if you are my brother, there is hope that my blood is not tainted . . . unless having a Spanish mother makes it so. Is that why you do not want me with you and Orlena?" The hurt and entreaty in the boy's face was plain to see.

"Never say it! I am proud to call you brother. It matters not who your mother was—or who Conal Quinn is," he added darkly.

"Then why, why can I not live with you?" the boy persisted with the singlemindedness of adolescence.

"Because the life I embark upon is dangerous—a road I would not have you travel. The men who ride with me are like Hoarse Bark and Cloth Fox, and now these few Jicarilla—they have no family, no one left depending on them."

"But you have Orlena and your baby," Santiago

said. At once he sensed a change in Night Wind's demeanor, even though his face quickly hid the tension.

"My child is the reason I ask you to return to the whites. Orlena is no longer at the stronghold. She has returned to the City of Mexico. Fray Bartolome was to escort her as far as his mission in Chihuahua City," Night Wind said. The bitterness and pain in his voice were unmistakable.

"But why? I do not understand. Orlena loves you. She carries your child—she is your wife!" The boy's world was being turned upside down.

"Yes, Orlena is my wife. Fray Bartolome married us before Conal brought me to Santa Fe in chains. But she chose to return to Ignacio to live the life of a lady. She would put her shameful mixed-blood baby in a convent orphanage."

"I do not believe this!" Santiago cried as he jumped up, but before he could run away, Night Wind's words stopped him.

"She told me this herself. We were alone together." He watched the boy crumple to the ground in bewilderment. He faced his younger brother and said, "I have given her reasons, perhaps. I kidnapped her and seduced her."

"I already knew that, but you married her among your own people. You love my sister and she loves you," Santiago said doggedly.

A look of anguish passed over the dark, chiseled face of the renegade. "It is finished, Santiago. She will tell you the rest of it when you rejoin her. Promise me you will go to Chihuahua City to Bartolome." At the boy's hesitation, Night Wind entreated, "You must protect my child until its birth. Then you will send word to me. I will make some plan about what to do after that. How I do not know. Only promise you will

NIGHT WIND'S WOMAN

watch your sister's babe and protect it from Conal."

"Yes, I swear that. None of us will ever live with him again," the boy replied with a catch in his voice. "But what of you?"

"I go to end it with Conal. If he is dead, he cannot harm you or my child." *Or touch Orlena?* some insidious voice inside Night Wind added.

"It will be dangerous. You are hurt. Will you at least let She Who Dreams attend your wounds first?"

Smiling at the boy, he reached out and held him firmly by the shoulder. "Yes, I too, make a promise."

When Santiago arrived at the mission, he was surprised at its rude simplicity. This was scarcely the lap of luxury Night Wind had bitterly told him his sister had chosen. He bade farewell to the two Jicarilla scouts who had accompanied him and dismounted uncertainly.

Before he could knock, the heavy wooden door swung open and a tall man with dark hair and piercing gray eyes looked him over as he motioned him inside. The Franciscan's face was wreathed in smiles, and the boy knew immediately that this must be Fray Bartolome.

"Welcome! There's no mistaking you, my son, even with those fiery locks shorn like a sheep's."

"I have my brother's eyes," Santiago replied defensively, not wanting to dwell on his father.

Bartolome assessed him shrewdly. "So, he told you, did he? Orlena knew naught of this."

"Is she here? I was not certain," Santiago said, relief flooding him as the priest ushered him and his weary mount into the courtyard.

"Your sister is here, but I am amazed to see you without your father."

"In time he may think to search for me here. We

must plan what to do, Father, for I would not have him find me, ever again."

Many things bothered the friar as he called Fray Alonzo and bade him rub down Santiago's weary mount and stable it with their mules. "What has passed since I was exchanged for you on the Taos Trail?" He dreaded hearing of Joaquín's death, yet felt certain it had happened.

"The Night Wind is free, Father." As the amazed priest showed him to the small cabin in the rear of the courtyard, the boy explained why he had fled Conal and gave the details of Joaquín's escape. When he came to their parting and Joaquín's bitter words about Orlena, Santiago faltered.

"I feared Conal would not keep his word to her, but it was her only chance to save him." Bartolome observed the boy's confused expression and said quietly, "We will speak of this only once so that you may understand why each of them did such terrible things to the other."

As he talked of Joaquín's childhood, his oath to kill Conal, and the twists and turns his revenge had taken over the years, the priest prepared a simple supper of cheese, bread, and sliced melons for the boy. Finally, after explaining the cruel letter Joaquín had sent to Conal and then Orlena's reading of it, he added sadly, "Part of this is my fault. I have never met a Spanish lady who could read. If I had not carelessly left it lying about, she would not have felt such a sense of betrayal."

"So that is what he meant about her reasons for deserting him," the boy said glumly. "But still she would not give over her own child to an orphanage and go to Ignacio. I know my sister. She could never do such a thing!"

"Orlena loves Joaquín still, in spite of the way he

intended to use her, but she parted from him under tragic circumstances not of her choosing, any more than they were of his."

By the time Bartolome had ended the tale with the death of the baby in the desert, the boy was crying silently. "It is not fair! It is not right," he choked out.

"Much in this life is unjust, my son. I do not pretend to understand why or to offer platitudes. We must be grateful that Joaquín and Orlena are alive, that is all we can ask now. I do know that your sister needs you. Joaquín was right to send you to her, even if he did so for the wrong reasons."

When Santiago saw Orlena, he understood what the priest meant. She sat in a small, solitary room, looking frail and wan in a drab black skirt and peasant's *camisa*. She mourned, not only for the child, but for her lost love.

Her eyes, dulled to an eerie yellowish shade, looked up at Santiago, scarcely registering surprise at his unexpected appearance.

For the next week, the priest and the youth tried in vain to bring her out of the lethargic grief that held her in thrall. She felt intense guilt over being duped by Conal into making the bargain that crushed Night Wind's love for her. Yet she had held doubts about her husband's feelings even before she played out the cruel scene in that mountain hut. The only good thing to come from their relationship had been buried in the northern desert.

Then one afternoon, someone rode in from that northern desert to shake Orlena from her lethargy, if not her grief.

Even after riding all day through driving wind and spring rains, Ignacio looked immaculate and poised as he stood before her that evening in Bartolome's cabin. He had bathed and changed into a maroon velvet suit before speaking with his sister. "You are well enough to travel. Either come with me to the City of Mexico or await the arrival of our devoted stepfather and see what he plans for you."

"Exactly what do you *plan* for me, Ignacio? Never have I known you to do a deed of kindness," Orlena countered wearily. Yet dread of Conal's unnatural desire for her battered at the shell she had built around herself.

He smiled pityingly. "If you remained so drab and lifeless, I would not bother, but I do trust you will outlast your grief."

She looked at him with eyes grown old beyond her scant nineteen years. "And if I do? I am still wed. You cannot sell me for an advantageous marriage alliance, Ignacio."

He shrugged philosophically. "Perhaps your outlaw husband will die. He came within a hair's breadth of it in Santa Fe. I will even take Quinn's whelp with us. It amuses me to thwart Conal Quinn," he said with one thin eyebrow arched as he flicked a speck of lint from his velvet cuff.

"Could it be we are your safe passage away from Conal's wrath?" Orlena asked cannily. Observing the tic in his cheek, she knew she had hit on the truth.

"Conal Quinn is being dismissed as governor of the province for malfeasance. He will have no power to harm me. I have the ear of the viceroy as a royal emissary." He paused and considered her. "Here in this wilderness he could do with you as he pleases. Who would say him nay? Your fine Franciscans?" he asked scornfully.

Thinking of Conal's touch and his cold lustful eyes when he had bargained with her, she shuddered. If he lost his post in Santa Fe, he would be driven and desperate. Blessed Virgin, what form of vengeance might he take on her? Worse yet, what might he do to the son who had rejected him?

"We will go with you, Ignacio," she replied tonelessly.

Spring 1789

The saddle leather creaked in protest as he shifted his weight. God's Bones, he grew too old for this! Days and nights spent in a hot, stiff uniform, riding all day through dust and sand, sleeping each night on the dry rocky earth. "But I am second in command under the Commandant General of the Eastern Sector of the Internal Provinces," he muttered bitterly beneath his breath. He took a generous swallow of brackish water and recalled the long, bitter battle he had waged last summer, and lost to Ignacio. His military record and the support of the *ricos* in the north had kept him from total disgrace. When he was dismissed from his post as provincial governor, he had petitioned the viceroy for the opportunity to hunt down and kill the Apache who had stolen his family.

That was what he had done this past year. His calloused fingers reached up to his sweat-stained, sunburned neck and caressed the necklace he wore. It fit well with his worn leather armor and thorn-ripped uniform.

"If you could see me now, my golden butterfly, all safely ensconced in the City of Mexico, what would you think, I wonder?"

Ignacio's political power kept her and even Santiago out of his reach. He had turned his back on them, too, cursing the boy who was his mirror image physically, but possessed the heart of a woman. Santiago had embraced that hated half-caste cur and his Lipan savages. Orlena had lain with the renegade and would have sacrificed her very life to save her lover!

"One day, when the Night Wind is dead, I will meet you again, Orlena. I swear on my oath."

Sergeant Baca rode up to him as he waited on the promontory, surveying the desolate plains. Not a trace of life stirred below. They had combed all of the Llano Estacado and ridden far south, even into Coahuila. Now they were back in Nueva Vizcaya. And still the Night Wind and his raiders roamed free.

The sergeant waited patiently. Captain Quinn's temper was always uncertain at best. "Well, Baca, what have you?" He broke the silence without looking at the sergeant.

"Perhaps more of those for your adornment, Captain," he replied with a black-toothed grin at the chain of human ears about Quinn's neck. The Irishman was not the only man to wear the trophies. Many of the seasoned field officers who warred against the Apache and Comanche gave a bounty for their ears, some even collected scalps. "We have found a village about ten miles west of here."

"Pah! Women and children. I seek the renegade and his raiders!" Conal turned his horse in disgust. "Let us finish this task and get back on Night Wind's trail."

The mission was quiet at this time of night. Fray Bartolome liked to walk in the garden just after vespers and cleanse his mind with the tranquility of nature. He had books to read, records to tally, many things to do, but tonight he felt singularly restless and lonely. Today a girl had died in the city—a *casta*, a child of mixed blood whom no one valued. She had been merely another Indian servant in a wealthy mine owner's household, unlucky enough to contract a fever.

NIGHT WIND'S WOMAN

His melancholy ruminations were suddenly interrupted by a familiar voice. "Still your habits do not change, Priest."

"Joaquín! I had feared you dead. It has been over six months since last I saw you." He inspected the nearly naked, bronzed savage who stood in the shadows beneath a spreading cottonwood tree. Now the half-caste had reverted completely to the Lipan he had been when the priest first encountered him. When Joaquín had come to take his child—the babe he was so certain Orlena would place in an orphanage—and found it had died, the last threads binding him to civilization had been severed.

The Night Wind had listened to Bartolome explain why Orlena and Santiago went with Ignacio to the City of Mexico, but the priest knew he no more believed the reasons for that than he believed Orlena still loved him.

"Why are you here, my son?" he asked gently. He had feared never to see this child of his heart again. "I have letters from Orlena and Santiago—"

"That is not the reason I am returned," he interrupted more abruptly than he intended. "I would hear of my little brother later, but first I have something—and someone—for you."

The priest walked swiftly toward his small cabin at the rear of the gardens. "What brings you here in the face of such danger? You could disguise yourself far better, if you wished." Joaquín's Apache breechclout and the arsenal of weapons he wore proclaimed him an outlaw. His hair was long and shaggy, held from his hard face by a leather band about his forehead. He looked like a killer. He was.

"I do not choose to be a tame Indian—or a white man—just now." Standing by Bartolome's rude wooden table in the cabin, he reached up to his belt and unhooked a large leather pouch. When he dumped its contents on the table, the mound of gold glittered in the dim light like a reflection from the altar in the Cathedral of Mexico.

"Where did you get this?" the priest whispered. "I do not want your blood money, Joaquín."

"It is from a mine in Sonora. I do not bring it as retribution for my sins. It is not 'blood money,' Bartolome." He paused and looked into the priest's face. "I have been finding children . . . children like me, in the mines, in the streets. They are *castas*, abandoned by both races. They cannot read or learn to survive, except by turning into outlaws such as I am. Surely you do not want that." A quirking smile tugged at his lips.

"You have stolen this gold," the priest accused him.

"Yes. I steal from the mines—gold, silver—and slaves. Children, my old friend. I have a ranch in New Mexico. You know the valley, where I took you after I ransomed you. Well, it is a good place to raise sheep and cattle. I have taken some of the older children and adult slaves there. I pay them to work the land for me. But there are many young ones—with minds as eager as mine to learn."

"Do they, like you, wish to learn so that they can revenge themselves on their Spanish persecutors?" the priest asked with a steel edge in his voice.

"No, they wish only a chance for a new life. Will you deny them?"

"What have I to do with this?" the Franciscan asked uneasily.

"I can supply the gold and silver. Wealth enough to buy books, food, medicines. But I cannot teach them love and patience. You and the brothers here . . ." He let his words trail away, then added, "There is a widow living outside Chihuahua City—Morena Girón. She has a large ranch and she, too, is a half-caste who would aid you in this work."

Bartolome hesitated. For the first time, Joaquín was not on a quest for vengeance but a mission of mercy. Yet the money to pay for it would be stolen. He remembered Joaquín as a beaten, starved child enslaved by those men he now robbed. Then he remembered the half-caste girl he had buried that day, her dark wide eyes forever closed, her chance for life erased. Perhaps this was a chance for such children as well as a new one for Joaquín.

"I will help you," he replied simply.

Chapter 20

When Bartolome saw the first children Joaquín brought him, he was aghast. If one wounded, abused, and starved boy had touched his heart fifteen years ago, a dozen such, some at death's door, left him stunned by human cruelty.

The first supplies he needed were medicines and clothing. The gardens the friars tilled at the monastery had to be greatly enlarged to accommodate an increase in their food supply. Once the critical needs were met, he secured more books and writing supplies with which to teach the children as he had taught their rescuer many years before. All these things were costly in labor and coin. For the gold and silver that various of Night Wind's raiders left with him, the priest was most grateful.

He had agonized for quite a while about accepting the wealth. His own Franciscan superiors were far away in the capital, and the bishop in Durango was not sympathetic to the plight of Indians. He finally concluded the best course was simply to apply himself to the myriad tasks that consumed his days from before dawn far into the night. His time was spent hiring *paisanos* to till their crops and build new shelters and schoolrooms, as well as training Fray Alonzo and Fray Domingo to begin keeping order among their new charges.

Simple things such as convincing a recalcitrant eight-year-old boy to bathe could be a knotty problem indeed when that child was a Comanche orphan whose only acquaintance with water had been in crossing rivers while pursued by soldiers. Eating utensils were often used as weapons at mealtime by many of the mission's new boarders. Worst of all, perhaps, was getting the children, raised without clothing in warm weather, to accept the strictures of European modesty in dress.

Chuckling at the primness of Fray Domingo and the naivete of Fray Alonzo when confronted with these challenges, the priest found this new life one for which he was willing to chance his scruples. Looking at the open window, he watched a confrontation between a plucky six-year-old girl named Green Leaf and a sternly commanding Fray Domingo. The girl was reluctant to relinquish her five-year-old brother for a much needed delousing treatment. He turned his attention back to the recently arrived pouch of mail.

The post was highly erratic, subject to the vagaries of Indian raids, corrupt government contractors, even lazy or unwilling militia who were often assigned the unenviable task of riding the length and breadth of New Spain with the mails. As he quickly perused the water-stained addresses, one letter caught his eye. It was written in a familiar hand—Santiago Quinn's!

Eagerly he tore open the seal. In the year since the

youth and his sister had left with Ignacio Valdéz under such tragic duress, the boy had become a faithful correspondent. Orlena, still in mourning for her dead child and lost love, wrote less frequently.

Their life with Ignacio had not been unpleasant overall. He was well favored by the viceroy. They had the shield of wealth to protect them, and the boy had resumed his studies with some fine tutors. It was Orlena, as lost and embittered as Joaquín, for whom he worried and prayed.

He read the letter once, then read it once more, carefully. Quickly penning a note, he rose from his desk and called through the open window, "Brother Alonzo, make haste! Send one of the older boys to the market with this message." The market in Chihuahua City was where Joaquín had spies who delivered information to him wherever he roamed. *Pray God they can reach him quickly!*

The City of Mexico, Autumn 1789

The garden, with its fragrant oleander blooms and brightly colored canna lilies, had become Orlena's refuge. Ignacio's estate was outside the city itself, yet was as large and lavish as any of the grand houses of the nobility who governed New Spain. Over the past year, she had grown to hate the cold splendor of its marble floors and velvet draperies.

Only the courtyard garden with its open access to the azure sky, the earth, and living, growing things kept her in touch with reality. How she hated the painted, bewigged, and jewel-adorned men and women at court functions. Ignacio insisted she be fitted with an elaborate wardrobe, refusing her even the decency of a period of mourning for the infant daughter buried in the desert so far away. Using Santiago's continued education and well-being as blackmail, Ignacio had forced her to participate in the lavish balls, hunts, and parties that amused the cream of New Spain's elite.

Her only protection from Ignacio's scheme to wed her advantageously had been the fact that she was married and her husband yet lived—until now. As she paced the garden's pathways, she twisted a passion flower in her hands, unconsciously pulling the petals from it. *What will I do?* The question hammered at her mercilessly.

So engrossed was she in her dilemma that she did not hear the catlike tread of her elder brother until his sibilant voice caused her to drop the flower, spilling petals down the front of her elegant rose silk day gown.

"So, have you come to your senses, little sister? I have had the viceroy's own confessor draw up the documents. With his majesty's backing, twill be a simple matter to see your highly irregular marriage to that savage set aside."

"My marriage was not forced—"

"Nor was it consummated, in spite of the bastard Quinn's bastard got on you," Ignacio interrupted with a hiss. "My patience grows thin, Orlena. I know the circumstances under which Fray Bartolome wed you and the half-caste. By canon law the marriage is of highly dubious validity at best. Only be grateful no one here in our circles is aware of who your husband was or how you came to be tied to him."

She fought the urge to claw his pale, cruel face. To Ignacio she was merely bait with which to lure the viceroy's nephew into marriage.

"I do not choose to sign over my life to yet another of your foppish cronies, Ignacio. Santiago has found a protector in our mother's cousin, Don Bernal Dominguez. He will see the boy properly educated.

No longer can you threaten me with our brother." She turned with her shoulders squared and faced him defiantly. "As for me, my dearest wish would be for you to free me of this endless turn of social life. I'll go to the sisters before I become Don Rodrigo's wife."

He smiled nastily. "Ah, yes, the good sisters. You could live as austerely with them as you did among the savages. There would be no man to touch you in a convent, would there, Orlena?"

"I want no husband pawing me, Ignacio. I have had enough of men and their treachery."

Before she could jerk away, he reached out and took a lock of her hair, which he twisted free of her highly piled hairdo. Yanking cruelly on it, he pulled her face to his until their eyes met, narrowed in mutual hatred. "So now even the sainted Conal's treachery has soured you. He still lusts for you, little sister. Of course, you could not wed your stepfather with the blessing of the Church, but . . . arrangements could be made. I do have communications with him now and again. It seems he has become one with the savages he hunts. He takes ears and scalps and decorates his body with them. He is quite mad, I think. They call him Colorado Quinn."

"They always did! Only I was too blind to see that side of him when I was an idealistic girl." Orlena knew what he was going to threaten her with, and her mind raced frantically to find a way free of the snare. "He does not want his son's leavings, Ignacio. Until he and Joaquín meet and one dies, neither will be free. And neither of them wants me."

He laughed silkily and patted her ruined coiffure. "You are mistaken, little sister; they *both* want you. I have offered you to Conal as lure. Who knows? If you are taken north by his soldiers and used as bait, perhaps he may gain his dearest wish—to kill his

Apache bastard!" With predatory satisfaction he watched her blanch.

"You would actually give me to Conal?" Her voice was flat with defeat. For months now, she had heard stories of Quinn's atrocities. Her only solace was that Santiago was forever free of his father's influence. She had taken care that the boy be sheltered from the grisly stories of Conal's worst exploits. She prayed that Conal Quinn would die in the wilderness that had stolen his soul—if he had ever possessed a soul. Turning her eyes to Ignacio, she said lifelessly, "You, not Santiago, should have been Conal's son."

"But I am not mad. Nor am I a savage steeped in gore. I am merely a practical man. I would, of course, spare you the horrors of living with Conal again, or of encountering your vengeful husband. Think you, sister mine, which is the worse—a respectable marriage with the viceroy's nephew, Don Rodrigo, or life as doxy to a whole garrison of Quinn's soldiers? I am certain the captain would be most generous in sharing you with his men."

Don Rodrigo was an overweight youth who stuttered and was afraid of horses. Indeed, his very timidity had kept him from pursuing a bride for so long that his exasperated uncle finally took matters into his own hands. Some said the gentleman was one of those afflicted with a preference for men, and the viceroy wanted to quash all such scandal. Perhaps the boy would not want her. After Joaquín's betrayal, she could never again bear a man's touch.

"Bring me the papers, Ignacio. I will sign the petitions. If the Holy See approves it, I shall wed Don Rodrigo."

He laughed in triumph, knowing the threat of giving her to Conal's soldiers would work—that and the possibility that the Night Wind might even fall to

Colorado Quinn, with her to entrap him. He caught her hand in a surprisingly swift, sure grip and kissed it with mock ardor. "I am your most obedient servant, dearest sister. Look for me on the morrow with the petitions to free you of this odious marriage with a savage!"

After he had departed, Orlena rubbed her hands together, trying desperately to wipe away the stain of her brother's touch. He was corruption personified — the quiet treacherous viper, while Conal, her beloved champion of childhood, was equally evil. He had hidden it well during those years in Spain, but she had been blind not to see it when they came here. Perhaps he *was* mad. She rubbed her aching temples and continued walking, thinking of the cruelest, most unexpected betrayal of all.

As if conjured out of the air, a familiar voice cut into her troubled thoughts. "You will not sign away the blessing Bartolome placed on our union, no matter how accursed it has become, Lioness." Joaquín slipped from the high stone wall facing the rear of the garden and dropped gracefully to his feet in front of her.

Orlena gasped in shock, frozen to the ground as she took in the hard, handsome face of her husband. His green eyes gleamed like polished glass in his swarthy face, which was now slashed by a cruel parody of a smile. "I only heard the last of that touching scene. Such devotion to your brother. What a fine pair you Spanish make, you and your elder brother. Does this Don Rodrigo know he would purchase used merchandise, pawed by a savage?"

"And so you are, although well disguised," Orlena replied, forcing her hoarse voice under control as she inspected him with contempt. His tall, lean body was as elegantly clad as any courtier's in a dark bottle-green velvet jacket and skin-tight buff breeches. His feet, normally encased in soft moccasins, were now sporting gleaming leather riding boots. He had clubbed back his straight black hair into a queue fastened with a green velvet ribbon that matched his jacket. The snowy lawn of his shirt front only served to contrast with his bronzed skin. Yet in spite of his swarthy complexion, he looked every inch a Spanish gentleman, if one with perhaps a predominate strain of Moorish blood.

When he moved near her, however, his pantherish stride and the wary movements of his narrowed eyes betrayed the savage lurking beneath the disguise. She stepped back as he came closer. "Once you came willingly into my arms and we were not even wed, Lioness," he said arrogantly, noting her retreat with satisfaction. *Let her fear me.*

"You deceived and seduced a foolish virgin for the sake of your vengeance. I am no longer that girl."

His laughter rang cold. "No, you are not a virgin. How many fine Spanish fops have you spread your legs for, I wonder? Are you with child by one of them? Must you now arrange to rid yourself of an unwanted half-caste husband so that you can wed your latest lover? Or is it merely to aggrandize Ignacio's political fortunes that you sign his papers?"

When he pulled her close with one arm, she reached up and slapped him with all her strength. Rage welled up inside her, infusing her with a vitality she had thought long gone. She flailed and struggled as he pulled on her hair. Pins went flying as the burnished masses of curls came tumbling to her waist. He ripped the sheer watered silk of her gown as he twisted her claw-like little hands behind her back, holding both slim wrists in one strong fist.

Finally she fell quiet, exhausted by her futile struggle. He held her tightly molded to the length of his body. They were hidden by the whispering embrace of low-hanging willow branches. His face was shadowed and barbarous looking as he lowered it toward hers.

Just as she opened her mouth to scream, he closed off her cry with his lips. Plundering her soft mouth, his tongue dueled with hers in a harsh, grinding kiss. He bore down, bruising her lips and Orlena could taste her own blood. Furiously she bit his tongue and was rewarded with a snarled oath as he released her from the kiss. The breath was still crushed from her lungs as he held her fast in a bone-crushing embrace.

"Bitch! You beautiful, conniving whore. Once I swore I would leave you to the vices of the idle rich and only reclaim the child that you rejected." She flinched at the mention of their dead daughter, but he shook with such repressed rage that he could not see it. "But now I have decided your freedom must be curtailed. Santiago sent frantic word to Bartolome that you would be forced into a terrible marriage after ours was dissolved. I see now how much Ignacio has had to *force* you to wed the viceroy's nephew!"

"I would have no husband—neither you nor Rodrigo," she hissed breathlessly.

"More is the pity then that you are already tied to me—and I choose for my own reasons not to unloose you!"

With that he tapped her a sound blow on her jaw, rendering her unconscious before she could scream. Since receiving the desperate plea from Bartolome, he had ridden for days to rescue his wife. Foolishly risking death, he had disguised himself as a *rico*, a mixed-blood rancher, visiting the capital on business, using the dangerous deception to gain entry to Ignacio's estate, where he could talk with Orlena and decide what to do about her plight. *Her plight!*

NIGHT WIND'S WOMAN

As he slung her unconscious body over his shoulder and stalked toward the rear gate to the gardens, he realized that this precipitous kidnapping was far from the rational plan he had intended. But as always, Orlena drove him past reason. He had desired her with a sudden painful stab when first he saw her in the garden, all gold and rose, so slim and elegant, the perfect Spanish lady. Then, upon hearing her words to Ignacio and watching her brother's parting gallantry to her, Joaquín had felt a killing jealousy seize him. He had wanted to hurt her as he had been hurt.

Orlena was his wife, canon law be damned! Ignacio, the viceroy, the whole Council of the Indies be damned! He would keep her until he tired of her! Effortlessly, Joaquín tossed her across his heavy, silver-inlaid saddle and swung up behind her, riding swiftly toward the shelter of the dense foliage beyond the estate.

"Where are you taking me?" Orlena finally asked. She had held her peace for as long as she could bear it after regaining consciousness. She was tied to a small, sleek filly and Joaquín held the reins, guiding them through the dense vegetation that lined the narrow, steep ravine. Insects bit her legs where her silk skirts had been hiked up so that she could ride astride. Her muscles cried out for respite from her cramped position, but she would not give him the satisfaction of begging.

He ignored her question, intent on searching out some hidden trail on the jungle floor. All day they had been riding north, descending from the fertile plateau of the capital into the green embrace of the tropical wilderness.

"We will die at the hands of bandits or savages— there are many hereabouts who do not speak

Apache," she added spitefully, wishing desperately to swat at a mosquito extracting a generous quantity of her blood. Her hands were bound, but in the isolated jungle he had not bothered to gag her, only warning her of marauding animals and humans if she cried out for rescue. Since coming to New Spain, Orlena had learned to be practical. But watching Joaquín's cold, silent profile as they rode wore on her nerves. With every jarring bounce on the heavy saddle, her scratched, bitten, and exhausted body cried for mercy. Orlena seethed until she had to speak. "Answer me, damn you! Where are we going?"

He turned and favored her with an icy smile, at odds with the steaming heat of their surroundings. "For tonight, to a small village not far from here. They will provide us with shelter, fresh horses, and something more suitable, if less fashionable, for you to wear," he added with a leer at one slim leg laid bare for the insects to feast upon.

As a concession to the heat, he had long ago shed his cutaway coat and unfastened the studs of his lawn shirt. It hung open, revealing the dark curling patterns of his chest hair. The sheer fabric clung to his sweat-soaked skin, molding across his broad shoulders. The breeches were equally indecent and distracting, fitting snugly to his lean, muscular thighs. His feet, unlike her silk-slippered ones, were encased in the flexible protection of soft leather riding boots. *Suitable clothes, indeed!* she fumed.

Good as his word, Joaquín was soon hailed by a small dark man of mixed blood, dressed in the usual *paisano*'s garb of loose, dingy white cotton and leather sandals. By nightfall they were settled in a small thatched hut on the outskirts of a rural village. Joaquín strode casually in the narrow door and tossed a coarse peasant's blouse and skirt to her. She was reminded of the clothes he had given her in New Mexico. Grinning, he seemed to read her thoughts.

"The skirts are full. Your legs will be protected from the insects as we ride."

"What is our final destination—the Lipan camp?" she asked with hope in her voice. Her foster parents would believe the truth when she spoke it!

"You will see when we arrive," was all he would reply.

When one of the old women brought a simple meal of beans, tortillas, and sliced fruit, they ate in silence. Wiping her sticky fingers on her ruined silk dress, she eyed the practical clothes, wondering if he expected her to change before his cold, disconcerting gaze.

Raising her chin stubbornly, she said, "I will not disrobe for you, Joaquín."

A chilling look flashed in his eyes, then a slow, lustful smile replaced the anger. "You stink, Doña Orlena, and your insect bites need attention lest you take a fever and die. You will bathe and let me treat you. There is nothing to reveal that I have not already seen, Lioness," he added in a taunting voice.

When he stood over her, she realized the futility of doing battle. She would only humiliate herself in front of a village full of people. Retaining the small measure of dignity left her, Orlena rose, clutching the clean clothing to her breast.

A path from the hut twined into dense foliage. In a sudden clearing lay a small pool fed by a stream that trickled from the crevices of a rocky ledge that jutted above the opposite side. The wild beauty of the scene would have enchanted her under different circumstances. Orlena recalled very well their earlier erotic ablutions!

This time Joaquín surprised her. Handing her a bar of soap, he turned his back and began unconcernedly to peel his clothes from his sweaty body. Lest his hard savage beauty again hold her in thrall, Orlena did likewise, quickly shedding her clothes. The water proved a much-needed refreshment, in spite of her unease in again bathing with Joaquín. The isolated pool was warm with tropical heat in spite of the dense canopy of trees overhead.

Orlena waded cautiously until she was hip deep in the water, then knelt and began to soap her hair. By the time she had rinsed it and lathered the rest of her body, her concentration was broken by a clean splash as Joaquín's body knifed into the pool from the ledge above. He emerged about ten feet from her, obviously familiar with the depth of the water to have made such a dive. "Finish with the soap and give it to me," he commanded as he shook clinging locks of night-black hair away from his face.

She did as he demanded, and he did not approach her, only lathered and rinsed his body, then paddled to the shallows and began to dry himself on a rough cotton cloth one of the village women had given them. She was already on the bank, assiduously avoiding looking his way as she dealt with the more complex problem of drying not only her body but the waist-length mass of her hair on one thin towel.

"Here, use this on your insect bites. It will kill the sting and prevent swelling," he said, handing her a small vial of an evil-smelling, oily substance. Grimacing, she accepted it. Rather than the carefully orchestrated seductive touching he had employed in his first journey with her as captive, this time he ignored her and donned fresh clothes without casting her a further glance.

NIGHT WIND'S WOMAN

Finally, after she had used the noisome medication on her legs and put on the skirt, she struggled to reach one welt in the center of her back before slipping on the blouse.

Gruffly, he took the medicine from her hand and said, "Hold your hair away so I may see." When she complied, he quickly and dispassionately medicated the welt, then refastened the cork on the vial as she drew the blouse over her head and tied the lacing in front with fumbling fingers.

They slept together on the rude pallet that night, much as they had on their first night in New Mexico, but this time she knew how useless it was to attempt escape from her vigilant captor. In moments she was asleep.

The journey north was long and torturous, quickly assuming a familiar pattern as they rode, ate, and slept together in strained, impersonal silence. She abandoned all attempts at engaging him in even superficial conversation. He would tell her nothing of his plans. Everywhere they stopped, he seemed to have a network of supporters who brought them fresh horses and food, as well as providing them with shelter.

In a few days, the cloying jungle lowlands gave way to more open higher elevations. The fertile valley of Mexico lay before them. Of course they avoided well-traveled routes and stayed to seemingly trackless back ways where no Spanish soldiers would find them. Only the Indians and *paisanos* who were Joaquín's friends knew of their journey. He seemed possessed of an inexhaustible supply of gold coin—stolen she surmised, but put to good use by the renegade.

Orlena was so exhausted by the pace at which they

traveled that she lost count of time. Every muscle and nerve in her body screamed for respite. And still she would not beg.

When they reached the outskirts of the city of Durango, she recognized where they were. This was at last familiar terrain that she had traveled with Conal so long ago on that fateful journey to Santa Fe. "Are you going to visit Fray Bartolome?" she finally dared to ask as they left the ramshackle Indian section of Durango and again struck north.

"We go to Chihuahua, but not to the mission," was all he would say. By the time they neared the end of their passage, Orlena was as sunbrowned and bedraggled as any *paisana*, which was precisely how she looked with a *rebozo* over her fair hair, dressed in dusty coarse cotton. Outside the city, just as they crested the ridge that overlooked its flat expanse, Joaquín veered their horses to the west. They rode for several hours into a small, fertile valley, picturesque in the lush grip of autumn harvest. Ripe peaches, enticingly blushed, hung from the trees, and fat, pale watermelons trailed along uneven rows of garden.

As they rounded a curve in the road, a magnificent adobe hacienda rose before them. All along the way, Joaquín had been greeted with awe and respect, but here the men and women tilling the soil seemed to recognize him as their don, a friend and protector. When he dismounted before the large, two-story whitewashed house with its red tile roof and elegant wrought-iron grillwork, a slim figure appeared at the front doorway.

She was elegantly clad in a rich, cream-colored riding habit. Gleaming masses of ebony hair hung straight and free down her back, flying like a silk curtain as she ran to greet him. She leaped into his embrace, looping her arms about his shoulders and

NIGHT WIND'S WOMAN

kissing him full on the lips.

When the long, joyous, and intimate welcome ended, Joaquín put her down, allowing her eyes to travel disdainfully up and down Orlena's grimy, crudely dressed person.

Smiling coldly, with one arm casually about the black-haired woman's waist, he said, "Morena, this is my wife, Orlena. Orlena, greet your hostess, Señora Morena Girón."

Her beautiful face held an expression as cold as his.

She replied, "Welcome to Hacienda Girón, Señora."

Chapter 21

Morena Girón was a *casta* and a striking beauty. Her slanted high cheekbones and rich ebony eyes were framed by a magnificent mass of black hair, which she wore pulled back from her high brow with ivory combs. The very severity of the hairdo added to her dramatic appearance. Now her eyes met Orlena's with such hate that the exhausted younger woman felt it like a physical blow.

Orlena's Spanish pride forced her to sit straighter in the saddle. Ignoring her filthy peasant's clothes, she tossed her tangled golden curls back and raised her chin, meeting the black-eyed glare with a cold amber one of equal ferocity. She looked contemptuously at Joaquín's arm about the *casta*'s waist and slid her leg over the saddle, dismounting in one fluid motion as Lipan maidens did, unassisted by any man's hand.

"Why have you brought me to Señora Girón's hospitality, Joaquín? It is quite apparent your Indian blood calls to hers. Surely my pale Spanish charms are tame by comparison," she said, striving mightily to conceal her humiliation. The beautiful *casta*'s place in her husband's affections evoked a raw pain in her heart that she would never reveal.

Morena felt Joaquín's arm tighten convulsively, then relax as he watched his wife dismount and confront them. *He still cares for her!* She said nothing, waiting to see what Joaquín would do.

He released Morena and slowly walked up to his wife, taking in her haughty demeanor. Only Orlena Valdéz could spend three weeks riding across jungle and desert, arrive in filthy rags, and yet look down on the formidable Morena as if she were an insect. Perversely, her pride pleased him almost as much as it angered him. He focused on his anger. "So, my base Apache blood calls to Morena's Yaqui blood, does it? And you, Lioness, are above such physical cravings," he whispered, contemptuous disbelief reflected on his face as he stood in front of her, forcing her to meet his eyes. "Show our guest to her quarters, Morena, if you please. The accommodations at the rear of the courtyard should serve well enough."

A slow smile of comprehension slid about the *casta*'s lips. "I shall have them readied, but first, perhaps a bath," she said as she sniffed the air about Orlena deliberately. "Then some fresh clothing. We look to be of a size . . . if I have one of my women take in the seams of the basque."

Orlena's face flamed at the insult, but she let the odious woman glide past her without a retort. When Joaquín motioned for her to follow, she hissed at him, "What will Señor Girón say when he finds you in his wife's bed on the morrow?"

He threw back his head and laughed. "No need for me to fear, Lioness. Morena is a widow."

They walked into the *sala* and Morena immediately excused herself, saying she would make arrangements for bath water and clean clothes for them both. "There is cool wine on the table, as always, Joaquín," she added warmly as she left the room.

Orlena looked about her, amazed to be in such elegant surroundings in the wilds of Nueva Vizcaya. The house was almost as palatial as Ignacio's outside the City of Mexico. The floors were polished adobe brick, not marble, true, but they gleamed with a rich luster and were covered by thick Moorish carpets of the finest quality. The walls were whitewashed, but no crude interior beams were visible. An Austrian chandelier full of fine beeswax candles hung from the high ceiling. The heavy oak furniture had been polished until it shone like satin.

She could not help but betray her surprise as she inspected the *sala* and looked down the long hall that stretched beyond the arched doorway.

Handing her a glass of pale red wine, Joaquín said coldly, "Augusto Girón was fifty-seven years old when he took Morena, a mere Yaqui half-caste servant girl, to his bed. She was fourteen."

At Orlena's look of horror, he continued grimly, "When his wife died childless and he became ill, Morena nursed him. It seems the local priest disapproved of their sinful liaison, and with his first wife departed, Augusto was exhorted to legitimize the union. He married her, but she paid a high price for her present wealth. While the first Señora Girón lived, she had Morena whipped and abused by her male servants each time her husband was away."

"And he did nothing when he returned?" Orlena asked incredulously.

Joaquín shrugged at her willful ignorance. "Who would he believe—his lady wife who told him she caught the girl stealing and punished her, or a mere Indian with lowly enough morals to entice the peasants to rape her?"

A wave of pity for the coldly beautiful woman washed over Orlena, but as she looked into Joaquín's accusing green eyes, she forgot Morena Girón. "Your hatred for the Spanish will always be between us, will it not, Joaquín?" she asked sadly, knowing the answer.

He swallowed the last of his wine in one fast gulp and angrily set the glass on the table. "My hatred of the Spanish, for which I have ample reason, is not why you chose to desert me and our child. You despise Indians, Orlena. We are the people without reason—beneath your fine civilization, unable to aspire to this!" His arm swept the richly furnished room with hostile contempt. Then he reached for her and pulled her into his arms. "How you must have hated yourself for feeling such base lust for an animal like me!"

Orlena's face flamed as she remembered her intense humiliation when she first had been attracted to the Night Wind. Feeling his arms about her, his heart pounding against her breasts as he held her roughly, she looked at his set face, hopeless misery reflected in her own. "You have exacted your revenge, even as you told Conal you would. Why do you want me now?"

"You are my wife, as I told Morena," he replied tightly. "No Spaniard takes from me—ever again. Not Conal. Not Ignacio."

Just then Morena reappeared silently in the high, arched doorway. Watching the crackling antagonism between them, she should have rejoiced, but Morena Girón's instincts had been well honed over the years. She could sense the frustration and want that lurked beneath their mutual contempt. "Your baths await," she said, causing Joaquín to release Orlena abruptly. Smiling at him, she continued, "Your tub is in the usual place, beloved. Hers is in the servants' quarters off the kitchen. Lena will show her to it and bring her clothing."

A young Indian girl curtsied nervously before them, her braids bobbing as she turned and indicated that Orlena should follow her. Morena moved closer to Joaquín and embraced him.

As Orlena left the *sala* she could hear Morena's voice echo down the hall after her. "I shall see to your bath, my bold warrior."

When Orlena was gone, Joaquín gently removed Morena's hands from his neck and said, "It is good of you to welcome me, Morena, but you know what we once were to each other is over. There is the work we share, but that must be all." He could see the pain and desperation in her eyes. Touching her cheek softly, he added, "I am sorry."

"It is her, is it not? You still love her after she has betrayed you and your child!" She twisted away, her voice harsh with anger. "You believe that foolish old priest Bartolome, who has fallen under her spell!"

He smiled sadly. "For all his irritating stubbornness, Bartolome is not a fool. He has given up speaking to me of her innocence. Perhaps he knows it is useless." He shrugged. "But she is my wife. I will not let Ignacio and Conal use her for their purposes. Who knows, mayhap I can bait a trap for Quinn using a golden lure?"

She snorted, unconvinced by his words. "As you will, Joaquín, but do not trust her."

"Little chance of that, Morena, never fear. Now, lead me to that bath."

"The room will serve, but are you not afraid I might escape?" Orlena said insolently, hiding her chagrin over being quartered at the rear of the courtyard. First that witch sent her an ugly gray dress with the bust let out by her seamstress so that it hung limply! In addition, she was given this room, far in the back of the grand house, away from where Joaquín would cavort with his mistress.

"You will never escape, Orlena. I will release you when it pleases me."

"So much for the lifelong bonds of the marriage sacrament Fray Bartolome performed," she retorted bitterly.

"You betrayed me, Orlena. You would have signed anything to allow your Church to free you so you might wed a Spanish nobleman," he said coldly.

She whirled on him in righteous fury. "I have slept alone this past year, husband. Can you say the same?"

A mocking glint flashed in his eyes. "So, you are jealous in spite of everything. Should I visit your bed this night, Lioness? Have you missed the crude rutting of this savage?"

"No! I want nothing from you, only an end to this humiliation. Parade your whores elsewhere, Joaquín!"

He grabbed her shoulders and shook her roughly. "Morena is no whore! You are the one better acquainted with the term, Doña Orlena!"

She jerked free of his bruising grip and slammed the door, then crumpled against it as the tears overflowed, scalding her cheeks. She could hear his footfall echo down the corridor. Did his room adjoin Morena's, or did he openly sleep in her bed?

Rubbing her temples, she forced her thoughts elsewhere. They were outside Chihuahua City in a small valley west of where Fray Bartolome's mission lay. If she could steal a horse, she might escape to beg his protection. But as she paced, Orlena reconsidered. They were married, and the priest still harbored some absurd notion that Joaquín loved her. He would only tell her she must return to her husband.

"I have nowhere to go," she whispered forlornly to the empty walls. Bone weary and feeling the effect of the wine on her empty stomach, Orlena walked dejectedly to the bed and lay across it. She was asleep almost instantly.

Hearing a light rapping at her door, Orlena sat up disorientedly, having no idea how long she had slept. Faint streaks of dying sunlight filtered across her floor from the western window.

"I have brought you a tray, Señora. Señora Girón felt you would be too weary to join her and Don Joaquín in the dining room." Lena's voice was muffled through the heavy wooden door.

Orlena roused herself and straightened her hair as best she could. There was no help for her tear-swollen face. She called out, "Just a moment. I was resting." Opening the door, she took the tray from the Indian girl without looking at her, merely thanking her quickly.

So, she was not even to be allowed to dine with them. "Too weary, indeed!" she mimicked scornfully. She sat the tray on the bedside table and uncovered it. Delicious spicy aromas of beef and green chiles, along with the pungent delicacy of tropical fruit and that lush fragrance of hot chocolate wafted upward. In spite of her empty stomach, all appetite had left her. Joaquín had abandoned her in this solitary room while he and Morena ate in the elegant dining hall.

He had truly lost whatever love he once felt for her—if indeed he did ever love her. Had her cruel act in the mountains killed it? Or, had it been a sham from the start, only a means to avenge himself on Conal as that insidious letter had said?

She reviewed their journey from the capital. After

NIGHT WIND'S WOMAN

the fierce, angry kiss that day in the garden, he had treated her with nothing but cold indifference, never betraying the slightest desire for her, even when she was naked in the water. He was tired of her. She was his possession, but one he valued only because his enemies wanted her. Mechanically, she picked up the fork and stabbed a small chunk of meat, eating without tasting.

Joaquín, too, had little appetite, although he forced himself to eat heartily for Morena's sake. She had had the cook prepare all his favorite dishes, and he did not want to disappoint her.

"Your wife is dangerous, Joaquín. Keeping her may lure Conal to you, but it may also bring her brother. They are two formidable enemies to fight at once," Morena said, studying his handsome face over the rim of her glass as she toyed with the crystal.

One black eyebrow rose in curiosity. "You have met Ignacio?"

She smiled serenely. "Do not let his foppish manner deceive you. He is as deadly as Conal and now possesses far more power. You know our work takes me to the capital on occasion. Even a *casta* gains admittance in some quarters."

He nodded grimly. "I know how valuable the information you obtain for us is to our cause."

She shrugged. "I enjoy besting those Spanish bastards."

"So do I," he replied grimly. "After a day or two of rest, we will leave here and head north into Texas. Conal serves under Ugarte now. When he learns I have Orlena, he will come for her, I think. Then we will settle it . . . finally."

"You *are* going to use her to lure him to you! Joaquín, he has many soldiers at his command— hardened men who will kill you, even Comanche scouts who can track you." Her liquid dark eyes were wide with fear.

"But I have Orlena. He wants her, and even more, he wants me dead. He has pursued me this past year with great singlemindedness. I tire of the game. I, too, have men who can kill and track. We are well matched, Morena."

She swore and threw down her napkin. "I hate that Irish pig!" She stopped suddenly and looked at him. "You want me to send word through my riders! I will not risk your life so, Joaquín," she pleaded.

"Yes, you will. My plans are well laid. I know the Llano Estacado and the Sacramento Mountains into which I will lead him far better than any white man alive."

"I cannot dissuade you, can I?" With slumped shoulders she subsided, recognizing the shuttered look on his beautiful face. The chiseled perfection of his Apache and European features had always stirred her. He was the most magnificent lover she had ever known, and tonight she wanted him. It had been far, far too long. Wetting her lips with the tip of her tongue, she whispered, "Your wife has refused to take her dinner with us. Let her sleep alone, too. Come with me this night, Joaquín. I will make you forget her!"

He kissed her hand softly and shook his head. "It would not be fair, Morena. After I married her in the Lipan ceremony, I explained to you what I had done. Then I believed she loved me. Now I know she lied, but she is my wife and I will take her with me to Texas. For now, I will not hurt you by promising what I cannot give."

"Then give me only what I ask—one night—no promises, Joaquín."

NIGHT WIND'S WOMAN

I should not have brought Orlena here, he thought angrily. He had wanted to hurt her by flaunting Morena in front of her, but he had not thought what his actions would do to Morena. "Let it lie, Morena," he said quietly. "I think it best if we leave on the morrow."

"What will you do with Orlena Valdéz after you have killed the Irishman?" she asked with a calculating look in her eyes.

The shuttered mask he wore earlier slipped for a moment. "I do not know. I went to rescue her at my brother's pleading. Santiago thought she was being abused by Ignacio." He laughed bitterly. "He mistook the matter. Perhaps I will return her to Ignacio's tender mercies. He can have this hellish match set aside and wed her where he wills."

She studied the look of tormented hunger on his face and knew he lied. The pain stabbed her with killing intensity. "She is no fit mate for the Night Wind. She will cause your death."

He smiled that devilishly blinding white smile. Like his green eyes, it was a reminder that he was Conal Quinn's son. "Someone surely will cause my death. Already I have cheated it too many times. Do not mourn too much for me, Morena." He stood up and took her hand, kissing the back of it in a light salute.

As she watched him walk from the room, the look on her face was no longer the vulnerable wistfulness it had been earlier. Now it was as hard as that of her dark Yaqui gods.

The ride to Texas would be hard on her. Already she was exhausted. He had planned to spend at least two more days here at Morena's place, but now he saw how impossible that would be. Aching with the sexual frustration he had reined in so tightly on their journey from the capital, he might weaken and give in to Morena's blandishments. "I will not use her as a substitute for what I desire," he muttered angrily.

Joaquín had wanted to punish Orlena's treachery by showing cold indifference to her. He was certain the Spanish gallants in the City of Mexico had fallen over themselves in pursuit of her favors. But now his need to humiliate her was exceeded by his need to bed her.

"This time there will be no subtle seduction, no gentleness," he swore through clenched teeth as he climbed the stairs to the room at the far end of the hall.

When Orlena awakened, the candle by her bedside had burned low. The hour was late. Again she had fallen asleep in her clothes. The wine and a full meal had done their work altogether too well. Looking down at Morena's hideous, cast-off dress, now a mass of wrinkles in addition to its ungainly fit, she began to unfasten the buttons angrily. "I shall at least sleep in a bed in comfort," she gritted out as she slid the gray linen over her hips and tossed it carelessly on a chair. The petticoats quickly followed. At least the sheer lawn undergarments fit, even if they were plain and well worn. Too small in the bust, indeed! She filled out the camisole just as well as that black-haired bitch!

Having no nightrail, she decided to sleep in the pantalets and camisole. There was a wooden-handled brush that looked to be clean on the bureau. Her hair was still tousled from her bath and faintly damp. Reaching for the brush, she struggled to untangle the dark golden mass.

Deep in concentration, she did not hear Joaquín silently open the door. He stood stone still, watching the rise and fall of her breasts through the gauze thinness of the camisole. Her spine was seductively arched as she raised her arms, working the brush through one long, tangled lock of hair, which she held away from her head with her other hand. Her thick lashes veiled her haunting eyes. He could feel the ache in his loins build to a mindless, hungry desperation, yet he remained rooted in the doorway, his breath swept away by her loveliness.

Sensing his presence, she jerked her head up. The brush dropped from her numb fingers as her eyes met his. Her lips mouthed the word *no* softly, then more forcefully as he stepped inside and closed the door behind him.

"Go to your mistress, Joaquín. Surely she meets your needs far better than I!"

"I choose not to involve Morena in our private war," he replied calmly, continuing to walk toward her, stripping off his jacket and carelessly tossing it atop her dress. When he began to unfasten the studs from his shirt and pull it open, she groped across the bed for the brush, seized it, and hurled it at him. He ducked effortlessly as she swore an amazing oath.

"For a highborn lady, you possess a low-class vocabulary, Lioness," he said as he continued his strip. His shirt joined the pile of their clothing as he reached down and took off his soft leather shoes, then slid the hose from his feet. When he straightened up, Orlena had jumped clear of the bed and was edging toward the large porcelain water pitcher and bowl on the wash stand.

"Do not, or you will clean up every sliver with your bare hands," he warned.

"All this time you have not touched me, you ignored me. Why now?" she whispered hoarsely.

"Why not? You are my wife. I am your husband. Have you missed my attentions, Lioness?"

"No! You but play cruel games with me and I despise you for it!" she cried, plastering her body against the rough adobe wall.

"Speak not to me of cruel games, Doña Orlena! You are the deceiver who excels at them!" With that, he placed his flattened palms against the wall as he pressed his body intimately along the length of hers, imprisoning her. His head lowered and he buried his face in her fragrant hair. Still damp and curling, it smelled of soap and her unique fragrance.

Orlena could feel his hot breath on her neck as his pelvis rotated crudely against hers. The slow, honeyed ache uncoiled low in her belly, unnerving her. She clenched her hands into fists, her nails biting into her palms in frustration as his seeking mouth found her bare throat, then trailed lower to her rising and falling chest. She was panting with want and hated herself for it! But his need was every bit as apparent. She could feel the hard probe of his erection straining through his tight breeches to press between her legs. Against her will, her thighs parted.

He laughed deep in his throat as one hand pulled roughly on her hair, turning her face up to meet the onslaught of his kisses. He savaged her mouth, forcing it open, invading with his tongue. As his lips molded to hers, his hips matched the thrusting rhythm of the deepening kiss.

Orlena rubbed her hands against the rough, whitewashed wall until her palms were bleeding, struggling to keep herself from responding to the white heat of his passion. Joaquín reached up and ripped the wispy camisole free of her breasts. The old fabric gave way easily, the only protest her gasp of dismay as his hand closed over one milky breast, gleaming in the moonlight. The pale pink tip hardened as his thumb stroked it. He gave a low, insinuating laugh as she tried to control herself, tried to pull back, knowing it was too late.

It had been too late when he first stood in the doorway with those hypnotic green eyes devouring her. Now he scooped her into his arms and flung her like a feather onto the rumpled bed.

"Would you not lose the pantalets as you did the camisole, remove them," he commanded as he unbuttoned his fly and worked the tight breeches down his long legs.

"They are your mistress's cast offs. I care not," she whispered, refusing to look at his splendid nakedness. Even so, the image of his bronzed body with its supple rippling muscles was emblazoned on her mind.

He was glad of her perverse refusal to obey his command, to give in to her own passions, he assured himself as he reached down and tore the thin cloth from her slim thighs. Looking down at the puckered points of her nipples, he could see the unmistakable evidence of her body's response to him. As he towered over her with one knee pressed into the mattress, a flush stole over her white skin. "If I reach down and touch you . . . so"—his hand rested tentatively on the curls between her legs—" you will be wet and aching for me, Lioness." His fingers splayed, then pulled together as they traveled from the dark gold mound to dip between her nether lips.

Orlena arched and bucked at the raw, primitive pleasure, unable to continue any pretense of indifference. Rolling away from the fierce ecstasy of his touch was nearly impossible, but she did so, coming up on the opposite side of the bed, crouched on her hands and knees. Each breath was labored as she bit off the words, "Get out of here! Go to your Indian whore!"

Grabbing a fistful of hair that hung over her shoulder, he yanked her back across the bed. "You *are* my whore!" He sank down on top of her, covering her body with his, driving his knee up between her legs as she writhed and kicked. "Spread your legs for me," he whispered harshly as his hands pinioned her wrists above her head.

The breath was squeezed from her body as his weight bore down on her. The will to fight suddenly left her and she lay limp and exhausted. Tears trickled from the corners of her eyes and she turned her face away from his.

Joaquín sensed the change from fury to tears and the hatefulness that had been coiled tightly about his chest loosed. He released her wrists and massaged them gently as his mouth rained soft caresses over her tear-streaked face.

She despised her weakness, crying foolish, womanish tears, surrendering so that he might humiliate and use her—better that he raped her than this, his tenderness, perhaps his pity.

He nuzzled her ear, then his tongue, velvety soft, lapped at the teardrops as he crooned low words to her, soft love words in Spanish and Lipan. When he had finished laving away the tears, he kissed the corner of her mouth ever so delicately as he shifted his weight from her body onto his elbows. Her breasts were no longer flattened against him, but now the hardened nipples brushed against his chest hair with each breath.

Centering his lips on hers, he kissed her softly, touching the closed seam until she parted it. His tongue slid in and she could taste the salt of her own tears on it. When did her hands reach up to twine in his long shaggy hair? When did she arch her aching breasts against the rock wall of his chest? He deepened the kiss as he felt her response. Her tongue dueled with his now, touching the familiar places of his mouth, gliding over his strong white teeth. One hand slid down from his head to his back, glorying in the flexed muscles with their satiny film of perspiration slicking her path.

Joaquín moaned as his engorged shaft rubbed between her thighs. Her legs instinctively clamped together, imprisoning it as she writhed up and down, driving him wild with desire. This time when his knee spread her legs apart, she pulled him closer and he slid into the welcoming heat of her body. A blinding kaleidoscope of sensations rioted through his body as he began to drive in and out of her tight wetness.

Orlena thought she heard him murmur, "At last, at last," but the words were indistinct and her own body, so long denied, clamored for more. She wrapped her legs about his narrow hips and rode with him. Her nails dug into his back, then slid up to sink into his shoulders as she followed the hard, rough rhythm of their mating. Her head thrashed back and forth in frenzied desperation as all too soon, she could feel the old familiar cresting—old, yet each time wonderously new. The completion began to build in waves, slowly at first, then faster and more intense until she could feel his shaft swell even more, joining her as he pumped his seed deeply inside her body.

Her anguished cry of ecstasy mingled with his ragged growl. Joaquín collapsed on top of her, his face buried in her tangled hair as she held him fast, unwilling to let reality intrude on the beautiful moment of unity.

"You will never leave me, Lioness," he finally whispered as he rolled away from her, pulling her to lie closely tucked against his side.

Feeling the comforting heat of his hard, long body cocooning her, Orlena stared sightlessly at the starry sky outside the window. *No, it is you who will leave me, Night Wind.*

Chapter 22

Morena Girón did not sleep well that night. After tossing restlessly in her lonely bed for hours, she arose to watch the sunrise. Joaquín often joined her in the courtyard. But this morning he was late, as she feared he would be.

Finally, at full daylight, he appeared in the doorway of Orlena's room, looking relaxed, satiated. The driving hunger and coiled tension she had sensed in him the day before were gone. He had spent the night making love to his Spanish wife! And she had obviously pleased him. Escaping back to her room before she was seen, Morena swallowed back her tears. *I had to know. Now what shall I do about it?*

Orlena awakened, feeling the loss of her husband's body heat. He was dressed and gone already. Perhaps that was just as well. She sat up and rubbed her head, recalling his anger and his passion last night. He had entered the room intent on rape, and yet the confrontation ended very differently than it began. She did not understand all that had happened, but she certainly did understand what she had done. Orlena Valdéz, casting aside all pride and shame, had welcomed him into her body, physically begged him to make love to her. And he had! Were they both mad?

After the first tender ecstasy, they had slept. Midway through the night, he had awakened her with soft caresses, pulling her lethargic body once more into his embrace. The second time she had not made even a token resistance, but melted sleepily, softly. Had she said she loved him? Probably. And with the sun, the Night Wind vanished. At the moment he was doubtless taking his morning meal with Morena.

"At least he slept all night with me," she whispered with a small measure of grim satisfaction as she felt the slight warmth of the bed linens where his body had lain. She slid across the rumpled sheets and stood up, shivering in the cool morning air.

A knock sounded. Knowing Joaquín would not indulge in such a formality, she wrapped her naked body in one of the linens and walked over to open the door a crack. She did not want a servant to see her shredded undergarments or the disarray of the room!

The timid young Indian maid stood there with fresh towels and a change of clothing in her arms. Her face wreathed in a smile, she said, "Your husband sent me with these. Hot bath water is on its way. I will assist you, if you wish."

Seeing the doeskin tunic and leggings, once hated Apache garments she would have scorned, Orlena gratefully accepted them. The soft leather was velvety and warm, beautifully tanned and cut for her slim body. At least she would dress in comfort now. These clothes were far more flattering than Morena Girón's drab castoffs. Whatever his feelings, her husband no longer seemed intent on letting his mistress humiliate her.

Joaquín was as confused as Orlena. He had awakened with her silken hair floating across his face as she turned in her sleep. Quietly, he had slipped from the bed and dressed, noting the telltale signs of their passionate night. Clothing lay strewn across the floor, and the bed linens were more off than on the mattress. For all she had fought him at first, she had given in quickly. Of course, he had been so moved by her tears that his resolution to take her with unfeeling cruelty had lasted even less time than her resistance.

Orlena Valdéz might feel degraded, ashamed of her base physical hunger for a half-caste's touch, but she had given up all attempts to hide her passion. It was as if no man had touched her since they were separated last year. Absurd! He dismissed the idea at once. The betrayal of his need for her disturbed him deeply, but what was done was done. They would ride for Texas this very day. Perhaps by the time he had finished with Conal Quinn, he would be able to quench his need for Orlena as well.

Joaquín broke his morning fast with Morena. Telling her farewell was proving difficult. Even though he knew it was a blatant delay of his departure, he agreed to ride with her to meet some of the former slaves who now worked in her fields and orchards.

By the time they returned from the morning's journey, Joaquín could see Fray Bartolome tying his mule near a tall cottonwood tree. He turned angrily to Morena. "I did not wish him here. He has been trying to convince me to forgive my wife her treachery. He believes her innocent. Now that she is here with me, it will cause nothing but trouble, Morena."

She shrugged fatalistically. "The priest comes and

goes. I do not command him. He does not command you. Perhaps he is here because of the school. I mislike his defense of her as much as you do!"

Fray Bartolome called out, "It has been too long, my young friend. You will not recognize Ana, she has grown so!"

Joaquín dismounted, then helped Morena down. When he turned to embrace his old mentor, the priest's warming smile made him forget his guilt and misgivings. Always it was good to see Bartolome.

"I will doubtless not recognize many of the children. You spoil and fatten them in your old age as you never did me when you were full of youthful zeal," Joaquín said jokingly as he hugged the big man.

"You have been off in the wilderness for six months, and this is the welcome I get upon your return! I have come with news of several children sent to Hurtado's mine, Morena," he said, turning to greet the handsome *casta*. "It is perhaps good that our best rescuer has unexpectedly shown up. I feared we might not be able to find men to free them before they are brutalized."

Morena's face lit up as she turned to Joaquín. "Now you cannot leave for Texas. You must stay and help us. I will care for Orlena," she added defensively.

"Orlena? Here? With you?" Fray Bartolome exclaimed. "What nonsense is this about going to Texas?"

Casting a dark glance at Morena, Joaquín turned back to Bartolome's smiling face. He sighed in resignation, saying, "Yes, I have Orlena with me. I would have spared you the worry of knowing my plans. You already spend too many hours upon your calloused knees. Say your prayers for the children, Bartolome, not for us."

"I will pray where I will. What our Blessed Lord

NIGHT WIND'S WOMAN

grants is up to Him. Where is Orlena? Is she well?" he asked as they walked inside.

A sardonic smile tugged at Joaquín's lips as he replied, "She is quite well this morning, I believe."

"Good. Then let me see her. Our parting last year was most painful for us both," the priest said. He hoped Joaquín's acceptance of his mediation augured well. The look of wounded fury he saw in Morena's eyes did not.

"Perhaps we should let the good father and your wife have a private reunion, Joaquín," Morena suggested.

Joaquín's face darkened as he imagined all the things Orlena could tell Bartolome in his absence. Of course, there were other things he felt certain she would confess to no one, not even a priest!

"I must go after these children, but first I will bring Orlena down to see her old friend," he said to Morena. "Are the children being held at the usual place in Chihuahua City?" he asked Bartolome.

The priest nodded and Joaquín darted ahead, up the stairs to get his wife.

Orlena stood at the top of the steps as Joaquín came striding up to meet her. Dressed in an open white shirt and dusty riding pants, he looked as elegant as any lord, his every movement graceful. She could not read the expression on his face as he approached her. She had bathed, dressed, and then worked up her courage to ask him what he planned to do with her. Now all the rehearsed speeches fled her mind as she felt his cool green eyes survey her from head to foot.

"The dress favors you, Lioness," he said quietly.

Nervously, she ran one hand down the soft, clinging doeskin. "Thank you. I—I do prefer this to Morena's clothes."

Realizing that the admission cost her dearly, he

nodded and simply replied, "I have been saving them for you." He did not add that he had brought them to the City of Mexico as a special present, which he withheld after he overheard her and Ignacio discuss ridding her of the inconvenience of her husband.

"I heard voices downstairs—"

"That is why I must speak with you. I have to go away, perhaps for several days. Bartolome is here and wishes to see you. Morena will offer you sanctuary while I am gone. Do not think to enlist the priest in helping you escape me."

Her heart became leaden in her breast. So he was already repenting their one night together. "I see. Well, I am at least rescued from Ignacio's trap."

"Do not hurt Bartolome by involving him in our personal war, Lioness," he warned again.

"As if I could talk him into letting me escape you now that he has his dearest prayers answered!" she said with stung pride.

His eyes were glacial as he replied, "You could convince the College of Cardinals that the Pope was Satan, I do believe."

"I will never hurt Bartolome!" *I have never willingly hurt you!*

Joaquín sensed something painful that she held back. Not wanting to leave her, he impulsively reached for her. His fingers dug into the soft doeskin, kneading her back, then tangling in her long golden hair as he tipped her face up and kissed her.

Orlena was at first startled, then warmed by his touch. She opened to him, returning the kiss, wrapping her arms about him and forgetting all else until he pushed her roughly away from him. "I must go now. Morena will explain everything."

"I can well imagine how she will relish the task," Orlena replied beneath her breath as she followed him down the stairs toward the sound of the Franciscan's beloved voice.

Seeing Orlena in the Apache clothes that she knew Joaquín had brought especially for her fanned the fires of jealousy in Morena. Even worse, the garments looked beautiful on her, as if she belonged in them. Morena watched the warm reunion between Orlena and the priest who had been her co-worker for the past year, anger and hurt growing apace. What was it about the Spaniard that bewitched all men?

"Joaquín, you must go if you are to have time to gather the men in the city and stop the soldiers from selling the children." Morena focused on discussing their plans.

The details of such an operation were familiar to all three of them, but fascinating to Orlena. She listened as they made the arrangements. With one quelling look in her direction, Joaquín said his good-byes and left the house, heading for the stables where Warpaint awaited. He had not kissed her good-bye—unless she counted the rough, brief kiss on the stairs. Looking over at Morena, Orlena knew the *casta* had noted his abrupt parting with satisfaction.

"I will leave you two to converse while I see to food and medicine for our secret guests," Morena said, then called back over her shoulder, "I will instruct the servants to prepare a midday meal for you, Father." She ignored Orlena.

Fray Bartolome noted with no surprise the veiled hostility between the two women. He had long known of the liaison between Joaquín and the widow. After his bitter parting with his wife last year, Joaquín had resumed his relationship with Morena. Still, it saddened the priest that Joaquín was using her in his revenge against Orlena. Both women were being punished for sins they had not committed.

Taking Orlena's hand, he drew her toward the kitchen. While they ate, she could explain what had happened since Joaquín had gone south to rescue her from Ignacio.

After they had settled in for a simple meal of tortillas and beans, they sipped their rich hot chocolate as Orlena told him about the way in which Joaquín had found her in the garden agreeing to Ignacio's blackmail. She held back none of the hurtful details about the ensuing journey north, culminating with her humiliation by Morena. She finished simply by saying, "So you see, Father, although he has saved me from my brother, he has not done it for love, but simply to thwart his enemies. Now he counts me among them," she added in a choked whisper.

Bartolome stroked his beard and considered. "So, Ignacio would dissolve your marriage. It was performed under highly irregular circumstances, without a dispensation for the collateral line of affinity, and it was not consummated . . ." Sensing her discomfiture as she lowered her head, he asked, "I take it you have left out one essential fact?"

"At least Ignacio can no longer use that as grounds for setting aside our vows!" she said hotly.

Fray Bartolome patted her hand. "Joaquín loves you, Orlena, no matter how bitter he is or what he thinks you have done. He would not have answered Santiago's plea and come for you if he did not care."

"He did it for his brother, not for me," she replied stubbornly.

Sighing, Bartolome decided that for now all he could do was change the subject. When Joaquín returned, they would have another discussion about Orlena. "How does your brother fare in the City of Mexico? I feared for him under Ignacio's influence."

She smiled. "No, we have at least been blessed that

way. Our mother's cousin, Don Bernal, is well placed on the viceroy's staff. He has no children and wants an heir. He is seeing to Santiago's education. Since he and Ignacio have always hated each other, I urged him to go live with Bernal."

"It has been lonely for you this past year, has it not?" The Franciscan's eyes were softened with compassion.

"Far more for me than for my husband, it would seem," she said with faint irony. "Tell me of these rescues of children from the mines." She wished not to dwell on her marriage.

"We mostly wrest them from their Spanish captors before they are sold in Chihuahua City. Not all are children. Sometimes peaceful Indians are enslaved for debt or other falsified charges. We do what we can. Adults and older children we attempt to return to their tribes, or if that is not possible, we find places for them to live and work. The Rancho Girón is very large and has need of many hands. The younger children are taught the skills with which to enter the civilized world. I have three of my Franciscan brothers from the mission helping me with the school. It is not far from here."

"All of this must cost dearly. You and Morena and Joaquín have a whole group of spies across the northern provinces reporting on captured Indians. Do they also tell Joaquín when rich gold shipments are being sent to the mint?" she asked shrewdly, with a teasing light in her eyes. "While we were traveling north, my husband had a great deal of money to see us safely along our way."

Bartolome, for once in Orlena's memory, looked abashed. "I prayed much over accepting stolen gold to pay for the school and the relocation of the freed captives. But when I remembered how Joaquín had come to me as a boy, I saw this idea of his as a far better way for him to spend his time than killing Spanish soldiers. The school may yet be a link between the Indians and the Spanish, Orlena."

"I would love to see it—and to meet these children. Perhaps I could help. That is, if Joaquín would allow it," she added sadly.

Fray Bartolome's mind was racing now. "You can read and write, I recall much to my chagrin—and you learned healing among the Lipan. There is a great need for you."

"These raids—they are dangerous for my husband, are they not?"

Bartolome shrugged. "Yes, but if we are to mend your relationship with him, we must show him the real Orlena. That will take time, and working with the Indians is a way to do this."

"It will not mend anything, Bartolome," Morena said from the door. Her cold words caused both of them to turn. "Joaquín plans to take her north with him to Texas—to use her as bait in a trap for Conal!"

Orlena's sharp intake of breath caused Morena a moment of bitter pleasure, but the priest quickly interrupted. "I will stop that, never fear," he thundered.

Morena shrugged, then looked at her rival with open malice. "What he does now is less dangerous than seeking death in Texas. Only take this woman away from here and he will have no means with which to lure Conal. Make no mistake, Conal Quinn is death himself!"

Morena's horrifying revelation about Joaquín's plans for her stunned Orlena. She had pleaded illness and left Fray Bartolome, spending the morning alone in her room. But the room itself evoked bittersweet memories of her husband's touch and her response to him. She could not bear to remain in it.

She had wanted his forgiveness. Forgiveness! Her cruel charade last year had saved his worthless life. He was the one who had set out to seduce and use her from the first time he learned of her relationship to Conal Quinn. Now he was conspiring to do so again. The part that hurt the most was her own stupidity in falling not once but yet a second time under his spell.

After several hours alone gathering her shattered wits, she decided to talk with Bartolome. He had heard with his own ears from Morena the extent of Joaquín's treachery. Even if he had married them, the priest could not expect her to obey her husband and remain with him to be used in his revenge. She washed her face, braided her hair, and went in search of her friend.

While Orlena was composing herself, Bartolome had done some earnest thinking and praying. Knowing Joaquín as he did, he did not doubt Morena's words, even though she obviously hated her lover's wife and wanted her sent away. Somehow Joaquín must be deterred from this deadly plan, for it was not only his own life and soul he endangered; the two women who loved him would be destroyed along with him and Conal. He had hoped the school and all the ill and abused who were brought there for succor might provide a solution to his problem.

When a pale but composed Orlena once more joined him, Fray Bartolome suggested riding out to see the Indian settlement. As they rode across the valley to where it was hidden far back in a blind canyon, Orlena was subdued and quiet. The priest watched her strained face. "We will not let him go to Texas, you and I," he said softly to her.

Orlena looked into the clear gray eyes she had

grown to trust so implicitly. "How can you stop him? He has said—so have you—that I am his wife. I must go where he wills or return to Ignacio."

Bartolome looked at the lush bounty of autumn that surrounded them. Fertile beauty in the midst of bloody violence. At times the will of the Almighty was obscure indeed. "Do you truly wish to dissolve the bonds with Joaquín?" he asked. His eyes never wavered from her face as he watched her struggle with her answer. He could see her swallow and force down tears.

"No," she replied in a tired, defeated voice. "You know I do not, but if I cannot have his love, I will not be his—his creature, played with and used against Conal. I will not go to Texas with him," she said with steel in her voice. Her old Spanish pride reasserted itself.

"Good," he replied simply.

"You—you will support me in this?" she asked with a small flicker of hope on her face. Then the light in her amber eyes dulled. "But how? You have tried to explain why I said what I did to him when Conal held us. He has refused to believe you all along. Now, after overhearing only the last of my conversation with Ignacio, he is even more convinced that I am an unfaithful wife. I am Spanish. For my white blood alone, he will never forgive me."

"For his own white blood, he will never forgive himself. Have you ever thought on that?" Bartolome asked quietly.

"Yes. But it only makes the problem worse. Everything that has stood between us comes back to his father."

"Well, killing Conal Quinn will provide him no solution, of a surety. But I think there is another answer. What a man sees with his own eyes goes much

NIGHT WIND'S WOMAN

further in convincing him of a truth than anything he is told—even by a priest!"

With that cryptic remark he turned his attention to pointing out the richness of the fall crops and the various men and women who harvested them. As they rode north toward the narrow end of the agricultural valley, the landscape was vastly different than on the high, barren plains of Chihuahua City. A narrow, twisting river flowed swiftly, zigzagging its way across the valley floor, supporting tall stands of cottonwoods and lush green orchards.

"Much of this land is owned by the mission. It lay fallow, deserted since the Indian uprisings of the 1760's, until we began to bring laborers into the fields."

"These people are ones you have relocated, former prisoners?" Orlena asked.

"Many, yes. Others have lived here for generations, the product of intermarriage between Spanish soldiers and traders with the Indian women of various tribes. But this valley is too close to the presidio for us to keep many escaped captives here. It is well concealed, but if too many strange pure-blooded Indian faces appeared, questions would be raised and it would come to the attention of the Commandant General in Chihuahua City. No, only the small ones at the school—which is very well hidden—remain here. Most are dispersed farther north to ranches and farms in New Mexico Province, some to Sonora." He paused, then said, "Joaquín has begun such a ranch in New Mexico, in the valley where Conal found you."

She looked incredulously at him. "Conal has spent the past year searching for him like a man possessed! He will use his soldiers to massacre everyone at that ranch!"

Fray Bartolome smiled serenely. "He would find

347

only a *rico* and his Indian workers if he should ever think to return there—which so far, he has not. Another pupil of mine, the son of a cobbler in the City of Mexico, did not wish to follow in his father's humble trade. Nor did he have a vocation in the Church, although he was a fine student, almost as bright as Joaquín. He loves being *patron* in the absence of the real owner. There is much about Joaquín's life this past year that will surprise you." He gestured to the sharp turn in the narrow road they followed. If not familiar with the landmarks as Fray Bartolome was, a casual traveler would never find the isolated trail to the settlement.

Orlena could hear the squeal of children's laughter after they rounded the bend. A series of long, low adobe buildings stretched like a small village across the open space between the narrow ravine walls of the blind canyon. Although rude and unadorned, the school, hospital, and houses were neat and clean with carefully tended vegetable gardens around the perimeter. Women in loose cotton skirts tended children, scrubbed clothing on the rocks by the side of a burbling stream, and performed other chores familiar to Orlena. This rhythm of daily life was the same in villages across New Spain, whether Lipan or Spanish. Men hoed the fields, repaired harness, and picked huge baskets of glowing purple grapes, which they carried to one large building on the edge of the village, a small winery.

"It looks so peaceful and prosperous," Orlena said in awe as they dismounted and were quickly surrounded by a hoard of children, Indians and *castas*.

Fray Bartolome hoisted two leggy boys up with effortless ease, but a small girl who shyly hung back watched the golden-haired woman in doeskin with great curiosity. "That is Ana. She is Lipan. Joaquín brought her here last spring. All her band had been killed in Texas, and she lay near death for a while."

Imagining what their daughter would have looked like, had she lived, Orlena felt a lump rise in her throat. She knelt and stretched out her arms, saying in their Apache dialect, "My name is Sun in Splendor, and I too am Lipan."

Ana hesitated only a moment before slowly inching her way toward the vision before her. The lady was white, but dressed and spoke as one of her people. Ana had missed her mother and sisters so much. The moment she touched Orlena's hand she found herself drawn into a sweet embrace. Ana returned the affection ardently, throwing small brown arms around Orlena's neck.

Bartolome watched the woman and child kneeling in the grass and smiled to himself. *Bless you, O Lord, it will work! You can heal them all!*

Chapter 23

Taking the prisoners from a handful of drunken soldiers had been a simple operation. Joaquín had a slash across his side from a soldier's saber, but he had felled the assassin before serious harm was done. Other than that tolerable wound, he was unharmed. If only such could be said of the captives they had freed, he thought with the painfully restrained fury that was his constant companion on each mission.

One fourteen-year-old girl stared vacantly across the open road before them. Raped repeatedly by the soldiers who had captured her at the Mescalero encampment, she had simply retreated into her own private world. She refused food and water and had not slept for three days. There was little hope for her survival. Another boy, barely more than a toddler, had watched his whole family hacked to pieces by the leathercoats. Joaquín had held him while he cried

NIGHT WIND'S WOMAN

himself into an exhausted sleep as they rode toward the mission outpost.

By the time they arrived, it was past dawn. The two scouts Joaquín had sent ahead signaled that the way was clear. As he rode into the compound, Joaquín noted the usual early morning activities around the school. Children ran laughing and talking toward the classroom building, where Fray Alonzo waited patiently, ready to begin the day's lessons. The men and women who tilled the fields and worked in the orchards were headed to their tasks, tools in hand. He waved to some, nodded quietly to others, and rode slowly toward the hospital building, where all newly freed captives were first brought. Almost all needed some medical attention.

When he swung down from Warpaint, the boy awakened and began to whimper. Joaquín stroked his shaggy black hair and the child subsided, sucking his thumb, eyes squeezed tightly closed. Joaquín's eyes were wide open, filled with chagrined amazement when he stepped into the long, crowded room filled with beds.

"What is she doing here?" he hissed without preamble at Morena, who sat tearing thin strips of coarse cotton cloth for bandages.

"Bartolome insisted your wife was a skilled healer," she replied, reaching for the boy who went willingly into her arms. He clasped his small chubby hands in her long hair as if she were his mother.

Without another word for Morena, he stalked to where Orlena knelt by the bedside of a young man, a *paisano* who had injured his foot while plowing. She was absorbed in washing the infected injury, ignoring the man who stood so menacingly above her.

"I would speak with you, wife. Come," he said,

turning arrogantly, expecting her to follow him from the crowded room filled with prying eyes.

"When I finish my morning rounds, I will join you in the kitchen. I expect you and your men are hungry," she replied matter-of-factly, not stopping her work.

He turned back, twisting sharply and reopening the seeping wound in his side. With a snarled oath of pain, he reached down and grabbed her wrist, causing her to drop the vial of ointment she was holding onto the pallet. "I am not hungry and I will speak with you—now." He yanked her up roughly and would have dragged her from the room, had not Fray Bartolome walked in at that moment.

Suppressing a smile at Joaquín's obvious irritation, the priest greeted him, ignoring Orlena's furiously angry face. Before she could voice her outrage, he said heartily, "I have seen your week's work. Well done, all considered. Orlena, too, has accomplished a fine week's work here at the school and hospital. Her Lipan herbal cures stop the fever and swelling that has killed many with simple cuts and puncture wounds. Wait until you see how she helps Fray Alonzo with the children. Ana loves her."

At the mention of the little Lipan girl, Joaquín stiffened. "I do not want Ana spending time with Orlena," he said baldly.

"Why? Do you think I will infect her with my Spanish blood?" she asked in a low, bitter whisper.

Releasing her wrist, he answered, "Your Spanish blood will lead you to desert her after she has given you her trust. I do not want Ana hurt further while you play at being a medicine woman."

"You hateful, bitter, twisted—" Oblivious of everyone around them, her hand flashed up to slap his arrogant, cold face.

NIGHT WIND'S WOMAN

When he reached out to parry her blow, he flinched at the sharp pain from the wound in his side.

Orlena could see him blanch and her eyes immediately traveled to his side, where a widening red ooze seeped through his torn shirt.

"I think your healing skills are about to be tested," Fray Bartolome said drily as he ushered Joaquín and Orlena toward the small room where they kept medicines and surgical tools.

She walked stiffly in front of him, her spine straight and her head held high. When she reached the door, she stepped inside, ignoring his muffled oath as he bent over to follow her through the low-beamed door frame. Orlena began opening several small flasks and pouches, saying icily without looking at him, "Take off your shirt and sit by the window."

He complied, gritting his teeth at the painful nuisance of the encrusted slash as it broke open further. When she turned, she nearly dropped the cloth she had clutched in her hand. "How long have you been traveling with that open wound?" she gasped.

"Three days. We had to be certain the soldiers pursuing us had lost our trail before we could return here." He flexed his muscles, stretching to ease the tight ache in his side.

Orlena's mouth went dry as she reached toward the heat of his body. Willing her hands not to tremble, she began to cleanse the dried, clotted blood from the ugly gash. She could see in the clear light of day what had not been visible when they made love. The fine white scars that had always crisscrossed his back were now overlaid with a newer pattern of similar weals. She knew they had come from Conal's abuse of him in the Santa Fe prison. It was miraculous he had not died of infection from the brutality. Santiago had told her of the sweatbox Joaquín had been forced to lie in after enduring the horrible whipping. Squeezing back tears and forcing her mind away from such horrors, she asked, "How came you by such a wound? The sword should have severed your arm before striking your side."

"My own arm was raised to strike a soldier in front of me when the wielder of the blade approached from the side." He could sense her reticence as she touched him. Perversely, it pleased him that she found his presence so disturbing. Of course, he found her presence here in his world disturbing, too. He did not care to analyze that.

"I must suture the slash," Orlena said nervously. *If only I can stop my hands from shaking!*

He turned his head to watch her thread a needle, his eyes calm and assessing. A slight smile quirked his mouth. "Once, long ago, Bartolome told me he would sew me up like skins on a tepee."

Her eyes traveled involuntarily to his other side, where the old bullet wound was faintly visible. How well she remembered his body! When her eyes met his, his expression indicated that he knew her thoughts. Feeling the heat of a flush staining her cheeks, she instructed him, "Lean against the back of the chair and take hold of the window sash to steady yourself."

Amused green eyes swept over her. "And who will steady you, Lioness?"

"The more you bait me, the more you shall pay the penalty, Joaquín," was all she would reply.

He neither made a sound nor flinched as she sewed. When she had finished, she stood up and walked to the small table where the clean bandaging lay. Grasping a length of it, she steeled herself and approached him to wrap the wound. As she reached around his broad chest, she could feel the rumbling vibration of his voice as he spoke.

"Did Bartolome bring you here?"

"I asked to come. I am needed here," she replied simply, continuing her work.

"But you are my wife. You go where I command you."

"To Texas as bait for Conal?" she asked bitterly.

"I must end it with him. He has become—"

"I know what he has become!" she interrupted fiercely, tugging on the binding until he winced in spite of himself. "Santiago knows what he has become. Mayhap we both know now what he always was beneath the surface. He wears necklaces of Apache ears and decorates his headquarters with scalps." Her eyes filled with tears, and she shuddered in revulsion. "I never want to see Conal Quinn again."

"That would be one way of saving his life," he replied coldly. "But I do not choose to leave you here."

"You still believe what your hatred dictates, do you not, Joaquín?" She stood up, looking at him with wounded fury in her eyes.

When she would have turned from him, his hand shot out and captured one slim wrist, again pulling her onto his lap. His hand tangled in her hair, cradling her head as he drew her to him. Green and gold eyes locked. He pulled her closer until the resistance of her hands against his chest gave way and she slid them up to encircle his neck.

"I believe I am bewitched by your golden sorcery," he murmured against her mouth as he claimed it in a hot, rough kiss.

Her fingers tangled in his shaggy hair, glorying in the thick coarse springiness of it as she felt the insinuating probe of his tongue, sweeping and caressing her mouth, melting beneath his heat. Her lips molded with his, following his lead as he deepened the kiss.

From the doorway, Fray Bartolome stood observing the heated embrace, a smile slashing his face as he noisily cleared his throat. "Er, I think our patient requires some bed rest, Orlena. Why do you not take the day and see to his needs." A light of devilment shone in the priest's eyes as he watched them jump apart.

Orlena stood up, feeling Morena's hate-filled black eyes peering at them from behind Bartolome's back. "Perhaps the widow Girón would rather accompany Joaquín to get his bed rest," she replied with icy sarcasm.

Morena slid past the priest like an oiled wraith, gliding into the small room. "I will make ready your old room at the ranch, Joaquín," she said softly, ignoring Orlena as if she were invisible.

"Well, there is enough for me to do here," Orlena said, starting to walk away.

Joaquín replied cooly, "Perhaps you are right. I will ride to the ranch with Morena. I trust, Bartolome, that you can see Orlena is returned safely this evening?" He watched his wife's back stiffen, but she did not break stride as she walked deliberately from the room.

Before she was out of earshot, he said to the priest, "Do not let her near Ana. The girl has lost enough now. She cannot withstand another desertion."

Orlena did not wait to hear Bartolome's soothing defense of her, but hurried back to her tasks in the room full of ill and injured people. All through the day she seethed, thinking of Joaquín and Morena alone in the grand ranch house. She knew they had been lovers

NIGHT WIND'S WOMAN

over the years and that the beautiful *casta* wanted him back in her bed. Perhaps this very afternoon she would get her wish. *Good riddance to them both! I will stay here where the children need me.* But what of *my* needs, her heart cried out.

Bartolome watched Orlena's rigid profile as they rode toward the ranch that evening. He felt her pain, yet lacked the words to console her. In his heart he knew Joaquín loved her, not Morena, but the problems between them must be resolved by husband and wife, not a meddlesome old priest. He had done his part by bringing her to work among the Indians. Now it would take time. *Time and the absence of Morena Girón from their lives,* he added silently, vowing to speak with the widow on the morrow.

From her window in the *sala*, Morena watched Joaquín's yellow-haired wife walk toward the house after Bartolome had departed. Seeing the way Joaquín kissed her with feverish need that morning had crushed her heart. Now her wounded fury had cooled to cold calculation. She smiled as she thought of Joaquín, asleep naked in her bedroom. After drugging the wine he drank with the meal she had served him, Morena had her servants take him to her room, where she stripped his unconscious body and covered him with a tangle of bed linens. She then left one of her silk robes lying by the bedside in a soft, suggestive heap. After his jealous wife had seen the incriminating evidence and gone crying to Bartolome, she would have him moved from her room before he awakened. Preening like a satiated woman, she walked quickly from the *sala* to the front door, her lines well rehearsed.

"You have returned early. Do the children begin to bore you?" she said to the startled blonde.

Orlena looked at Morena's loose hair and the open buttons at the top of her basque. *She is only trying to vex me.* "I believe I will return to my room and bathe before dinner," she said calmly, ignoring the hateful *casta*'s reference to the children.

"I'll have your bath water brought up," Morena said with false solicitude. "Oh, use the front stairs. The servants just put down fresh whitewash on the back stairs."

Although a prickle of apprehension ran up her spine, Orlena shrugged carelessly and turned toward the wide polished steps in the foyer.

Joaquín was dizzy and his head ached even more abominably than his side, which had subsided to a dull throb. He shook his hair from his eyes and gingerly sat up, trying to orient himself. The last thing he remembered was eating luncheon with Morena and feeling suddenly unwell. Looking around the large, opulently appointed bedroom, he immediately recognized the purple velvet draperies and imported Louis XV furniture. Most especially he recognized the bed. Morena's bed. He turned his head toward the window. It was approaching dusk. Cursing Morena and her wiles, he struggled to disentangle himself from the covers, only to discover that he was completely naked save for the bandage Orlena had wound about his midsection. Orlena!

As if he had conjured her up, she appeared rooted in the doorway. For all her haughty Spanish pride, his wife could not conceal the anguish that flashed across her face before she turned silently and fled down the long hallway.

When he tried to rise and pursue her, his knees buckled and he fell back onto the heavy mattress. Swearing at the jarring ache in his side, he rose more carefully this time, holding on to the chair by the bedside.

Morena stood in the hallway, watching him wrap his lean, swarthy body with a linen sheet.

When he looked at her, the green fire in his eyes scorched the smirk from her face. She backed up a step, then stood her ground defiantly. "You can see she knows of our relationship. She does not trust you. It is because she is as faithless as any harlot in the City of Mexico, most of whom have fine Spanish titles," she said with contempt.

"What Orlena is or is not does not concern you, Morena. She is my wife and I will deal with her." He walked to the doorway and grabbed her, yanking her roughly against the wall. "See you have a servant fetch me clean clothes. And Morena—never again interfere between me and my wife." His voice was low and soft, but the cold words held a palpable threat.

Orlena stood shivering in her room as the maid filled a copper hip bath with hot water. The spring air was brisk; her nerves, not the weather, caused her chill. Her first impulse had been to ride to the mission and denounce the perfidious adulterers to Fray Bartolome, but pride held her back. *I will be forever damned before I just crawl away and lick my wounds!* She quickly decided to remain at the ranch, at least for the night, to bathe, eat and sleep as if she cared not a whit what Joaquín and his harlot did. Convincing herself that such was the truth was a more formidable task.

When the maid had finished filling the hip bath with water, Orleña sank gratefully into its soothing warmth to soak the chill from her body. Her days at the hospital and school were long and arduous, yet never until today had she felt so drained. She laid her head against the back of the hammered copper tub and closed her eyes. Immediately the dark, writhing bodies of Joaquín and Morena appeared in her mind's eye, entwined in a passionate embrace on that big bed. She squeezed her eyes tightly to force away the vision, then willed herself to sink deeper into the tub and relax. Concentrating on Ana's radiant face helped. Her hand groped half-heartedly about the low table beside the tub until she found the soap. Working up a lather with a small cloth, she began a slow langourous scrub.

That was how Joaquín found her when he reached the room, eyes closed, long mane of golden hair trailing to the floor behind the tub, her delicate face in relaxed profile. Hypnotized, he watched her small hands run the cloth up and down each slim arm, then over those elegant high breasts, slicking her skin with perfumed, silky water in slow, delicious strokes. He forgot to breathe.

Silently he closed the door and slipped the bolt, then shed his open shirt, peeled away his trousers and kicked off his moccasins. Still Orlena lay back in the tub with her eyes closed, making low rippling noises in the water as she raised one slim leg, then the other, and massaged them with the cloth. He crossed the carpeted floor and knelt beside the tub, then reached over and closed his hand about her ankle, holding it aloft for inspection. "Perfect," he breathed.

Orlena's eyes flew open and she tried to yank her leg free, kicking ineffectually at him. His long fingers wrapped like steel about the fine bones of her ankle, holding it virtually immobile as she splashed and thrashed.

"Let me go! Return to your Yaqui—she obviously suits you better," she hissed. When she reached her nails out to claw at his face, he bent her leg up against her chest and grabbed the long trailing mane of her hair, giving it a hard yank. She quieted, held in a most awkward and humiliating position, hating her helplessness as his cool green eyes dispassionately roamed over her wet, naked flesh. "Are you never satiated? Or do you wish to compare me to her?" she asked in contempt.

"If that were my intent, I could long before now have done it, Lioness." He loosed the cruel grip on her hair and lowered her leg back into the tub. When he removed his hand from her ankle, he slid it deftly up her leg, over her thigh and across her belly, splaying his fingers beneath her breasts, then softly, quickly, brushing his palms over the hardened points of her nipples. She gasped, half in fury, half in pleasure, unable to disguise the sound, much as she wished to do so. Her eyes searched his face as he became absorbed in caressing her responsive body. The look of naked desire and desperate hunger that she saw weakened her resistance. *He is as powerless to fight this thing as am I!*

But why did he return to Morena's bed first? She did not resist as he pulled her from the water and wrapped a soft linen towel about her. After he scooped her into his arms and carried her, still dripping, to the bed, he laid her on it. Only then, when he stood above her with his hardened sex straining proudly toward her, did she protest, pushing against his chest when he began to lower himself on top of her.

Quick as a hare fleeing a coyote, she rolled from the other side of the bed to the floor. The towel came unraveled and she yanked at it, but this time he was too fast for her, seizing it and wresting it from her. She reached for the coverlet on the bed to hide herself from his hypnotic gaze, but he sank one knee onto the bed and held it firm. "This is foolish, Lioness. Come here," he whispered thickly.

"No! Does your lust know no bounds? You have just come from Morena's bed!"

"Where I slept alone, drugged to unconsciousness!" He interrupted her angrily.

Her eyes narrowed in disbelief. "I saw you naked, tangled in her sheets—"

"Forget Morena and her schemes. You but play into her hands with your foolish jealousy," he interrupted as he stalked her slowly, rounding the bed and backing her into the corner between it and the wall.

"I am not jealous," she spat, knowing how patently ridiculous the words sounded, even as she spoke them.

His reply was a low, husky laugh as he pounced, pulling her against his hot naked flesh and enfolding her in a hard embrace. He kissed her neck and trailed his scorching mouth up her cheek to her temple, her fluttering eyelids. Then slowly, deliberately, he brushed her mouth, daring her to refuse him.

Orlena fought a losing battle, wanting desperately to believe his words. Morena was scheming enough to have done as he said, yet she still mistrusted Joaquín's own confusing motives. She opened to him, pressing her lips to seal with his in a searing kiss.

Was this what she had instinctively wanted? To lure him to her as she lay soaking decadently in perfumed water? Orlena refused to answer her own tortured thoughts as her palms traced a course up his hard-muscled shoulders to reach about his neck. Her fingers tangled in his long, coarse hair and she clung to him.

Joaquín could feel the damp, silky heat of her body, still warm and fragrant from the bath. He groaned and rotated his hips against hers, holding her small buttocks against his lower body with one hand as he raised her against his aching shaft. When he was certain of her surrender, he picked her up once more and returned to the bed.

This time, when he lowered his body over hers, she held him fast, opening her legs eagerly to invite him into her softness. With a moan caught deep in his throat, he sank into her wet, welcoming sheath, stroking slowly, then plunging faster and harder as his golden Lioness locked her slim legs around his hips and arched against him in hungry invitation.

He felt ready to explode, buried deeply inside her, but gritted his teeth in concentration as he slowed to allow time for her to join him. Her release did not take long. With but a few long, slick strokes, he heard her ragged gasps as the involuntary contractions of ecstasy seized her. She clawed at his back and thrashed her head from side to side as he renewed his powerful thrusts, faster and faster until the world evaporated and he felt hurtled among the stars. He cried out her name and collapsed on top of her, panting and sweat-soaked.

As the haze of passion gradually receded, Orlena ran her hands gingerly over the bandages about his midsection. "Are you hurt? The stitches—"

A low, raspy chuckle rewarded her tentative question as he made a reply muffled in her tangled hair. "Your stitchery is as fine as that of the best seamstress in the City of Mexico. It remains intact in spite of our exertions. But now I am weary and would rest." With that he rolled off her, pulled her against him, and yanked the coverlet across their naked bodies.

Joaquín fell immediately into an exhausted sleep, but Orlena remained awake. She felt warm and secure held thus. It was not fair that he should have such power over her when she had none of his love or trust in return. He desired her, but did not believe in her honor or fidelity. Yet as long as they were together, might not this be a chance to restore what they had shared in the Lipan village? She closed her eyes and dared to dream.

As Morena stood outside their bedroom door, torturing her soul by listening to the sounds of their passion, she admitted at last that Joaquín would never leave his wife. He was in thrall to the golden Spaniard and no matter what her treachery, he would keep her. Finally, unable to bear it any longer, she slipped quietly down the hall to her own room. She must save Joaquín from the Spanish bitch. But how? Then she remembered her conversation several weeks earlier with Joaquín about Orlena's brother Ignacio. A tremulous smile worked its way across her wide, mobile mouth, then broadened into full-fledged laughter, laughter which did not reach her cold, obsidian eyes. She rang for a servant and gave instructions to have her clerk meet her in the library the following morning at eight.

Several hours later, a discreet knock awakened Joaquín and Orlena from their sound sleep. Joaquín sat up, wincing from the pain in his side as he called out none too civilly, "Who is it?"

The young maid, Lena, nervously identified herself and said she had a tray with dinner for him and his lady. Orlena slid beneath the covers as Joaquín calmly instructed her to wait with the food. He rose from the bed and walked to where his trousers lay in a heap. Donning them with a small grimace of pain, he slipped the bolt on the door and admitted the girl. Without even casting a glance at Orlena in the tangled bed, she set the tray on the table by the window. Lena quit the room in silence, ignoring the discarded clothing and spilled water in her path.

Joaquín stepped over to the food, removed the napkin, and smelled the fragrance of roast spring lamb and a casserole filled with spicy vegetables. "Come and eat, Lioness. You must be as famished as I."

Hating the fiery flush that burned her cheeks, Orlena rose and walked quickly to the armoire, where a cast-off robe of Morena's hung. Sliding the frayed blue linen over her body, she belted it and walked to the table.

They fell upon their food with the same ravenous abandon they had exhibited for each other earlier. Joaquín had barely consumed any of the drugged luncheon Morena had served him and Orlena had not eaten since early that morning.

As they shared the food in silence, each considered how to gauge the other's feelings.

Joaquín felt his physical victory over his wife was a pyrrhic one. He had admitted being duped by Morena instead of letting his wife assume he had bedded her. She was jealous and in his desire to have her, he had let slip his own vulnerable need for her—a foolish way to repay her treachery indeed!

Orlena watched his shuttered face from beneath lowered lashes, still hoping that there was a way to rebuild their relationship. Finally, wiping her fingers on the napkin and daubing at her kiss-swollen lips, she dared to speak. "What do you plan to do with me, Joaquín? Are we really going to Texas to entrap Conal?" She raised her eyes to meet his coolly assessing gaze.

"I would end it with Conal. He has hunted me

relentlessly this past year. His mind is unhinged, Orlena." He seemed to hesitate, uncertain of his next words. "But I do not want you harmed by him," he finally admitted.

Her heart gave a queer, light lurch in her breast at that small concession. "If you go after him in Texas, it will be dangerous for you, too. And, Joaquín, Bartolome is right. You cannot kill your own father. The stain on your soul would eat at you."

"The stain is in the blood of that bastard which runs in my veins. That is what gnaws at my very guts."

"If we left here and went to California, perhaps—"

"No! There is nowhere he would not follow. Anyway, I do not believe you would willingly go with me to that distant wilderness any more than I believe you want to remain here amid sick and injured Indian children," he said, watching her face for a reaction.

Orlena slammed down her napkin and stood, nearly overturning the chair in her haste. "Will nothing ever penetrate the wall of hate you have erected about you? I love those children! Ana is . . . she could have been . . ." Her words faltered as she remembered the unnamed infant girl buried in the Chihuahua desert.

At first her words did not register, but then he recalled Bartolome's description of his daughter's death. "Ana is Lipan. She has nothing to do with you," he said coldly.

"So was my daughter a Lipan—or would you deny your own flesh and blood?"

"It was not I but you who chose to deny our child! You would have left her to the care of the nuns!" The pain of that betrayal over a year ago was far more raw than the new wound in his side.

He rose and reached angrily for his shirt. Slipping it on, he fastened it as he slid into his moccasins. Orlena stood stunned by his monstrous, willful blindness. She began to deny his accusation, but the words choked her, dying in her throat as he stalked out of the room without another word. The bitter tears fell freely as she sank back onto the chair and cradled her head on her arms. Everything between them was hopeless.

Chapter 24

As instructed, Morena's clerk, Benito, reported to the library early the next morning. He sat writing methodically while she paced the length of the long, book-filled study, carefully composing the letter in her mind before speaking each sentence aloud. She had never learned to read and felt no loss for it. "When you have finished, repeat it back to me, Benito."

The clerk's quill scratched for several more moments as she tapped her fingers on the oak desk in impatience. Then he cleared his throat and began in a high, wheezing voice to recite all the emissary's titles and the formal salutations that were appended to it. Morena waved him to omit them and read the body of the text instead.

Taking another breath into his obese body, he continued, "It is my most happy duty to inform you that I have located your missing sister, who was abducted by a dangerous half-caste raider called the

Night Wind. Having tired of the poor girl, he has left her in my care at Rancho Girón and ridden on. If you but hasten to Chihuahua City and thence to me, you will find her unharmed. She tells some fantastical tale of his being wed to her, but owing to the strain under which she has lived and to the delicacy of her reputation and your own, I have, of course, said nothing of this to anyone. You may rely on my discretion. Your obedient servant—"

"Yes, yes," she interrupted him with a wave of her hand. "That will do nicely. Post the letter at once." She calculated that it would take her Indian rider at least a week to reach Ignacio in Mexico City. Then it would take Ignacio a minimum of two weeks to reach the ranch and reclaim his errant sister after he received word of her location. That allowed her time aplenty to send Joaquín on an errand of vengeance which would put him safely out of Ignacio's way.

"You mean your spies have found that filthy little Frenchman?" Joaquín asked Morena incredulously as they shared an early morning meal in her elegant dining room. "Ever since he betrayed Bartolome to Conal, I have searched for him. He hides like a gila monster beneath a rock, only waiting to sneak out and strike from behind."

"He is dangerous. You must be careful. Luis tells me he has seen him in El Paso del Norte, but that was several weeks ago," Morena replied. "He was released from prison in Sante Fe last year without the blood money Conal promised him," she added maliciously. "Ever since, he has been hiding, afraid of your wrath."

"As well the one-legged little pig should be. Mayhap I will cut off his other leg for him and see if he can sew it up and walk on two wooden stumps."

"Only be careful. He has friends and he is cunning,

Joaquín," Morena said as she placed her hand over his. The past weeks had been strained between them since her unsuccessful attempt to drive him from Orlena's bed with her trickery.

Bartolome continued to defend Orlena to Joaquín and insisted she was needed at the school and hospital. Joaquín had brooded and argued with his old friend, but he and his wife remained in the valley . . . and in spite of the hostile crackling tension between them, they slept together each night.

Soon, Joaquín, she will be gone. When you return with Pascal's scalp, I will console you for the loss of your faithless wife. Before Morena could say anything aloud, he rose and squeezed her hand affectionately.

"You are a good friend, Morena, and now I must ask a boon of you. Bartolome insists Orlena must continue to work with the children. Watch her comings and goings and keep her here." He hesitated, then shrugged in perplexity. "I am not certain if she speaks the truth, but for now, I would have her wait here for my return."

"I will care for her well, Joaquín, never fear. I give my word on it." Her black eyes met his green ones levelly.

He nodded silently, accepting what he believed to be a difficult declaration from her and left the room to prepare for a long, hard ride to El Paso.

Orlena did not take her meals in the dining room with Joaquín and Morena, but preferred the company of the cook, Esperanza, who fixed her a simple breakfast each morning in the kitchen. As she sipped a cup of rich chocolate, she brooded over her confusing and seemingly hopeless relationship with Joaquín. Each day he went about his own business, helping Morena and her men with the management of the large ranch, spending time with Bartolome on the complex affairs of their Indian resettlement, and riding off to Chihuahua City to glean information around the presidial headquarters about gold shipments and troop movements.

As she worked at the school, she thought with dread about the time when he would drag her away to Texas, a lure to entrap Conal Quinn. At night she returned to the ranch to share his bed. They spoke little, and when they did it inevitably ended in an argument, usually over Ana. Ana, the beautiful bright child she had adopted in her heart as her own. More dearly than anything, she wanted to keep the child with her, but she feared even asking Joaquín, knowing he would refuse her.

The cruel impasse could not long continue. It seemed the only thing she and Joaquín could share in harmony was their bed. If she was held in thrall by that ancient, mysterious bond, so was he—small consolation when there were no words of love or kindness to bless their physical union. Bartolome continually advised her to keep doing as she was, working with the children, tending the sick and loving her husband in her heart of hearts. But, that aching heart cried out, for how long?

Her sad reverie was abruptly interrupted when Joaquín walked silently into the large, warm kitchen. Startled, she splashed her chocolate onto the table when he spoke. "I must leave you for a while, Lioness. Will you miss me?" His white teeth gleamed in a rakish smile, but his green eyes mocked her.

"I assume I am to remain here and wait with no further word until you deign to return."

"Ah, so you will miss me," he said with a chuckle, reaching out to pull her from her stool into his arms. His shirt was open and he wore buckskin pants and Apache moccasins. With little change of clothing on the trail, he could easily transform himself from tame Indian into Lipan raider.

Orlena could feel the sinewy muscles of his body as he pressed her against him for a swift, hard kiss. Her fingers slid inside the open shirt to curl into the hair on his bronzed chest. She was rewarded by the acceleration of his heartbeat. Orlena ignored the old cook, who turned her back with a conspiratorial wink. Daring to experiment, she opened her mouth for his kiss and gentled its roughness, tasting of him and letting him taste the rich chocolate that had just warmed her tongue. For a moment, he seemed to forget all else—his sudden departure, their surroundings, his mistrust of her—as he deepened the kiss. She could feel the pressure of his erection as he held her hips pressed to his.

For one mad moment, he nearly gave in to the impulse to sink with her onto the kitchen floor and make love to her one last time before leaving. Then sanity reasserted itself in the form of Luis Toda, Morena's foreman, who cleared his throat loudly as he stood in the doorway. He was to ride with Night Wind and introduce the raider to Morena's agent in El Paso.

Joaquín untangled his hand from Orlena's silken hair and slowly released her, all the while struggling to bring his body under control. He thought he detected the faintest trace of a feline curve to her lips and womanish pride in her power to arouse him. A blaze of anger flashed across his face, then vanished as he looked at the pulse throbbing at her throat. He placed his fingertips softly against it and whispered, "You, too, are victim, Lioness." With that, he turned and walked through the doorway without a backward glance.

Orlena stood watching him ride away on Warpaint,

NIGHT WIND'S WOMAN

uncertain whether to feel triumphant or desolate.

City of Mexico

Ignacio Valdéz sat with his head thrown back, massaging the bridge of his long, thin nose, an affectation he often assumed when stalling for time. The man who had brought the Girón woman's letter waited in an adjacent chamber while the viceroy's nephew, Rodrigo Colón, sat across from him, impatiently squirming in a large velvet chair.

The boy tended to corpulence and excelled at stupidity. Any of the well placed older men at the Spanish Court who would have taken his virginal sister to wife would have been far preferable, but there was still an advantage in currying the new viceroy's favor. Ignacio had recently invested heavily in several tracts of land, grants from his childhood companion, now a weak young king. He needed Indian slaves to work the lushly rich lands and someone trustworthy to oversee his holdings here when he returned to Spain, a journey that could not be undertaken too soon for his liking. Young Rigo would provide the perfect solution. He was malleable and honest, and with his powerful uncle's backing could administer the estate.

Only one minor difficulty presented itself—the absence of the golden-haired bride. He had, of course, made no mention of Orlena's disappearance before she could sign the petition to the Holy See. In fact, he had forged her name, rather artfully, if he did say so himself, and sent it on to Rome via special emissary. He told Rigo and the viceroy that his sister was so distraught over her unhappy marriage that he had sent her to seek solace with the holy sisters until the issue was settled.

For several months, while the Spanish king's political influence was wending its way to Rome, the story had held fast, but now the ardent young swain, doubtlessly prodded by his uncle, wished to meet his prospective bride. Questions regarding Orlena's marital status were most certainly being raised by the viceroy. Ignacio looked through pale lashes at the boy whose pudding face ill concealed his petulance.

"Don Ignacio, why do you not simply send to the holy sisters and request a brief return to your city house for Orlena? We—that is, I—have never met the beauteous lady. I understand such delicate matters with the Church take time, but at least we could begin to plan our nuptials." He looked into the cold yellow eyes of the older man and suppressed the urge to stamp his foot. Valdéz actually looked amused at his earnest entreaty! *No doubt he thinks me naught but a rude colonial!*

Assuming the most placating air he could muster, Ignacio smiled. "I shall write my sister forthwith, Don Rigo. You are right. She must look ahead to new joys, not back to old tragedies. I shall personally escort her from the convent to your esteemed presence!"

When he had finally gotten rid of the bumbling colonial, he had Morena Girón's half-caste shown in. He must gamble everything on the truth of her letter now. Surveying the expressionless savage, he said coldly, "Your *lady*"—he paused to emphasize the dubiousness of the term—"had better have my sister. I would see Orlena unharmed, safely returned to this house within a fortnight. If she is in any way damaged, or if she is not in Chihuahua City after I make such an arduous journey, I shall be most unhappy. Do I make myself quite clear?"

NIGHT WIND'S WOMAN

At the savage's sullen nod, he felt an irrational urge to fling his inkwell into the shuttered bronze face. White men of all classes and temperaments he could read and intimidate, but there was something about the accursed Indians from the north that left them impervious to his powers.

"When would you leave, Don Ignacio?" the half-caste asked flatly.

Looking at the papers scattered across his desk, he cursed his errant sister for the thousandth time and snapped, "Early on the morrow!"

As Ignacio and his hand-picked soldiers thundered off that morning, Santiago Quinn paid a rare visit to his brother's city house. He had been hearing distressing rumors at Don Bernal's house. Only last night his mother's cousin and several other of the viceroy's officers had gathered for dinner there. When they thought him dismissed for his studies and out of earshot, they discussed the viceroy's nephew, Don Rodrigo Colón, and his pending marriage to Orlena.

Santiago knew she had not signed the petitions, and he had believed her safe with Joaquín in the north. But Don Bernal himself spoke of the boastful Rigo's mother planning a large ball to fête her son's new fiancée the very next month. What was Ignacio up to? Santiago was determined to find out. As he sat in the closed carriage and watched through narrowed eyes, the line of horsemen with Ignacio bouncing unhappily in the lead, rode away.

"He must be journeying far to the north where there are no roads, else he would never ride," Santiago muttered to himself in contempt. For all his fine riding horses back in Spain, Ignacio had always preferred the comforts of a well-sprung carriage. He must have found Orlena and Joaquín! Or he was off to threaten Fray Bartolome in an effort to recover their sister. Calling out instructions to the driver, he only prayed he could ride as swiftly as a Lipan warrior once he was able to secure a horse and enough provisions to see him all the way from the City of Mexico to the Franciscans in Nueva Vizcaya.

Blaise Pascal hated Texas almost as much as he hated New Mexico, but neither was as bad as the filthy, sweltering little pigsties along the Rio Conchos in eastern Nueva Vizcaya. After a year of hiding and existing by his wits, the wily Frenchman was finally in reach of his goal. He had secured a shipment of guns in El Paso, old and defective, yet with samples from each box that would fire. These he would sell to traders on the gulf in return for passage to New Orleans.

When Quinn imprisoned him and then Valdéz interrogated him, he had been certain of death. But after Conal was relieved of his post, the new governor had freed him. Of course, no mention of the five thousand pesos owed him was ever made and he was politic enough not to press the issue. Sooner or later, the escaped Night Wind would learn who had betrayed the priest to Conal, and then his life in New Spain would be worth less than one of the defective guns he was selling.

Stealing was not easy when a man had only one good leg with which to make a hasty escape, but Pascal was a clever card cheat and a shrewd bargainer. He soon resumed his illegal trading expeditions to the Comanche of Texas, scrupulously avoiding any contact with Apache bands who might report his whereabouts to Night Wind. But sufficient cash to get him east of the Sabine remained out of his grasp. Until now.

NIGHT WIND'S WOMAN

The last he had heard, Night Wind was in Chihuahua. He himself had only shaken the dust of El Paso del Norte from his clothes this past week. In another week he would reach the coast and his assignation with the French merchantmen. Of course, it meant crossing within a scant one hundred miles of Chihuahua City. He had to drop south and then head east to the Rio Bravo and cross into Coahuila—Lipan territory. Sweating, he assured himself that it was not where the raider ranged. Night Wind preyed upon gold and silver mines in western Nueva Vizcaya. "I will be well away before I must ever see him again—not to mention that madman, Conal Quinn."

The fat little Frenchman considered the captain with a shudder of revulsion. He did what he had to, to survive, but Colorado Quinn truly enjoyed his work killing Indians. When Pascal left El Paso, the Irishman was at the presidio for a brief respite from his relentless pursuit of savages. The captain scoured New Mexico, Texas, and Nueva Vizcaya for Night Wind, who seemed to be everywhere—and nowhere. Pascal had seen the curling brown trophies of ears adorning Quinn's neck—from a discreet distance in a crowd the day Conal rode in. The next day, the Frenchman rode out.

His devoutest wish was that Quinn and his cub would kill each other, but he did not plan to remain in New Spain to see it. He sat in the small, stuffy room that passed for a cantina, sipping the foul, local *aguardiente* and wrinkling his nose at the congealed brown mass of refried beans on the chipped clay plate in front of him. Outside, a coyote howled in the distance and the Rio Conchos snaked its way to the Bravo.

Pascal and the three Mexicans who rode with him had stopped for the night at this desolate way station.

He watched a large gray spider crawl up the corner of the wall and debated sleeping in the chill desert night rather than using the dubious facilities of the cantina's sleeping rooms in the rear.

Suddenly, the cold prickle of a knife blade pressed menacingly against his neck. He stiffened and attempted to turn his head, but the blade pressed harder, stopping any movement.

The crudely built cane chair creaked in protest beneath his weight as he squirmed. "Who are you? What do you want?" he whispered in Spanish, looking about for his companions, who had left the room.

"You know well enough what I want, Blaise," a familiar voice replied softly.

"Joaquín!"

"Just now I choose to be the Lipan, Night Wind, not Father Bartolome's pupil. You do remember Bartolome, the gentle man of God you betrayed to Conal, do you not, Blaise?"

"I am innocent! Why do you accuse me? Is it because Conal imprisoned me while you were in Santa Fe? I can explain—"

The blade drew a thin trickle of blood that ran an uneven course over the layers of fat and whiskers on Pascal's neck, dripping onto his buckskin shirt. He grew silent, but his mind raced.

"You have saved me a long ride, old friend," Joaquín said conversationally. "Imagine my surprise when Hoarse Bark and Cloth Fox encountered us on the way to El Paso with the tale of a wooden-legged Frenchman trading guns along the Conchos."

Hoarse Bark walked silently in front of Pascal, smiling evilly. "You sell guns to the Comanche, our sworn enemies, white man. But I have heard from many that you do us a service. The guns do not fire,

NIGHT WIND'S WOMAN

but explode in the user's face."

The patrons of the cantina listened to the conversation and observed the raiders. Dressed in buckskin trousers and heavily armed, several of the strangers looked to be full-blooded Apaches. Their half-caste leader closely resembled the description issued by the presidio soldiers of the Night Wind. No one in the tiny isolated village would help the Frenchman. They watched impassively as the renegades departed with their captive.

One man stood by the doorway, watching the riders head off with Pascal. A pity. He had hoped to turn a good profit from the guns, but now the Apaches had taken the prize. He knew they would kill his partner. Still, it might not be a total loss. He had learned before they left El Paso that Colorado Quinn was headed southeast along the Bravo. Perhaps there might be a reward from the Irishman for such recent news of the renegade's location—if the captain from El Paso still harbored such an unnatural obsession for the one called Night Wind.

Orlena stooped to pick up the slop bucket from beneath the bed. Unexpectedly her stomach churned, and she sat back on her haunches until the sudden seizure abated. Having worked in the hospital and tended terrible injuries for the past six weeks, Orlena knew she was not squeamish. Doggedly, she picked up the heavy bucket after dragging it clear of the bed where an Apache boy slept. He had been terribly beaten and starved. As soon as she finished cleaning up the row of beds, she must try to spoon some more broth down his throat. As she hefted the bucket and walked slowly down the aisle, the malaise began to pass.

Observing her from the door, Fray Bartolome walked toward her and took the wooden pail from her hands. "This noisome stuff is too heavy for you. Why do you not go and prepare your poultices for the patients with fevered wounds? I will take care of this."

Shoving the sleeve of her loose white blouse above her tanned elbow, Orlena smiled wearily. "I am fine, and the pail is not that heavy. I must have eaten something for breakfast that disagreed with my stomach. A most unusual occurrence, I assure you."

"And yesterday?" Bartolome prompted. "Then, too, you shoved your midday meal about, refusing to eat. Do not fear for Joaquín. The journey to El Paso is long and they may ride farther than that." His face clouded. "On the trail of vengeance, he knows infinite patience. He has only been away a fortnight. It may be far longer, but he will return for you. I am certain of it," he said with conviction.

Orlena smiled as they walked outdoors. The day was as golden as her hair, warm with the kiss of autumn. She took a deep, calming breath and said, "He has left me many times, Bartolome. Once, in the Lipan village, I hoped that we could build a life together . . . but we have done too many cruelties to each other." Her voice choked.

"And lost the child of your love, I know," he replied gently. "But have you considered that the Lord often gives even when he inexplicably takes away?"

Orlena looked into his clear gray eyes, trying to read the cryptic remark. Slowly, comprehension dawned. "You must have read as much of those Jewish physician's writings as you did of St. Francis." Her hands unconsciously moved to her belly in a protective gesture. "It has been scarcely two months . . . I am not certain."

Bartolome's smile was beaming. "I am not certain

either, but is it not something to hope for again?"

Her face was radiant. "Yes, yes it is. I was so desolate when I lost the first child. Now, if I can give Joaquín another, perhaps it will help mend things at last."

"I am certain of that. Only give him time, Orlena."

Chapter 25

Time dragged interminably for Joaquín as they rode toward Chihuahua. He could still see Blaise Pascal's smashed and shredded face after the Biscayan steel musket exploded, leaving him writhing on the earth, begging the Night Wind to kill him and end his agony. Much to Hoarse Bark's disgust, he had ordered the Frenchman shot instead of letting him die slowly.

The raiders had made Pascal fire half a dozen of the old muskets, whose barrels were infamous for exploding upon firing. With each shot that echoed across the empty desert air, Pascal's round face beaded with more sweat. Joaquín knew he understood their game. They would make him load and fire until the old steel betrayed him. By the time the trembling, pleading outcast fired the fatal gun, Joaquín had grown sick of the whole affair. He only wanted to see his treacherous former ally dead and return to Orlena.

Orlena, his golden woman. As he sat staring into the

flames of the campfire late that night, he realized that he had not even thought of Quinn in days. Was she blunting his desire for revenge? Certainly in the past two years since he met her, she had filled his thoughts far more than anyone else, even Conal. His vengeance had focused upon her when she and Conal betrayed him. His hatred of her had kept him alive in that prison sweatbox when thoughts of Conal's perfidy could not have done so.

Bartolome had told him how Conal had blackmailed her, but he had not believed it. Beautiful, innocent-eyed Orlena could charm birds from trees. *Even tame the wind?* the thought came unbidden. She turned every man she ever met into her creature. For all his boasting to Conal about enslaving her, he knew that Orlena had won her own victory. She might be powerless to resist his physical appeal while he held her captive, but even when he was separated from her, she held him in thrall. Tomorrow he would see her again. With each day spent traveling across the trackless wilderness, she called to him.

As they rode into the neck of the lush valley west of Chihuahua City, he again considered the priest's explanation about what Orlena had said to him when Conal held him prisoner. Did she indeed lie in the foolish hope of saving his life? Perhaps to save the life of their child, which Conal could also have threatened? But then, why the words with Ignacio that he had overheard in the City of Mexico? She had offered him no defense for her actions then. But considering how little he believed her the first time, why should she have tried?

Joaquín mulled over his warring emotions but came no closer to an answer. She worked tirelessly with the Indians at the hospital and adored the children at the school. Ana loved her to distraction, and Orlena seemed to return that feeling. "Still she is my prisoner. Perhaps living with me is preferable to the fops Ignacio would saddle her with if she returned to him," he muttered to himself as the fertile landscape surrounding Rancho Girón came into view. Suddenly he felt a sense of urgency. He must talk with his wife and find out the truth. This war between them must not continue.

Inside the big hacienda, Morena paced furiously, her black eyes flashing with anger at the presumptuous Spaniard who was nothing more than a prisoner here. *A temporary prisoner,* she thought with a smile of satisfaction as she said, "I told you not to bring any of the children here. It is too dangerous."

Orlena stood by the *sala* window watching Ana play with the kitten she had given the child as a special pet. "Ana is only a little girl who dresses as a *paisana* and speaks perfectly clear Spanish now. No one would possibly suspect she was ever a captured Lipan. I plan to keep her with me," she said defiantly to the beautiful brunette.

Morena scoffed. "Had you best not ask your husband's permission first, Spaniard? For all your highborn lady's manners, you are still his prisoner."

Fighting the flush of anger and humiliation that her adversary's truthful accusation evoked, Orlena replied with disdain, "I am Joaquín's wife, no matter that his *former* mistress might wish it otherwise." With that, she turned and walked from the room. The warm, fresh air of the courtyard with its sparkling fountains and laughing child beckoned her.

Morena stared with slitted eyes at the proud golden head, held so regally as the Spaniard walked away. "Soon you will be gone and Night Wind will be mine once more," she whispered on the empty air. Just then, a commotion out front distracted her from her scheming reverie. Perhaps Ignacio had arrived already! She glided down the hall, smoothing the folds of her red silk gown. She must be very careful how she handled him so as not to endanger either Night Wind or the rescue mission.

Before she reached the front door, it swung open and Joaquín strode in, dusty and travel-stained in old buckskins and soft moccasins. She froze in horror. "Night Wind! Why have you returned so soon? That wicked Frenchman is going to escape," she quickly added, covering her blurted question as best she could.

His harshly chiseled face looked weary, but the green eyes burned with a hidden flame. Brushing aside her burst of questions, he replied simply, "Pascal is dead. Where is Orlena?"

Before Morena could think up a lie with which to get him to leave the house, he overheard a shriek of childish laughter and the soft chuckle of his wife's voice from the end of the hall. She and Ana were heading to the kitchen. Ignoring Morena, he walked with purposeful strides toward the sound of the laughter.

When he reached the kitchen, he found Orlena and Ana kneeling on the floor. A small black-and-white cat was between them, lapping greedily from a bowl of cream. The scowling cook looked up at him and shrugged silently, then padded out the rear door to check the fires in her bread ovens.

"Orlena, he is so splendid, all black-and-white patches, just like the Night Wind's stallion," the girl said as she stroked the soft, fluffy fur. The kitten continued to drink, but began to purr loudly.

"You cannot call such a small sweet thing Warpaint," Orlena said with such warmth in her voice it held Joaquín immobilized in the doorway. She had once used that tone with him, long ago.

"No, I suppose not," Ana said consideringly. "But listen to how he sings to us. I know! I shall name him Sweet Singer for his lovely purring."

"Not a warrior's name, but a fine one," Joaquín said as he stood studying Orlena's reaction. Her eyes darkened to deepest amber as she looked at him, while Ana leaped up and flew into his arms with a squeal of delight.

Gone was the shy, frightened child who lived haunted by death and violence. In her place was this beaming little girl with liquid brown eyes that danced with happiness. He knew Orlena had wrought the change in the child. As he hugged her, his eyes never left his wife's face. If only he could read her emotions as easily as Ana's.

Orlena felt her heart turn over as she watched her dark lover toss the child up in the air and then hug her. A broad smile slashed the chiseled perfection of his swarthy face, and his green eyes glowed with delight as he and Ana lapsed into the Lipan dialect. Orlena listened as the child sang her praises. *Does he believe anything good about me?* Slowly she stood up, uncertain of what to do, wanting to run as artlessly into his arms as Ana had, yet afraid to risk rejection or scorn by doing so.

The kitten was noisily pushing the clay bowl against the side of the adobe wall as he licked the dry bottom furiously with a small pink tongue.

Setting the girl down, Joaquín said, "Ana, Sweet Singer appears to have finished his meal. Perhaps you should take him into the courtyard for a bit while I speak with Orlena."

Obediently the child scooped her treasure up, ignoring his mewling protest as she patted his full belly. "Greedy little one. You will make yourself sick," she whispered as she slipped out the door.

Joaquín and Orlena stood facing each other across the kitchen, both afraid to break the spell by speaking. She longed to touch his beard-stubbled cheek. He longed to run his hands through her golden hair. All at once, the paralysis broke and they rushed into a fiery embrace, devouring each other with kisses. He tangled his hand in her hair and pulled it aside, baring her neck to his voracious lips as she ran her splayed fingers inside his buckskin shirt, kneading and caressing his hard chest, thrilled at the wild pounding of his heart.

When he scooped her up and carried her out back to the cook's garden and orchard, neither of them saw Morena standing in the door with her fists clenched at her sides.

When he reached the lush foliage of a row of peach trees, he set her down and took her hand in his. Surprised by the cessation of passion, she walked with him through the orchard, bemused and expectant. He seemed to be gathering his thoughts. Although bursting with her own special news, she held back, waiting for him to speak his piece.

"Lioness, I have missed you," he began softly, stopping in midstride, unable to resist touching one of the loose golden locks lying across her shoulder. "Bartolome was right. You are good for Ana. I can see how she blossoms beneath your tutelage."

"I would keep her with us, Joaquín," she said quietly. She looked into his face and waited.

"Is there to be a future for us, Lioness? Do you wish to remain a half-caste's wife?"

More than anything! she wanted to shout. Instead, she said, "Will you continue to raid and risk death as you have, always searching for vengeance, Joaquín? Where will we find peace and safety for Ana—for *our* children?" she added softly as her hand unconsciously rubbed her belly. Already she was certain it swelled with a new babe.

He became very still. "You carry another child?"

"Are you not pleased?" she asked, stung at the hard edge to his voice. "Will it interfere in your blood feud against Conal?"

He looked at the outraged set of her beautiful little face. "Are you not pleased might be the better question, Lioness. With a mixed-blooded babe, you can never return to your old life."

"I am not the one refusing to give up my old life. You are! Your hate comes before our love, Joaquín," she accused.

"Love, Lioness? Is it so? Or are you merely a prisoner of your lust and its consequence?" He reached out and touched her hand, pressing it against the slight rounding of her belly.

Tears filled her eyes, but she blinked them back, refusing to humble herself further before this arrogant savage. "Lust you call it. Mayhap you are right, Night Wind. But I will not shackle you. Go search out your father and kill him—kill each other! I care not."

She turned away from him and made to run for the house, when a cold deadly voice froze her to the earth.

"He need not search me out, Butterfly, for I am here," Conal Quinn said as he stepped from behind a tree. "Always it seems I arrive too late to rescue you from my bastard's touch. A pity the child shall know no father."

Joaquín shoved Orlena behind him and reached for his brace of pistols, cursing himself for the careless preoccupation that had allowed this catastrophe. Conal motioned and several armed soldiers materialized from behind the smokehouse at the edge of the orchard. The half-caste continued to hold Orlena

NIGHT WIND'S WOMAN

behind him, but made no move to withdraw his weapon. "How did you find us?" he asked in icy calm.

A slow smile spread across Quinn's face, twisting it grotesquely as he looked into his son's cold green eyes. "'Twas simple enough. When you killed Pascal, his partner came sniveling to me, looking for the oblivion of a fast drunk. For a few coins—quite a bit cheaper than Pascal was wont to charge me—I found you had ridden from the Rio Conchos for this valley. I knew you would not endanger the priest by staying with him, but then I remembered the beauteous Morena. Pity I did not recall her affection for her kinsmen sooner, but I have dispatched a dozen men to take prisoners at the house, even as we speak."

"So, coward that you always have been, you will have your men torture me while you watch. This time, *Captain*"—he emphasized the demoted rank scornfully—"why not end it once and for all—you against me?"

"The winner, of course, gets the golden treasure here," Conal said with a leer at Orlena. "I have always misliked taking chances where none was warranted, but after this past hellish year, I owe you your death—and her to witness it," he added bitterly. Withdrawing his broadsword from its scabbard, he motioned for his men to stand back. "You always showed a savage's craft with that knife. Drop the pistols to the ground and let us go blade to blade—the length of mine in exchange for your youthful stamina."

A grimace distorted Joaquín's features. He did as Conal bade, tossing the brace of pistols in his belt to the ground and moving clear of Orlena. "Fair enough. I know your word is worthless, so I will not ask that your men spare me when I kill you. My only consolation is that you will never touch my woman."

Shirl Henke

"No! Joaquín, you cannot kill your father, no matter what he has done. Conal, for whatever love you once bore me and Santiago, do not do this. Joaquín is your son!" She turned from one to the other as the two men began circling like wolves. Plainly, her plea was useless. She stood back, eyeing the Spanish soldiers, praying that some of Joaquín's men had accompanied him to the ranch. If only they would hear the outcry and respond!

Conal drew first blood, using the advantage of his longer weapon, but the nick on Joaquín's arm was only superficial. He feinted left, then parried right, grabbing Conal's sword arm and sweeping in to slash his right thigh a telling bloody length before they broke apart. The two men circled, each looking for an advantage. Conal, older and more seasoned, had the advantage not only of a sword but also of the leather armor across his chest. To kill him, Joaquín would have to come in low and gut him, a dangerous, nearly impossible feat. The half-caste's only other alternative was to deflect his opponent's sword and lunge for the throat, another risky maneuver. Joaquín, younger and faster, was dressed in lightweight buckskins and an open cotton shirt which afforded little protection, yet allowed him far freer movement. Still the relentless broadsword wielded by Conal's strong right arm was a formidable weapon, and Joaquín was soon covered with wounds oozing blood. None were deep, yet the uneven contest was taking its toll.

Orlena stood motionless, her mind racing and her eyes scanning the soldiers. Then her gaze locked on one of Joaquín's carelessly tossed pistols lying in the tall grass at the base of a peach tree. She inched toward the gun, all the while watching the soldiers.

Suddenly, Joaquín gained the advantage by sliding behind the low-hanging branch of a tree just as

Conal's sword came down, only to hack a deep gash into the green wood. In the instant it took him to free it, Joaquín's knife opened another crippling slash across Conal's left leg.

"Now you truly look like Colorado Quinn," Joaquín taunted.

Conal only laughed. "So do you, mongrel!"

Orlena made a swift lunge for the pistol, but the lieutenant caught sight of her from the corner of his eye and jumped to intercept her just before she could reach her prize. As the soldier wrestled her to the ground, Joaquín again ducked beneath a limb.

"You run like a cowardly savage. You are half white, at least. Stand and fight!" Conal swore as another small branch slapped at him, momentarily blinding him. In that instant Joaquín was on him and they rolled to the earth between the rows of trees. The half-caste's fingers locked on Conal's sword wrist, immobilizing the weapon. He smashed Conal's arm against the ground and the sword went flying. His knife now flashed toward Quinn's throat for the kill.

"No, Joaquín, you cannot! They will shoot if you kill him," Orlena cried, struggling as the lieutenant yanked her brutally to her feet. Both of his men prepared to fire on his command.

Joaquín held his blade at Conal's throat, his knee against his father's leather-armored chest, choking the breath from him.

"Kill me and die, bastard! I'll meet you in hell to finish this battle," Conal ground out, his green eyes glazed with hate.

"Shall I spare you all the moral dilemma? I assure you I have no qualms whatsoever about killing my beloved stepfather."

Ignacio's voice cut across the sound of the men's labored breathing and Orlena's struggles. Everyone froze as the indolent courtier strode nonchalantly into the clearing. Half a dozen men flanked him with drawn weapons. He made a barely perceptible motion to one man, who instantly raised his musket and shot Conal.

The slug smashed into Conal's face, splattering Joaquín with blood and the sticky grayish matter he knew to be brains. He waited a beat for the order to kill him. When it was not given, he stood up, ignoring the ruin that had been Conal Quinn.

"You have had a man killed whom you could never beat in a fair fight, Spanish fop," he said with cold contempt, waiting to see what the mercurial courtier would do next and praying his men and Conal's had heard the shot.

Ignacio chuckled mirthlessly. "Pity I've robbed you of your kill, but don't be pettish. As your estimable father said, you may rejoin the battle in the next life. I fear I have need of my sister—without the annoying encumbrance of a husband, no matter how irregular the technicalities of the marriage. Killing you here in the wilderness will save a good deal of time petitioning the Holy See."

He paused and looked from Joaquín to Orlena, who was yet struggling in the arms of Conal's soldier. "You have my leave to set her free, or face the same fate as your captain," he said conversationally to the lieutenant. He felt supremely confident, certain his soldiers outnumbered Quinn's presidials, not knowing of the men Conal had sent into the large hacienda. The lieutenant immediately released Orlena and stepped back, near where the discarded gun lay in the grass. He had no illusions about how long the courtier would allow him and his men to live.

Orlena turned to Ignacio with loathing on her face, restraining the urge to fly at him. If only she could divert him until Conal's soldier reached that gun, Joaquín might have a chance to slip into the trees and escape. "This avails you naught, Ignacio. Killing my husband will not kill the babe he has given me—and this time no one will take it from me!" She walked up to him, intent on grappling with him before he could issue any further deadly orders, but her plan failed. With lightning speed, he struck her a vicious blow, knocking her to the ground.

"Now I have even greater incentive to kill your savage," he snarled, motioning for one of his men to shoot the half-caste as he had Quinn. The soldier leveled his pistol at Joaquín, but before he could take aim, Morena raced into the clearing, screaming for Hoarse Bark and Night Wind's raiders to follow her. She threw herself in front of Joaquín and wrapped her arms about his neck just as the gun exploded.

Joaquín could feel the impact of the ball as it slammed into her back. Her grip tightened, then loosened as she whispered, "I am sorry, beloved. I only wanted Ignacio to take her away . . . forgive me." She slid to the earth as chaos erupted all about them.

Joaquín dived quickly across the open ground to where one of his discarded Miquelet Lock guns lay. Ignacio, who stood rooted in terror with an elegant Ripoll pistol clutched in his badly shaking hand, raised it and aimed at the moving target. Both men fired at once, but only Joaquín hit his mark. The shot slammed into Ignacio's chest, knocking him against a tree trunk, where he slid slowly to earth as a large red stain spread across his shirt. Ignacio Valdéz could never abide the discomfort of armor.

The Apache raiders, who had freed Morena from Conal's soldiers at the hacienda, poured into the orchard. With savage war cries, they fell upon the remnants of the two Spanish forces. The special troops from the capital who had escorted Ignacio were in disarray, but Conal's hardened presidials, having escaped the Apaches at the house, fought viciously. As his men raced across the garden into the orchard, the lieutenant who had held Orlena once more grabbed her before Joaquín could reach them. She kicked and bit as the leathercoat dragged her toward the cover of the trees.

"Hold, Night Wind, else your woman dies," he hissed, but Orlena twisted in his arms and knocked the gun away from her head. It discharged harmlessly into the air as she squirmed free and Joaquín pounced.

The two men went down, her bloodied husband at a distinct disadvantage against a fresh opponent wearing armor, but Joaquín moved with amazing speed. Before the dazed soldier could free his cumbersome broadsword, Joaquín's knife had done its work, slashing cleanly across the lieutenant's throat. In a blur, the half-caste sheathed his blade and rolled up. Grabbing Orlena's wrist with one hand, he extracted the half-freed sword from the dead man's scabbard.

He held her behind him as he cut down another soldier, then dragged her in a fast trot toward the house, calling out in Lipan for his men to disengage and scatter.

Conal's and Ignacio's soldiers still outnumbered the raiders even though the Apache had inflicted sizeable losses on them. The savages melted into the trees, leaving the leaderless Spanish in chaos.

"We must reach the corral where Warpaint and Morena's best horses are kept. No one will catch us then," Joaquín said as he slipped into the kitchen and headed down the long hall toward the front door.

"No! I must find Ana first. We cannot leave her, Joaquín." Orlena struggled against his iron grip.

He appeared to consider for an instant, thinking the child would not be noted or harmed until Bartolome could come for her, but one look at Orlena's stricken face convinced him to relent. If any harm should befall Ana, he would never be forgiven—or forgive himself.

"Where is she?" he asked.

"Her room is upstairs next to mine, but when she is frightened, I have found her in the cook's pantry, hiding with her kitten."

Following the path of her eyes toward the narrow wooden door in the far corner of the kitchen, he moved toward it, never relinquishing his hold on Orlena's wrist. "Ana, it is Night Wind. Are you here, little one?" he called softly as he opened the door. The creaking hinges and the kitten's squeal blended as a small body clutching the furball raced into Orlena's arms.

"I heard soldiers. Then Morena crying and cursing," she sobbed as Orlena tried to comfort her.

Joaquín, who had finally released his hold on his wife, now scooped up the child with her kitten and called out, "Follow me quickly lest they find us, Lioness. I do not think either Conal's or your brother's soldiers would be well disposed toward you right now!"

Chapter 26

They rode for several hours, but no one pursued them. Once he was certain of their escape, Joaquín shifted their course from dead west, arcing back to the northeast.

"Can we not go to Bartolome and warn him of what has happened?" Orlena asked as they paused by a stream to drink and refresh themselves.

"With Conal and Ignacio dead, no one will bother Bartolome. I will send him word when we reach our destination," was all he would say as he picked up the sleeping child and carried her to his big piebald stallion. "Can you ride for another hour or so if we slow our pace, Lioness?" he asked.

"Do you care if I lose this child, too, Joaquín?" The moment she spoke the words she wanted to call them back.

His face, open with concern, shuttered closed, the

expressionless Apache facade once more in place. "Leave it at this, wife—I care as much as you do." With that he kicked Warpaint into a slow canter, never looking back as she mounted her gelding and followed him. When they reached the low flat area where underground springs bubbled up into a shallow lake, the rustle of short shaggy pines and tall grasses welcomed them. Exhausted, Orlena slid from her horse. She helped Joaquín dismount with Ana and her kitten, both soundly asleep, and took the bundle from him.

Joaquín watched Orlena tenderly walk with the girl to the water's edge and sponge her face to help her awaken. The golden woman and the small dark child murmured low in warm conversation, petting the kitten and laughing together as he built a fire. Feeling perversely left out and angry with his wife, he interrupted them, saying, "This is woman's work. While I go in search of our dinner, tend this fire and get the cooking utensils from the saddle packs." Without a backward glance he strode away, carrying a length of finely braided rope for a snare.

"Where are we going, Orlena?" Ana asked with a catch in her voice. "I will miss the school and the holy brothers, especially Father Bartolome."

"So shall I, little one, but I am certain Night Wind will take us somewhere safe where we shall be happy," Orlena assured the child, praying it would be so. *At least where Ana will be happy.*

Dinner that evening was quiet, with Joaquín saying as little as possible except to talk with Ana about her kitten. To Orlena he only gave commands. Rather than create an ugly scene in front of the child, she followed his hateful if not unreasonable orders about making camp and preparing for the night. She and the child shared a bedroll with Sweet Singer. Joaquín slept alone.

As they slowly wended their way north, the tenor of the journey did not improve. Five days out, they were rejoined by half a dozen of Joaquín's men at a prearranged rendezvous point. Hoarse Bark was still cold to Orlena, but the new Jicarilla recruit, Manuel, was friendly, as were the others, an odd mixture of Apaches and mixed bloods, all of whom held their leader in awe. That a Spanish noblewoman was his wife seemed in no way inappropriate to them, but they did not know the story of how Night Wind had secured his white woman, either, Orlena thought bitterly.

Every night they slept apart, every day they exchanged thin civilities, and every hour Orlena died a bit more. *Bartolome was wrong. Even this new life I carry will not bring him back to me. He does not want me.* She laughed and smiled with Ana and the other men, but withdrew into an aloof shell around Night Wind.

Joaquín battled within himself as they journeyed toward their final destination. He did not want to reveal his true feelings to Orlena for fear of her rejection. She had been the one to renounce him when he was taken off in chains to die. She lost the child she had told him she did not want, and then insanely cast the blame on him! And now, bound to him once more by another child, she seemed no more favorably disposed to want a life with him than before.

The threats of Conal's sick desire and Ignacio's scheming plots were ended. If not for being a prisoner of her woman's body—and her own lust—she could be free of him. She could return to the City of Mexico, even to Spain itself, and live away from the taint of her

NIGHT WIND'S WOMAN

Apache lover. Ignacio had been right. Their marriage was irregular enough to be easily declared invalid.

A man tormented, he watched her from a distance, trying to decide if it was worth risking the pain of another rejection by baring his heart to her. Perhaps Bartolome had been right and she had tried to bargain for his life with Conal last year. Even now, with Conal Quinn no longer controlling his life through consuming hate, he was still a prisoner.

I am a prisoner of love, not hate, now, he thought. Was one as hopeless as the other? Certainly he had felt no triumph in Conal's death, none of the fierce savage joy he had expected over the years when revenge had kept him alive. He felt only an odd sense of relief, almost a loss of purpose. Perhaps that was why he was clinging to Orlena now, holding her captive and taking her to his ranch. He vowed that when they arrived he would keep her there until the baby was born. Then, if she wished to leave him and his offspring, he would free her. *But can I let her go?* The thought haunted him, waking and sleeping.

Digging graves was a hot chore, even on a cool fall day. Bartolome wiped his brow as he surveyed the work of the farmers dragged from their fields by the soldiers whose leaders and comrades had been slain. The priest had just helped an elderly conscripted gravedigger finish his assigned task when the poor man almost fainted from his exertions. So many dead. Bartolome could not regret the inevitable fate of Conal Quinn, or even the ignoble end of Ignacio Valdéz, but there were so many others—Spanish soldiers and even some of Night Wind's raiders, who had been killed in the bloody skirmish. Saddest of all was the tragic betrayal by Morena Girón that had precipitated the carnage. Her soul's fate troubled him deeply, but she had given her life in atonement, saving Joaquín. He prayed the Lord would consider that. Today he would say a funeral mass for all of them, believers and unbelievers, for he could not know among the Apaches who had been baptized and who not. All would have his prayers.

Many were in need of them, none more so than Quinn. One of the soldiers told the priest how his captain had died. Bartolome thanked God in his heart that Joaquín had not killed Conal, who was, from all reports this past year, quite mad. If only the pestilence of hate did not infect the son as it had the father.

Sighing, he trudged from the large field toward the rear door of the mission. It was time to don his vestments and say the mass. The graves were completed, open wounds in the earth waiting to be filled with the blood and bones of the poor benighted mortals who now reposed in the mission's chapel.

Bartolome was half through the mass when he looked up at the small assemblage where the dead outnumbered the living. He saw a dusty, exhausted Santiago Quinn sink white-faced to his knees in the rear of the chapel.

As soon as the last words of blessing were spoken, Bartolome motioned for his acolytes to attend the altar while he walked to the crude wooden bench where the boy sat. "This is not an auspicious time for you to arrive, my son." He paused, looking at Santiago's glassy-eyed expression. "You know your father and brother are dead?"

"I know Conal Quinn and Ignacio Valdéz are dead," the boy answered flatly. "I would know if Orlena and Joaquín are alive. Where has he taken her? Are they safe?"

"They are unharmed, escaped cleanly. Do not fear for them. There is much I would tell you, but this is not the time or place. I must finish the burials by consigning the remains to the earth."

"I will await you here, then. I fear I have no desire to pray for Conal or Ignacio, Father," Santiago replied quietly.

When Bartolome returned, Fray Alonzo had brought Santiago a hearty repast of roasted beef and fresh vegetables. The youth sat alone in Bartolome's cabin, shoving the food about on his plate, his usual voracious appetite gone.

"You must talk about your feelings, Santiago. He was your father, and in his own way he loved you well," the priest said as he sat down across the crude wooden table, said grace silently, and dished up a portion of the food for himself.

The boy's bright green eyes, so like Conal's, filled with tears. "Time is distorted in this place, I think. It seems a thousand years ago that we came here. He was so different in Spain. I thought I knew him. So did Orlena."

"And you were wrong," Bartolome added gently. "I told her once, long ago, that Conal was really two men, one the loving father you both remember from childhood—"

"A childhood we have both put behind us," Santiago interrupted bitterly.

"Yes, that is the way of growing up. Often it is painful, but you will find no benefit in dwelling on the hurt Conal did you and your sister. Let that part of him die. Let the good memories remain. At least you have many. Joaquín has no such consolation."

Santiago looked into the wise, sad face of the priest. "I will try, Father, but it will be difficult." He took a few desultory bites of food. "Tell me of Joaquín and Orlena. How did they escape? Where are they? I would see them both again."

"Joaquín has a ranch far to the north in that isolated valley where he brought me when the exchange was made last year. It prospers now. He has taken his wife there, I am certain. With Conal dead, they will be safe. They await the birth of another child."

Santiago's eyes glowed with the first animation Bartolome had seen the youth exhibit since he arrived. "I am to be an uncle at last! But it is a long journey to that valley. If Orlena lost this babe—"

"She will not. Joaquín loves her and she him. Ignacio cannot undermine their marriage now. Certainly no one in New Mexico will," Bartolome added with a twinkle.

"I would go see them and find out if I have a nephew or a niece," he said. Excitement made his adolescent voice crack.

"It is a long journey for a boy alone. You are most fortunate to have arrived here unharmed. Do not tax your guardian angel further, my son. We will hear from them in due time. Then perhaps they will come here or you may journey there, but for now I imagine your Cousin Bernal in the City of Mexico is beside himself with worry for you. Should you not return there and resume your studies?"

They boy hesitated, recalling several brushes with death along the dangerous trail to Chihuahua City. As usual, Bartolome was right. Cousin Bernal would be frantic. He sighed. "I suppose you are right. But I would send a letter while I am yet here for you to post to them. You do have ways of contacting them, do you not?"

Bartolome smiled broadly. "Never fear. I have my ways."

New Mexico Province, Winter 1790

The beauty of her surroundings never ceased to awe Orlena. The climb of several thousand feet into the lush valley had been made at a far more sedate pace this time than on her original hasty journey with the Lipan. She sat on her horse, surveying the tall stands of cedar and spruce. The air was cold and tangy with the scent of the trees and wood smoke from the fire in the ranch house below her.

The ranch house. Her home. Its central courtyard was surrounded by the wide, low building of sparkling white adobe. The flat roof, with its open beams, once so ugly to her, now seemed a thing of rare symmetry and beauty. As soon as Joaquín had brought them here last fall she had fallen in love with the place, set like a gem in this high, fertile valley. The man who ran the place in Joaquín's absence, Pablo Rivas, welcomed them and proudly showed his employer the fat herds of sheep and the wild cattle he and his Indian vaqueros had accumulated.

Joaquín Quinn had perversely decided on using his father's hated surname now that Conal was dead. Pardoned by the new governor of New Mexico, he was now a *rico*. If their life was not one of lavish opulence such as Orlena would have enjoyed at the Spanish court, it was nonetheless one of great physical comfort. She had servants in the large warm house, fresh wholesome food, even lovely gowns and cloaks sewn from the finest fabrics available at the trade fairs. She had Ana and soon would have another child of her own. The cycle of her life as a rancher's wife was filled with vital and interesting work, encumbered by none of the hardships and dangers of her days with the Lipan. But she did not have her husband's love.

Joaquín slept with her, making it plain ever since he brought her to his domain that she must accept his touch, yet expect nothing of trust or affection, only the physical satiety he chose to give her. Last night, in spite of her swollen belly and feeling fat and ugly as he disrobed her, she had again given in to his hypnotic caresses, lost in the savage passions they seemed destined to unleash in each other.

"We're both prisoners," she murmured to herself as she sat on the gentle old mare, the only animal slow and even-tempered enough for her to ride in her advanced pregnancy. After their languorous interlude last night, he had done as he always did, turned from her in the big wide bed, rolled over, and fallen fast asleep. No words of tenderness passed between them. Indeed, they spoke no words at all but for the terse conversation necessary in discharging their duties as *patron* and *patrona* of the ranch.

Joaquín's unreasoning mistrust of her remained an aching wound that would never heal. She had agonized and finally written to Fray Bartolome about their plight. He counseled patience and prayed that the birth of their child would soften her husband's heart. Orlena doubted it. He was as cold as the snowy landscape before her. A late winter storm last night had spread a dusting of silvery white snow across the valley. The mare picked her way carefully down the trail toward the warm haven of the ranch house.

Soon it would be dark and Lupe would have a fragrant pot of stew bubbling on the hearth. Ana and Sweet Singer would worry about her. Joaquín would worry only about the babe. Sometimes she feared he did not even care about his child, but only felt a duty to provide for it and its mother. Knowing how she hated it, he rode with his renegades far from their valley into Nueva Vizcaya where rich caravans traveled. She was sympathetic to the captives they freed, but Joaquín's continuing need to punish the Spanish frightened her. He would always be driven by hate, which left no room for love.

Entering the rosy glare of the large, high-ceilinged kitchen, Orlena immediately looked for Ana, who was usually playing about the hearth while Sweet Singer was under the fat cook's feet.

"Where is Ana, Lupe?" She shook her soft woolen cloak free of snow and hung it on a peg near the fire.

The cook's eyes widened in consternation. "She is not with you, Doña Orlena? She left here several hours ago, bundled up for a ride, carrying that pesky cat. She said you were up on the ridge and she could see plainly to ride up to you. I did not—"

"Where is Joaquín?" Orlena interrupted impatiently as icy fingers of fear seized her heart. She had seen no trace of Ana and her pony on the wide, open trail down to the valley floor.

"The *patron* is not come in yet. Mayhap he is still down by the corrals where they work the newly captured mustangs."

Grabbing the cloak quickly, Orlena flung it about her shoulders in a flourish and vanished down the hall toward the courtyard, the closest way to the corrals.

Joaquín was soaked with sweat in spite of the chill evening air. The frozen ground jarred his bones with every stiff-legged bounce of the half-broken stallion. Just as the big brute began to tire and trot around the corral with reasonable docility, Orlena's cries set his ears back and he began to skitter.

Cursing, Joaquín dismounted and turned the reins

over to Manuel. "Rub him down and feed him well." He turned expectantly toward the sound of her voice, angry with her for such exertion. She was gasping for breath and holding her belly as he reached her in long, ground-devouring strides. "What is wrong?"

"Ana is missing! I have searched everywhere. She rode up to meet me on the ridge, Lupe said—but I never saw her!" She paused and sucked more air into her lungs.

Joaquín began issuing orders for a search, then turned to Orlena, "Go back to the house and wait. It grows dark and we must hurry. Another storm is blowing in."

"No, I can ride—"

He shook her, then scooped her into his arms and began to run toward the house as if she were no more than a doll. When he reached the front door, he put her down and shoved her toward Lupe. "Keep her inside. Lock her up if you must!" Turning to Orlena he said, "You will not endanger my child by riding into a blizzard!"

Knowing he was right, but hating the cold, preemptory way he impressed the fact on her, Orlena watched him lope back to where Vitorio was holding Warpaint's reins. Joaquín swung gracefully into the saddle like the Lipan raider he was. At his signal, the men spread out, riding in diverse directions as the darkness and the storm drew nearer.

Joaquín remembered Orlena's words about the ridge trail that Ana supposedly took to intercept her. He had instructed the men to fan out all along the ridge and then backtrack toward the valley.

Darkness fell and the snow blew in again, like a white wildcat, clawing at his buckskins. He rode up and down the trail but found not a trace. Tracks on the dark, snow-blown ground were invisible. Finally, exhausted and dispirited, he sent Vitorio and the other men in for food and a thawing out. Unable to face Orlena's tear-streaked face if he returned without the child who had become her surrogate daughter, he rode up the ridge once again. Suddenly he remembered a steeper, far less passable way up the cedar-lined mountain, far too dangerous for his pregnant wife. Would a foolish child in a hurry attempt it?

His hands were too numb to feel the reins as he kneed Warpaint off the steep trail down the first small ravine. When he reached a dead end there, he backtracked and tried the next break in the timber. After a day working horses and being soaked with sweat, he felt his teeth chattering and his breath freezing in his lungs. Ignoring the pain, he persevered, thinking of Ana, so small and alone in the dark and the cold.

The trail was almost at the crest of the ridge and Joaquín despaired, with no other ideas about where to search, when he saw Ana's pony. It stood back in the shelter of a thick stand of spruce trees, almost invisible but for its white markings against the dark green boughs. In an instant he dismounted and walked to the skittish beast, calling in Lipan and then Spanish for Ana.

Orlena paced the *sala* floor, then walked to the front window again. Her vigil had gone on since late afternoon, and now it approached dawn. The storm had worsened through the night. Finally the howl of the wind quieted and the air cleared of sleeting snow drops. The vaqueros were saddling fresh horses down by the corral, preparing to ride out with the first faint streaks of light. Then she heard it over the dying wind—the soft plod of Warpaint's hooves, interspersed with the loud squalls of Sweet Singer.

With a cry of joy, she threw open the heavy oak

doors and raced into the yard. Joaquín sat hunched on the big piebald with his precious burden swaddled in a blanket. Ana was scarcely visible, but Sweet Singer's patchy black-and-white head stuck out and his red mouth protested loudly.

Vitorio ran up to the horse and took the blanket-wrapped bundle from Joaquín, handing the child and her cat to Orlena. She hugged the girl, crying and questioning at the same time as they walked toward the front door.

"What happened to you? You are nearly frozen!"

"Sweet Singer jumped down and ran after a rabbit up on the steep trail at the end of the valley," the child said miserably between chattering teeth. "I chased him for a long while before he returned to me and then it was very dark and the wind was blowing. We hid beneath a big spruce tree where there were lots of heavy limbs to protect us from the snow. That is where Night Wind found us."

At the mention of his name, Orlena looked back at her husband, remembering how wet with sweat and exhausted he had been yesterday evening. Just then, his knees buckled and he slid to the ground where Vitorio caught him. Orlena handed Ana to the cook and reached out for Joaquín, who steadied himself and muttered, "I am all right, just numbed with cold. See to the child." Already Ana was shivering in Lupe's arms as the big woman vanished into the house with her and the protesting cat.

"Heat some bricks for her bed quickly," Orlena called after Lupe. Turning to Joaquín she said quietly. "Thank you for saving her. Are you certain you are all right?" She longed to touch his frozen face, but his forbidding expression stayed her hand.

"I will go to the kitchen and warm up. I could use

some hot soup. You and Lupe see to Ana first."

Ana needed all the skills Orlena had learned from She Who Dreams. In fact, as she undressed the frozen child and bundled her into a warm bed filled with heated bricks, Orlena prayed that the medicine woman would come to take charge. "But she is not here, and I am."

Forcing herself to be practical, she rubbed the child's frozen arms and legs, restoring circulation, then kept her warmly covered in her room with a blazing fire roaring in the fireplace.

Lupe quickly brought a large bowl of broth, which they tried to induce the child to drink. However, exhaustion won out over hunger and Ana drifted into a restless sleep, once assured that the mischief maker, Sweet Singer, was there to cuddle with her.

"At least the rascal helps warm her body," the cook said sourly as she took the untouched broth back to the kitchen.

"Did my husband eat? Is he all right?" Orlena called after the shambling Mexicana.

Lupe's blackened teeth showed as she smiled broadly. "The *patron* ate a hearty meal at the kitchen table. Warmed and fed, he will be fine. Do not worry about that one. He is strong as a stallion."

Relieved that Joaquín was unhurt, but embarrassed by Lupe's obvious sexual innuendo, Orlena returned her attention to the girl.

A short while later, Joaquín came into the small, warm room to check on Ana. He had dark circles beneath sleet-reddened eyes and looked ready to drop from exhaustion. "How is she?"

"I do not know. She is too tired to eat and I know she needs strength after her ordeal. I fear lung congestion and fever. She is so small . . ." Her voice faded.

"Do not work yourself into an illness. Lupe and I can help with her. You have the babe to think of, too," he said sternly.

She whirled in anguish. "You are a fine one to talk, weaving on your feet after twenty-four hours on horseback out in the hellish cold. Go to bed! I will not overtax myself with one little girl."

He nodded bleakly. "I will rest a while, then check on you."

As the day wore on, Orlena's fears grew. A rattling cough began in the child's throat and spread lower to her lungs. By evening she was ablaze with fever. She instructed Lupe to bring icy water and lots of clean rags to bathe Ana. They would try to bring down the heat burning her small body. The night would be a long vigil of cooling rub-downs combined with nourishing broth.

Hours passed as Orlena wrung out cloths again and again, her fingers now stiff with the cold as she persisted in her treatment. *If only She Who Dreams were here to give me guidance!* Suddenly Orlena remembered the time Joaquín had nearly died in the Lipan camp when Quick Slayer's knife made the evil scar on his side. She called for Lupe.

When the old woman appeared in the door, Orlena asked about the cherry trees in the orchard. She described the pieces of bark She Who Dreams used for her fever infusion and sent the cook off to gather the necessary materials.

Joaquín came in about the dinner hour, obviously the better for a day's rest. He watched Orlena sponging the child and spooning the cherry bark infusion between her parched lips. The scales finally dropped from his eyes. This was the real woman, his Lioness, who had saved his life in the same manner in the

Lipan camp. She had worked as hard at Bartolome's school and hospital, but he had been so blinded by jealousy and his own guilt that he had refused to see what everyone else did.

Oh, my golden Lioness, what have I done? He looked down at her haggard face, her shoulders slumped by weariness, her belly heavy with the child of their passion. He had abducted her in revenge, not once but twice, and now she was chained to him by the child and Ana. She loved Ana; he admitted that now. But could she love him? Could she ever forgive him?

Sensing his presence, Orlena looked up. He had rested and changed clothes, but still he looked like a brigand with a stout growth of beard and his long straight hair loose about his face. For all that, she thought him the most heart-stoppingly splendid man she had ever seen. But the scowl on his face looked forbidding. What went on behind those glacial green eyes?

"You will harm yourself and your child. Go to bed and rest. I will care for Ana," he said softly.

She stood up angrily, her hand going at once to the stiffened ache in the small of her back. Rubbing it, she glared at his arrogant face. "You will never believe I care for Ana or that I cared for our child—the one who died in that awful desert! Can you not see that Ana is that daughter I lost? I love her, I love her, damn you!"

She began to sob, pounding furiously on his chest with hard little fists as he tried to calm her. He was unable to say anything, for pain squeezed the breath from him. Finally she subsided into exhausted hiccuping and he scooped her up into his arms and carried her down the hall to their bedroom. Calling for Lupe, he instructed her to see to her mistress.

Shirl Henke

Then he returned to Ana's side.

I love her! The words echoed in his mind as he spooned broth into the feverish child's mouth and bathed her with cold rags. Orlena loved Ana and blamed him for the terrible death of their daughter. Now he had put her at risk again, here in the wilderness, overworked and carrying another Apache baby. All of her life she had been forced by men to do things against her will. First by her father, then Ignacio and Conal, but most of all by him. He had been the cruelest betrayer of all, using her as a pawn in his twisted vengeance. No matter that he had enslaved her senses as he had boasted to Conal. She would never have chosen a bastard half-caste renegade to husband.

"Ah, Ana," he sighed to the tossing, feverish child, "when she is recovered from the birth, I must let her go back to Santiago in the capital. She may choose to take you and my babe with her . . . or not . . . I do not know. Only this I do know . . . if I offer her freedom, I will lose her."

He steeled himself for the emptiness ahead. The best, the only way to survive, was to avoid her. He must no longer claim her body in passion. He would sleep apart from her. Given how near it was to her time, that should not be unreasonable anyway.

When in the middle of the night, she appeared to spell him with Ana, he said quietly, "Her fever is broken. She will live, Lioness. You may sit with her. I have matters to which I must attend."

He cleared his belongings from their room and moved them into another one down the hall. Then he went into his library and sat down at the large oak table to compose a letter to Bartolome. Given time for it to reach him and for him to summon Santiago,

NIGHT WIND'S WOMAN

Orlena should be able to travel when they arrived here to collect her.

"If I do not touch her or look at my child, I shall bear it better," he vowed to himself. It was time to go raiding again. Perhaps a quick, clean death might mercifully claim him.

Chapter 27

You will harm yourself and your child. The words haunted her. He would never forgive her foolish deception. The adobe shack stood like a bleak, ugly symbol of that night of betrayal, of the death of his love. From then on, it had become only vengeance. Had not the past month's agony proven this to her? Joaquín had deserted her bed, coldly announcing that she was near her time and he would not harm the child by lying with her.

"I am fat and ugly to you," she had accused him, throwing up to him his involvement with the beautiful Morena. He doubtlessly blamed her for his mistress's death.

Orlena stared at the adobe hut, walking toward it without watching the overgrown path. Her foot caught on a vine and she jerked it free, intent on her misery as she reached out to touch the rough walls, now warmed by the spring sun.

NIGHT WIND'S WOMAN

She had tried to tell him she loved him and chose to live her life with him, but he had quickly cut her off, saying her speeches could wait until the child was born. Then she might well see things differently. The coldness in those green eyes erected a barrier she could not breach.

She came to herself, realizing she was pounding on the rough wall. Her hands were scraped raw and bloody, and she was sobbing uncontrollably. Suddenly a warm gush of water ran down her legs, and a dull throbbing ache spiraled from her lower back around her pelvis to clutch at her abdomen. The baby! But it was nearly a month too soon! Terrified of losing yet another child, she huddled down by the wall and hugged herself in misery. She was alone, with no one to help her in this desolate wilderness but Lupe and a flighty young *casta* serving girl named Rita.

Joaquín was gone on one of his dangerous missions. He had seemed to court death these past months, even more than he had when Conal was alive. He might never come back. She forced that terrible thought from her mind. But it would be days or weeks before he returned. Would his child be alive or dead? She began to pray, squatting in a huddled heap, feeling the warm rays of the spring sun soothing her as the pain dissipated. At least this was not the ragged waves of agony that she had endured when she lost the first child.

Orlena squeezed her tear-stained eyes tightly closed, then opened them suddenly, sensing a presence in spite of the soundless calm of morning. She Who Dreams stood before her. Blinking her eyes, Orlena refocused, and still the mirage was before her. "I am having a dream," she whispered to herself.

The vision smiled. "That is a good sign," the old

woman said in Lipan. "I always hoped you would be so blessed."

Orlena felt the tight constriction about her belly ease. Taking a deep breath, she stood up and reached out to touch the very solid body of the old woman. "It is truly you! You are here!" Tears ran down her cheeks again, but this time they were joyous as she hugged She Who Dreams fiercely.

The old woman returned her embrace and then began to walk with her, slowly retracing their steps toward the house. The twisting creek flowed rapidly, filled with spring rains that almost overflowed the narrow log bridge. As they traversed it, She Who Dreams carefully guided Orlena's awkward footsteps lest she trip and fall into the rushing icy waters. When they reached the other side of the stream, Orlena faltered and stiffened again as another contraction hit her.

"Walk slowly," She Who Dreams said. "It is good for you and the baby." The calmness of her voice seemed to infuse Orlena with a sense of relaxation and security. She was no longer alone.

"How did you find me? Is White Crane with you?" she asked eagerly.

She Who Dreams smiled mysteriously and her round face looked beautiful for a moment. "I have always known you would one day need me. The vision I had guided me here when the time was right. Your father remains with our band, for he must keep hotheads from foolish raids that might bring the Comanche or the Spanish to find us. One day you will come to see White Crane and all your friends. Little Otter asks of you often," the old woman said with a smile. "Her baby grows fat and walks now."

Recalling the birth of Little Otter's baby, Orlena knew that what was happening to her was different.

NIGHT WIND'S WOMAN

But before she could even ask the question, the wise old woman answered. "This young warrior is eager to see the world. He kicks much, eh?" At Orlena's affirmative nod, she continued, "That is why the waters have left your body. He has begun his descent early. The laboring will be difficult but quick. He will be small—but lusty and of good health," she added to reassure Orlena. "A worthy son for Night Wind and Sun in Splendor."

Smiling ruefully, Orlena realized how good it was to hear the Apache tongue and to hear her Lipan name. "So, you know this is a manchild. I had hoped it would be so."

"Because you have lost a daughter and then regained one in Desert Flower, the one you call Ana," She Who Dreams said sagely.

"You are amazing, my mother," Orlena replied. "Ana never told any of us her Lipan name. Desert Flower. It is as lovely as she is herself. She has filled the void left in my heart by my daughter's death," Orlena added quietly.

They continued to walk, toward the gardens behind the big ranch house. Spring had given new vitality to the neatly tended rows of melon vines, squashes, and peppers. Seeds burst into life to bear fruit, even as Joaquín's seed planted many months ago in her was doing.

"You hope this child will heal the breach between you and Night Wind. That part of your heart has remained empty. I saw that he would turn from you in pain, but I would know all of the reasons this has happened," She Who Dreams said as she supported Orlena through another, more intense contraction. In a moment they resumed walking again.

Orlena took a deep breath and then began her tale of all that had befallen her since she left their camp to meet her husband in this valley. It seemed so long ago now. She Who Dreams took in every detail, nodding and grunting from time to time, seeming to be fitting together in her mind many pieces of an intricate design. By the time Orlena had finished her tale of death, betrayal, and misunderstanding, the old woman seemed to reach a decision.

Before she could speak, Lupe came running from the house, across the garden toward her mistress. Looking askance at the old Lipan woman, she said in Spanish, "Don Pablo says these are Don Joaquín's family from—" She gasped as she took in Orlena's water-logged skirts and the way she held her belly as she walked. "The child is coming, *patrona*! You must come in the house and lie down at once."

Orlena smiled as the contractions again eased. "No, Lupe. Not just yet. I am doing fine. This is my foster mother, She Who Dreams. She has birthed many babies and knows well what to do. You must make those who traveled with her welcome and prepare food. Have Ana help you and keep her occupied. My mother will tell you and Rita what must be done for me when the time comes." As another, even more intense contraction began to build, Orlena muttered beneath her breath, "I pray the Blessed Virgin and White Painted Lady it will be soon!"

In her broken but serviceable Spanish, She Who Dreams issued some simple instructions to Lupe. With one look at Orlena who nodded her confirmation, the cook departed for the house, muttering to herself, "Never have I heard of such a way for a lady to have a child! If only Don Joaquín was here."

If only Don Joaquín was here. The cook's words echoed in Orlena's mind over and over during the next two hours as she gave birth. As She Who Dreams had said, the process was swift, but the final few moments of the delivery were fraught with intense pain. Also as the medicine woman predicted, the child was small, a lustily bawling baby boy.

When she took the little bundle, all bathed and swaddled from She Who Dreams' hands, Orlena felt the vital life in him as he cried. His little face was dark, like his father's, with the same inky hair, but the dark locks had a faint curl to them, as her golden ones did. All babies had pale eyes, but she suspected his would likely turn green or amber in a few months. Her breath caught in her throat as she rocked him and let his greedy little mouth pull on her breast. "He is strong and beautiful, just like his father," she whispered as she drifted into an exhausted sleep, propped up with the nursing infant held between a mound of pillows in the big bed.

She Who Dreams smiled at Lupe, who was forced to return the courtesy. At first shocked at the barbaric way of birthing a baby by squatting like a *paisana* in a field, the cook had to admit that the birth went faster and less painfully than the usual method of letting the mother lie in a soft bed for hours, sometimes days of laboring.

"She must rest now. Prepare hot food and fresh goat's milk for her when my daughter awakens. I will watch her."

Lupe nodded and retreated, already knowing better than to argue with this intimidating woman who seemed to know what she was thinking before she even uttered a word!

The raid into Chihuahua netted them a fine cache of gold and freed several dozen Apache captives. The Night Wind rode at the head of his men, but as they neared the small rich valley, he felt no sense of triumph. He had sent Hoarse Bark to Bartolome's mission with the gold and the Indian children. The adults traveled with him. Several of the Jicarilla had kin among those bands roaming northern New Mexico. Others wanted to work at his ranch. A few of the young men were eager to join his raiders. He saw a life of emptiness stretching before him without Orlena and their child. He had been robbed of the driving force of his hate. It had died with Conal Quinn. Love could not replace it now.

He thought constantly of Orlena, her golden beauty haunting his dreams as he tossed restlessly on the hard, rocky earth each night. Her time was near now. He had been gone for nearly a month. Perhaps Santiago would arrive soon to take her away. He sat rigidly on Warpaint's back and tried not to think of it. When the long, low outline of the house lay before him, he swung down from the stallion and handed the reins to a beaming Pablo, who ran from the corral to greet him.

"Welcome home, Don Joaquín!" Bursting with the news of the *patron*'s splendid son, he restrained his overwhelming desire to blurt it out. Such was not his place. His lady should show him his son. How surprised he would be!

With a faint look of annoyance at his employee's exuberance, he walked toward the ranch house, feeling lonely and out of humor. When he entered the front hall, She Who Dreams walked from the *sala,* as at home in the big house as she would have been in her summer wickiup. His eyes first widened in amazement and pleasure, then narrowed in suspicion and fear. "Why are you here? Orlena?" His heart squeezed with dread.

"Your wife is fine. I am here because she had need of me," she replied cryptically. "Come with me."

NIGHT WIND'S WOMAN

Without a backward glance the old woman turned and walked down the hall with her charge following warily.

When she quietly opened the door to the master bedroom, Joaquín stood rooted in the hall, staring at Orlena, who sat in a large cane chair facing the courtyard window, nursing a baby. He could see the thick black hair and coppery skin so dark against the paleness of her milk-engorged breast. Every fiber of his body ached to rush to her side and touch her, to hold his own flesh and blood, the babe he had sworn not to look upon, the child he must give up.

"Is he not splendid?" She Who Dreams asked proudly.

Hearing the sound of her voice, Orlena raised her head from the dreamy reverie in which she had been drifting. Her mouth formed a small "oh" of surprise as she cradled her son's head against her breast. The look of shock and anguish on her husband's face choked off her joyous words of welcome. Embarrassed at her nakedness, she covered her breasts and stood up stiffly. "Here is your son, Joaquín. Would you not examine him?" Still he stood frozen in the doorway, his face shuttered and unreadable.

"He is healthy and strong, even if born early," Orlena said to him as he tried to divide his attention between two irresistible sights—his wife and his son.

He wanted to betray none of the longing he felt for either. "Have you chosen a name, Lioness?" he asked neutrally.

Cut to the quick by his coldness and lack of interest, she replied levelly, "That is for you to do, both by Spanish and Apache custom."

He nodded. "Then he shall be called Bartolome. Perhaps he will grow to be a man of peace. That should please you." With that, he turned sharply on his heel and walked down the hall to the room he had been using, calling out to Lupe for a bath and some food.

She Who Dreams watched Orlena crumple back into the chair, soothing the fretting infant who seemed to sense his mother's anguish. Her amber eyes glistened with tears as she looked into the kindly brown ones. "You see how it is. He cannot bear to be near us. He does not want us, Mother."

She Who Dreams had observed the whole scene in silence. Now she said, "Or perhaps he wants too much and is afraid to reach out, lest all be taken from him."

Orlena gave a derisive sob. "He is the one who takes. He stole me from my family in Santa Fe and again took me from the City of Mexico. I am his to keep . . . if only he wanted me or his son."

"Perhaps he believes you do not wish to stay. He has stolen you and forced you to become his woman, to bear his children. A man of pride such as the Night Wind would not want a wife he had to hold prisoner. Think on it and let him consider what it is he plans to sacrifice." She added cryptically, "Soon you will be given a choice. Only make the right one and all will be well."

"Can you not make that beast go faster, Father?" Santiago asked in disgust as the priest's mule ambled in a leisurely pace along the mountain trail. Spring glowed about them, reflected in the golden sky, the flowering cacti and the sweet perfume of rain-washed grasses.

Bartolome seemed curiously unconcerned with the youth's impatience to reach his sister. "This poor animal is doing the best he can under the considerable

NIGHT WIND'S WOMAN

burden he must bear. We will reach the ranch in time enough to see your nephew born."

Santiago's face darkened. "I mislike the letter Joaquín sent you. It is not natural for a man to reject his own child. I thought he loved Orlena, that he would protect her from Ignacio. Now I am not at all certain. Mayhap he can never forgive any of us for our Spanish blood," he added with a touch of sadness underlying the anger in his voice.

Almost sixteen years old now, Santiago had grown to a man's full stature in the past year, even if his voice still cracked and his level of patience was equally erratic. He had received several letters from his sister, filled with details about the ranch, yet oddly devoid of references to her husband and their marriage. He read between the lines that Joaquín often left her alone and that the misunderstanding born of Conal's treachery had never been mended. Nothing Bartolome could say in his correspondence to Santiago dissuaded the youth. He had arrived in Chihuahua City weeks before the fateful letter from Joaquín reached the priest.

Once Bartolome read it, he, too, had become troubled. Time alone together awaiting the birth of this child had not mended the rift as he had prayed it might. Joaquín's stubborn pride and all the emotional scars of childhood still plagued him like demons. He felt his beautiful Spanish wife did not love him, but had been trapped into remaining his wife because of her pregnancy. His offer to give her over to her brother and allow their highly irregular marriage to be dissolved was based on those fears.

Bartolome sighed wearily at the folly of youthful nobility. While thinking on the subject of misplaced zeal, the priest looked at his companion's set face.

Shirl Henke

Santiago, of course, had totally misread the whole situation, but since Bartolome had been unable to convince either Joaquín or Orlena of the truth of their feelings, he felt it useless to try and convince a stripling lad. He would simply have to rely on his instincts and Santiago's good will when they arrived at the ranch.

"At least I will be able to baptize the baby," he told himself as he rode slowly up the steep, twisting trail toward the skyline where the verdant Sierra Blanca met slashes of white clouds and azure skies.

As they rode into the valley, Bartolome had the odd feeling that they were expected, but not by Joaquín. They were a month early for his summons because of Santiago's premature arrival in Chihuahua City. Someone else wanted them there. But who? He dismissed the thought as fanciful and reached for the water flask slung across his saddlehorn.

Joaquín was alone in his room soaking in a large copper tub. He could cleanse himself free of dust, blood, and sweat, but how could he live with the guilt? Again he had failed her, leaving her alone to face an early and difficult birth. She had miscarried once because of the hardship of this wilderness. He should have known it might happen again. But he was so intent on avoiding her that he had taken a coward's way out and deserted her. He thanked whatever deities listened to one so cursed as he that She Who Dreams had come to help his Lioness.

He shifted in the big tub, letting the hot water soothe away the ache of dangerous days and restless nights on the trail. What was he to do now? Bartolome and Santiago would not arrive for weeks. He must somehow retain the wall he had built with such exacting precision between him and Orlena. His passions would explode and he would take her again if he came near her. The physical bond that enslaved him also held her in thrall. He must not let it torture either of them any longer.

But the boy—his son! He had a son he was dying to hold, yet he sat in a tub of rapidly cooling water, drinking himself stuporous to keep from becoming attached to his own flesh and blood. His heart cried out to do as Strong Bow had done with his child, as all Lipan fathers did, carrying their children out beneath the open sky and presenting them to the world. But he could not do that, he concluded bitterly.

He reached for the glass of *aguardiente* and swallowed the bitter stuff in one swift gulp. It did not help. The image of that tiny dark head was burned into his brain. He cursed bitterly, not even able to get decently drunk! Joaquín stood up and wrapped a towel about himself, heading for his bed. As he passed out from alcohol and exhaustion, he made himself a promise—on the morrow, while Orlena was out of the room, he would visit his son just one time.

Dawn came, merciless with spring brilliance. Joaquín squinted his eyes against the glow of fuchsia, orange, and amber on the eastern horizon. Yesterday he had learned from Vitorio that Orlena was recuperating rapidly from the birth. She rode every morning now, as soon as she had attended to her infant's feeding. He must hurry and dress if he was to see young Bartolome while she was taking her exercise.

The icy water in the basin loosened the cobwebs from his brain as he splashed his face. Shaving was an ordeal because of too much liquor and a severe case of nervousness. His hand actually shook and he cut himself with the blade. Cursing, he forced himself to calm down and finish the task.

By the time he had completed a hurried toilette and dressed simply in buckskin leggins and a linen shirt, the sun was a golden ball climbing high in the azure sky. He watched Orlena ride away from the corral, wearing a Lipan tunic and leggins, doubtless a gift from She Who Dreams. How magnificently his Lioness rode, with her golden hair trailing behind her in the spring breeze like a blazing banner unfurled. "I must not think of her," he muttered to himself as he turned from the doorway and walked slowly down the hall. She Who Dreams was watching the baby, he knew, but he could deal with her. She understood his heart and would not force him to endure useless prattle about the painful situation between him and Orlena.

When he entered the master bedroom, his eyes glanced past She Who Dreams and fastened on the tiny bundle lying in the crib, kicking beneath the covers. Detecting a quiet smile wreathing her face, he ignored it and nodded tersely to her as he approached the baby.

"I have come to examine my son as is Lipan custom," he said without preamble.

"He has just eaten and is sleepy. He will not cry if you hold him, I think," She Who Dreams said noncommittally as she stared out the window, seeming to search for something on the horizon.

Joaquín knelt by the crib and pulled back the blanket. His hand seemed to dwarf the infant, yet with unfocused blue eyes the baby instinctively reached for his hand. One tiny, perfectly formed set of fingers fastened about his thumb.

"How strong he is!" Joaquín exclaimed before he could stifle the words.

NIGHT WIND'S WOMAN

She Who Dreams remained impassive, staring out the window. "It is your duty to present him to the sky and the four winds," she said quietly.

Joaquín hesitated. This was not a Lipan village. "He will be raised as a white man. His blood is more Spanish than Apache," he equivocated.

She Who Dreams snorted, showing some animation as she turned to him. "Sun in Splendor is my daughter and your mother was Lipan. That makes your son fully one of our people. We choose who belongs, Night Wind. Give him his Lipan name and show him the world."

Joaquín's hands trembled as he lifted Bartolome from the crib, carefully supporting his spine and head the way he had watched the men of his village do with their children. The baby kicked and squirmed, but did not cry. The burble of a yawn made his small pursed mouth widen into an "O". Then his little grasping fists fastened on his father's shirt and he clung tightly. Joaquín rose on shaky legs and walked from the room toward the open courtyard. All the while the thought hammered in his brain, *Fool! Fool! You only make the parting more painful.* But he knew he must do this, on his honor as a Lipan warrior. Even if raised by the Europeans, he would have his Lipan naming.

Standing in the blazing morning sun, Joaquín shielded the infant from its intensity and looked about for inspiration. What was his name? Just then Ana came running around the side of the porch, headed across the open courtyard in pursuit of Sweet Singer. The black-and-white furball had grown into a handsome young cat who stopped his headlong race and began to twine against Joaquín's legs.

"Night Wind! She Who Dreams told me you returned last night. How glad my heart is! Is not your son beautiful?" Ana stopped in front of Joaquín, who knelt down and gave her a warm hug with one arm.

"Yes, Ana, he is beautiful. Today I present him to the sky and the four winds," he said with a catch in his voice as he arose.

"What will be his name?" the child asked as she scooped up the groveling, playful young cat.

Looking at Sweet Singer, Joaquín suddenly smiled and said, "He has grown into a fine strong lion cub. I think the same will be true for Bartolome, here. He is the son of a Lioness. His childhood name will be Lion Cub."

She Who Dreams stood in the shadows of the courtyard porch as Night Wind went through the ritual of presentation. She and Ana watched without making a sound. When Night Wind had finished and turned back to the house, the old woman had vanished.

Lion Cub was tired now and fretting softly as his father returned him to the empty bedroom. Joaquín looked at the big bed where Orlena lay each night now, alone. He shook his head, trying to rid himself of such troubling thoughts, and laid the baby in his crib. Almost at once Bartolome was asleep, but the strong little fist still clung tightly to one of his father's fingers.

Joaquín knelt and watched him sleep for a long while, emotionally drained from the naming ceremony and the bonding that had irrevocably taken place the instant he had touched the child. "So strong, even as you sleep, my cub," he whispered as his other hand stroked the fine cap of curly hair on the infant's head. "Your mother is strong, too, with the courage of a lioness. Be like her and make her proud of you."

Orlena stood in the hallway, transfixed as she watched her husband kneeling by the crib. *Tears!* Her emotionless half-caste, the pitiless renegade, was shedding silent tears as he spoke to his son. She Who Dreams had been right! Knowing she could not let his pride suffer if he found her watching this most private scene, she melted silently away from the room and walked outdoors. She must speak with her foster mother, but first she had much to ponder.

Chapter 28

Soon you will be given a choice. Only make the right one and all will be well. Orlena turned She Who Dreams' words over in her mind as she walked across the courtyard. What choice? How could she convince Joaquín that she loved him? That she wanted to remain with him and raise their son here in New Mexico?

Ana ran up to her, interrupting her thoughts with a barrage of questions about the naming. He had taken Bartolome outdoors and named him the Lion Cub! A horrifying thought flashed into her mind. Did he wish to keep only the son who shared his Apache blood and rid himself of the Spanish mother? In spite of She Who Dreams' assurances, Orlena was once again stricken with doubts. "Enough of riddles and waiting games," she muttered. "Ana, go watch over little Bartolome," she instructed the girl. "But first, tell Joaquín I wish to speak with him in his study."

NIGHT WIND'S WOMAN

She paced back and forth, working up her courage as she waited for him. "It would be like him to dismiss my request and simply refuse to appear," she whispered bitterly to herself. Her voice echoed in the large, masculine room. A rough oak table and chair dominated the austere study, which was backed by a simple bookshelf. She ran her hands over the heavy volumes —well-worn copies of Caesar's *Gallic Wars* and Tacitus' *Germania* as well as the less predictable plays of Lope de Vega. There was also one slim copy of the life of St. Francis, with the spine scarcely bent. More of war and power, less of the simplicity of trust and love—that was the way Joaquín had lived his life, she mused sadly.

Joaquín stood before the study door trying to prepare himself to face Orlena. Since his chilly greeting to her upon his return, he had hoped she would be inclined to avoid him until Santiago arrived to take her away. Her sudden summons left him feeling especially vulnerable. He had just come from laying his son in his crib, vowing that he had touched the infant for the first and last time. But if he did not face her now, when? Sooner or later they must have done with this painful travesty of a marriage.

When he opened the door and stepped inside the room, his face was shuttered and calm. Orlena jumped at his quiet entry, then forced herself to assume a facade of coolness.

"Well, what is it you wish to discuss that cannot wait until my day's work is done?" He stood poised on the balls of his feet, every muscle in his body flexed, yet deceptively indolent to a casual observer.

Orlena had become far too intimately acquainted with him over the years not to recognize the tension coiled inside him. What she had never been able to discern was the meaning of it. *He is angry,* she thought with a blaze of temper herself. How dare he be angry when he had gone off and left her alone to give birth to their child, then returned to treat her so coldly? "What I wish to discuss, Joaquín, is far more important than a day's work—work I might add, that Pablo and Vitorio do well enough while you are off risking your life in the south!"

He scowled. "I have no time for your angry lecturing. I do what I must." He turned to leave, but her words stopped him.

"I wish to discuss our future, husband. Or does such a trivial matter as the life of your son hold so little interest for you?"

He whirled furiously, his mask of control slipping. "My son holds *all* my interest!"

"So I am given to understand. Ana told me you came this morning while I was out and named him. When I tried to show him to you, you acted as if a bath and hot food were infinitely more significant!"

"That is absurd! I rode in late and was completely amazed that the babe had come a month early," he replied defensively.

"Yet the fact that I was great with child did not stop you from riding out in the first place—or from staying away for weeks on end," she accused him, pouncing on the weakness she found in his argument.

"Always it returns to my savage heritage, does it not? I ride out to rob your precious Spanish, to rescue Indians from their cruelty. I did not intend to desert you or our son."

"Is it that you would not desert your son, but would rid yourself of me? I know what you believe of me, Joaquín, but Bartolome is my son and I will never give him away—any more than I would leave Ana." She paused, praying for him to deny her accusation.

His jaw worked, clenching and unclenching. How to

NIGHT WIND'S WOMAN

say what he must say? "You need not leave Ana or Bartolome. You may take them with you, Lioness, if that is truly what you want," he said quietly.

Orlena stared at him, stupefied with amazement. "Take them and just leave?" she choked out. "Leave you to your vendetta! How you must despise my Spanish blood that it taints our son, even Ana by her affection for me!" She quivered with anger. Tears began to well up and she rubbed furiously at her eyes, brushing them away.

"I do not despise you, your blood be damned, Spanish witch! I love you! But I will not hold by force what I cannot have freely given!"

Orlena's breath caught in her throat. Her mind reeled as his shouted words penetrated her pain and anger.

Down the hall, Santiago heard Joaquín and Orlena's voices raised in anger, but he was unable to make out the words they hurled at each other with such fury. When he and Fray Bartolome had ridden up to the ranch house, She Who Dreams had detained the priest to explain all that had transpired. But the old woman had urged him to go inside and speak with Orlena and Joaquín. Taking a breath for courage, Santiago strode purposefully down the hall toward the sound of the argument and swung wide the door.

The two of them stood on opposite sides of the big table, confronting each other like two combatants. Orlena's face was tear-stained and she looked dazed and incredulous, as if Joaquín had just struck her a blow or said something she could not comprehend. Joaquín's fists were clenched, resting on the table as he stared at her, his powerful chest heaving with anger that flashed in his eyes as he turned from his wife to the intruder.

Orlena, too, tore her eyes from her antagonist and

stared at her brother. "Santiago, how did you come here? Why—"

After months spent journeying through dangerous wilderness, carrying a brace of Miquelet Locks had become second nature to the youth. Looking at the blazing green eyes and set jaw of the Night Wind caused him to pull one from his sash. He cocked it and pointed it at Joaquín, who was once again an unreadable stranger.

"I was summoned a month hence, but it seems I have arrived none too soon," he replied grimly, noting the ragged, breathless quality of Orlena's voice and the way she was trembling.

"You are early, but I am glad you have come so precipitously," Joaquín responded.

"I wonder at that, Brother. When I first pleaded with Father Bartolome to send you as her rescuer, I did not dream that you would abuse your wife!" He glanced from Joaquín to Orlena. "I am bidden to escort you away from here—anywhere you wish to go. We can make a home in the City of Mexico with Don Bernal or we can return to Spain."

"And I may bring my son and Ana with me? Is that the arrangement the two of you have made?" she asked, her mood shifting mercurially from trembling anger to an oddly smiling calm. *Soon you will be given a choice.* Now she had the answer to her foster mother's riddle—the answer to so many things that had vexed her over the past years.

"That is what your husband wrote Bartolome before the child was born," Santiago replied dubiously, the gun still trained on his brother. Then his eyes widened at her words. "The child! It is a boy? Is he well, Orlena?"

She smiled serenely, like a well-fed cat, as she slowly rounded the table and walked over to stand beside her tall young brother, so gravely holding that ridiculous pistol on her husband. "Yes, young Bartolome is well. She Who Dreams will show you your new nephew. Give me the pistol, Santiago, and leave this half-caste rogue to me. Make haste, for I would finish our conversation in private!" She reached out and took the weapon from his hand.

Slack-jawed in amazement at the sudden shift in Orlena's emotions, Santiago did not resist. Something was decidedly wrong! Joaquín's face remained shuttered, his body rigid. Blessed Virgin, she would not shoot her own husband, would she? "Orlena, come with me and let us prepare to leave," he began hesitantly.

Her smile was blinding and devilish now as she replied, "I think not, little brother. You had best heed my instruction, else you will be shocked by what I will do next."

"You would not shoot him?" he cried, aghast.

"That depends on how well you both can follow instruction. Now, do as I say and seek out your nephew. You will find that he is quite splendid, I think." She almost shoved the tall, russet-haired youth from the room, then closed the door behind him and leveled the pistol on Joaquín, who remained motionless, his expression inscrutable.

He watched the amber light glint in her eyes as her lips curved in a wicked smile. "Come here. Take off your clothes," she commanded boldly.

His lips, too, became mobile as he replied with a devilish gleam in his eyes, "Think you this is the best place, Lioness? At the mountain outpost, we had at least a pallet in the room . . . of course, there is this table." He gestured to the paper strewn surface behind him. "Or, do I misread your intention?"

Her face became serious as she lowered the gun. "I

love you, Joaquín. I will never leave you, not for all the gold a whole fleet of Spanish galleons carries. But"—she raised the weapon again and walked provocatively toward him—"I may lose patience if you dally longer. I could just graze you to prove my point—and have you at my mercy."

His heart felt as if it would burst from his chest. "I only wanted to offer you freedom, Lioness," he whispered huskily as he reached out and took the gun from her, tossing it onto the table.

"Now you see that I am free to choose, Joaquín, and I have chosen," she whispered as she looped her arms about his neck while he swept her into his arms and carried her toward the door. She stopped kissing him only long enough to reach down and pull open the latch. He walked down the hall to the last room at the far corner, where he had been sleeping alone the past bitter months.

Santiago rushed toward the courtyard where She Who Dreams had just carried her sleeping grandson to meet his namesake. The Franciscan held him and stared gravely into the tiny face of young Bartolome. "So, he has been named the Lion Cub according to your Lipan custom. Now I think it would be fitting for him to be baptized according to our Christian custom. What think you, Grandmother?" His clear gray eyes danced merrily as he looked from the content infant to the shrewd old woman.

She Who Dreams smiled serenely. "Your ceremonial washing did not harm Night Wind or Sun in Splendor. I think it cannot harm their children either."

"Children, eh?" He chuckled. "You are an optimist to hope for more children." Then he paused and studied her face carefully. "Unless . . . you were the one who knew we would arrive this day! Do you read the future, Medicine Woman? I have heard some of your people possess such gifts."

"Spirits do not always tell all—only what we need to know," she replied with deliberate vagueness.

He smiled. "And you know all will be well for Joaquín and Orlena?" He looked up at Santiago's flushed face as the youth approached them hesitantly, his eyes transfixed by the sleepy baby. "I take it your sister is not in need of rescue?"

Santiago shrugged helplessly, still staring in awe at the child. "I do not understand any of it. When I heard them arguing, I"—he hesitated in embarrassment—"I drew my pistol and told Orlena I was taking her away from here. I offered her a safe haven and a fine life with Cousin Bernal."

"Which she refused," Bartolome interjected gently.

"She did more than that! She took the pistol from me and leveled it at Night Wind. I feared for a moment she would shoot him—"

Fray Bartolome's laughter interrupted the mortified youth. "Never fear that, but I do believe our bold raider is in for quite a surprise—one that he will vastly enjoy," he added, continuing to chuckle.

"Orlena told me to come out here and see my nephew," Santiago replied, looking eagerly at the swaddled bundle that now began to fuss and kick.

She Who Dreams took the infant from Bartolome and thrust him at the curious, yet hesitant, youth. "Here. You must hold Lion Cub."

"I have never held a baby. I am afraid I might hurt him. He is so small. . . ." Santiago was forced to accept the wiggling infant from the insistent grandmother. Almost at once, young Bartolome sighed and again drifted off to sleep, held by his entranced young uncle.

* * *

Joaquín set Orlena down inside the bedroom door. While he slipped the bolt, she clung to him, her arms wrapped about his neck as she rained soft, nibbling kisses about his face, throat, and chest. She could feel the slamming of his heart against his ribs as he enfolded her in his arms and pressed her tightly to him.

"I have missed you, my Sun in Splendor," he whispered hoarsely as he buried his face in her tangled golden hair.

Holding his face with her soft slim hands, she said simply, "I love you, husband. I will have no other." Her eyes met his and she felt a thrill of recognition as she stared into their fathomless emerald depths. At last she could see behind them, into his soul. What she beheld robbed her of breath.

"I have loved you for so long and I have been too frightened to confess it, even to myself. To love is to let go of all the old hates. Ever since I was a boy, Bartolome has told me this would be so, but when it happened—with you—I was afraid to do as my heart bade me. When I stole you from Conal, you stole my heart. I have done cruel, foolish things to you, Lioness. Do you forgive me?"

"You already have your answer, for you stole not only my body, but my heart, too, Joaquín. We have both misunderstood, but time comes full cycle. We have the chance to begin again. All those who would harm us are banished. We are free."

"Then let us begin again," he whispered as he lowered his mouth and devoured her lips. "You commanded me to take off my clothes," he said raggedly when at last they broke off the kiss.

"When a lioness commands, best beware her claws," Orlena said as she ran her nails lightly down his chest, pulling open the soft cotton shirt.

NIGHT WIND'S WOMAN

Joaquín quickly shed it and kicked off his moccasins, then began to unlace his buckskin pants, saying huskily, "You see how well I obey your command." A smile twitched at the corners of his lips. "With far less resistance than you gave me when first I ordered you to disrobe."

She smiled and ran her hands over the dark, sinuous contours of his chest and arms. "I said I would disrobe for my lawful husband . . . and so I shall." She watched as he peeled down his tight breeches. Then she stood back to inspect his naked male beauty. He was magnificent, bronzed and slim, his sculpted face softened by love. Orlena began to tremble with desire.

"It has been so long—so long, my love," she said softly as she began to pull her buckskin tunic over her head.

Joaquín stroked her breasts through the sheer cotton chemise that still shielded them, hefting the swollen globes, feeling the nipples harden at his touch.

She gasped softly at the exquisite sensations and then said unsteadily, "You must see to my leggins, I fear, for I have not the strength to unlace them."

He lifted her effortlessly and carried her to the bed where he sat her down and knelt at her feet. With nimble fingers he untied the buckskin laces and pulled the leggins free. Tossing them in the corner, he said, "You see how obliging I am, Lioness. Not only do I disrobe myself, but you as well."

His long tapered fingers worshipped her pale silky flesh as he took the last of her clothing from her body. When she was as completely naked as he, he ran one hand across her flat little belly in wonder. "Our babe made you swell so, I feared for you, Lioness, but now . . ." His roving fingers moved higher to the heaviness of her milk-laden breasts. He was rewarded by a sharp intake of her breath as she pulled him down to suckle and taste of their bounty.

"I will rob my son of his dinner," he whispered as she moaned and arched against him.

In answer, Orlena pulled his head up to kiss him. Their legs and arms entwined as they rolled across the wide soft bed. Her long golden hair wrapped about his shoulders like a mantle as they deepened the kiss, their tongues dueling and their breaths mingling in frenzied passion. Orlena bucked and writhed against the hardness of his phallus, eager for the joining of their flesh, but Joaquín slowly quieted her, holding her above him as he lay on his back. He struggled to speak.

"I do not want to hurt you, Lioness. The birth was—"

"Nearly two months ago. I am completely healed," she interrupted, boldly reaching down to grasp his shaft and stroke its steely hot length until he was robbed of all reason. He reached up and positioned her above him with her legs straddling his hips.

"Stop me if I hurt you," he whispered raggedly as he lowered her onto his hard, velvety sex. She slid down with desperate hunger, slickly enveloping him. Once seated and fully impaled, she dug her hands into his shoulders and tossed her hair back to brush and tease his thighs. Involuntarily he arched up and she moved with him, pulling him closer, deeper.

"The only hurt has been waiting for this, beloved." She rose as he guided her hips with his hands, his fingers digging into the sleek muscles of her buttocks. Orlena rode him with savage intensity until he stilled her runaway passion by holding her against him as he struggled to regain control. She sobbed in frustration, then melted against him, bending down to kiss his lips. When she felt his arms again strain to lift her and

NIGHT WIND'S WOMAN

resume their pagan ride, she quickly accommodated her hips to his thrusts.

Burying her face against the straining tendons where his neck met his shoulder, she muffled her cries of ecstasy and met the long-awaited, aching crest. Feeling her climax, Joaquín released all control and thrust wildly, swelling and exploding deep within her, adding even more to the intensity of her release. Her nails clawed into his shoulders as she felt him spill his seed high and hot in her womb. As the convulsive, exquisite pleasure gradually subsided, they lay fused together, sweat-soaked and panting, satiated so utterly in body and soul neither could move or speak.

Yet they communicated in the lush silence of the room, lying on the bed, simply holding each other. When they finally regained their breath, he gently rolled them to lie on their sides, facing each other, still intimately joined. "Will you always be so eager to obey my commands?" she asked him in a throaty purr.

"As long as they lead to this end, your every command is my devoutest duty—and delight," he replied. His hand brushed some strands of tangled gold from her face as he caressed her cheek. Their breaths mingled as they kissed softly, gently.

With her thick, dark lashes veiling her eyes, Orlena whispered, "Never have I known such peace as I do now . . . Yet"—her eyes flashed open and met his—"I would not chain you with my fears for your life. The Night Wind must ride to free our people."

"You and our son will keep me here far more often now, but I honor your bravery and your love for the Indians, Lioness."

"We will work with Bartolome. I will do what I can to help with resettling those who are rescued." She hesitated and tightened her arms about his shoulders.

"I was jealous of Morena, Joaquín, but I am sorry for her death. She loved you and did not mean to betray you."

"I know that is true, my love, but I used her ill, bringing you to her home where it could cause naught but hurt for you both. Do not blame yourself, for it is more my fault than anyone's that she is dead. But we can carry on the work she and the good father have been doing."

Orlena suddenly stiffened in his arms. "Father Bartolome! If Santiago is here at your request, so must the priest be, too!" She reddened in mortification. How long had the lovers been closeted away since she sent her brother off to see his nephew?

Reading her thoughts, a laugh rumbled up from his chest and he rained light kisses across her heated face. "I think Bartolome is quite politic enough to wait until we choose to show ourselves. I am certain he is already well met with She Who Dreams, bargaining for the baptism of his namesake."

"Think you he will win?" she asked teasingly.

"She Who Dreams is a very tolerant woman," he replied, then drew her back into his embrace. "Now, let us see to making more children for the good Franciscan to baptize."

Orlena most willingly complied with her husband's proposal. Now their future stretched toward the horizon, as vast and full of promise as the fertile valley where they lived.

AUTHOR'S NOTE

The theme of this book is integrally related to La Leyenda Negra, the Black Legend of the Spanish Conquest of the Southwest. The war between Spaniards and Native Americans began with Cortez and continued down through the centuries. Both sides were guilty of appalling cruelty, but if the Spanish stand indicted more strongly in this story, it is perhaps because I share the heroine's rather idealistic view that as men of the Enlightenment, they should have behaved better. One of the most perplexing problems historians must analyze is the role violence plays in the birth of any new culture. In spite of—or mayhap because of—this savage scene, *La Raza*, the new Indian-Spanish race, was born.

Conal Quinn and Ignacio Valdéz are representative of the worst excesses of the Europeans; Cloth Fox and Quick Slayer are their Apache counterparts. But to balance the killers, there are men of peace like Bartolome and women of tolerance like She Who Dreams. With my protagonists, Joaquín and Orlena, European and Native American values clash head on, but love triumphs over hate. Anyone who has seen the murals of Diego Rivera in Mexico City will understand what I have tried to do in this story.

I chose the Lipan Apache as my hero's people for a variety of reasons, chief among them being the role women played in their culture and their monogamous marriage customs. I found a number of sources helpful in learning about this remarkable tribe. The standard authority on the Apache is Morris Opler, who edited the *Apache Indians* series. Volume X on the Lipan was especially valuable. Andree F. Sjoberg's article, "Lipan Apache Culture in Historical Perspective," in volume nine of the *Southwestern Journal of Anthropology*, enlightened me about their methods of hunting and gathering, their medical skills, and their burial practices. For visuals, I highly recommend Thomas E. Mail's *The People Called Apache*. *The Handbook of North American Indians*, Volume X, gives a detailed account of "Apachean Cultural Patterns." As a primary source, I found the Garland Series on Indian Captivities, Volume 107, "Bucklew the Indian Captive," to be an excellent firsthand account of a man held by the Lipan. As to how Native Americans fared at the hands of Europeans, L. R. Bailey's *Indian Slave Trade in the Southwest* was highly informative.

The Southwest's violent and colorful history has been well chronicled by a wide variety of historians. Max Moorhead is their dean, a man who has devoted a lifetime of study to the Spanish borderlands. *New Mexico's Royal Road* and *The Presidio: Bastion of the Spanish Borderlands* are two of his works on which I drew heavily. Marc Simmons' *Spanish Government in New Mexico* is a fascinating and detailed analysis of the political and economic system of the Spanish military and its vital role in the conquest of the Southwest.

For information on how the people of New Mexico spent their daily lives, Oakah L. Jones, Jr.'s *Los Paisanos* is a fine resource, not only for its insight into that province, but as a window on the rank and file of

NIGHT WIND'S WOMAN

Spanish settlers across New Spain. *Old Santa Fe* by Ralph Emerson Twitchell paints a vivid portrait of the legendary city of the Holy Faith, Spain's farthest outpost in her Internal Provinces.

I love to hear from my readers. All letters with S.A.S.E. answered. Please write to me at:

                        P.O. Box 72
                        Adrian, MI 49221

Shirl Henke

TERMS OF SURRENDER

SHIRL HENKE

"Historical romance at its best!"
—*Romantic Times*

Devilishly handsome Rhys Davies owns half of Starlight, Colorado, within weeks of riding into town. But there is one "property" he'll give all the rest to possess, because Victoria Laughton—the glacially beautiful daughter of Starlight's first family—detests Rhys's flamboyant arrogance. And she hates her own unladylike response to his compelling masculinity even more. To win the lady, Rhys will have to wager his very life, hoping that the devil does, indeed, look after his own.

_3424-7 $4.99 US/$5.99 CAN

Dorchester Publishing Co., Inc.
P.O. Box 6640
Wayne, PA 19087-8640

Please add $1.75 for shipping and handling for the first book and $.50 for each book thereafter. NY, NYC, and PA residents, please add appropriate sales tax. No cash, stamps, or C.O.D.s. All orders shipped within 6 weeks via postal service book rate. Canadian orders require $2.00 extra postage and must be paid in U.S. dollars through a U.S. banking facility.

Name_____
Address _____
City_____ State _____ Zip_____
I have enclosed $_____ in payment for the checked book(s).
Payment <u>must</u> accompany all orders. ❏ Please send a free catalog.

LOVE A REBEL... LOVE A ROGUE
SHIRL HENKE

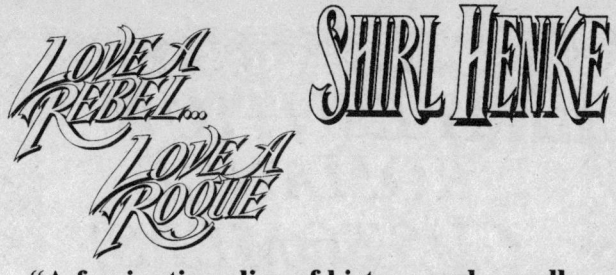

"A fascinating slice of history and equally fascinating characters! Enjoy!"
—Catherine Coulter

Quintin Blackthorne will bow before no man. He dares to despise his father and defy his king, but a mutinous beauty overwhelms the American patriot with a rapturous desire he cannot deny.

Part Indian, part white, and all trouble, Devon Blackthorne will belong to no woman—until a silky seductress tempts him with a passion both reckless and irresistible.

The Blackthorne men—one highborn, one half-caste—are bound by blood, but torn apart by choice. Caught between them, two sensuous women long for more than stolen moments of wondrous splendor. But as the lovers are swept from Savannah's ballrooms to Revolutionary War battlefields, they learn that the faithful heart can overcome even the fortunes of war.

___4406-4 $5.99 US/$6.99 CAN

Dorchester Publishing Co., Inc.
P.O. Box 6640
Wayne, PA 19087-8640

Please add $1.75 for shipping and handling for the first book and $.50 for each book thereafter. NY, NYC, and PA residents, please add appropriate sales tax. No cash, stamps, or C.O.D.s. All orders shipped within 6 weeks via postal service book rate. Canadian orders require $2.00 extra postage and must be paid in U.S. dollars through a U.S. banking facility.

Name_____
Address_____
City_____State_____Zip_____
I have enclosed $_____ in payment for the checked book(s).
Payment <u>must</u> accompany all orders. ❏ Please send a free catalog.
CHECK OUT OUR WEBSITE! www.dorchesterpub.com

ATTENTION ROMANCE CUSTOMERS!

SPECIAL TOLL-FREE NUMBER
1-800-481-9191

*Call Monday through Friday
10 a.m. to 9 p.m.
Eastern Time
Get a free catalogue,
join the Romance Book Club,
and order books using your
Visa, MasterCard,
or Discover.*

Leisure Books

Love Spell

GO ONLINE WITH US AT DORCHESTERPUB.COM